D·E·S·I·R·E·L·E·S·S

A NOVEL OF NEW ORLEANS

THOMAS YORK

VIKING

VIKING

Published by the Penguin Group
Penguin Books Canada Ltd, 2801 John Street, Markham, Ontario, Canada L3R 1B4
Penguin Books, 27 Wrights Lane, London W8 5TZ, England
Viking Penguin Inc., 40 West 23rd Street, New York, New York 10010, USA
Penguin Books Australia Ltd, Ringwood, Victoria, Australia
Penguin Books (NZ) Ltd, 182-190 Wairau Road, Auckland 10, New Zealand
Penguin Books Ltd, Registered Offices: Harmondsworth, Middlesex, England

First published 1988

Copyright © The Estate of Thomas York, 1988

Printed and bound in Canada

Canadian Cataloguing in Publication Data

York, Thomas
    Desireless
ISBN 0-670-81940-9
I. Title.
PS8597.055D48 1988   C813'.54   C87-094829-6
PR9199.3.Y674D48 1988

British Library Cataloguing in Publication Data Available
American Library of Congress Cataloguing in Publication Data
0-670-81940-9   Desireless   88-50106

Desireless *has nothing true in it.*
It is a totally invented story.

"MOMENTS TO REMEMBER" by Al Stillman and Robert Allen
Copyright © 1955, Renewed and assigned to Larry Spier, Inc.,
New York, N.Y. and Charlie Deitcher Productions, Quogue, N.Y.
Reprinted with permission.
"I SAW THE LIGHT" by Hank Williams
Copyright © 1948 by Acuff Rose Music, Inc., and Hiriam Music,
Inc. Copyright renewed.
Copyright © 1948 by Fred Rose Music, Inc. Copyright renewed,
assigned to Aberbach Enterprises Ltd., and Fred Rose Music Inc.
(Aberbach Enterprises administered by Rightsong Music, Inc.)
International copyright secured. All rights reserved. Used by
permission.

for David Swords in New Orleans
Jewish Diane (wherever she is)
and the nine black sisters

CONTENTS

Downtown
New Orleans

Map by Brian Lehen

Mississippi River

FRENCH QUARTER

N

GREATER NEW ORLEANS BRIDGE

D·E·S·I·R·E·L·E·S·S

Thou blind man's mark, thou fool's self-chosen snare,
Fond fancy's scum and dregs of scattered thought,
Band of all evils, cradle of causeless care,
Thou web of will whose end is never wrought;
Desire! desire, I have too dearly bought
With price of mangled mind thy worthless ware;
Too long, too long asleep thou hast me brought,
Who should my mind to higher things prepare.
But yet in vain thou hast my ruin sought,
In vain thou mad'st me to vain things aspire,
In vain thou kindlest all thy smoky fire.
For virtue hath this better lesson taught,
Within myself to seek my only hire,
Desiring nought but how to kill desire.

—Sir Philip Sidney

I. THE LANDSCAPE OF DESIRE

Well, then, shall we not be right in saying that if a person would wish to see the greatest pleasures he ought to go and look, not at health, but at disease?

Plato, Philebus

CHAPTER 1

It wasn't clear where the bus was going. Looming out of the dark and reeling past were dirty stucco houses, bungalows with peeling paint, boats for rent, an isthmus of trees against a desolation of water, a lacing of bridges, causeways, railroad bridges, shipyards. He peered out the bus window. It was night, and drizzling, but flickers of light from the gas stations and jiffy groceries enabled him to read the larger signs: Gulf Coast Baptist Temple, Deaf Revival Kingdom, Hy Times, COLD BEER, Delchamps Food. . . . Somewhere since Mobile the bus had left the freeway and was traveling the scenic coastal route through blind night and intermittent squalls. Confederate Inn, Alamo Plaza, Broadwater Beach Golf Club, the turn-off for Keesler Air Force Base and churches, churches, churches, darkened and set back from the road in clumps of palm and live oak draped with Spanish moss. Mexican food, Flamingo Motel, a pedestrian overpass for "Guests of Gulf Towers Only" with a blind man, white cane lit up by the bus headlights, standing at the roadside underneath the overpass. Gulf Coast Coliseum and William Carey College loomed and disappeared, followed by the Jefferson Davis speech site—historic marker—flanked by two lawn-ornament deer, the worse for wear and weather, blindly gazing Gulfward. Across a narrow strip of dirty sand and dirty water the long unbroken pencil stroke of the Gulf Islands in the distance was blotted out by blackness, and lost in the squall line was the far horizon. All that could be seen to seaward were black spars of harbored sailing boats against black water, and clumps of stunted palm trees moored in sand.

The bus was taking Hwy. 90, but without stopping at small towns along the way. This seemed strange, but no stranger than the truck careering down the wrong causeway, its brights getting closer and closer, until the bus swerved, missed it, and drove on. Or the woman sitting next to him, pretending to be half asleep while snuggling into him—he was by the window—as though to peer out at the passing of blind night along the Gulf, all the while massaging, then unzipping him and wriggling herself up onto his lap. Moving together with her as they both gazed out the window at the Gulf, the strange become familiar was still strange. But no stranger than the black man at daybreak on the outskirts of Atlanta: the bus gearing down for a traffic light, slowing, not quite stopping, the black man bursting from a doorway ten yards distant in a dead run for the bus, when suddenly around the running black six whites—policemen? plainclothesmen? Dixie mafia?—materialized with handguns gripped in both hands, blasting at the head of the black who crumpled in mid-stride beside the bus, below his window. He saw it—soundlessly enacted through green-tinted glass: one moment the bus was gearing down to stop, then the black appeared, the whites appeared, the whites gunned down the black, the bus drove on. He saw it then as he saw now the huge marker stone, NEW ORLEANS EAST, and a mausoleum bordering a swamp. Then a crenellated turret with flags, à la King Arthur, on the edge of swamp and fronting a bayou flanked by shacks on stilts. The marker stone and crenellated turret were neither more nor less strange than the black outside Atlanta or the truck on the causeway or the woman on his lap. Strange, too, that no one else on the bus—including the woman stuck to him and pretending to be sleeping—had noticed, or remarked, the careering truck or the gunned-down black man. Wonders were many, none more so than another. Hwy. 90 had become the Chef Menteur, and he was entering the city now. Street names, vaguely familiar, were beginning to whizz past: Chantilly, America, Desire . . . Through the green-tinted glass of the bus window he was approaching a city underwater. A flood of obsession and street names rushed at the window, beat against it, raced away: Pleasure, Abundance, Desire . . . Entering the Project now. So long as he formed no connections, no associations, no linkage with the outside, he could function. The bus geared down and stopped. He blinked at the markers over the stoplight—Florida and Desire—and fought back a wave of remembrance. Black teenagers lounged on all four corners, outfitted in bizarre hats, fancy jeans, and plastic raincoats which glistened in the changing traffic lights. Then the bus was moving and he was in motion, along the waterless canal which bounded Desire Project. There weeds grew, though he couldn't see them, out of garbage and dead dogs; he was sure the city hadn't cleaned it, sure it wouldn't, and that was near to forming a connection . . . The bus pulled up at Elysian Fields and Rampart.

The woman on his lap started awake. With exaggerated intimacy, uncertain of response, she pretended to be half asleep and snuggled into him. It hadn't been his idea, it had been hers, somewhere between Ocean Springs and Pascagoula, to pull down her panties and unzip his fly and wriggle herself onto his lap while pretending to peer out the window. It hadn't been his idea, but he'd gone along with it. Now she was stuck to him like a stamp.

The woman, thirtyish and fat around the bottom, snuggled closer. He gripped her by the hips and unstuck her. She pulled up her panties, straightened her skirt, and settled in beside him.

"Honey," she cooed in a whiny voice, "We in Nu Orleens, honey?"

He glanced at her with irritation. Not unpretty, just uncertain. A tail looking for a dog to wag. Next she'd want to know his name, where he was staying. "That's where we are," he said. "New Orleans."

Intimidated by his tone, she gazed out the window. Then, as the submarine street signs and a mausoleum swept past, she turned and snuggled up to him. "I never on a bus before, I swear. I never with no man, outside my husband."

He lurched as the bus turned off Rampart onto Tulane. He followed through the lurching motion and stood up, caught hold of the rack above, and got his grip. "So long," he said, and started down the aisle as the lights inside the bus switched on and the driver swung the bus into the terminal driveway and announced over his microphone, "New Orleans."

The vague sense of an appointment, pending or missed, plagued him as he left the bus, and, walking quickly past the terminal, he glanced in through its window at the wall clock: ten o'clock. But that was all behind him: meeting people, being met, comings, goings, deaths and entrances, being late or early, being clocked. He stood for a moment indecisive on the sidewalk, the avenue before him black with wet, smoking. The rain which like a brushful of deck paint, flat and black, had swept across the city had stopped now, leaving every building, every surface, covered. Nothing glistened under the street lamps; the street, sidewalk, and city smoked with wet and smelled of asphalt. A cab pulled up, and idled. Not much traffic on Tulane, no one walking. Glancing downtown toward Rampart, then up Tulane past Charity and

Hotel Dieu hospitals, he fished a penny from his pocket, flipped it, watched it fall, then started walking slowly up Tulane away from town.

Black nurses in white uniforms—shift change at Charity—debouching from Emerge and down the stairs onto the sidewalk, languid and loose-limbed and loudly talking in their rich and mellow voices: "Gurl, ah seen that ol' whitey goose at chu!" "You seen nothin', you a goose." "Doan chu lie, Japonica! I tell Charles on you." "Charlie doan give a shit. He say ah'm the rankest sow in town." Deep-throated laughter, and, before he thought not to, he found himself gazing across the street at the unlit facade of the sleazy lunch counter where Valerie had been working when he returned the first time. It was empty now, the steel-bar shutters drawn, but before he recollected where he'd been and that five years had passed, he glimpsed himself inside and at the counter, on a stool between black men, black nurses seated at wire tables, the only white (as he was always, around Valerie, the only white), the counter dark and wet with stains and spills from empty and half-empty Coca-Cola glasses, as with one arm, smoothly black, she removed the glasses, while with her other hand she swabbed the counter clean. Drawing a cup of Luzianne coffee and thrusting it at him, sloshing, she said: "Why you comin' round here, Jimmy, after all this time?"

"I'm back, I came back, Val."

"What chu come back for?"

He met her gaze—her wide-eyed, worried gaze, masked in impassive black—and shrugged.

"You cain't live in this town, Honey, you cain't live nowhere!"

And dipping the rack of dirty glasses into a vat of boiling water, with a violent jerk she pulled them out and set them up to dry.

He trained his gaze back on the smoking street. New
Orleans was founded on a delta, the delta overlaid a swamp,
the swamp seeped away to the water beneath it, and the
water bled to the Gulf. Who knew where from there? Who
cared? He crossed Galvez, the avenue more desolate, the
neutral ground seedier than he remembered it, and held in
check a tide of remembrance. Not that it was painful, it
wasn't—no more than a broken bone was painful after it
knit, just enlarged. A break, a fall, a sudden shock, the
memory of vulnerability: the outer banks with water slopping
over. Beyond the outer banks, beneath the bridge . . . flat
black like the souls of sinners or the smoking street.

Flintlike he set his face to the night air, watched two
enormous cockroaches skitter across the sidewalk, sidestepped to avoid crushing one and walked along Tulane toward
Carrollton. Each street name—Gayosa, Salcedo, Telemachus
—lapped at the levee of his memory, every intersection
threatened an encounter. If not with the Sibyl of Salcedo
Street who, black and fat and sitting in a junked car seat in
her vacant lot surrounded by wrecked chassis, remembered
everything and everyone—his mother, Lee Anne, Valerie—
and who recognized him the last time he returned, she said,
by the way his head wagged as he walked, from side to side,
against the clapboard church; if not with her, then with Fred
Turk, who the last time he came back had got religion:
"Preston, you remember, on th' tenor sax? He's not playin' th'
blues no more. Me neither." Pointing as he talked to "Jesus
Christ the Light of the World"—an unpainted shack beneath
the Broad Street Bridge. "Ah moved from th' back to th'
third row now. Ah ain't sanctified yet, but ah'm studyin' it.
They all got th' spirit, but th' full revelation don't come to
me till I gets home and studies it. Then th' fullness comes, you
mought say. Ah'm there in a wonder." Wonders were many,

but none more wonderful than . . . the wino sitting on the littered sidewalk in front of a steel-bar-latticed shop front, a nearly empty bottle of red wine in his lap, both hands clasped around its neck, a smudge of ashes on his forehead: "Mardi Gras is over, fren', and all our Mardi Gras, forever . . ." He walked quickly, beset by an invisible host of lesser ghosts and petty tormentors, nattering, buzzing, and bleating in his ears, past Broad and, two blocks over, the Broad Street bridge—an abandoned overpass: the main traffic in lost souls had been re-routed. A city bus passed, Elysian Fields bound, a strong-armed Negress at the wheel. Was Valerie still a bus driver? Was this her route? The Sibyl would know, but he was safely past Salcedo, head wagging as he walked from side to side, impelled uptown along Tulane.

The thought of an appointment came more strongly to him now, mixed somehow with a sense of permanent loss. He considered turning around, retracing his steps down Tulane, or two blocks over, along the slums and overgrown railroad tracks and rat-infested weeds of Perdido, toward town and the *Vieux Carré* and the Napoleon House—the Nap House where he would almost certainly end up tonight, so why retreat from it? Why, if not to keep some appointment, meet someone? Though he was far more likely to see someone he knew, someone who remembered him (if only the waiter) at the Nap House, than he was by proceeding in this direction where, the shops all closed, the streets deserted, he saw no one, not a soul.

At Carrollton, he decided, he would turn around, or take the trolley downtown, via St. Charles. That way he would have made a wide sweep of his old haunts, paid his respects, so to speak, scoured the Garden District for ghosts, and would still wind up at the Nap House. As he neared Carrollton and spied the palm trees, black at the trunks and steaming with wet, outside the Fontainbleu Motel, he eyed the pink-tiled, neon-lit structure with a strange brackish taste in his mouth—as though he had walked through a desert and crawled up a hill and found, like the SHELL refinery across the river with the first blinking letter blacked out, an ersatz oasis. There was nothing especially New Orleanian about the Fontainbleu, nothing especially anything; it was, like the Ho-Jo, the Flamingo, or the Gulf Towers, a motel that had hosted a shoot-out or two and a million or so contraceptions.

He turned in at the entrance and walked through the lobby, past the bar, through the shuttered portico opening onto the piazza with palm trees and swimming pool, and looked out on the court which was shrouded in shadows by palm fronds and the pool lights refracting up through the still water. Only one guest sat now in the darkened court, where Lee Anne had sat. In that chaise longue Lee Anne had sat the last time he saw her—five, it felt more like a million, years ago: before the murderous bloodlet of marriage had run, through the slough of *nisi*, to the absolute gulf of divorce; after the Thorasine and electro-shock and the twenty-seven-day "cure" at DePaul's and two years in Mandeville, Lee Anne faithfully hunkered beside the hospital bed where he lay strait-jacketed, shrapneling words into his ear like "Momma," "love," "forever."

He wondered vaguely, briefly, who is she being faithful to now? Lee Anne, his keeper and ex, Southern belle and slut, playing scales all night on her violin to punish him and scratching his opera records in a fit of jealousy. Lee Anne was always being faithful to someone—the garbage man, the furnace man, the anonymous voices on the phone in San Francisco—finding someone to be faithful to. He wished her no ill. He had watched the palomino prance while being dragged by the stirrup through the B-grade movie of their marriage. He had only just escaped by jumping off:

> And I who share their torment, in my life
> was James Antoine Girard; above all
> I owe my sorrows to a savage wife.

Etched in the mausoleum stone that Larry's super-salesman brother said he'd sold him on the layaway plan. Had he? When had he?

Why not?

Stifling a yawn and setting down his grip, he stood at the entrance to the motel's inner court, the occupied chaise longue turned toward the pool, the light from the pool refracted through water and shattered by shadows of palm fronds. He was more tired than he had expected: the sixteen-hour bus ride to New Orleans, the effort of resisting memory. Beyond it all, around it all, he had the haunting sense of an appointment . . . pending, missed, with the sense somehow of permanent loss if it were past; and it almost certainly was past, of that he was nearly certain. . . .

The solitary guest in the chaise longue beside the pool stirred in the shadowy light, and he saw now that it was a woman. She leaned forward, her back to him, to pick up something from the deck, and the way she moved, the shape of her shoulders, the swing of her hair, stirred in him the stab of recollection—her gestures were Lee Anne's!—but he knew his mind was playing tricks on him. Often on returning to someplace, he saw heads he thought he recognized, voices he thought he could distinguish—usually from the rear and at a distance. Memory was faulty after a dozen or so electro-shocks and several hundred drunks. Still, the haunting sense of an appointment missed, the fact of being once again in New Orleans, the familiar landscape of the Fontainbleu: all combined to produce in him a powerful impression that the woman in the chaise longue with her back to him was a familiar part of his past: like a tree, or a house, or a part of a hand, that she was known to him, and he to her. Perhaps he was even supposed to be here, scheduled to meet her; perhaps this was the appointment he had a vague sense of, and yet could not remember having made. . . ?

He advanced across the dimly lit piazza like a swimmer against tide, and sat down in the only other chair, a lawn chair about ten feet off and at right angles to the chaise longue. Now he could study the woman's profile, which she held for him as for a painter, silhouetted against the green light of the pool.

He sat in silence for a minute, two minutes.

"Lee Anne," he ventured.

The woman didn't answer, didn't turn to face him. Leaning forward to pick up her belongings, she stood up. Certainly she resembled Lee Anne: her body lithe and long-waisted; her long swan neck surmounted by a strong, but classic, face; her nose, too, was Lee Anne's, and her long blonde hair—a perfect stand-in for the Palomino, if not her. The thought that there might be more than one woman capable of making him suffer depressed him. But, in the dark . . . he couldn't even tell if she were white . . . she might be a redhead, have a wig . . . she might be a man. . . . He stood up too and hazarded one last attempt, why not? The woman standing there might not be Lee Anne, but then again she might be; and what was Lee Anne anyway, but a name, a memory, a shadow? What was life but a succession of such shadows, each resembling the last?

"Lee Anne," he said impatiently, "it's me, Jimmy, I've come back."

"Well," she said, turning to face him so that her whole face was in shadow, "you're late."

"I just got into town . . ." he began, then cut it short. He wasn't at all sure that it was Lee Anne. And he was beyond that age when he took it for granted that he could, if he wished, bed down any woman. It was lagniappe if a woman of style went for him. Mostly it was the ex-models, ex-stewardesses, and ex-topless dancers, the marginal women who played the cracks, or a stylish bitch who was slumming. As for Lee Anne, the voice wasn't quite hers, and the woman's face was still in shadow.

"I'd planned more of a reception for you, but . . . you're late and my husband said I should come anyway."

"Your husband?"

She responded with a shrug and started off across the courtyard. He followed, more curious about the fact that she was married than about who she was. As he shambled dutifully along after her, his gaze scrutinizing her long-legged, long-waisted back—she had on a silken peignoir over a two-piece swimsuit—and the wide, winglike shoulders sheathed in blown-dry not-quite-blonde hair, he did what he'd sworn he would not do: he ransacked his memory for a clue to this meeting. Had he told Lee Anne, ever, that he was returning? How could he, when he hadn't known himself? Had he ever asked her to meet him? Why would he? Had he communicated with her, or any mutual friend, within the past five years? No, he hadn't, he was pretty sure he hadn't, not even with his mother . . . least of all with his mother.

"This reception," he called after her, stopping to pick up his grip, "I hope it's not like old times."

"No Early Times," she said without stopping or turning,

"and no Old Crow, if that's what you mean." It was what Lee Anne might have said.

She kept walking, and he followed her: up two flights of zigzag stairs and along a thinly carpeted balcony overlooking the courtyard from which they'd just come. The palm trees and swimming pool and deserted deck chairs below looked very much, now that he gazed down on them, like the furnitureless scene in his mind's eye that he had pictured in recurring dreams since leaving New Orleans: an inner court-yard, like this one, surrounded by doors, like these, with himself on a balcony, or a bridge, looking down on a pool, or a river. Maybe here, and not at the Nap House, was the place of assignation; and his appointment, if he had one, with her . . . ?

She stopped at one of the numbered doors and unlocked it, then waited for him to come up. As she held the door for him he saw her face clearly—Mediterranean, with the broad forehead and high cheekbones and aquiline nose he considered classic—giving this woman, with her head thrown back, Lee Anne's air of disdain and of being a Catholic and cold. But there were differences, too: her swarthier skin and darker hair and . . . something he couldn't pinpoint—her air of contempt? or was it fatalism? he was uncertain . . . One thing was sure, she wasn't Lee Anne.

As he came up to her, she said, "No, not like old times."

He entered the room while she held open the door, touch-ing her hair as he passed. A strand or two detached itself.

"That leaves many possibilities," he said.

She followed him in, locked the door, and leaned against it. The neon sign blinked "Fontainbleu" just outside the window. She pulled the blinds, and switched on the night-light.

"Almost all, I should think."

There was nothing distinctive about the motel room: 316 was like 317, 318, or a room at the Alamo Plaza, or Gulf Towers. But something about the woman he sensed, he continued to sense, was different: not age, but ennui seemed to have brushed her so that she did not disappear into the bathroom, she did not even glance at the mirror as she passed from the door to the bed. No self-conscious touching-up or nervous patting of her hair distracted or delayed her from her duty, about which, as she kicked off her shoes, she seemed purposeful. He had concluded that, whether or not she was a prostitute, she wasn't his ex, when she said: "I was waiting for someone. He didn't come. You did. It's that simple."

She had flounced down on the bed and leaned back on her elbows and was looking over at him, her head and torso forming one continuous unit, one flowing line with the room full of shadows and half-lights—the neon sign blinking outside the window, the night-light beside the bed. In the strobe-light effect of the blinking neon, as she lay back on the bed and began unbuttoning her peignoir, she reminded him of some Greek god or goddess, surfacing from a river, the feet and hands and hair chopped off, submerged.

In the mirror he watched her: exposing, button by button, the long V of neck and swimsuit top, the shadowy torso and belly, the swimsuit bottom which she hooked her thumbs in and drew down over firm, well-muscled thighs and long legs, then kicked off. Her stomach and the pelvic line extending down from it looked concave and inviting as she leaned on her arms to slip off the peignoir; then she lay down on her side and felt behind her for the swimsuit snap.

"This is different," he commented.

"Different from what?" she said sharply.

"From last time, other times."

"There was no last time, and there won't be a next time.

It isn't my habit to meet strange men by the pool and take
them to bed. As I said, my husband told me to."

"Your husband," he repeated softly, "do I know him?"

She gave a rueful little laugh, as though the idea were
preposterous. "I hope not," she said, and sat up in bed and
looked at him. "He doesn't know you, that's for sure. All he
knows is that I'm here, and that you—or someone—is with
me."

"I'm not sure I understand," he said.

"I'm sure you don't," she said, and again laughed ruefully.
Then, looking at him critically: "You could take your own
pants off."

He did as he was told, standing up and stepping out of his
trousers, while the woman, sitting on the bed cross-legged
and naked but for her unsnapped swimsuit top, watched him.
Impatiently, and with a trace of resentment, she said: "Last
night I met a man who interested me—just a guest of the
motel. He'd wandered down to our party in the patio. I
danced with him, and later I went with him to his room—
this room. When I woke up this morning he wanted to know
my name and where I lived, but I was content to leave things
as they were. I kissed him goodbye, and went home."

"He didn't follow you?"

"No, he didn't follow me. He was content, too; maybe
even relieved . . ."

He had sat down on the bed beside her and was drawing
off the swimsuit top which had, unnecessarily, shoulder
straps. As she hunched forward to slide the straps down her
arms, he saw without surprise that she had small breasts . . .
like Lee Anne's.

"But my husband," she said scornfully, "my husband
wasn't content to leave well enough alone."

"He threw you out?"

She scoffed again, a mocking sound which made her breasts jiggle. "Hardly. Husbands don't throw wives out, now in New Orleans, not in the New Orleans I come from . . ."

"Gentilly, I suppose."

She ignored his gibe. "Wives may ask husbands to leave, but husbands don't throw wives out. That's too crude."

He longed to see her breasts jiggle again, and to fondle them while she laughed. For dangling breasts he felt no fondness—perhaps because neither his mother nor Lee Anne had large breasts—and what an inconvenience they must be! Whereas this woman . . . For no apparent reason he regarded her more critically. Her hair, for instance, which he had at first thought blonde and blown-dry, like the Palomino's, then not-quite-blonde and limp with the humidity, he saw now was streaked with old dye and was darker at the roots than at the ends, where it was sparse and getting sparser; it was in fact falling out, for several strands had adhered to his mouth since he touched her breasts. Was this, and not her lack of vanity, why she hadn't gone into the bathroom or brushed her hair in the mirror?

"I don't know why I'm telling you this," she said abruptly. "You don't deserve an explanation. I'm here, that should be enough."

"It is," he said, and slumped sideways onto the bed, inviting her to lie down with him. She stretched out beside him, and thrust herself up against him. There was surprising strength in her arms, and in the way her hands clutched his back and held him close he sensed an urgency near to desperation; desperate, too, the way her legs enwrapped him and her stomach muscles tensed to lock him in the socket of her pelvis. He had never been to bed with a woman so strong, never grappled with a woman athlete; and it struck him that women must experience this each time they had sex. For him it was like lying with . . . a man. In New Orleans . . . something he'd forgotten until now: the drag queens on Canal, and in the Quarter. He touched her, lightly, to make sure, and heard a little intake in her breath . . . she was all right.

"I got home," she said as she kissed him, and continued to talk between kisses, "and got in bed with my husband . . . this morning . . . and he said, 'Where have you been?' . . . I told him, and told him how I had left . . . and that I was home now . . . with him, and he said . . . 'You can't do that!' . . . 'You can't just leave the guy like that!' . . . 'Go back,' he said, 'Go back tonight!' . . . so here I am." The smell of her breath and the taste of her mouth reminded him of the prostitute, also a patient, at DePaul's. He turned his face to avoid her mouth as he felt his shorts being drawn down, his groin being ransacked. A complex of associations assailed him, an imbroglio of shadows, crossed identities, and ghosts: her shadow exerting weight and pressure, his body without heat or desire; the ghost of Lee Anne behind and this nameless woman around him, their breasts and torsos interchangeable, almost; but the texture of her hair and the smell of her breath and the sound of her voice were different from Lee Anne's. And her teeth. She had, he saw now, a pronounced overbite, her upper jaw extending out over the lower so far that the teeth would not close. It was especially prominent when she laughed. It reminded him of a skull laughing.

"Here," she said, moving forcefully over and down, "let me love you." She began, gently, and he was surprised to find himself responding. Was it because she was anonymous, or because this was New Orleans? Cesspool, sumphole, miasmal swamp that it was, everyone in New Orleans ate oysters and drank bourbon and stayed up all night and in rut the year

round. Even the roaches and rats grew bigger here, repro-
duced more often ... 'The Big Easy,' they called it: a
suppurating lesion, an open sore, a river, turgid and dark.
And he had come back, not to resist it, but to flow with it:
down the river of regret, through the delta of desire, to the
gulf of oblivion, why not? He felt himself being sucked dry
and drained, nerveless and juiceless, a bone without marrow,
a stone. . . .

"There," she said, moving up alongside him, "but you're
making me do all the work. What's the matter?"

"Nothing." He considered mentioning the woman on the
bus, but thought better of it. Which was she, she might ask:
the night's, or the afternoon's, spittoon? He wondered himself
why he wasn't more lively. If he was capable of being
excited, this anonymous goodwife was capable of exciting
him. "I come and go," he said.

"Well, how about a little more coming and a little less
going?" She thrust once or twice at him, vigorously. "Think
you can manage that much?"

"Sure," he said, and did, but all the while his mind
remained abstracted, his sense of the woman with him nameless and impersonal, while his body did mechanically what
the situation called for. And at that moment, slick with sweat
in the woman's embrace in room 316 of the Fontainbleu, his
déjà vu illusion of familiar strangeness burst: it came to him as
she came, and he failed to, that the woman he was with was
no more like Lee Anne than he was like her lover of last night,
and that this entwining of their bodies and commingling of
juices was no more consummation than his animal encounter
on the bus. And it struck him in his moment of revulsion—
with the visceral impact of a systemic reaction—that the
reason for the woman's fervid vigor, falling hair, and fetid

breath was what he had seen again and again in hospitals, convalescent homes, in the state nuthouse at Mandeville, and even at DePaul's, but never yet in a motel: cancer and chemotherapy.

"She is dying, Girard, dying"—the voice of one of his tormentors, not nattering now in his ear, but seriously pleading in his skull: "And if you were to kill her—now, at the moment of her soft cry, her pitifully brief ecstasy—she would die in desire and in duty to her husband. You would be doing her a favor . . ." "Girard," whispered another inner voice, "what if you were to die in her arms, cut off in the empty waste and middle of your life in this seedy motel room? How would you like that?" . . . The image of the black man bursting from the doorway—legs churning, arms pumping, blood pulsing in a headlong, thrusting, ten-yard lunge for the last bus—into the ring of handguns: his head exploding and his body crumpling . . . Why were sex and violence twinned in his mind, their two heads joined at the hip and at the shoulder? Having died once, and after that the treatment, his only desire this time around was to die desireless.

He felt his breath squeezed out of him; he came. They both lay spent like swimmers, gasping, while locked within her scissor-grip his little thinglet withered.

"You're dying, aren't you?" he said, staring past the woman at the blinking neon light.

Fontainbleu . . . Fontainbleu . . . Fontainbleu . . .

"What if I am?" She laughed scornfully. "Aren't we all?"

With a shudder which he didn't bother to interpret, the woman slid away from him and traipsed into the bathroom, closing the door behind her, locking it. He could hear water running as he put on his clothes and picked up his grip, and when he left the room her bath was still running.

CHAPTER 2

All along St. Charles, from the trolley window, he saw the mansions of his childhood, dark and tenantless, condemned. Black hulks against the midnight sky, their backs against the river, in among the live oaks and magnolias festooned with Spanish moss, the soon to be demolished mansions sat: each one a family crypt and archive, sprawling, spacious. Old families, such as his. The Garden District where, after his mother left his father, he had grown up.

A man without a nose got on the trolley. He watched the man pull out a wet bandanna and wipe repeatedly the glisten-ing center of his face. The trolley clattered past Napoleon Avenue. A block away the darkened structure of St. Stephen's, where he had spent three years in tie and pants and uniform disguised to others as a "Crusader." Gathering speed, the trolley clanged him past the sidewalk tables of Fat Harry's: there, a tenth-grader and truant, he had opened a *Times-Picayune* and read the charges laid against his father by his mother.

All that was a long time ago, and all that remained were a few newspaper items in the archives and some street signs . . . Louisiana, Washington, Jackson, the Irish Channel, where one miserable hot summer in a slave-quarter garage, when he'd returned to New Orleans the first time, wedged in with blacks and Bohunks, between Camp and Coliseum, behind St. Mary's Street he had survived. . . . Strange, how all that rat's maze of memory had vanished, disappeared without a

21

trace, the moment he had left New Orleans; and how it came back now in flashes and fragments, sloshing over the levee of forgetfulness he had thrown up, at the signal markers of the street signs.

Felicity, Polymnia, Euterpe, Terpsichore . . . close crowded streets of dismal shotgun houses, their fronts no wider than a row of drunks stretched out. House fronts flush with the sidewalk: no lawns, no stairs, no alleyways, not even a crawl space between each blockful of house fronts and the dingy, ill-lit bar on every corner . . . Corona's Bar, where he'd taken Lee Anne the first night in Billy Bland's car; a night to remember, or was it? From such harmless evenings and happy hours, drink in hand, the long dark night is fashioned. Clattering past the purple K&B, just closed, where he and Larry went for Early Times, their nightly half-gallon; in ambush at the turnstile stood Lee Anne: a long sweeping stroke of her hand, begun at his chest and falling hopelessly, gropingly down the length of his shirt, grazing him. Larry, embarrassed, had said to her, "I'll drive you home." Then, as he ushered her out through the turnstile: "She still loves you, Girard."

Melpomene, Thalia, Erato, Clio . . . clattering past Calliope and the Jerusalem Temple where as a grade eleven "Squire" he'd taken Peggy Grue to *Laissez Perret*; before that to Valencia, Friday nights for four years—child's version of polite society—and Peggy Grue had gone on to McGhee's, a debutante. . . . Memory was safe, smooth, deep as the waters above one's head, as the darkness all around. Mistaking the past for the present or a phantom for flesh and bone—that was to be shunned at all cost.

The trolley, which had not slackened speed since Jackson Avenue, clattered and clanged hellbent for Lee Circle, as though threatening the bronzed old gentleman to get off the track. At the last moment the trolley braked and shunted around the base of General Lee, passed the 7th Circle Lounge, the Hummingbird Lounge—noisome dens—and dog-legged down to Carondelet, then picked up speed and power for the straight run to Canal. Twelve fifty-five by a Falstaff clock through the window of a dive, winos sprawled in doorways and spread-eagled on the sidewalk. Trolleys stopped at one o'clock—last run. Past Poydras with its wide neutral ground and shiny office buildings. Carondelet a canyon now between tall walls of buildings (not too tall: skyscrapers sank in swamp), a man-made canyon running as the river ran, turning as the river turned, connecting with Canal which had a ferry.

On Canal across from Royal he got off and waited for the lights. A few blacks lounging on the corner at the flood-lit menswear store, while one bag lady jay-walked, toting her bags. A blind pencil vendor went through his ritual: cane forward, foot forward, step, shake can twice. Nobody near him. He went through his routine again, shaking his tin can. The lights changed and Girard crossed Canal Street, broad and garishly lit with, somehow, a green tinge as though it were underwater or steeped in humidity. From this festering center New Orleans like ringworm had spread. New streets had sliced like a butcher's knife through old estates whose owners never dreamed the city would reach them. But the city had followed the river, and the river was a worm, and the worm turned where Canal Street intersected it to form an ox-bow, and from that ox-bow the city spread.

Across Canal he entered the French Quarter, though most of its architecture was Spanish, from the days before the fire. A few buildings had escaped destruction, and bore the marks —burn marks in Lafitte's Blacksmith Shop, water marks with 1794 scrawled in red on the stucco—but he had never

frequented Lafitte's, or any of the bars on Bourbon Street.
Like a man rushing to a fire he covered the first block off
Canal, and turned the corner onto Iberville, a great thirst on
him.

The faded stucco underneath the portico still read
"Martin's Bar—est. 1827, Gentlemen Only," but the place
had changed, grievously changed. He peered in through the
open double doors to where the stand-up bar for a century
and a half had supported planters in their panamas, then
merchants, bankers, businessmen, then sailors, winos, and the
wrecked hulks of human dereliction in a slow decline to its
present clientele. Reluctant to credit what he saw and heard
—the voices and forms of young blacks, male and female,
bumping to the thumping of a jukebox—he stepped inside
and stood facing the bar, hedged in by four or five sticky,
drink-spilled, food-stained tables with straight-back folding
chairs around them. The once-elegant ship's paneling bar still
sported beneath its brass rail the copper pissatoire, into
which generations of men, while guzzling beer on tap and
discussing important topics—who had a better right hook,
Dempsey or Corbett? who would win this year's Sugar
Bowl, LSU or Alabama? would Petitbon carry the Green
Wave all the way? was Ali the greatest fighter who ever
lived?—had simply opened their flies and, without the inconvenience of having to break off drinking or talking, pissed . . .
The copper gutter was still there, but green and corroded and
clogged with junk-food wrappers, crushed cigarette packs,
empty beer and pop cans, and uneaten fragments of food,
while noisome smells of greasy fried foods hung in the noxious
air. . . . Here his father in his broker's suit and Panama hat had
taken him as a boy, into this manly stand-up bar with the
pissatoire where women weren't allowed (no special prohi-
bition was required to keep blacks out), and had sat him on

the bar among the men—Colonel Manning and Dr Conway and Father Desjardins, and others, many others—while they drank and talked about important topics, from time to time relieving themselves . . . The bartender, a raffish little man, just off a ship or from a de-tox center, seeing him standing among the tables staring at the bar, yelled: "Get'cha somethin', bud?" The jukebox stopped its thumping and black couples turned toward him, leering softly while loose-jointedly shuffling toward the tables in the Negro-smelling, heat-afflicted air.

Fleeing the evil-smelling, degenerated den, he walked quickly across Iberville and up Exchange into the Quarter. The Napoleon House he could reach by way of Royal and its antique shops and Spanish balconies, or Chartres with its sailors' dives and dark wooden doors flush with the side-walk. But Bourbon with its bars and strip shows was the Quarter, and the Quarter was New Orleans—had the right of first night, anyway, the pustule where the worm first turned—so he walked up Bourbon, senses jangled as he knew they would be by the gaudy lights and blaring music of the strip shows, barkers hustling, and a black dwarf dancing in the street; tamale vendors, horse-drawn taxis, and religious hucksters; by the sounds as he passed bar after bar of Dixie-land, progressive jazz, blood-rock, funk, and polka; with the smells of hot tamales, horseshit, candied apples, and stale beer. He passed quickly through the crowd which thronged the street and sidewalks, tourists ambling slowly, jeering softly, gathered in embarrassed knots at open doorways to peer in; the barkers opening, then closing their show doors like mollusk shells, revealing wet pink flesh flood-lit and multiplied by mirrors, palpitant—a passing glance, come in, pay and come in . . .

Passing Sinbad's with a quick glance through the doorway,

the barker with his hand out, hoarse and sweating, a fast spiel, electric organ grinding funk inside, a fat girl in high heels and G-string dancing . . . he stopped and jostled his way back through the crowd around the door to look again. Only one or two patrons seated at the bar which, backed by mirrors, was a stage; the fat girl on the stage looked vaguely familiar . . . the barker pulled the door to: "Now or never, frens, only two bucks cover. Pure Cajun maid's 'bout to begin, con-tinuous . . ." The raspy voice drowned in electric organ, the neon sign blinked "Sinbad's." The knot of onlookers moved on to gape next door, and he was left with the barker who looked over and past him, then cocked his head and thrust out his palm, "One buck for you, pal," and opened the door. He paid and passed in, avoiding the topless waitress as he slouched in a seat near the door, in the shadows.

In the shadows he sat silent and soberly watching the fat girl on stage shake and shuffle, shimmy and thrust through her number. She had three or four sequences of moves and had run through them all several times before the organ released her. Toward the end of each sequence she would glare at the organist, a wizened little black man who grinned back at her, then played cadence after cadence, keeping her working. She would shrug and grow listless, abstracted, would almost stop, then begin to move mindlessly one more time through her routine of thrusting and shaking, bending and swaying, arching her back and holding her silicone breasts. Watching her work was painful, like watching a cow being prodded with an electrical goad down a chute. At last the sadistic black, who had been playing "Sometimes I'm Happy" in King Curtis style, completed a cadence and let her go, sweating and stumbling, to the end of the stage, where another girl walked on to take her place. ". . . con-tinuous enter-tainment," he could hear from outside, "pure Cajun

maid's 'bout to begin . . ." The organ player lit a cigarette
and took two or three drags in rapid succession, keeping his
eye on the thin black girl who stood dumbly on stage, eyeing
him dully. Then, with both hands loud on the keyboard, he
filled the air with electric funk; the black girl crouched and,
standing in place, began to twist and writhe upwards and
outwards like a cypress tree out of a swamp . . . He was
reminded, by her swampy contortions, of nothing, flat black
nothingness. . . .

He was watching the black girl and wondering when her
sinuous routine would exhaust itself and become repetitious,
when the fat girl, a wraparound skirt and cutaway blouse
over her G-string, shambled up to his table. She was bearing
a drink tray. There were—he counted them—three other
patrons, all male and each of them stranded amid a sea of beer
bottles and empty chairs. She had come to his table first.
"Drink, Mister?" she said, pronouncing the syllables slowly
as though she were drugged or retarded. He studied her face
in the half-light (vapid), as he already had studied her body
(heavy): a burden to her as she was to the world . . . what
had made him come in here? The girl's face, now that he
looked at it closely, bore not the slightest resemblance to
Vicki's; the one other time he had been in Sinbad's, when
Vicki was dancing, was five, six years ago . . . "Does a girl
named Vicki still work here?" he asked. Then, when the fat
girl stood mutely waiting, "Vicki," he said again, "does she
work here?" The girl glanced fearfully over her shoulder
toward a door at the back where a broad-shouldered, brutish
man stood, arms folded across his chest, then looked at him
blankly and said again: "Have a drink, Mister?"

The black girl on stage was still mechanically corkscrewing up from her inner swampland, the organ still grinding, the
organ grinder still grinning. Pointless to have come into this

place, this ill-baited trap with the pitiful girls and the shotgun stage and the bouncer at the back. The Quarter was full of traps, rat traps, and like a rat from the river he was making his way from one to the next, not using his head but shoving his body through one hole in the wall after another—hadn't he learned enough not to? The girl was still waiting. He waved her away with one hand and got up and, stumbling over a chair in the dark, pushed past the barker and through a knot of onlookers into the street, Bourbon—street of cathouses and watered-down whiskey—and started walking, past "Famous Door" and "Teaserama" and, spying down St Louis Street the four-leaf clover over "Molly's Irish Pub" where Gill, the one-armed sea captain, if he were in port, would be passed out, walked on another block to Toulouse before he turned toward the river.

He steered straight for the Napoleon House, stopping only once to piss against the Louisiana Fisheries Department. Standing up against the darkened building, in among the bushes under a magnolia tree, its roots exposed for fifteen feet in each direction, he could see a block away the inauspicious facade of the Napoleon House—unchanged since 1832 said the sign—and down the street beside it, between it and the blackened hulk of Jax Beer brewery, loomed the shoulder of the levee, holding back the broad and muddy Mississippi. Beyond the levee, which he could see, ran the river which he couldn't: the sluggish, snakelike river—all the way from Minnesota to the Gulf of Mexico—draining middle America, cesspooling here at its delta all the silt and shit from above . . . all the carcasses and chemicals and open sewer lines from Paducah and Memphis and Vicksburg and Baton Rouge—trunk as well as tributaries: the Arkansas, Ohio, and Red rivers . . . New Orleans was the sumphole for them all. Living in New Orleans was like standing underneath an open toilet. If only there were one thing to forget (Lee Anne) or to avoid (alcohol), one river (the Arkansas) to swim . . . but it seemed the entire drainage system with its freight of conglomerate waste was pressing at the levee of his mind and rising with alarming speed to flood and drown him. . . . He lurched across the Fisheries Department yard, stumbling over the exposed magnolia roots, and running catty-corner across Toulouse and Chartres streets darted like a fish out of a net through the open double doors of the Nap House.

Immediately he felt at ease. The easement of a fat man when he sinks down in a chair, or of a sailor when his ship slides into port—all this and more the atmosphere conveyed to him the instant he entered. The uncrowded mahogany of the short bar, the tiny inlaid tiles of the floor and the wooden-bladed ceiling fan turning lazily, the illuminated portrait of a dead waiter over the bar, and the white-shirted forms of the leisurely waiters who seldom made haste and never bumped into each other: these smoothly functioning and familiar sights consoled and calmed him. Small electric candles depending from old stucco walls cast fingers of light through the main room, and from the inner room he heard the thin, scratchy sound of a string quartet emanating, he knew, from the ancient turntable with the pile of classical records beside it, and the yellowed sign: "Please wait until record is finished." Without bothering to look into the inner room, or the enclosed patio at the rear, he took a seat at a table near the double doors which opened onto the sidewalk, facing Toulouse. The clock in the window of the bar across the street showed 1:30.

The waiter he recognized: old and white-haired and with a huge belly, standing quietly beside his table, pencil poised over a tab. "An old-fashioned," he said—here, where they knew how to make them, with water, not soda, and the

bourbon not watered down. He stared out into the street as
the waiter—whose name unaccountably came to him: Felix
—silently scribbled his order and moved away. Along the
lamplighted street a black street cleaner with a huge
mustache-broom moved slowly but rhythmically, sweeping a
pile of refuse toward a bin marked "American Waste." Few
people were out on the street at this hour, and the Nap House
was nearly deserted. Felix padded across from the bar, bearing a tray, and set down his old-fashioned, then withdrew to
his chair against the wall beneath the illuminated portrait of a
dead waiter.

From the inner room over the thin sound of strings he heard
guffaws and a deep booming voice. Voices were distinctive,
though he had somehow misplaced the sound of Lee Anne's;
his own, too. Two men sat, several tables away, quietly
talking; other than them, he was the sole patron in this front
room. The bartender stood in the shadows at the far end of
the bar, and Felix dozed in his chair, the lone waiter. It had
been here at the Nap House at this very table a dozen years
ago, as he had sat and sipped old-fashioneds with Floyd, that
Floyd had guffawed like the man in the next room and
advised him to make Lee Anne—what were his words?—
"Truly unhappy. Offer her insecurity. You can always get a
divorce." Was that the decisive moment, or was he deluded?
Had it been predetermined, set up, arranged—a conspiracy:
all of them breathing together, against him—or did he choose
her? The man in the inner room chortled again: a sound
familiar, but heartier and hollower than he remembered, if he
remembered, Floyd's mirthless snorts. Too often tonight he'd
mistaken one for another, superimposed on superfluous
strangers names and identities, and invested degenerate
creatures with obsessive meaning—all in a vain and futile
longing for a meeting, to be met: by whom? and for what

purpose? Must ghosts, like cotton brokers, reason? Did spirits explain? He laid both palms flat on the table and stared at the drink before him. Bowing his head slowly he brought his nose even with the rim of the glass and, closing his eyes, drew a long deep breath through both nostrils, inhaling the aroma of the whiskey. The smell—of bourbon, sugar, and orange—was heady beyond imagining; the taste would be heavenly, no? He lifted his head and, steadying himself, directed his hand which had darted automatically toward the glass to his shirt pocket instead, from which he pulled a pack of cigarettes, extracted one, and lit it, staring all the while at the frost-beaded, amber-colored glass. "Hail Mary, full of grace," he mumbled, as he picked up the saturated orange slice and, putting aside his cigarette, placed it dripping in his mouth. ". . . thy womb Jesus. Holy Mary, Mother of God, pray for us . . ." He had picked up the glass and now held it out before him, as if toasting an imaginary guest, or consecrating mass-wine. ". . . now and at the hour of our death. Amen." He drank, first a tiny sip and then the tumblerful, tipping the glass higher and higher as the amber liquid drained into his mouth and down his throat. . . .

The party was breaking up in the next room. With a stertorous snort Felix started awake and lumbered up from his chair to deliver their bill, announcing "last round" as he passed Girard's table. An enormous man preceded by two women in evening dress came through the doorway between the two rooms. Idly he stared at Floyd. He was certain it was Floyd though the huge man flanked by women and filling the double doorway bore little resemblance to the Floyd he had known a dozen years ago. Involuntarily, like a patient in a waiting room whose name has been called, he stood up: aware, suddenly, of his shabby, travel-stained clothes, and that for all his dereliction, dissipation, and glances into

desolation, even madness, he was still much fitter, less debau-
ched, and probably more sane than the massive hulk in a
white linen suit bearing down on him, a well-dressed woman
on each arm.

"Floyd? Floyd 'Dragon' Boudreau."

The big man stopped and stared through horn-rimmed
glasses. The women towing him, abruptly arrested in their
progress through the bar as by a huge drag anchor, stared idly
at each other, waiting.

"Why, I do believe it's Girard. Are you a ghost, or what?
The last time I heard tell of you, Jimmy, you'd jumped from
the Huey P. Long Bridge—unsuccessfully, I believe."

"A tug picked me up."

"Ladies," announced Floyd in a stentorian voice, while
old Felix peered over his glasses at the tableau and the
bartender watched from the shadows, "meet an old friend of
mine, James Antoine Girard. He comes of good family. James,
on my right, Mavis. On my left, Lee."

The two women regarded him as debutantes might regard
a black porter, and under their scrutiny he was more than ever
aware of his baggy pants and travel-stained shirt.

"Oh, is this . . . ?" the woman named Lee began.

"It is," Floyd confirmed. "But what I want to know,
Jimmy, is how is what's-'er-name?"

Girard shrugged. "God knows," he said.

"That's what I find is the problem these days, God knows
all and tells nothing." Floyd peered at him through folds of
fat and horn-rimmed glasses, leeringly: a look, Girard remembered now, as distinctive as the guffaw. Yet for all his bluster
and bravado, they were frightened eyes—little boy's and
bewildered eyes entrapped in a huge body.

"You've put on a bit of weight, Floyd."

"You noticed. Twenty-five stone I weigh now. For the

untutored," he turned to each of the women, "that's midway between three and four hundred." He chortled, then moved with surprising speed to the door and called "Taxi!" A cab materialized out of the darkness. "Come, girls," he called, and Girard was left standing while Floyd saw the two women into the cab. Then the cab disappeared, blending again into blackness. Girard laid a bill on the table. Floyd's hand, its knuckles buried in fat and a diamond ring choking one finger, closed over his. "Don't spoil them. I paid. So where are you staying?"

"Uptown," Girard said vaguely.

"You're lying," the big man said bluffly. "You're probably en route to the Greater New Orleans Bridge to try your luck again."

"My luck's run out. I'm waiting for the rapture."

"I heard that slogan," Floyd said softly, "in a black church once. Don't look surprised. I'm not above attending church, even a nigger church, on business. Tell me," he leered, peering obscenely, "is searching for a second death the same as waiting for the rapture?"

Girard, feeling suddenly the whiskey he'd just drunk, the first in months, and belittled by Floyd's mocking raillery, bristled. "Listen, Floyd, I'm tired, I'm broke, and . . . you presume too much."

"I know, I know," Floyd boomed, the whole of him except his eyes enfolding Girard and steering him by one arm toward the door. "I know it's presumptuous of me but, in a way, I was waiting for you. I've been waiting for you for five years." He peered at Girard apprehensively, his eyes still keeping their distance. "I've got something that may interest you. Let's go to Jed's."

Girard balked.

"Embarrassed?" Floyd inquired solicitously. "You always

did run yourself down. Come on, Jimmy. I'll buy you a drink,
maybe two. Your favorite tune's still on Jed's jukebox."

They walked up Chartres to the lot where Floyd had
parked his car. The dome of St. Louis Cathedral loomed
silent and dark over them like a black marker in a black gulf.
Directly across was Jackson Square: General Jackson riding
his horse.

"You see that horse?" Floyd said. "Front feet rampant
indicates that Jackson died in battle, whereas in fact he died
of natural causes in the summer of 1845. Then there's
Beauregard, the manificent statue of General Pierre Gustave
Toutant Beauregard at the entrance to City Park—uptown,
where you're staying, Girard. His horse has one hoof raised,
by which we surmise that Old Beau was wounded in battle.
But, no, nary a scratch did Bory sustain, and he expired in his
bed in 1893. Really, Girard, hard to know what to believe
sometimes—don't you find?"

They had reached the car, a Mercedes. "Little something,"
Floyd said, unlocking the door, "from my first wife—the
bitch." They got in and he turned on the motor, a rich hum,
and drove over the curb, no bump at all, into the dark street
where the Negro pushing his broom, the whites of his eyes
caught by the headlights, swept slowly and rhythmically
toward them American waste.

"Somvabitch," Floyd muttered, veering the powerful car
sharply at the scared black. He guffawed as the street cleaner
dropped his broom and leaped wildly out of the way. "Keep
the uppity bastards in their place," he said thickly. "By God,
this is a dead town, Girard."

CHAPTER 3

"Jed's American" at Lowerline and Freret. The motorcycle
shop on the corner, the dingy "Rooms for Rent" above. They
parked beneath the faded arcade on the oil-splattered drive of
the motorcycle shop, then walked past the alleyway, narrow
and boarded on both sides, which led around to the back of
the bar and up a fire escape to three seedy rooms and a toilet.
   "Fond memories," said Floyd, standing on the sidewalk
underneath Jed's bulb-lit sign which was under the cardboard
"Rooms for Rent" sign.
   Each event in itself was, if not fond, tolerable. Here where
he'd banged Lee Anne twenty-odd times that weekend in the
bed in the room in whose window behind green plastic
curtains the "Rooms for Rent" sign stood, while Floyd came
and went, procurer and voyeur, bringing them oysters to
swallow and beer to swill between heats. Each event was
itself and irrevocable: Lee Anne claiming until that weekend
to have been a virgin (except for the weekend before, in Billy
Bland's car), then insisting on calling her "Daddy" in
Gulfport from the phone downstairs in the bar and telling
him—while the panicky bartender shakily pointed the snub-
nosed .45 at Girard and yelled, "Get that slut outa here! Men
only upstairs. You think I don't mean business?"—that she
was "committed," "engaged," "in love, truly, Daddy," the
bartender cocking his handgun and waving it wildly with
both hands just six feet away at Girard's stomach, trim in
those days . . . each event led ineluctably to the next in a

series of groping steps (blind) down a fire escape (dark) until like Dick and Jane (the faithful Spot fetching them beer and oysters) they had clattered over the garbage cans in the alley, alerting the testy barkeep. . . .

"I try not to think about things," Girard said. "Things don't think about me. One thing, if you think about it, leads to another."

"And here we are—without thought, or mind, or memory . . ."

"Or money."

"Everyman, I will go with you, and be your guide . . ."

"To Jed's." They both said it together, like a ventriloquist and his dummy, and entered the two dark, narrow rooms partially partitioned with burlap, a bar in one and jukebox in the other, crunching underfoot the littered peanut shells. Girard slouched onto the end stool at the bar, the weight of his shoulders hunched forward onto his elbows, and studied the photo taped to the mirror over the bar. Tulane's '65 team —the last to have a shot at the Sugar Bowl; the 1935 team was the last to win it—the photo frameless and faded, the faces youthful and blank—except Mason's: his face was hard, the face of a pro even then; his hand securely on the pigskin as on a possession, something to hold to, to run with . . . And he remembered running with Mason round and round inside the Sugar Bowl, sweating off in ins-and-outs and sprints and jogs, like wringing out a wet jersey, the weekend fraternity booze; then watching Mason run on, from stadium to stadium, in team after team down the years—Houston Oilers, Green Bay Packers, Oakland Raiders, Los Angeles Rams—while he, hung over and in a frenzy to evade the draft after college, planted his ID on a corpse washed up by the Mississippi, only to be swallowed by Lee Anne . . . And there she was! Homecoming Queen of '65, victorious season, with the captain of the team (Mason) escorting her mid-field amid

bouquets and princesses and jerseyed jocks (Girard). Lee
Anne and Mason: that was one he'd not inquired into too
closely, but the image of her shimmying at the homecoming
dance with her escort's hand on her as on the pigskin, while
he drank, and they disappeared, merged in a flash like a
picture too painful to look at with the bed directly above him
and Lee Anne sprawled, legs spread, for a day, a night, and a
day, receiving him time and again in a wad of wetness and a
nexus of goo, the Palomino cleft and chafed sore by his wet
little mess . . . no, no victories since '65, only a bag of
shrimp, a barrel of beer, and a wilderness of women—the
tramp on the bus, the anonymous goodwife in the motel, and
how many others like them? . . . He watched morosely in the
mirror the juke in the next room, old like its tunes, flash on
and off, yellow and purple, though some of its yellows like
pulled teeth were missing. Then Floyd's bulk blocked the
machine and its armature clicked; Floyd at the bar ordering a
pitcher and peanuts.

The bartender drew off a pitcherful of the urine-colored
draft, sliced the froth with a knife, and set the overfull vessel
on the bar. Floyd's fat fingers clasping its handle and the
handles of two frosted mugs, peering over his glasses and
cocking his head at the table toward which he would steer,
then passing, pitcher of beer and trencher of peanuts in hand;
while Girard sat darkly watching him and hearing as he
passed the sound of Hank Williams, twangy and bright, from
the jukebox:

> *I saw the light*
> *I saw the light*
> *No more darkness*
> *No more night . . .*

And, darkly silent, slouched at the bar in Jed's American
between the photos on the mirror of Mason with the football
and Mason with Lee Anne and the spectacle of Floyd attacking peanuts, Girard remembered Jed and arm-wrestling for
pitchers and Jed retailing the story ("Wanna hear th' story?
He prob'ly ain't heard th' story. Wanna hear how Hank died?
Really died? I'll tell ya, I was with 'im.") of driving
Williams's spanking new '53 Cadillac Fleetwood through
Oak Hill, West Virginia, to keep a New Year's Eve date in
Canton, Ohio, Jed the chauffeur with Williams at twenty-
nine a shriveled alcoholic in the back seat, clutching the gold
record he'd just got for "I Saw The Light," Jed trying to
steer the Cadillac while struggling with Williams who was
clambering over the seat and opening the glove compartment
with the hypo in it, plunging the needle into his arm and
pumping air into his million-dollar veins, screaming all the
while "There ain't no light! There ain't no light!" . . .

> *Now I'm so happy,*
> *no sorrow in sight*
> *Praise the Lord*
> *I saw the light.*

A black face, hesitant, appeared at the door. "Get that
black somvabitch out of here! Where's Jed? By God . . ."
Floyd, his mouth filled with peanuts and beer, continued to
mutter: ". . . piss poor. Dixie, shee-ut, Jed's pulling a fast
one, this weak piss is Jax." Floyd quaffed a mugful; poured a
second, and downed it; poured a third. Girard came over and
sat down at the table. "A man has to have a great thirst to
drink here, an indiscriminate thirst," Floyd said. He poured a
mugful of beer for Girard. "A bourbon man, as I recall. Gone

to gin, myself. Gin and menthol cigarettes," he made a face indicative of the depths to which he'd sunk, then lit a Salem, took a drag, and made another face. "Gin and tonic, gin and soda, main thing is to stick with it once you've begun." Floyd dribbled a fistful of peanuts into his upturned mouth. "Gin and peanuts good too, though personally," he intoned as he munched, "I prefer sausage with beer—witness my Teutonic belly. You're keeping fit, sober too, though I can remember you drunk; in fact, I can hardly remember you not drunk."

Girard regarded the pitcher of beer on the table. If he had been drunk he couldn't have run the levee and walked down Jefferson Highway all the way to the bridge. If he hadn't been drunk, if he hadn't downed in quick succession two highballs and a triple bourbon, he wouldn't have set out; or, having walked and run all the way to the bridge, he wouldn't have kept walking out on the bridge and, without breaking stride, gripped the railing with both hands and jumped. "I'm not drunk now," Girard said, "I'm sober."

"You haven't got the money not to be," Floyd pronounced, and quaffed his third mugful. "So why did you come back?" He belched.

The wall clock over the jukebox . . . was missing! For an instant, Girard almost panicked. Then he realized it was the angle he sat at; always before he had sat at the bar. He waited for the patron who stood at the jukebox to move, the ratchet to click, the yellow bulbs to light up the clock face: five minutes to three. He had left the house on Pitt Street while it was still dark; he was picked up five minutes past sunrise. The *States-Item* said the next day that he was rescued "two hundred and fifty yards downstream from the Huey P. Long Bridge at 5:55 A.M." And he felt again, as "The Streets of Laredo" began, the grip of the current and corkscrewing eddy

impel him—up, or down? he wasn't sure—but on toward the
drone of a powerful engine, felt again his fear of the prop;
then popping out on the black swirl of surface, the stench,
and gasping for air; then the crew and curses and his father's
Navy greatcoat caught by the gaffhook; his back dragged up
over the fender; men grappling, groping into each other, their
faces . . . the world is the sea, the church is the boat, men are
fishes . . . he remembered the tugboat. . . .

> For I'm a young cowboy
> And I know I've done wrong

Floyd looked pleased, making the connection, as Girard
knew he would, between his unanswered question and
Mitchum in *Pursued*, between the streets of New Orleans and
of Laredo. He finished the beer in the pitcher and leaned
heavily onto the table, shattering peanut shells with the
weight of his elbows.

"Listen, Jimmy, you've got friends in this town, you still
have. But I'll level with you. When I heard you were going
around with that black chick—not that I'm fastidious in such
matters, you understand, but going around openly in New
Orleans with a black, and to black bars . . ." Floyd shook his
head. "Then, when you called me and asked for a gun—not
that I couldn't spare it: I've got one on me now." He showed
it: under the white linen suit coat and silk shirt, beneath an
enormous roll of stomach fat, in a black belt holster. "But
when you called me here, to that phone," he pointed an
admonishing finger, first at the phone, then at Girard, "and
asked for me, by name, then for a gun—this on the night of
your ignominious swim, with your name on the news and
your picture on the front page the next day—well, suffice it

to say that I've doubted your sanity, James, your sanity and your good breeding. Are you sure, quite sure, there wasn't somewhere along the way, at the sugar plantation perhaps, a Haitian in the woodpile? And where has all this vulgarity got you, but back to New Orleans and Jed's?'' With the finger he had been pointing, Floyd picked his nose; then, producing a monogrammed silk handkerchief from his hip pocket, wiped methodically his finger, his nose, and lastly, his glasses. "And a fell place it is too," he muttered, holding his glasses up to the dim light and squinting, "a loathsome place, without light.''

Girard sat sullenly watching him go through this ritual, sensing somehow, though there had been no hint, that Floyd's next words would be the ones he was waiting for, the words he had come back to hear . . . like fish to the net, or a dog to vomit . . . a word to the dead, from the dying. . . . With calculated unhaste, Floyd completed his toilet, replacing in his hip pocket the soiled handkerchief.

"Actually, Jimmy, all that I just said was horseshit.'' Floyd put his glasses back on and fleered at him—like a priest who has macerated the host and then holds it, hoarding it. Take, break, bless, give; Floyd was short on the giving, the blessing too. "But one can't be too careful, can one?'' Floyd said, blinking—or was it a wink? He folded his soft hands before him, fat fingertips touching. The large diamond ring on his right hand, fourth finger, caught the pale yellow light from the jukebox. "The fact is, I have a small business proposition to make you—for our commonweal, of course . . .''

"Of course.''

". . . which I trust you will treat, ah, discreetly, more discreetly than has been your wont. I wonder . . .'' Floyd glanced around them, assessing their decibel level and the

distance between them and the silent bartender and the one
other occupied table. "I wonder if we should . . . ?"
"The levee?" Girard said.
"Your penchant for water astounds me."
They drove the ten blocks to the levee, Girard having
scandalized Floyd by suggesting they walk. Floyd locked the
car and they crossed railroad tracks, then trudged up the
sandy, weed-choked slope. The sky hung close and overcast,
humid as just before rain, but down the other side of the levee
through a tangle of drowned trees and dense willow bush
they could see the smooth black of the river—blacker than the
deadheads it made cutlines around, smoother than the banks it
surged against—the river flowing as it always had flowed,
toward the Gulf it had always flowed into. Wordlessly, they
began to walk slowly upstream, along the levee's bald top.
Here Magdalena had launched the last day, springing like a
young doe out of the willows and following him home on his
run—forever would he flee and she be chaste?—triggering
Lee Anne's jealous wrath, his escape from the house, his early
morning walk, his run, his jump . . .

> And I who share their torment, in my life
> was James Antoine Girard; above all
> my error was to scorn a savage wife

—was the inscription his stone should bear, if he had a stone,
if it had an epitaph.
　　Fifty paces or so along the levee, the swish of the river the
dominant sound, putrefaction the prevalent smell, Stone
broke the silence: "Have you ever felt there were too many
people, Girard? I mean, in this vigorous city?" He indicated
with a sweep of his arm the sleeping slumtown below them:

shanties and shacks hunkered up at the base of the levee, squalid and yardless and dark, with here and there the shuttered light and muted hum of a black-windowed neighborhood bar, each shanty sheltering slumbering pickaninnies, each shack containing an oblivious bus driver, dock worker, guard, with his freshly pressed uniform on a chair by the bed and his earth-colored woman beside him; beside her the grandparents, uncles and aunts, brothers and sisters, families and hangers-on, clans and outcasts, a whole parish asleep in houses below river level. A city founded on bog, trusting to sandbags. Somewhere a dog barked; another dog answered; a chorus of yip-yapping curs. "Have you ever wished you could help to eliminate some of humanity's suffering? Or, more to the point, some of suffering humanity?"

Girard stopped walking. "This hardly sounds like you, Floyd."

"That's what everyone says. That I seem to be out for myself. People sense that about me. When I approach some nubile Newcomb sophomore out for a midnight stroll in the park—she wants to be raped, or she wouldn't be there— when I say, 'May I film you being sexually assaulted beneath this live oak tree with the festooning Spanish moss, using codex infrared and a zoom lens?'—then she opens wide her little O of mouth, that mouth the world is waiting to see gagged with a black paw; up go her hands to her little pips of breasts, those breasts the public is waiting to see brutally exposed; she squeezes her legs together, those legs the industry is waiting to see forced open and abused—in short, she screams, she flails out, she flees from me. From me! Into the bushes where, doubtless, she gets what she wants and maybe her throat cut in the bargain. It hurts my business, it hurts me. Consequently, I haven't been making many movies of late: just the same tired old still-lifes for the sex mags—faded white housewives on the polar bear rug; Mavis and Lee, the lesbians you met, coupling on tiger skins—that sort of thing. I need a new angle, fresh subjects."

"Try filming disasters, floods, fires."

"Too much competition," Floyd replied, "and too much trouble. No, I've got an idea—no script yet, but an idea—for a feature-length movie. I've even lined up distribution and funding. But I'm having trouble casting it. I lack your charm, Girard, the little Dick Whittington way you have about you, I lack that."

Girard was walking again, his nostrils assailed by the stench from the river as it swished past in the dark. More rain and the river would flood the city, less rain and the city would be overcome by pestilential stench.

"And, due to my peculiar position," Floyd went on, "as trainer of the N.O.P.D. in small arms, a little civic service I perform—which, incidentally, entitles me to carry a gun at all times, and to shoot rioting blacks—due to that, too, I am unable . . ."

"Spare me, Floyd."

"Actually, I had in mind your black concubine, the Miss Black New Orleans of a few years back, what's her name?"

"Valerie?"

"Valerie. She'd be perfect. I can see her in it, and a very demanding part it is too, requiring, you might say, her all."

"When did you ever see Val?"

"Oh, I've seen her, I've seen her—maybe driving her bus, maybe waiting on tables—never mind where. Think you could get her?"

"I thought you didn't consider blacks human."

"I don't mind doing business with them. Strictly business. By the way, I suppose I should mention, it's a snuff movie; but I'd make it worth her while. You might even wish to, ah, snuff yourself out, Girard—in a meaningful and remunerative way, you understand—none of these impulsive moonlight swims, these ludicrous tugboat rescues.''

Floyd stopped walking and lapsed into silence, waiting. The ripples from a deadhead caught Girard's eye and he traced them, with difficulty, back to the source. The air was so humid that he was drenched, and Floyd's suit had turned dark with sweat stains.

''I hope I strike a responsive chord in you, James, when I admit, openly, that your past actions and present demeanor, coupled with your charm in dealing with the fair sex, have emboldened me to make you this offer, as an earnest of which I here and now give you five hundred dollars in cash—a small retainer, tax-free, of course—an incentive for you to look into the matter and to approach the ebony lady.''

Girard felt his hand brushed by bills in a bundle, a bank strap around them, and hearing Floyd say ''strike a responsive chord in you, James,'' wondered as he sensed himself enter deep water whether he was moving upstream or down, and if up to the surface, or down to the bottom, whether he would reach the Gulf sooner or later. . . . He felt himself sinking down, down, like a Greco-Roman wrestler with his legs chopped off, submerged. Was there a fatal combine of forces, some secret New Orleans krewe, pursuing him to use him, whom they had destroyed once already, as an agent of their destructive will? There was no way to know, no way Floyd could have known, of the Fontainbleu incident of five hours past, with the woman in the bed and the knife in the mind and his fantasies about death and dying . . . Yet, the appoint-ment he had sensed pending all night, and the past he had thought was behind him had intersected here at the edge of this river whose blind flow allured and whose power as-suaged him. He struggled not with flesh and blood—a fat

man, priestlike and pale, in a sweat-stained white linen suit
—but with powers, with rivers, with Mediterranean icons
and African images implacable and black as the storm that had
swept through the city and threatened to do so again. As
Girard's hand enclosed the bundle of bills and he felt smooth
black water engulf him, he heard himself asking idly: "You
want a suicide, is that it?"

"A predictable accident will do," Floyd replied, "one I
can film."

"Why not fake it? I mean, it doesn't make sense, Floyd.
Special effects are sophisticated these days."

"And expensive. It makes dollars and sense. Not only is
there the cost of production, there's marketing too. What
chance would I have, even if I did have expensive special
effects, of breaking into the market with just another porn
film? What I need is a certifiable death—the death of a
beautiful woman: what Poe called the only true subject for
Art. Then you've got something."

"What? A murder charge?"

"The legal and technical end's my department. You only
need to get the girl. Ah, James, you get the girl in the end,
and it couldn't happen to a nicer fellow." Floyd had turned
and started to trudge back. "Can I give you a lift anywhere?"

"I'll walk."

He could still call out to the receding fat man, or run and
overtake the blob of blackness Floyd was fast becoming. He
could stuff into his chubby hand the wad of bills and say,
"No thanks, no deal." But the flow of the river—not the
money, which he still held in his hand—seemed to mesmerize
him. He heard the motor starting, Floyd's car leaving, and he
was left alone on the levee, looking down on darkened
shanties similar to Valerie's mother's place, the occupants'
suspirings almost palpable in the close night air; while on the

other side, ominously hissing and gurgling and slopping, the river drained the land like a huge open vein into the warm bath of the Gulf.

In spurts, as a wrestler sweats, it started to rain. He found himself running, running along the levee toward the Huey P. Long Bridge: thinking, then muttering, then shouting to himself as he ran in the rain, "There ain't no light! There ain't no light! There ain't no light! . . ."

CHAPTER 4

From where he lay, on a bed near the window overlooking the street, he could see through the top of the hickory tree to the street below and the house across the street. The street was paved but narrow, the sidewalk raised and cracked—cracked by the roots of the hickory trees and raised by the flood of water which every spring, when the rains began and the gutters clogged and the drains backed up, stood knee-deep in the streets. Now the sidewalks and the street were dry, the gutters alkaline with the imprint of old leaves, the trees between the sidewalk and the street not bare, but not bushy either. He lay propped up on the bed by the window looking down through yellowed clinging leaves at the house across the street.

There were several houses across the street, all shotgun style, with narrow frontage, narrow wooden steps leading up to narrow porches and, behind the porches, long and narrow wooden floors (the floors a crawlspace off the ground, because of frequent flooding), roofed with corrugated tin and flanked by long blind sides, which from his place across the street he could not see. And there was a black Baptist church on the corner, with a mausoleum occupying the square block beyond it. Except for the church, he looked out from the only second-storey window on the block—at the closed breech of the shotgun house directly across the street.

On whose porch a gangling black girl, eleven or twelve years old and with braided kinky hair, sat shelling and eating

shrimps from a brown paper sack, while drinking Coke from
a quart bottle . . . elixir of life, Coca-Cola, whose wetness
and sweetness and acidity could burn a hole in your stomach,
or a black hole in the sheet . . . powder burns, Larry said,
bustling about in his intern's outfit at eight o'clock in the
morning, shit, shower and shave, brush teeth too with tooth-
paste, paste of tooth . . . open up, open up now, a little light
on the subject, see if you've contracted carcinoma of the
mouth yet—wider, ahhh—care for those who can't, or
won't, themselves: now off, off to Charity . . . the black girl
across the street sitting on her porch, dropping limp shrimps
whitish pink down her upturned orifice, washing them down
with Coke; "I'd rather have a radical throat in New
Orleans" would make a good cancer ad . . . the bustler back:
forgot to tell you, fellow with no nose—worse luck, no eyes
either, precious little face—suicide, of course; if only these
people would learn how to squeeze, how not to jerk, the
trigger . . . keeping him alive, though—science and yours
truly—keep you posted, ciao . . . the girl on the porch
swallows the last of the shrimps, rummages through the wet
paper bag, crumples it up and tosses it into the bushes;
wonder how they're keeping him alive and is he black, no,
white, no, whitish pink with little bubbly spots like car-
bonating Coke, all turning gray in the air . . . powder burns,
Larry said, and "You wouldn't believe what a shotgun
muzzle, stuck in the mouth and fired with the thumb, can do
—but the gullet's intact, and the brain" . . . happy thoughts
before breakfast. . . .

Other black children walking and running down the sidewalk; the black girl gulps down the last of the Coke, grabs a
book, goes skipping out the gate to join them. A young man,
tall and black, comes running from the house, taking the stairs
at a leap and hurdling the low wire fence. "Pooky!"—a voice

from inside the house; a black arm out the door, a brown paper sack in the air. Torquing from the waist Pooky fields the sack by arching his upper body over the gate, then tosses the sack and catches it behind his back and goes on tossing and catching it with rhythmic twists and turns, singing to himself, down the Hickory Street sidewalk and across Short Street toward the streetcar stop on Carrollton . . . neutral ground with palm trees running, though the streetcar shunts at St. Charles, all the way to the levee which holds back the river which flows to the Gulf. But if it seeps and spreads before reaching the Gulf? . . . "Thinking while you run on the levee is like drinking in the Quarter," Coach Fatty says. "Here at Tulane winning is not a life or death matter, it's more important than that."

The Angelus bell from Mater Dolorosa—Our Lady of the Drowned—spread through the air like depth charges; in New Orleans matins at nine o'clock, earlier everywhere else. A tall, thin, older black man, anywhere from thirty to fifty years old, comes quietly out the door, which he carefully closes behind him, down the stairs one at a time and, his hand on the gate, stops to speak to a frowsy black woman in a colorless wrapper who sweeps an adjoining porch; then he opens the gate and, pausing to check the tires of a new model yellow Oldsmobile parked in front of the house, closes the gate behind him and walks in the same direction as did the young man, but sedately . . . Sickle-cell anemia, said Larry, her father's already bought one from my brother, already installed in the Mount Moriah mausoleum up the street. Well, who lives forever? Who lives? Who . . .

Already the morning, sickly and yellow, was spilling over the rusty housetops into the gutters of Short Street. Along Hickory, Negroes passed, languid and slow, shuffling along the sidewalk. A mother, shambling and vapid, waiting at intervals for her child to catch up; two women struggling with sacks of groceries; a fat black youth, steatopygic, dressed in a security guard's uniform—is that you, Droopy? —waddled toward Carrollton and the K&B where he worked. All moved slowly, listlessly, beneath the hickory trees along the broken sidewalk.

A large brown woman in a starched white uniform, beige stockings on her stout legs, her hair coiffured in such a way as to make her seem even larger, taller, and orange-colored rather than brown, sweeps majestically out of the house across the street, crosses the tiny porch in a single stride, descends the stairs and lets herself through the gate, half-turning as she passes the frowsy black woman next door (who now sweeps leaves from the sidewalk) to drop like a leaf a word in her direction, then opens the door of the yellow Oldsmobile and stands alongside it, surveying her street, her house, her car, gets in her car and drives off. The neighbor woman stands for a moment watching the yellow car leave. She gives one or two halfhearted sweeps with her broom, looks listlessly up and down the street, then slowly mounts the steps to her porch, sweeping dispiritedly one step at a time, and goes in.

From where he lies on a bed near the window overlooking the street, he thinks: "Nothing has changed, not even her mother's hairdo or the next-door neighbor's wrapper, nothing." He raised himself slowly from bed, and with an effort put on his shoes; his clothes from the night before, wrinkled and damp, were still on him. New Orleans, in spring and with the sun overcast, was damp, humid and damp, short-shirt-sleeve weather. He slumped back on the bed again, waiting . . . for a report, by phone, on the faceless man ("gullet good, brain gone, still holding on—ciao") and the sale of mausoleums in New Orleans (big market here, but how many cities under sea-level?). In New Orleans, Corpus

Christi, Galveston, coffins float up to disturb the living. Laid out in a mausoleum Valerie's father would turn to mud, not dust. Good man, a good man and black . . . and because he was in a black brass band, his departure would be filled with juice . . . Goodman Black here liquefies. . . .

He could scarcely remember what it was like to be dry: lying on his mildewed bed which Larry bought when he moved (on this bed, in other times, lay Valerie; in better days, Lee Anne), watching the parade of blacks (Pooky, Droopy) like leaves from the trees drifting down Hickory Street between the black mausoleum and the trolley track, which ran past Our Lady of the Drowned on its way to the levee which held back the river . . . a long time underwater with bells and the blaring of trombones and trumpets and tubas and cymbals and drums boomed by wizened old black men in fancy regalia dirge-stepping from Mount Moriah Black Baptist Church down Short then along Hickory—the saints marching in, the saints carried out—Valerie's father leads this parade . . . but had there ever been a time when he had been in that number? He couldn't remember. And memory now, in the sickly light of what was passing as present, memory no longer posed a threat but a promise, unattainable, past. . . .

He did not really want to see her . . . he wanted always to see her as he saw her the first time: hosing her car as though it were on fire while hotfooting it on the asphalt of Hickory Street with the green garden hose like a garter snake in her hand, her white shorts and white halter drenched and dull beside the sheen and shimmer of her skin nimbused by rain-bows, her Afro glowing like live wires . . . then stalking exuberantly up the stairs and standing proudly on her porch, arms akimbo in the hot New Orleans sun, to exult in her steaming, gleaming car which was fire-engine red, with across its shiny trunk "CHEVROLET" in bold black letters, and across its chrome grill "VAL".

Now he lay propped up in the mildewed bed looking out through the dingy window, waiting and watching to see her walk out on her porch and stand . . . would she still stand arms akimbo, with a defiant look on her face; then stalk exultant down the steps and boldly cross the street to her car which, though it still bore the inscriptions "CHEVROLET" and "VAL," had a crumpled left front fender and its dented trunk wired down? . . . Or would she, like the others—her sister, brother, father, mother, even the frowsy neighbor woman in the colorless wrapper—listlessly gaze toward the house in which he lay, half lay, in the bed beside the window, hiding and watching, not wanting to be seen . . . because to be without desire, without heat or passion and unsubject to change, was more desirable than pleasure which was transient or the pain of memory; and memory, whatever else it might be, was seeing without being seen: the furnitureless space in the mind's eye, unflinching, trained on the breech of a shotgun house from which the blind emerge, blinking. . . .

He started. The Angelus bell, long and drawn out, twelve times and a half—was it noon? Jed would be opening up now, letting down the awning and sweeping out the peanut shells from last night; and this morning when he and Floyd . . . He suddenly felt hungry and sat up on the edge of the bed. He couldn't remember when he had last eaten; then he remembered: Mobile. Money—he fingered the bills in his pants pocket—none in Mobile; a wad now. He fished in his shirt pocket for cigarettes—the package was wet, the cigarettes brown—lit one and took a deep drag. Floyd's was a market approach, nothing personal. Valerie could buy in, or stay out. He was the middle man, pimp, procurer—exchanging loyalty for lucre, practicing despair. If he were successful, what would he gain? If he failed, what could he lose? . . . nothing . . . nothing. If Valerie bought in and it went badly,

Floyd would scramble for higher ground. Where would he
go? He got up and went to the bathroom which always
smelled musty . . . wet towels in a corner, mildewed shower
curtains, ammoniac smell from the toilet . . . the neat little
Jewish girl with short hair that Larry brought to the party
(nurse from Truro, no name) sitting, her crotch exposed,
peeing—"Excuse me. There's a latch there, you know."—a
hundred people outside the latched door, his nose in the
cockpit of pleasure, his tongue . . . what made memory, and
such fugitive food, so delicious? Certainly not the taste, acrid
and tart; nor the smell, urinary . . . could there be in such
flashes the memory of memory, the pure present tense of two
dogs? Or would consciousness always be drowned in the
slime of a pulsating vulva? . . . He extinguished his cigarette
in the toilet and opened the medicine cabinet. Three cockroaches skittered in different directions among nostrums that
Larry had filched. Watch them, admire their resourcefulness
—indestructible, nearly. "A cockroach can live for ten
years," Larry said, "in the refrigerator lining, or the toilet
bowl—without food, or heat, or light, or air—he needs only
moisture." From the clutter of bottles he retrieved Larry's
razor, soaped the hollows beneath his cheekbones, and
shaved. Then he went through the kitchen and out the back
door, down the rickety stairs that clung to the rear of the
house in a tangle of mirliton vines, the shriveled fruit as he
descended the stairs falling and plopping below him:

and we go,
and we drop like the fruits from the tree,
even we,
even so . . .

through the gate which let onto the sidewalk, and across Hickory Street. . . .

He knocked again, louder this time. The neighbor woman opened her door and peered out at him—is that you, Frobena? Peekaboo!—gave a startled look, and vanished. Valerie's inner door being unlocked, the latticed outer door opened a crack—black face with white eyes staring at him— the latticed outer door shut. Valerie's sister padding noiselessly into the house's recess to tell her. The outer door chain being unfastened, the door opening . . . he stepped inside.

He could see, before his eyes had grown accustomed to the dark, the whites of her eyes and her gleaming teeth; she was standing in the center of the small, dark room, which was made smaller, darker, by the massive couch and easy chair with wine-colored cushions and the wood-stained walls and floor. Before he could speak she motioned him to silence, and pointed: on the couch, hedged round with cushions and blending with the plush upholstery, lay a sleeping picka- ninny. She took his hand and led him from the room, through a bedroom (darker, dominated by her mother's double bed on which lay sleeping two more children) into a third room containing three cots and a crib (on one cot sat her sister, nursing a baby; as Valerie led him through the narrow room, the sister squeezed past them into the front room) and on into the last of four rooms, the kitchen, with a toilet and a tub partitioned off in a back corner. Valerie released his hand and slumped down in a straight-backed chair beside the breakfast table; he sat down on the other kitchen chair. The breakfast table was vinyl and the kitchen floor linoleum, and his eyes had grown accustomed to the dark, so that now as she sat facing him, wearing a flimsy cotton housecoat, he could see

her Negro features and the glossy jet-black skin of her face and
neck and arms. But his senses were assailed now, not by the
sight, but by the smell of her, and not of her alone but of the
house through which he'd passed and now sat down in,
breathed in with every breath he took—the strong, slightly
acrid and organic smell of upturned earth, of fecundating sex,
of fertile bottomland and river delta. And seeing her, and
smelling her, he remembered not just that he had left her, but
why: because desire, once yielded to, was bottomless, and
there was that about her which she could not contain nor he
possess—a vibrance, atavistic, Afric, which disturbed him.

"Well?" Her voice, when she spoke, was as he remembered, resonant. "So Jimmy's done come home agin, come
home to Nu Orlunz. You look like you need feedin'."

"I could eat," he said.

"Mama's left some food out, had her circle here for dinner
yestiday, le's see now," she got up, pulling the flimsy cotton
housecoat around her and holding it to her as she opened the
oven door, "they's fried chicken, an' black-eyed peas, an'
mashed potatoes an' gravy, an' . . ."

"That'll be fine," he said, getting up to go to the bathroom.

"I'll put some coffee on," she said, "an' clothes. When you
flush that turlet, jiggle th' handle. The light screws on."

"I remember," he called, closing the door behind him and
hearing the oven door shut and her footsteps leaving the
kitchen. Then he reached up and screwed on the naked light
bulb and confronted like a calcified corpse in the corner the
open toilet seat where . . . while he had sat out front with her
father, sitting and smoking silently in the front room—the
only sound, her piercing shrieks; the only smell, ammonia—
she had crouched screaming on the toilet seat, her mama
kneeling before her, holding her legs open while she pulled
the wet grass and bloody packing-crate filler which had been

blessed by the old voodoo woman, pulling it and with it the fetus, until it came, the roots caught and it came, her mama holding and she retching all over her mama—the little blue-veined thin-membraned curled creature with fingers and toes all bloody and strangled with grass. . . . He unzipped his fly and waited a long time, squeezed out a few drops, and flushed—remembering to jiggle the handle—and thought: "How could she have been so naive?" But then, he had been naive also, in some ways more naive than she:

"If it's just for a night, it's not worth it. No black man would take me out, an' I'd be wipin' counters the rest of my life. It's not worth it. You don't even know me."

"But I'd like to, I'd like to give it a try. Not just for a night, you're not just a night's or an afternoon's spittoon; you're a woman, a beautiful, black . . ."

"I'm black, you don't have to tell me. That's me, an' I'm not ashamed. But you would be."

"I'm not."

"You will be."

The toilet continued to run and he jiggled the handle again. Then he reached up and unscrewed the light bulb, and opened the door. Valerie in a short-sleeved white work uniform was standing, her back to him, at the oven, spooning out from two steaming pots a plateful of food.

"You want pig's tails?" she asked over her shoulder.

"What?"

"Pig's tails, they's pig's tails in Mama's peas—you want some?"

"I'll try some, I guess."

"Humph." She glared at him, spooned out a big gob onto his plate, then set the plate down on the table. "Now don't you go tryin' nothin' you ain't had before, you always did have a weak stomach. Coffee's comin'."

"You're not eating?"

"Gotta go to work. Jackie's watchin' th' babies. We done had a slew of 'em since you been round, Jackie 'n Sheelita 'n me, even Yulanda. Seems last year was a year for havin' babies round here. Nobody missed out, 'cept Mama."

He sat down at the table and started to eat. The food tasted astonishingly good. He finished the first plateful and Valerie spooned up a second, poured coffee for both of them, and sat down.

"How's your father?"

"Got th' black disease. An' you know that jazz band he plays with? Ol' men comin' by all hours t' see how he's makin'—Mama's 'bout fed up. It's hardest on her. Now tell me, 'fore I take off for work, how's Jimmy?"

He nodded, his mouth full of food.

"We had good times, didn't we? Ain't nobody had as good times as we did. 'Member when you took me to that guy's place out by th' airport—th' one with th' alligator tanks— an' called me a black hole in th' sheet? You was awful cruel to me, Jimmy."

Girard washed down the food with some chicory coffee, thick and sweet like molasses. "You were a black hole, Valerie, you still are—the black hole I fell into, and am still climbing up out of."

"Hogwash! You been in so many, you done got confused. Your black hole weren't me. Maybe it were th' river, or maybe your own mind. I'm th' only thing normal ever happened to you, an' where did it get me? I'm th' one in th' hole"—she held up both hands to call the kitchen to witness —"th' same black hole I was in."

"You should have used something, Val."

"Yeah, I should of—a .45. That night I come to you askin' for money, twenty-five measly dollars to help with th' doctor . . ."

"Your second abortion."

"That's right, the one my mama still don't know about. Well, Joe . . ."

"Your friend the longshoreman."

"My husband, my ex-husband now. He say if you didn't come through with th' money, he'd person'ly put a hole through yore white hide."

"He didn't."

"That's 'cause I told him you paid. But I swore to myself then and there, I ain't never gonna scrounge again. Joe was good to me when I was in trouble, an' you was goin' out with all them white girls, gettin' over on us. I never should a' married him, but I wanted to get outa here, you know how bad I wanted outa mama's house."

Her last words were delivered point-blank and Girard felt, this time on a full stomach, the guilty backwash and a nauseating undertow dragging him down. Then he told himself that this particular levee had washed out years ago and that loyalty, though it might still exist, was a coffin that had floated up when the mausoleums flooded. Guilt was a corpse.

"I seem to remember something like that," he said vaguely. He was aware, as she sat glaring at him, smoldering with an old bitterness, that the white uniform which she'd put on for him—though many black women wore white uniforms and looked sleekly desirable in them—was for her an emblem of shame. After five years, still dressed in mourning. And he wondered idly, if he took her then and there, on the kitchen floor, in among the sleeping pickaninnies and the pig's tails, would it cancel out an old debt, or contract a new? Would it matter? So many babies conceived, aborted, born—black babies, white babies, brown, high- and low-yellow babies— so many dugs sucked, sucked dry, and not enough blood let,

not nearly enough . . . New Orleans a pimple ripe for bursting to see what color the pus. . . . "Listen, Val, I don't know
what your situation is, and I don't want to know. But it looks
like you could use money."

She flounced up and started clearing the plates. "Do we
stack, or is we quality?"—in honeyed tones, with a little
curtsy—"I'll tell you one thing: Miss Black Nu Orlunz don't
mean a thing once you're caught sleepin' with a white man,
'cept you can't get a job nowhere an' if a thief or a rapist ever
recognize you you'll get shot lower down than th' stomach.
Sure, I could always use money—black money, white money
—so long's it's green, I could use some. You know where
some is?"

"I do, but it would mean a few pictures—a few dollars for
a few pictures." He waited.

His dirty dish in her hand, she stood and looked at him.
"You've done stooped that low. You look th' same, you even
sound th' same, but you ain't th' same. Time was I said you'd
never pass me by, you'd never deny you knowed me. But that
was a while back." She shrugged, and turned to the sink and
started running some water while putting away the food.

"Shall I set up an appointment," he said, standing up.

"Sure," she said. "Sounds easier than servin' food. Anyway, I'm like them channel swimmers, smeared all over with
erl—cain't nobody see the real me."

Girard left her, her back turned to him, at the sink, the
sound of running water and the smell of sleeping bodies,
palpitant and black, pursuing him as he groped his way
through the dark house.

II. GIRARD LOSES HIS WAY

As long as a thing is being corrupted,
there is good in it of which it is being
deprived; and in this process, if
something of its being remains that
cannot be further corrupted, this will
then be an incorruptible entity, and to
this great good it will have come through
the process of corruption.

Augustine, *Enchiridion*

CHAPTER 1

Memory knows before imagination remembers, knows ineradicably within itself the terrain over which it has traveled. Try though it may to efface and erase, to live in the pure present tense and sheer middle, the barbs in the flesh have been fastened and the sensors set to alarm. Knows before it remembers the resonance of a black voice, his mammy's when as a boy of seven one hot August night after supper he escaped from his bedroom—shinnying down the clematis-choked drainpipe over the carriageway between the big main house and the Colonial addition—and made his way through the droning of cicadas and odor of dampness along the tall dark stalks of sugar cane (the river a hundred yards off, but hidden by the levee) to the sounds and smells, stronger and older, that drew him: the washtub bass and one-strand on the wall of the shotgun house (flanked by others, each identical: imitation-brick tarpaper outside, bare cypress boards inside; a front porch for sitting on out of the heat, and a chicken-run under the house) where his mammy with her pungent smells and late-night cooking lived. Childless except for him, she lived with Jasper, and Jasper, a battered old guitar across his knees, sits on the porch with his legs drawn up. When he sees the boy dart from behind the cane curtain to the hard-packed earth beneath the chinaberry tree, he strikes a chord.

"Com'ere, son." Strikes another chord. "You know th' diff'rence 'tween bein' sanctified an' what we calls th' blues? This here's th' blues." He plays a progression of chords, very

animatedly, grinning up at Love as she emerges from the house
and stands arms akimbo on the porch, glaring down, first at
Jasper, then at the boy in the yard.

"Whar you hidin', boy? I gets in trouble if you be here."

"Let'm be, Love," Jasper says. Then to the boy: "Love
here's been sanctified, so she don't hear no blues. If I's to play

> *Baby, please don't go.*
> *Baby, please don't go.*
> *Baby, please don't go back to Nu Orleens—*

she wouldn't hear me."

Love raises her strong black arm as if to swat a fly and
Jasper quits singing and strumming.

"But I tricked 'er, son, I tricked 'er—jes lak yore daddy
done tricked me. Yore daddy . . ."

"Come on here, ah'm takin' you back home." Love coming
down the porch steps, alarming roosting chickens underneath,
black arm outstretched.

"Yore daddy, he in sugar—am ah right? All this here,"
Jasper waves a languid arm in a fading arc, "b'long to yore
daddy—am ah right?"

"Doan listen to 'im." Love, with a firm grip on the boy,
starts marching him off to the big house.

"Yore daddy, he ain't sanctified, an' he doan sing no
blues," Jasper yelled, striking the guitar for emphasis.

"My mother's sanctified!" the little boy, struggling in
Love's arms, yelled back. "My mother sure is sanctified—you
bet! Isn't she, Love?"

"You mamma shore is somethin', all right. But it ain't
sanctified. I tole you not pay him no mind. You come on,
now."

. . . and memory knows before imagination remembers coming home to the big house: his mother alone in the Empire sitting room, sitting dramatically on the stiff-backed S-shaped love seat beside the baby Steinway, the fingers of one hand resting on the Steinway's wood, her long Napoleonic index finger tapping as she speaks: "I was just about to send the sheriff out," she says, indicating without looking at it, the chiming clock atop the cypress mantel. "Your father's locked in with his accounts, as usual. He has cut himself off from the business," she spoke each word ruefully, "the business of getting and raising children. And I . . ." She broke off to face the boy full on: his mother, his beautiful mother. "Why do you do this to me, Jimmy? I am a sick woman. Have you no pity? If it weren't for Love here . . ." She looks at Love, a searching look between a glare and a plea, then presses her long index finger against the wood of the Steinway so long and so hard that it leaves a mark in the mahogany. "I'm not feeling myself tonight," she says, regaining her poise and retrieving her hand from the Steinway to hug herself as though she were chilled, though it is hot. "Put Jimmy to bed, will you, Love?" And presents her face, her beautiful face, to be kissed.

. . . remembers hearing as he and Love ascend the spiral staircase the strains of opera from behind his father's locked door: the strange words and lush sounds leaping the carriage-way from the little room where his father spends most of his time—a simple Colonial-style room with a cot and a desk and his father's plantation accounts and his records. Love tightens her grip and shakes her head at the boy's attempt to bolt free, not missing a step as she shuffles on up to the head of the stairs where his sister, not sleeping, but pretending to sleep until she sees who is coming—just Love and him—starts shaming him with her two index fingers (she has long

ones just like her mother) and taunting him as Love marches
him down the hallway past her bedroom: "Shilliky pooky,
pull out your horns! Shilliky pooky, put out your eyes!"
Already she has had her picture in the *Times-Picayune*—standing hostess-like in a bell-shaped hoop skirt with lace sleeves,
brown hair in ringlets, their colonnaded big house in the
background framed by live oaks—the caption reads: "Southern Elegance. Linda Girard, 14, pictured here outside her
parents' plantation near Burnside, La., is living proof that the
elegance for which the South is justly famed can still be
found. She will be making her debut at the Carnival of Rex
next February. Photo by A. Antoine." James Antoine Girard,
7, as he is marched past her room to his own, sticks out his
tongue.

. . . remembers too most vividly being alone in his own
room, his head toward the river, his feet toward his sister's,
which was the master bedroom (ever since he could remember, and certainly since the addition was built for his father,
his mother had slept downstairs in the guest bedroom—
"Nearer the ground," as she put it, meaning the grounds, for
she often went walking at night under the live oaks or along
the levee, and once she had caught him on his way through the
canebrake to Love's; his father, of course, slept at the back, on
the hard little cot in the bare little room that smelled of pipe
smoke and sounded of opera, neither of which his mother
could stand or would tolerate in the big house—"I know I'm
only a guest here, in your father's house, but I *won't* be
insulted!"): so that his cognitive map of the house in which
he grew up disguised to himself as a child, while memory
seeped into him along with the sound of his father's operas
and Jasper's delta blues, was of himself lying alone in his big
bed with the eight-foot-high tigerwood posts, staring up at

the sixteen-foot ceiling whose central design, a lumpy medallion of horsehair and plaster (scrolled there by a journeyman
builder in 1821, so his father said), was neither symbolic nor
scary; while his sister slept the sleep of self-conscious pretti-
ness (to her everyone was either a spy or an admirer); with
his mother out roaming the grounds at night or striding free
on the levee (his father locked in his room smoking his pipe
and playing *La Sonnambula* or *Lucia di Lammermoor* or *Norma*);
with Love and Jasper and the rest of his father's tenants living
their secret lives behind the curtain of cane they planted each
year around Easter, and cut and stripped and ground then
hauled to the sugar refinery at Houma every year around
Christmas; while at his head the river flowed—past Burnside
and Convent and Gramercy and New Orleans—to the Gulf
it had always flowed into. (Though he could neither see nor
hear it as he lay on his bed in the dark, he could sense the
river's ceaseless flow—like his mother's restless stride—past
his head, almost through his head.) So the map in his mind of
where he lived as a child was bounded by river and canebrake, and restless, dominant women—one black and one
white—with his father and Jasper alone with their music,
and himself and his sister (who was seven years older than
he) understudying their future parts in this doomed pavane
which seemed to revolve around them. When the music (like
the silence at table) grew too turgid, or the prancing (his
father's term for his mother's walks along the levee) too
intense, they would escape—his sister upriver to Ashland
Plantation, and he into the water turret next to the house.

It was cool in the water turret, cool and cubic. The
diamond pattern in the brick work, where loose bricks had
been removed, enabled him to see—when he stood on tiptoe
and peered through the lowest diamond-patterned slit—all

that was going on around the house: his father in his room above the carriageway, when he moved across the window; his mother in the guest room or the Empire sitting room; Love crossing back and forth between the dining room in the big house and the kitchen in the Colonial addition; from time to time Jasper coming to see Love, or his uncle Armand calling on his mother. All this he could see through the diamond-patterned slit, while hearing the attendant sounds of opera from his father's room, Love's cooking from the kitchen, his mother's summons, "Love!"—could see and hear without being heard or seen. And gradually, as he turned eight, then nine, the pattern he was watching warped and changed, as though the bricks had shifted: his uncle Armand's visits to his mother became daily, his mother's prancings on the levee were nightly, his father's ventures from his room became so rare that he was virtually a prisoner (Love taking food to him three times a day), while his sister went away and stayed at Ashland for weeks at a time, only coming home on weekends and for clothes.

It was on one of these weekends that he saw her, not in her high-throated, full-bodied bell-skirt with lace sleeves, nor in the ghastly gray skirt and white blouse that she had to wear to the nun's school, but sunbathing bare-buttocked in the yard beyond the live oaks and the riding paling. In the moment when she turned, as on a spit, from sunbathing her back (gathering the swimsuit top against her breasts, but not quickly, not self-consciously) and lazily, languidly, her body full of warmth and flushed with sun, she dawdled in the turning and let her swimsuit top fall to the ground, exposing her quick breasts and tufted crotch—an object, and seemingly content to be an object—while he peered through the dia-mond-patterned slit of the turret, both a spy and an admirer: in that moment of sunripeness he saw her, and it was like peeking through the lattice of the gazebo when they were children, except that she was vulnerable now, having breasts and pubic hair to cover, while he was safely hidden in a brick-lined turret, as completely walled-in as he was concealed.

The end came suddenly, as suddenly as a surveillance site being spotted from the air and blown up. It happened in the same summer he turned ten. His sister, seventeen, had started entering the baton-twirling competitions which would be her forte in the beauty-queen contests—Miss Sugar Cane, Miss South Louisiana, Miss Baton World, and, finally, Miss Louisiana—she would go on to win within the next five years. There was little kerfuffle surrounding Linda's small triumphs, which went largely unnoticed at Homewood. He would see her strutting around the riding paling, flinging her baton up between the live oaks and catching it when it came down; then she would be absent for a weekend; and when next he saw her in her drum-majorette's outfit it would sport a new ribbon—blue, all her ribbons were blue.

One Sunday the summer he turned ten he had gone out to spy on the big house and to lie in wait on Linda's return from Houmas, or Lake Charles, or Baton Rouge, or wherever it was she had gone baton-twirling. As he approached the water turret he heard moaning from inside. He couldn't believe his ears! Until then he was convinced that no one else knew of his hideaway, not even Love. Maybe it was some branches rubbing against one another, or some animal, maybe a possum, had squeezed inside and got trapped. He opened the little door and his eyes, adjusting to the diamond-latticed dark (like hundreds of slant-eyes looking in, like being inside a fly's head), spied Linda! In her drum-majorette's shorts and cape she lay on her side hunched up in a fetal position, hugging her knees while rocking back and forth, and with

every rocking motion she cried "Mamma . . . Mamma . . .
Mamma! . . ."

He stood in the door through which sunlight poured,
gaping, not knowing whether to run get their mother, or . . .
And then Linda, seeing him stand there frightened and starting to cry himself at her distress, opened her arms to her little
brother, who ran to her and buried his face in her neck.

"It's all right, it's all right, Jimmy," she soothed. And
now she was consoling him for the fact that their mother
never went to her contests.

"She just has her own life, that's all. Not that she don't
love us, just . . ." James Antoine Girard, aged ten, nuzzled
closer into the softly heaving breasts of Miss Sugar Cane cum
Miss Baton World.

"I begged and pleaded with her, but she wouldn't come.
She's never been to anything I'm good at, and now she says
we're movin' to Nu Orlins, just like that!" Linda snapped
her fingers. Her warm breasts jiggled underneath Girard's left
cheek.

"Well, I'm not goin'! I swow I won't leave Homewood for
Nu Orlins!"

Until that moment, snuggled into Linda's breasts while she
rocked him back and forth and bitterly complained ("Mamma
can't do me this way, her an' Uncle A."), he had never
thought of New Orleans, except as a place downriver which
the Father of Waters passed as it passed him, and as the origin
and destination of the stern-wheelers which plied the half-
mile-wide chocolate-colored river and hooted when they
passed Homewood.

He would not remember New Orleans until he moved
there with his mother and his sister to the house on Henry
Clay. The house was not far from the Garden District ("not
far enough," he heard his father say) and, like Homewood
seventy miles upriver, it was only a stone's throw from the

levee. Once installed in the house he would remember trips to
town and sleeping alone in the cramped single bed without
cornerposts beneath a ceiling eight feet high that threatened
to crush him it was so low, while his parents in the next
room sat at the round oak kitchen table and argued late into
the night. He would remember those earlier trips when, the
summer before he entered grade five, he was moved to the
house in town, and forced to wear a uniform and attend St
Stephen's Elementary, a prep school for St Stephen's
Academy, when his father's strained voice and long silences
were no longer as near as the next room, even in argument.

Those earlier arguments had mainly to do with his uncle
Antoine (though for a time he thought it was himself), and
shortly after they moved to town his Uncle Antoine moved in
with them and shared his mother's bedroom, though she
denied this—even when Uncle Antoine was late in getting up
and fixing himself the Turkish coffee he always drank, she
would deny that he had slept there, or, at any rate, that they
had slept together. "Your Uncle Antoine dropped by before
breakfast and fell asleep," she would say; or "Your Uncle
Antoine has to go to Houma today, and I told him he could
stay over," or some such transparent lie. And so it went, and
so it had gone, for years: his mother, for some obscure reason
of her own, saying, in effect, "believe me, not what you see,"
and his sister and himself, after a brief period of bafflement,
disbelieving both. His father did visit, but since the move to
town coincided with the divorce he didn't visit often; then,
after the newspaper article, he didn't visit at all, though he
would call on the telephone, and write occasionally—the
envelope addressed in his father's cramped hand to "Master
James Antoine Girard, Esq., 1406 Henry Clay, NOLA"—to
arrange a meeting in Audubon Park, or at Monkey Hill, or at
the zoo.

The newspaper article which marked the end of his father's

visits to the house—a full-page ad, really, with a fluted column at the bottom which read: "*Advertisement paid for by friends of Mrs. Irene Trepagnier Girard*"—came out on a school day and was not shown to the boy, though he noticed that his mother was upset and that his Uncle Antoine was more in charge than usual. Even before he left for school the telephone had started ringing, and when he got to school the taunts began: two grade nine boys who often badgered him to entertain them with "them big words, man!" this morning pestered him about "them women, man!", and other boys seemed to cluster in the hallways at their lockers in small squads of whisperers, or gigglers, with him the object of their fun. He knew it was serious when in Father Haloquet's French class the anemic Jewish frailty who wore glasses and a little cap on Fridays cast a sympathetic look in his direction. Period three was occupied by a pep rally in the auditorium. The band played a tune he had heard on the radio, followed by the Key Club quartet. Suddenly a parade of students with a huge banner in hand ("St. Stephen's Crusaders") encircled the humming, harmonizing quartet, the supposed sons of the Four Freshmen. The lead-singer called up his grandmother, the maker of the banner. An emotional display between the two, followed by a tear-filled speech. All this amid thundering shouts and applause, students jumping up and clapping above their heads, speeches being made by teachers. Then followed the drama of introducing the football players, who crouched in position and did a mock skirmish on the gym floor. The head coach, then his assistants, introduced. A film about "Taking Risks" shown. The national anthem sung, followed by a pledge of allegiance. Another, yet another message prompting students to buy SAC cards (which would enable the holders to attend football games, dances, and other student activities for less money)—the whole rally was directed toward the marketing of SAC cards—concluding with a standing ovation and the band's rendition of the school song.

He managed to get away in the crush around the football team that followed the pep rally, and once out of the gym he walked quickly down Prytania Street to Napoleon Avenue, then turned left a block to the purple K&B on St. Charles Avenue. Here he bought a newspaper, something he had never done before, and he wasn't sure which one to buy. But the Negro boy hawking the *Times-Picayune* seemed less offensive to him than the wizened old black with rheumy, bloodshot eyes sitting in attendance on the *States-Item*, and spitting often; besides, the paper his mother and his uncle subscribed to was the *Times*. So he bought one, standing in the sun in his khaki uniform and tie, fishing in his left pocket for his lunch money and handing it to the Negro boy, who handed him a folded *Times* and rolled his eyes; then hurrying with his paper across Napoleon Avenue to an empty sidewalk table outside Fat Harry's where, feeling as his sister did that everyone around him was a spy, he turned the pages of the paper, scanning them, until finally on page B-17 he saw his name, Girard— his father's name—and down at the bottom of the full-page spread with borders like the ones announcing funerals, bankruptcies, and election promises, his mother's signature, Irene Trepagnier Girard. He read quickly, so as to get the gist but not suffer the full brunt of his mother's ad.

TO THE GOOD PEOPLE OF NEW ORLEANS, A DECLARATION:

WHEREAS Mr. James Allemands Girard, a man I know well, having borne two children to him while residing with him on his holdings at Homewood near Burnside, Louisiana, is a man whose credit, like his reputation, is in dispute; and

WHEREAS the said Mr. Girard, although separated from me for nearly a year now, continues to importune the Holy Roman Catholic Church and our Primate, His Excellency, the Most Reverend Phillip Labranche, for a divorce settle‐ ment favorable to himself, in order to shore up his credit; and

WHEREAS he maligns me and misrepresents my character to the Archbishop and all other Christians in New Orleans, and threatens to sue for the custody of our two children:

I THEREFORE DECLARE Mr. James Allemands Girard to be a scoundrel and no Christian gentleman, and I dissociate myself from him entirely;

FURTHERMORE, I offer in defense of my action, which is neither precipitate nor vengeful, the following provoca‐ tions which I suffered while residing at Homewood with Mr. Girard from October, 1938, to August, 1955:

I DECLARE that the said Mr. Girard, while cohabitating with me, his lawful wife, did entertain guests of the opposite sex in his room and did on more than one occasion commit adultery, to my certain knowledge, as follows: on or about the night of March 16, 1955, with a woman named Lucy, and on or about the weekend of April 3–5, 1955, with another woman named Norma;

I FURTHER DECLARE that Mr. Girard, while still within the bonds of Christian wedlock, did on numerous occasions during the years 1951–1954 take trips to New Orleans where he kept a mulatto concubine whose first name is Thalia;

FURTHERMORE, he arranged to meet, and did meet in

compromising circumstances, without my consent or the knowledge of their husbands, the following persons: Mrs. A.D. Tureaud, Louisa A. Conway, Narcisse Landry, Roberta Manning, to name but a few;

FINALLY, in view of the fact that throughout these seventeen years Mr. Girard acted the part of neither husband nor father, nor of responsible provider, but kept himself locked in his room where he entertained women friends, and took trips to town where he kept a Negro mistress,

I HEREBY DECLARE myself aggrieved in spirit and outraged that such behavior should be countenanced; I withdraw myself and my children from his scandalous influence; and I respectfully warn his creditors that Mr. James Allemands Girard is a bad risk.

Regretfully,

(Mrs.) Irene Trepagnier Girard

Some of the names, he knew, were heroines from his father's operas; one was a street name in the city where his father had done business—"Thalia," between Melpomene and Erato, was where the sugar broker's office was (he had gone there with his father many times); and some were actual names of real people—Mrs. A.D. Tureaud, for instance, at Union, and Miss Louisa A. Conway of Whitehall, and Narcisse Landry at Tippecanoe House: these were all owners, or the wives of owners, of plantations adjoining Homewood. Even Colonel Manning's wife at Riverton was included on his mother's hit-list. Whether all of the names corresponded to actual persons he did not know, nor did he know whether his father had had dealings with all, or some, or none of them.

Not only did he not know, but nobody else would know either, including his mother; though she thought she knew, and had told the world which now thought it was in the know. Perhaps even his father didn't know, or, if what his mother said were true, perhaps he had lost count and was reduced to impotence and imbecility in his room at Homewood. Maybe that was the explanation—the Occam's Razor Father Durieu, S.J., invoked in Catechism—to the whole mad show of the last few years: crucial years to him, but wasted for his father and mother who were at war. Still, it seemed unlikely to the boy, from what he had seen with his own eyes from the water turret, and heard with his own ears from his bedroom at Homewood, that his father had ever got closer to Narcisse Landry or Roberta Manning than Hoffmann to Olympia, or Parsifal to Kundry. The only woman that he knew of in his father's life, aside from his mother, was Maria Callas, who nightly serenaded his father in his room and greeted him morning after morning in the guise of Norma, Lucia, Alceste, Aida, Turandot, Butterfly, Tosca, etc. And what man could wish more? His father showed good sense, he thought, in having the best of her on records and leaving the rest of her to others; for his part, he would never have anything to do with any woman who had not been dead at least a century.

But for now, sitting in the sun outside Fat Harry's with the paper spread before him—the son of the Don Giovanni thus indicted, the offspring no less of the Queen of the Night—the prospect of returning to school was like a public pillorying. In school (the school his mother said she'd moved to town to send him to, away from Burnside and the niggers: "When Love left I just couldn't stay at Homewood"), in school which was a rat race concerned with sociality and scraps of knowledge, in preparation for a bigger rat race concerned with fame and money, he walked down endless corridors of plaster filled with people, all of whom knew who he was, who his mother said his father was, and who his mother thought she was—Mrs. Irene Trepagnier Girard, New Orleans socialite and Christian martyr. If his mother were to die today, struck down perhaps by a bolt from God, he wouldn't shed a fucking tear. "Gone to heaven," he'd announce to his preceptor, "heaven, Sir."

The big clock on St. Anselm's commenced to strike and he could see a block away the front line of Crusaders walking briskly down the steps then surging to the street and running toward him. Panicky, he quickly folded the paper and started walking down St. Charles away from the school and the squad of ruined boys bearing down on Fat Harry's. Casting a hurried glance over his shoulder as he tossed the paper into a trash bin, he turned left at the Baptist Church on General Pershing—away from the school, his mother's house, and church-bell-chiming consciousness. The Crusaders were coming, invading his childhood, showing it up for the lie that it was. He couldn't remember, as he tore at his tie and ripped the buttons off his uniform, ever having laughed as a child. He couldn't remember ever having played as a child. He couldn't remember ever having been a child, except when he was, as he yearned to be, safely hidden in the water turret at Homewood watching it all—his father's procession of fancy women, real or imaginary, his mother's prancing on the levee after dark, their internecine strife that was tearing him apart —through the diamond-patterned slit of the brick wall. His mother and his father were selfish people, Southerners. He had had a rotten childhood, he knew that.

CHAPTER 2

And memory knows before the event, as though the event were an afterthought, and the reporting of it a formality, like a document announcing the war's end after the armies have gone. So he was not surprised when, two years after his mother's declaration, he saw his father's picture in the *Times-Picayune* with the headline: "Burnside Man Leaps to Death from Huey P. Long Bridge." Dressed in what his father had always called his "broker's suit" (it was the suit he'd wear when he went to see his creditors, or the sugar broker down on Thalia) and his Panama hat ("What's the name of this tune, Jimmy?—'You scream, I scream, everybody want ice cream!'"), his father's thin face between the broad brim of the hat and the wide lapel of the suit looking like it was trying to speak to him. But he didn't have time to study the picture. He was dressed in the stars and bars (modeled on those of the Confederacy) of a St. Steve's junior classman and on his way out to school when he spied the announcement; his first thought was that his father had something to say, and his second was that it was a shame that for lack of a bridge near Homewood—Jimmy Davis's "Sunshine Bridge" was under construction, but not yet finished—his father had to travel all the way down to New Orleans, almost to his mother's doorstep, to commit suicide. But he didn't say anything because his mother, though she doubtless had seen the newspaper, had not yet devised her response to it (his Uncle Antoine was still sleeping, and she would need to consult him) and was pretending she had not seen it. So he too pretended not to have seen it and left the house walking stiffly and feeling, though the air was warm and the ground dry as he walked through Audubon Park, strangely cold and wet.

Gardenias and hibiscus were in bloom, their heavy scent drugging the air, and the Old Man's Beard, or Spanish moss, which hung from the live oaks along the path and from the cypress trees in the pond, put him in mind of walking underwater: swept forward by an undertow while his dangling legs tripped on cypress roots and his gaping mouth swallowed silt. He did not feel threatened by this sensation, but curiously reassured, as though the worst that could occur had occurred, and he was still in motion. Then suddenly he was running, from shade tree to shade tree across the well-watered greens and along the wilted fairways of Audubon Park golf course, the water from the sprinklers in his eyes, toward the spire of Loyola Cathedral; and he was cursing her and all cunts as he ran, weeping wildly and beginning to breathe air and walk on ground again as, stumbling, he sprawled on the fairway, gasping convulsively for breath. "My mother is a bitch. My mother is a bitch," he kept repeating over and over to himself. "My mother is a first-class bitch!"

On St. Charles Avenue he bought a paper and as he walked along the neutral ground, while trolleys clanged and clattered past, he leafed impatiently past headlines about the Gulf of Tonkin, *Rolling Thunder*, and 500,000 boys not much older than he was being drafted to go to Vietnam. Baffled and frustrated that he couldn't find the piece he sought, he turned to the "B" section, where he spied the picture of his father in his broker's suit, and read: "James Allemands Girard, 44, of Burnside, La., leapt to his death yesterday from the 150-foot-high span of the Huey P. Long Bridge. Business and domestic troubles were cited as factors in the former sugar cane

planter's decision to take his own life. According to friends of
the deceased, Mr. Girard had been plagued of late by creditors, and had suffered from declining profits resulting from
last season's rains which spoiled the sugar crop and depressed
the molasses market. Mr. Girard was a member and past
president of the New Orleans Opera Society, and a former
grand master of the Krewe of Rex. He was a graduate of
Tulane University (class of '37), and a scion of the Girard
family who built Homewood plantation in 1817. In 1938 Mr.
Girard married Irene Trepagnier. He is survived by a son,
James Antoine, and a daughter, Linda. Funeral arrangements
. . ."

He did not go on reading because he did not want to know.
He would not go either to his father's funeral to hear lies and
eulogies, or to St. Stephen's to be taunted and interrogated
by his classmates, then called up by the preceptor and sent
home. But out on the streets, in his stars and bars uniform
with the grass stains on it, he was sure to be picked up and
returned to the imprisonment of his mother's custody. He felt
like a soldier who had been absent from a great slaughter, and
spared, but the enemy was in control now, and her control
reached everywhere: no one was neutral, the whole city was
in collaboration with her; even the trolleys trundling along
the neutral ground were filled with her spies, and churches
and schools on the street corners were her headquarters. Nor
was there any denying which side he was on—if he were
asked, as he would be—he was on the losing, the lost side.
With an aloneness whose anguish he had never felt before, he
longed to be hidden in the water turret at Homewood; but it
was nearly seventy miles upriver, and he was in the uniform
of a schoolboy. There was no one he could trust now, he had
had only one ally. There was no place for him to go now, nor
did he foresee any place in the near future. It would be this

way for a long time to come, perhaps always, and there was nothing he could do about it, nothing—except keep moving as the river moved, and reconstruct the water turret in his head: his skull the brick, his brain the water, and his eyes the diamond-patterned slits. Peering narrowly through closely lidded slits at the world of trolleys, houses, cars, he turned at the corner commanded by the Presbyterian church down State Street toward the river.

Parallel rows of shotgun houses, turreted emplacements, widow's walks, and picketed redoubts confronted him. Closer to the river was what resembled a walled fort with shotgun shanties flanking and investing it, and on the river the stern-wheelers and ocean-going ironclads plied their way upstream and downstream, enforcing the blockade. Caught in this stranglehold of commerce and complicity, with comfort the reward and death punishment for serving or resisting it, the citizens he met out on the street—a black governess with two white children, an elderly white man wearing a Panama hat and holding a cane, two nuns encased in black habits, and a class of a half-dozen handicapped children shambling along in orderly file behind their uniformed black nurse toward the zoo—all seemed oblivious to the desperate dilemma they were in. At Tchoupitoulas he hesitated, then turned upriver toward the park and his mother's house, a half block behind the line of idiot children. There was no hope of his running the blockade, or breaking the siege-ring, or bolting the long docile line of uniformed boys, not yet. Breaking out would require luck and cunning, and he would need an ally—one trusted by the enemy but loyal to him. At Webster the black nurse held up her hand and her charges jerked to a halt. He watched as she marshaled them across the street—chiding this one, encouraging that one, never doubting where she was heading or her ability to take them all with her. Never

doubting . . . It would have to be a woman, he knew; his
future ally would have to be female and approved of by his
mother, otherwise he would never break out. . . .

With the advent of consciousness what is seen is perceived,
and what is perceived is immediately known; there is no need
to remember because all that is known is simultaneously
present. Instead, there is need to select from the onslaught of
faces and facts, stories and structures, clamoring to be ac-
knowledged, and to screen out false consciousness. Whatever
is not true to one's own need to know, whatever does not
touch on the personal pain that brought on consciousness, the
wound over and around which knowledge encysts, is to be
screened out as false. Whatever cuts through, due to luck or
mischance, is given the weight of real knowledge.

Beside the fountain dedicated to the Blessed Virgin Mary,
amid a hundred other girls in graduation dresses, at midday he
saw her: her body flushed with vibrance and her face with
radiance, so much so that even in the noonday heat and May
humidity her hair, which was done in ringlets, had sprung
free in wild curls, not drooped and straightened like the other
girls'. She was standing at the center of a gaggle of Sacred
Heart girls—she was the center, as the statue of the BVM
was the center of the fountain—when he walked over to her,
spoke to her as though there were not twenty other girls
around her. He was among a hundred other boys in uniform,
guests at the afternoon graduation tea for senior girls at
Sacred Heart; and now the boys of St. Stephen's and the girls
of Sacred Heart who for twelve years had been trained to
avoid one another were being forced to mingle for an afternoon and to pair off for the graduation dance that night. But
he was not shy and he was not tongue-tied when twenty faces
turned toward him, for he spoke only to the one girl in the
center:

"May I escort you to the dance tonight?" he said. "I'm Jimmy Girard."

The girl regarded him as though she too were oblivious to everyone except him. "But you don't know me," she said, "you don't even know my name."

"I know you're the only one here for me, and if I don't ask you soon, somebody else will. Billy Bland over there, or Hart Davis," he pointed to the two all-State footballers, "and then you'd have a miserable time because they'd talk about you to their buddies. With me you're safe from locker-room talk. I don't have any buddies."

She looked quizzically at him. "Suppose I don't care what others say. What then?"

He shrugged. "All the better," he said, and began to withdraw from the ring of intently listening girls.

"I suppose I'll go with you," the girl said quickly. "I'm Lee Anne—Lee Anne Vipond—from Gulfport, my daddy's from Gulfport." They scrutinized each other's faces in the bleaching, debilitating heat by the Sacred Heart fountain. Then she stepped forward from her circle of ladies-in-waiting and took his arm. "We've only got from now till midnight to get to know one another," she whispered.

They skipped out on the tea and boarded a trolley (not the only couple to do so) and went to Corona's in the Irish Channel, where they played "Honky-Tonk Angel" on the jukebox, and where Girard had too much to drink, but not so much that they were not able to pile into the back seat of Billy Bland's '55 Ford to go to a roadhouse across the causeway, and then to the yacht club on Lake Pontchartrain's far shore. Here they left Billy Bland and his date and boarded one of the many yachts that were tied up and made love, the first time for either of them—a fumbling, frustrating, nervous encounter in which Girard came twice before he was inside,

and Lee Anne never came—but now they knew each other
and got back in the rear seat of Billy Bland's Ford and were
driven at high speed back over the causeway and parted, the
girls to Sacred Heart and the boys to St. Stephen's to dress,
and arrived, boutonnieres and corsages in place, at the dance
at nine o'clock to be greeted by nuns and priests in the
reception line.

As they filed into the reception hall, where the band
backing the "Sons of the Four Freshmen" was tuning up,
Girard and Lee Anne were the first to dance—like royalty, or
newlyweds: the other couples waiting an appropriate length
of time, then following them out onto the dance floor—while
the band played and the Sons sang "I'm Always Chasing
Rainbows." This was followed by "Angel Eyes," "Day In
—Day Out," and a host of other favorites, concluding at
midnight with the song that brought tears to many eyes and
sent senior girls, who throughout the evening had hugged
senior boys dressed in stars and bars, to the sidelines to hug
nuns dressed in black habits:

Tho' summer turns to winter and the present disappears,
The laughter we were glad to share will echo thru the years.
When other nights and other days may find us gone our separate ways,
We will have these mo-ments to re-mem-ber. . . .

So Lee Anne was graduated, then Girard, and that summer
before college they spent together—in the back seats of cars,
at the Viponds' cottage, even on the Audubon Park golf
course—exploring each other's swollen surfaces and secret
recesses through the joys of genital and oral sex. That fall they
entered college together: she Newcomb, he Tulane—the cam-
puses adjacent, the courses (or some of them: music apprecia-

tion, fine arts and tennis) cross-registered. Each noon they met for lunch at the Newcomb cafeteria where Lee Anne, five feet eight and only 128 pounds, ate only meat and that in small portions. Slim, svelte, and possessive, with a mass of blonde hair framing her hawk's face and swan's neck, she accompanied Girard in his NROTC uniform to the door of all his classes: "The Hungry One," his English professor dubbed her. On one occasion when English 102 lasted for over an hour, she climbed up on two chairs perched precariously atop one another in the hallway of Gibson Hall, and peered in through the transom over the door. "I see it is time," Dr. Adams announced wearily. "The Hungry One awaits you, Mr. Girard."

Behind, beside, around him—everywhere but inside him—Lee Anne seemed to surround him. When due to her urgings he joined a fraternity, the Delta Kappa Epsilons, Lee Anne became a Delta Phi Epsilon. When in his sophomore year he was elected to Phi Beta Kappa, so was Lee Anne. When as a junior he became captain of the NROTC drill squad, Lee Anne became the unit's "Best Lady." And while he was second-string quarterback for the Greenwave football team (during his junior year he was red-shirted and primed to take over from Richie Petitbon, who would graduate that year), Lee Anne was Homecoming Princess and slated the following year to be Homecoming Queen. Moreover, his sister, Linda, who had been Homecoming Queen the year before he entered Tulane, became Miss Louisiana and then runner-up to Miss America while he was in his junior year—the same year Linda graduated from Tulane Law School. And these three women—Linda, his mother, Lee Anne: each of them formidable in her own right—kept in close communication about him: monitoring his movements, apportioning his time, determining what he ate, where he slept, what he thought. One morning after he had stayed overnight at his mother's house, he overheard his sister talking on the phone, laughing and lapsing into Southern speech patterns that sounded just like his mother's. When finally his sister called him to the phone and he picked up the receiver, he heard Lee Anne and his mother on the extension continuing the three-cornered conversation they'd just been having with Linda, and Lee Anne was affecting his mother's speech too. He listened.

"You c'n have him tonight, honey," his mother was saying, "I had him last night."

"You sure did. He won't be up to much, the two of you get through with him."

"Oh, he'll be up to once, sweetheart, though last night Jimmy was so tired he tumped his sweetmilk over."

"His sweetmilk! His bourbon, you mean."

"I disremember, honey. He was feelin' sickish when he came home, and took some crackers in his sweetmilk. You know how to treat him, I guess. If you don't, nobody does. Nobody since Love left . . ."

He put the receiver down carefully, went back to the bedroom to collect his few things, and started to leave the house. As he passed the phone again, he could hear them gabbling away, their voices sounding like the clicking of teeth inside the bone-shaped receiver. "They're all alike," he thought. "They're all alike." "Bitches!" he yelled at the black thing—the clicking inside stopped. "Mindless bitches!"

So it was not without warning that he entered in his senior year what he would afterward call his "Big Sleep." Most of it, nearly all, was spent in a little cubby-holed bed in the garret overlooking the Southern Baptist Hospital on Napoleon Avenue—Les's garret with the lions out front. He needed a roommate to keep Lee Anne at bay, and not only Lee Anne but Coach "Fatty" Carboat (whose favorite saying was "Winning is not a life or death matter, it's more important than that"), Commander Kent and Lieutenant Staples of the NROTC unit (the Commander would wait downstairs by the lions while the Fleet Marine Lieutenant bounded upstairs to see that everything was "Copacetic, A-Okay—not an inspection, Mr. Girard, just an informal inquiry"), and Professor "Duckie" Knox, his former math professor and faculty adviser to the ROTC and NROTC units and the football team (who, although he was always goosing the boys when he visited their locker rooms, and pumping Girard for details of his sexual exploits, was the only professor Girard was willing to see). And since he needed a roommate, Les, who styled himself a Bohemian and a playwright, in that order—with his acerbic manner, his slovenliness, and his obsession with opera (in addition to the fact that he did not have, and would not tolerate, a phone)—filled the bill perfectly. Having to go through Les to get to Girard deterred most, as it had in freshman football when Les ran interference for him. But there were a few, especially Lee Anne, whom it took, not Les, but Jussi Bjoerling to drive off.

Girard would be lying in his little cubby-hole of a bed, as he did for at least sixteen hours each day (redressing the balance whereby, as the Golden Boy on the football and drill fields, the Young Lion in the fraternity and debate team, and the Southern Gentleman when in classes and with Lee Anne, he had scarcely gone to bed at all during his first two years at Tulane), when in stalks Lee Anne—no more the solicitous helpmeet with worshipful glances and encouraging gestures, as at first; all that had given way to harsher emetics, as in wartime the primary virtues (loyalty, courage) remain, but the less highly prized ones (civility, patience) give way—her hawk's face swooping down on him, her hands set to seize and shake him awake: to duty, to the drill field, to her. Having swept past Les, she stoops down and grasps the unresponsive Girard. Suddenly there sounds, like a swift sword, the thrilling tenor voice of Jussi Bjoerling:

> *Svani per sempre il bel sogno d'amore*
> *L'ora è fuggita*
> *e muoio disperato!*
> (My dream of love is now dispelled forever;
> I lived uncaring,
> now I die despairing!)

As abruptly as she swooped down on him, she stops, not due to aesthetic appreciation, but because she can't stand opera, and especially opera so loud. She makes a few wrathful gestures, mainly with her feet, since she has covered her ears with her hands; and while Les stands guard at the record player, ready to block any lunge in that direction, Girard covers his head with the sheet, turns to the wall, and curls up in a fetal position, protecting his kidneys with his elbows. After a few desperate, badly aimed blows, Lee Anne leaves the garret—frustration showing in every angle and limb of her body, fury unspent. Les turns the record player down and stands by it, smiling. "Time for your daily pick-me-up, Girard," he says, and puts on *Cavalleria Rusticana.*

The sound of the music comes to him, his head still turned to the wall and hidden beneath the sheet. Turiddu's "*Bada, Santuzza, schiavo non sono di questa vana tua gelosia*" (I warn you, Santuzza, I will not stand for your jealousy), answered by Santuzza's "*Battimi, insultami, t'amo e perdono ma è troppo forte l'angoscia mia.*" (Beat me, insult me, I still love you and pardon you, but my anguish is beyond endurance). It is the 1953 recording with Bjoerling and Milanov, Bjoerling near the end of his powers, Milanov at the height of hers, and the voices he had heard as a child while hiding in the water tower (Caruso, McCormack, Tibbett; Galli-Curci, Schwarzkopf, Callas) blend effortlessly into the two he hears now, as the two anguished spirits address him—personally and directly —as though they were there with him, singing sorrowfully and threateningly to him, Girard, in his bed:

Santuzza:

La tua Santuzza piange e t'implora
come cacciarla così tu puoi?

(Your own Santuzza weeps and begs you;
how can you treat me like this?)

Turiddu:

Va, ti ripeto, va non tediarmi
pentirsi è vano dopo l'offesa.

(I told you to go, you make me tired!
It's too late for penitence!)

As the music reaches a crescendo of threat and of anguish, of jealousy and deceit, even damnation, Girard slowly rises from his bed, blinking, knowing in advance how it will end, both the day and the opera (Les is at his desk in the other dormer window, writing: he will stay that way most of the day, his back to Girard, gazing across Napoleon Avenue at the Southern Baptist Hospital, remembering dialogue for a play based on Girard and Lee Anne): another day of waste and beauty, another wasted day. At 2:30 P.M., to the clack of Les's typewriter, Girard is beginning to think about breakfast when Duckie Knox arrives.

"Well, how was she today, Jimmy?" The cheery old faggot who walks like a duck waddles over and puts his hand fondly on Girard's shoulder. "Say, you're getting fat, boy. That LSU line'll make mincemeat of you. How goes the great sleep, Jimmy-boy?" He sits down, still fondling Girard's shoulder and upper arm. "Eugene O'Neill's still at it, I see. What say we go get something to eat. Come on," he rises abruptly, "get your pants on, fat boy!"

At the Camellia Grill on Carrollton, while Girard has an omelette and toast, Duckie Knox from the next stool lowers his voice (and his hand, which grips Girard's knee now), and leans toward Girard's slowly masticating jaw: "You'll never be able to pull it off, Jimmy. I don't give a damn about Lee Anne. Fuck her—I presume you do. Is she good? Does she like sucking cock? Boo Mason told me . . ." Girard stops chewing. ". . . never mind that now. I was talking to Commander Kent this morning. They're ready to boot you out of the unit, but that's not the worst, boy. You'll be drafted in the same breath, sent as a shave-tail to some navy tanker off Pensacola. You want that? They can do it, boy. They're paying your way, remember, with that crummy scholarship. You could have had any number, but you took that one—you're stupid, Jimmy! For a bright boy, you're stupid—just like Lee Anne, you could have . . ." With exaggerated deliberation, Girard lays down his fork. "Never mind, never mind . . . the main thing is you've got to get off your fat ass! Go over and talk to the Commander, and while you're at it go see the Dean." Resting his case with a hearty slap on Girard's back, he stands up and waddles over to pay the bill. A few steps only, but the splay-footed old gander in the bunched seersucker suit and frowsy tie, his eyes magnified behind thick glasses, resembles nothing so much as a drooped barnyard fowl a few rungs down on the pecking order. Girard's bought breakfast sits in his stomach like a furball.

Outside the air-conditioned Camellia the warm October air wilted them. A stone's throw away sat the levee, squat and smooth, like a breastwork hiding a murderous trench, or a longed-for ford: "Let us cross over the river and rest under the shade of the trees," he could almost hear the dying Stonewall say. Instead, "Better report for practice this afternoon, boy," Duckie Knox shot over the top of his car. "Coach Fatty's fit to be tied. LSU in six weeks and his star quarterback in a Wagnerian dream-sleep. You check with Coach Fatty, Jimmy-boy, you hear?" And with that he ducked in his car, switched on the air-conditioning, and surged out into Carrollton Avenue. Girard watched him angle onto St. Charles and then down it toward Tulane and the Sugar Bowl, the Garden District and his mother's house.

North along the levee flatboats and pirogues were tied up in among the willows, the chocolate-colored shallows lapping at them. A crowd of seagulls scavenged in the wake of a rusty tanker screwing downstream. He started running, on legs weak and shaky from disuse, the furball in his stomach feeling more and more distinct as, plunging forward, he broke out in a nervous, sour sweat. When he came in sight of Ochsner Clinic about a mile upriver, he could see the levee off to his left where it turned the hairpin and, glinting against the westering sun as though it were ablaze, he saw the bridge. Less than a mile distant and more than 150 feet high, up above where gulls scrapped and beyond the infirmaries and playing fields of lost and violent souls, he beheld the bridge with a nausea that had him sprinting, then bent over double with retching, on the levee overlooking the river flowing both ways: toward him and away from him and, as he crouched like an animal vomiting at the neck of the hairpin curve, through him. "Never," he resolved as he retched up the greasy eggs and buttered toast and jam, "never again will I eat with that bastard!" Then, as the words formed themselves in his mind, his mouth spewed them out with the vomit: "Never again will I eat!"

So he entered the climax-phase of his Great Sleep, in which not only did he not rise from his bed, but he would not eat, either. Lee Anne grew worried, changed her tactics, and sat beside Girard's bed each day for hours while Les played "*Lasciami dunque, lasciami. Invan tenti sopire il giusto sdegno colla tua pietà.*" (Get away from me! Don't think your pity is going to pacify me!) from *Cavalleria Rusticana*, and Mimi's coughing arias from *La Bohème*. Girard began to show symptoms of hepatitis, and Les's play, without any overheard dialogue to be incorporated, moved in the direction of the theatre of menace and a new title: "Refrigerated Deathlessness." By the end of November—the weekend of the Tulane–LSU game—Girard had shrunk to 140 pounds, his complexion was sallow, the whites of his eyes jaundiced, and all the small bones in his face visible. Still Lee Anne arrived daily, disguised to herself as his nurse, as earlier she had been virgin and, briefly, virago. And lying unresponsive in his filthy bedclothes, his face turned toward the wall, abstracted from his lungs and heart and kidneys (but not his liver), which functioned independently of him, Girard fancied he could sense in the woman sitting by his bed hour after hour that terrible paroxysm of the female of the species, but not confined to her: "Love," they called it, while it wrecked their lives, consumed their vitals, and deranged their minds—Love: which made of formidable women slavish creatures, and of stupid shop girls termagants—still they all called it Love, and understood each other and were sympathetic, even with a rival, so addicted to this state of abasement, this mad frenzy, that they would help out one afflicted if they could, not hoping to heal her, but to be struck themselves, as by an epidemic of head-lice. Love. Nor was it confined to females as, say, sickle-cell anemia was to Negroes, or trichinosis was to hogs, or tularemia to rabbits; but it was resident primarily in them and carried by them, as distemper was primarily in dogs or pinkeye in polled Herefords. Its signs he'd come to recognize and could see coming: the fervid glitter in the eyes, the vibrant flush of the whole body, the terrible focus of the entire being (like staring down the almost incredible barrel of a 156-caliber Big Bertha as it is ponderously wheeled around and targeted on you); could see coming but could not always sidestep or escape the killing-zone: if not annihilation, then mutilation, or at least the superficial scratches, bites, and abuse that went with it, and the scars. He had some of the scars of love himself, for he had been "in love" with Lee Anne for two weeks that summer before college, and he remembered with revulsion now the awful, anxious, vicious way of it: a state so dread and devastating and degrading he wanted never to experience it again. He was, he reckoned as he lay in his bed, the object of Lee Anne's hawk-eyed vigil, still suffering the after-effects and the fallout from that May-day idyll three full years ago. With his face to the wall where three months earlier his back had been, he had renounced all hope of recovering from his brief descent into love.

On the first day of December, in an interlude between operas and above the desultory clack-clack of Les's type-writer, Lee Anne announced her departure. She leaned over to speak in Girard's fetid ear, while Les scrambled to put on a record. And hearing as he lay in a listless stupor the strains of Turiddu's farewell (*"Mamma, mamma! . . ."*) counterpointed with Lee Anne's—the male voice terminal and from a great

distance, the female voice tentative and at his ear: the two
voices vying to say their goodbyes, the one poignantly, the
other demanding response—he let their cadenzas and caden-
ces, the music of art and of life, flow over and through him:

E poi, mamma, sentite—
s'io non tornassi,
voi dovrete fare da madre a Santa,
ch'io le avea giurato di condurla all'altare.

There's nothing more I can do, Jimmy.
I love you, and I always will,
but I'm going now and I won't be back
unless you call for me. I'm sorry, Jimmy.
I've called your mother. She's coming tomorrow.

With a momentous sigh reminiscent of those for which Sarah
Bernhardt was famous after the amputation of her leg caused
by the death scene in *Tosca*, Lee Anne departed. A murmur of
voices could be heard in the distance, a woman cried shrilly
that Turiddu was killed, Santuzza gave an anguished shriek
and collapsed, and Mamma Lucia reeled and fainted. Girard
lay as before, his breathing labored and erratic, pulse weak,
eyes closed, while from the folds of his bedclothes a sick-
sweet smell ascended, like ambergris.

Les padded over and eased himself into the chair Lee Anne
had vacated. In the dimly lit garret he sat silently, as if
waiting for a scene-change, before launching into his obliga-
tory *recitativo accompagnato*, which began in Girard's mind with
an emphatic "*Deh!*" accompanied by a G minor chord. "If
there's a worse place than Hell, you're in it," the amateur
playwright began. "Nobody is a friend of yours, let's face it
—you're a lost soul, Girard. How you got that way I don't

know, and I don't want to know. You've got a choice of
keepers, that's all—Lee Anne or your mother. It amounts to
pretty much the same thing, but I'd take Lee Anne. You can't
fuck your mother. You can't resist her, either. She'll slap a
restraining order on you, and you're in no shape to resist. Lee
Anne's devoted. You may say your mother's devoted, but it's
not to you; it's to some idea of you as a child, or of herself as
your mother. Lee Anne's devoted to some idea of what you'll
become, of what she'll make of you. It's not you in either case,
it's never you, but that's Pirandello. Anyway, it's time you
got up and went with one or the other—not everyone has a
choice of keepers, Girard—unless . . ." Les's voice lowered
and Girard could hear, or imagined he could, the tonic chord
lengthening into chromatic decay. ". . . unless you decide to
make a job of it." From the sheath where he had kept it
concealed he produced, while Girard turned feebly to face
him, a long, thin, stiletto-type knife, which he held up to the
light, sighted along, then offered to Girard haft first. "Morality may perhaps consist solely in the courage of making a
choice," he recited to a submediant A minor. Les continued
to hold out the knife while Girard, panting slightly, raised
himself on one elbow to stare at it. The bones of his face, not
so prominent due to the scraggly beard that covered them,
gave him the look of a Third World priest, or an ascetic; his
eyes, when he opened them, were wide, bright and jaundiced; and he spoke, when at last he did speak, in a husky
whisper through blistered lips with a dry tongue: "I'll get
up," was all he said.

So Girard made the mistake—was it his and did he make
it, or was even it predetermined by others?—of planting his
ID on a corpse in the Mississippi, so as not to get drafted
when he went AWOL from the NROTC unit, and of going
with Lee Anne to San Francisco: not the plantation by that

name, only a few miles from Homewood, but the city of that name two thousand miles from New Orleans. There, while Lee Anne taught music in a Catholic girls' school and gave private lessons on the violin, Girard regained his health: running daily from their apartment on Greenwich Street near the naval base, down the hill through the columned ruins of the 1905 World's Fair to the foot of the Golden Gate Bridge, then along the ocean front by the yacht club which faced Alcatraz. And as he ran past naval barracks, through ersatz Roman columns to the access ramp of a bridge bigger even than the Huey P. Long, and for more than a mile in sight of Alcatraz—the water always intensely blue and whipped-up white around it, and the motor launches bearing uniformed personnel back and forth, from the mainland to the rock, from the prison to the yacht club—he began to experience the nearly constant sensation of being pursued while he was running—which caused him to run all the harder—and, when he was not running, of being followed.

The identity of his pursuers was never clear, but often they were in uniform and always they were women. Once they tried to trap him in a cul-de-sac in the wooded and hilly naval base, but he managed to hide in a ravine and, when they had passed, to clamber over the ten-foot-high barbed-wire-topped fence, nicking himself only slightly. On another occasion they chased him onto the Golden Gate Bridge, converging behind him in two groups to block his exit; but the bridge was completely shrouded in fog, and he managed to lose them.

He started to drink, at home and alone, steadily and addictively every evening—not only on evenings that Lee Anne was out teaching violin—from the time when he finished his run until bedtime. His pursuers, who were unable to catch him when he was running, seemed disinclined to follow him when he was drinking, through he knew they were there, just beyond the invisible boundary which marked his alert and alcoholic control. This little sphere in which he felt safe —his room, with a cot and stereo in it—was avoided by Lee Anne, especially after he quit playing opera and began listening to jazz for five or six hours each evening, a routine broken only by trips to the bathroom and to the kitchen. Wrapped in the floppy old maroon terry-cloth bathrobe which had been his father's, with his own green T sewn on the back, he moved with the precise, lunging steps of a drinker who knows where he is going, because he has been there before, from his cot to the urinal to the ice-box and back again to his cot, like a rat in a box or a squirrel in a cage, supremely self-confident and ahead of himself—his mind already rehearsing the motions his body moved to perform—until his sleeve would catch on a door knob, or his slipper snag on the stoop. Then he would curse and savagely smash or kick the offending object. If Lee Anne were present, she would shrink from him, but she was not often present. Once she cornered him in the bathroom to confront him about his drinking, and he smashed his hand through the wall, breaking plaster, lath, and all the metacarpals of his right hand against a four-inch stud. After that, she avoided him. He would return to his cot after his little trek through the empty house, a cast on one hand, a fresh drink in the other, and listen for hours in a warm, torpid haze to Kid Ory, Jelly Roll Morton, Sweet Emma, Jack Teagarden, Percy Humphrey and "Slow Drag" Pavageau, getting up only to relieve himself, refresh his drink, and turn over the record. And gradually, as he listened over and over to "Basin Street Blues," "Sugar Foot Stomp," "Burgundy Street Blues," "Muskrat Ramble," and "King Porter Stomp," he came to know what it means to miss New Orleans.

He missed the freedom of it, and the familiarity: taking a beer standing up at Martin's Bar in the French Quarter, and pissing when he felt like it in the marble tiled *pissatoire* which guttered beneath the brass rail where the men-only patrons stood. And the women, he missed the women of New Orleans and the sensuous sensation of being surrounded by easy black, brown, and high-yaller women wherever one went—along Canal Street, on the "Freret jet" bus or the St. Charles trolley, in Schwegman's Giant Super Mart—wherever, even the churches: he missed the Gloryland Mt. Gillion Black Baptist Church of New Orleans where Love used to take him, a little white boy, when she had him in tow and had to do something with him. In his little room on Greenwich Street overlooking Alcatraz, remembering "The City That Care Forgot" while he listened to Dixieland and drank Early Times, there was little about New Orleans that he did not miss: even his mother and her friends, his sister and her friends, and the bitches and princesses who frequented "Jewcomb" and "Jewlane" seemed to him tolerable, or at least avoidable—like carnivores, who were all right so long as you weren't on their menu. He was not, anymore, on Lee Anne's.

So, beginning in San Francisco, and as a result of his drinking and listening to jazz as he drank, he and Lee Anne began sleeping apart and then, at first he suspected and later he knew, Lee Anne started sleeping with others. She would come home while he was out running, and leave before he got back. While he was out on his one, unvarying route (she knew his route, and she knew when, within a minute or two, he would be passing through the naval base, the World's Fair ruins, the Golden Gate Bridge ramp, or alongside the yacht club), she was at home preparing to go out on the many roads that lay before her. Once back from his run and confined to his room and the solitary, alcoholic round that made up his evenings, where she might have gone today, or where she might go tomorrow, was impossible for him to guess. The places they might have gone and the things they might have done together were all occasions for contention. He was confined while she was off prancing (as his mother used to on the levee, while his father stayed locked in his room), and short of lying in wait for her, tracking her down and retriev-ing her—which dogs did best, and which his own pursuers kept him from doing—he had no alternative to the solitary confinement he had imposed on himself, to which she had added a new punishment: jealousy.

Now and then a window would open, through which she would peek in, say something taunting or mocking to him, then quickly disappear, and the window would close again—on her, on her world, on San Francisco—leaving him in the dark, with his bourbon and jazz, confined to his room and consumed by jealousy. His pursuers were mostly men now, in pairs, always in pairs—two men, sometimes a man and a woman. They crowded around him like Mormon elders, they turned up on street corners and at strategic spots on his run like Jehovah's Witnesses. Perhaps they were FBI agents, perhaps lovers, perhaps both. But rather than accost any of these paired pursuers, who seemed to be joined hip and shoulder as though they were born that way, joined, and rather than confront Lee Anne with accusations of infidelity, which she would simply deny, he stayed in his room and listened to jazz and drank.

And eventually, perhaps inevitably, it occurred to him to wonder whether there might be some link between his sense of being pursued and Lee Anne's pursuit of others, between his sense of being besieged and the fact that she was always absent. Was his paranoia simply a result of her prancing, and was the jag she was on with her nameless, faceless, countless lovers (this did not mean there were many; there might be

only one, or none) related somehow to the conspiracy that
hunted him? The real hunt—the ongoing, unrelenting one—
could it be that it was between him and her? Might all these
others—his pursuers, her pursued—be supernumeraries? Or
was the fact that his ID hoax had been discovered and that he
had been indicted in absentia for draft evasion (Duckie Knox
had sent him word) sufficient to explain his mine-sweeping
mind-set while running, his fortress mentality when in his
room? The Tet Offensive, which had shocked the American
public the previous spring, and a new president's pledge to
bring home the first 25,000 from Vietnam, gave him little
attacks of hope. But the U.S. was mired in a mercenary war
which over half a million conscripts had been drafted to fight,
and more would be required. The news blared at him every
day. The FBI twins would be after him now: raiding the
places he stayed in, infiltrating Lee Anne's love life, and
swarming all over the Castro and Haight-Ashbury in search of
slackers. In the *Festung Girard* of his own thoughts, his obser-
vation post having become a slit-trench, his water turret a
besieged fort, he asked himself whether his enemies were one
or many, already knowing who and how many his friends
were ("Nobody is a friend of yours, let's face it—you're a
lost soul, Girard"); and he came to the startling conclusion
that, by his own fault, by his own grievous fault, he had once
more underestimated love.

He had underestimated love once before, to his damage:
when his father had relinquished and his mother possessed
him; now he had done so again, perhaps to his ruin, with Lee
Anne. It was not the pretty face one cherished, he knew; it
was the face one had destroyed. If Lee Anne with this new
virulent strain of love was intent on destroying herself, it was
so she could blame him; and she was destroying him in the
process. False consciousness swamped him like a river in flood

surging over and threatening a levee. He resolved when he saw her to propose a new start: he would quit drinking, and she would stop prancing, and they would return at term's end to New Orleans.

CHAPTER 3

To New Orleans they came, where there reeled all about them a city forgetting its cares and drowning its sorrows. A hurricane had just hit, and everywhere trees were uprooted, cars stranded where their engines had drowned, and the bars and taverns and clubs on each block were crowded with patrons from noon until dawn.

"It's like there's been a war here," Lee Anne said as they drove up St. Charles, then turned onto Carrollton Avenue. Girard, slouched on the passenger side of her new yellow Fiat, looked at the shattered palm trees and warped trolley tracks and said nothing.

"Look! There's Uncle Caspar's," she said. "Oh, pity the poor live oaks!"

Girard peered out at the *chevaux de frise,* which entrenching Confederates had simply called "sheep racks"—in Vicksburg, Port Royal, and Atlanta; New Orleans they'd surrendered without firing a shot—guaranteed to impale, or at least to delay, attackers. The trolley track was torn up as effectively as if Sherman's wreckers had marched through. With a *Times-Picayune* clutched in his hands, the classified "Houses for Lease" section turned uppermost, he kept watching for street signs: Jeanette, Birch, Green, a sign missing, Cohn . . . "That must have been it. Do the block."

They turned right off Carrollton, right again on Short. Where Hickory intersects Short Lee Anne braked the Fiat.

"We-ell," she began, "the stucco needs painting . . ."

"The hickory's still standing."

"There's a mirliton vine in the backyard. I can make gumbo."

"And a black Baptist church on the corner. No sleeping on Sundays."

They looked at each other and laughed, nervously; Lee Anne leaned over to kiss him, but he leaned away.

"It'll do," Girard said in a husky voice. "Just don't tell my mother we're here."

So Lee Anne leased the bottom half of the house at the corner of Hickory and Short (a Tulane med student named Larry lived upstairs), and commenced her daily routine of furniture-shopping on Magazine Street and job-hunting downtown. Girard stayed home listening to records—sometimes opera, at other times jazz—while watching the black family across the street come and go from their house, the black congregation come and go from their church, the "Whites-only" patrons come and go from their club, while he himself came and went on little walks daily: to "Mr. Sal's" grocery on Green Street, where a cluster of black children always lounged at the entrance, waiting to be admitted one by one through the iron-bar latticed front door at which old Mr. Sal stood, his sallow face covered with stubble and a dead cigar clamped in his mouth; along Carrollton Avenue, where crews of black men in blue uniforms repaired track at a leisurely pace and, amid much laughter and talk with the drivers of cars passing by, removed shattered palms from the neutral ground; down Hickory Street, where gangs of black men in gray uniforms sat on gravestones talking and laughing, occasionally bestirring themselves to resod the graves and realign the crypts in the mausoleum across from the Whites-only club. After three days of walking and watching, passing the club with its smell of flat beer and hot jazz from inside, he came home and put on a Bix Beiderbecke record, watched out the window while the good-looking black girl across the street hosed down her fire-engine red Chevrolet with the name "VAL" blazoned across its chrome grill, opened a beer and drank half of it; then he got up shakily, put the record away, and called a number in the *Courier* which advertised "AA—24 hrs."

"Hello. My name is Roy and I'm an alcoholic. Need help?" a well-oiled voice said.

"When and where are your meetings?"

"Where you coming from?"

"Carrollton and Claiborne."

"Okay. You know the K&B on Oak? Actually it's on Carrollton."

"Right."

"Well, there's a Methodist church just down the street. That's where we meet—use the side entrance."

"When?"

"Tonight, tomorrow night, every night. Usually a guy will settle on a couple of nights weekly, but I'm there every night, eight to ten. Like I said, I'm Roy. What's your name?"

"I'll probably be there," Girard said, and hung up.

He chug-a-lugged what was left of the beer and went out, locking the door after him. The sun was hot and the air humid as he walked down Hickory, ahead of himself and feeling for the first time since San Francisco an acute headache from the beer he'd just drunk. When he reached Carrollton he hesitated briefly—the trolley tracks were still torn up and palm fronds still littered the neutral ground—then turned toward the levee, quickening his pace. He scrutinized the Methodist church as he passed it, locating the side door, but did not break pace until he came to the K&B on Oak Street, where package liquor was sold. Entering the air-conditioned drug-store the first person he encountered was Droopy, the fat black boy who lived next door and who shambled up and down Hickory in his security-guard uniform. He was dressed in the white nylon shirt and black pants and motorman's cap of his office, his vast bulk at ease as he leaned on his elbows on the turnstile railing. Droopy struggled up as "Mistah James" clicked through the turnstile, then settled down again, the rolls of fat around his belly conforming to the railing, which shifted slightly in the concrete floor.

There was a line-up at the liquor counter, and the good-looking black girl from across the street was in it. Dressed in a stiffly starched short-sleeved white uniform, she held in the crook of one smoothly black arm a gallon decanter of Gallo, while her other hand grasped (the same way Love strangled a chicken) the neck of a bottle of Royal Red. Girard stood behind her, waiting to order hard liquor. She didn't speak, he didn't speak, the girl at the cash register gabbled away and rang up the sales as slowly they moved up in line.

Finally, "Val," he said quietly. Droopy, who was well out of earshot, shifted his vast bulk to watch them—as though a picket line had been crossed, or a voice verification test failed—but without disapproval, or curiosity, or even interest. "I know the name of your car," Girard finished lamely.

"Me an' my car's named the same," she said, white teeth flashing like enameled knives. So dazzling were they, and so sharply did they chop, that involuntarily Girard felt his penis shrivel. "I'm Valerie. You lives cross't th' street, don't you? I seen you at Mistah Sal's once't."

"I go there sometimes."

"Ever'body do." She stood holding her bottles, a thin line

of perspiration forming on her upper lip, which was chocolate-colored shading off to pink inside her mouth. Strong white teeth, large brown eyes, hair like a thousand coiled springs or live wires piled high in an Afro.

"You a nurse?" he asked.

"Why you say that? Oh, this ol' thing," she said, flouncing a satiny black arm in her tight-fitting white uniform. She laughed heartily, huskily. "You mought say ah'm in food—most of us is, if we're not guardin' things, like Droopy over there." The line moved up two places and she turned to advance, flinging over her shoulder: "Ah'm down at Schweickhardt's—you know it? Come in sometime an' ah'll make you lunch, a dollar ninety-five."

Her turn came, and she paid; then Girard's. The white woman at the till hefted a half gallon of Early Times onto the counter, put out her palm for money—$7.90—which she tossed with two quick motions into the cash register, then slid the bottle into a K&B purple sack which she stapled shut, glaring at him the whole time. Droopy was impassive as he clicked through the turnstile. When at last he emerged into the sudden sheet of heat outside, the purple paper sack nestled in the crook of his arm, he watched Valerie in her flame-red Chevrolet tear out of the parking lot, then screech to a stop beside him.

"Ridin' in VAL begins when, if you flinch, you get out,' she said. "Wanna ride?"

He got in and the car leapt into motion, Valerie accelerating down Carrollton with the angle of her body in line with the left headlight, as though she were afraid he might rape her, with one eye on the road and one on him. Their purple K&B sacks sat between them on the imitation leather seat-cover, and two little gewgaws dangled and jounced from her rearview: a plastic Jesus and what looked like a glass eye with a hole pierced through its pupil. "You a Catholic?"

"Why you say that?"

He stretched out his hand to touch the jouncing Jesus and she veered the speeding car away from him. Black workmen on the neutral ground made signs of mock alarm, grinning broadly.

"Oh, that ol' thing. Mah auntie is. Ah'm Baptist, we're all Baptist. She's a Lesbeen, too. Here you are, mistah, Hick'ry Street." The Chevrolet screeched to a stop. It definitely needed a brake job.

"Jimmy," he said, picking up his parcel. "Sometime I wouldn't mind going to church with you, if it's allowed."

"You mean it? Sure it's allowed. You really mean it? We don't go to that church on th' corner."

"I know," he said, getting out. "I've watched you."

"Ten-thirty Sunday," she said. "Ah'll take you, Jimmy. Ten-thirty."

"I'll be ready."

The car lunged forward as he stepped back, then squealed in a wide U-turn across the neutral ground, over the tracks, and sped up the opposite side of Carrollton toward the levee. He watched it—the plastic Jesus and pierced evil eye jouncing along in the chrome-plated VAL—and it seemed to him he was entering another world, one that he'd been away from for a long time, ever since Jasper quit singing the blues and Love left . . .

> Love lift-ed me,
> Love lift-ed me,
> From the bonds of si-in,
> Love lift-ed me-ee.

In her freshly laundered deaconess's uniform she stood, three other women identically dressed standing at their stations in the church, around the Reverend Reed in a black suit, black shirt, black bullet head with bloodshot eyes and sweating face set flat on neckless shoulders, as the Reverend Reed commenced, while they sang, clapped hands high overhead and swung their hips, his Sunday seizure: she with the others singing, clapping, circling him; stepping back and throwing up her arms in mock affright; then laying hands on and upholding his huge bulk—a sweating shaking black man, veins bulging and eyes rolling and facial muscles twitching, in convulsion now and slavering as the Holy Spirit slew him— four sisters dressed in white supporting him and singing all the while, "Love lift-ed me-ee."

He watched throughout the two-and-a-half-hour service only her, and she watched him watching her, glancing at him through the spray of the huge black preacher's slaver, through a latticework of lines of force about the rictus of the Word: the effeminate and idolater and adulterer and many mo' is damned. His little guppy mouth she watched, his child's pink hand. When then she asked him after church—he the only white in a hundred or so blacks on the steps of The Original Morning Star Black Baptist Church of New Orleans, and staring at her the whole time, at her and at Elder Griffin's star-shaped gold tooth—if he wanted a ride home, she knew the instant he got in, his fish-white hand still on the door, that the Reverend Reed who frightened even her, and she carried a gun in her purse, hadn't scared him off.

"Now ah'm lost an' ah know it," she said, grinning broadly.

"We may both be lost," he said, "but no one will be damned." It was in reference to the sermon, and he talked softly and slowly, silkily she thought—about the church, the

Reverend Reed, the singing—almost as though he'd never been in church before. When she asked if that lady, the one they called "the Palomino," was his wife, he said yes, yes she was, but she would be leaving; for him even to be in a car with a black girl would be reason enough for her to leave, but she was leaving anyway. Then he asked her if she would go out with him, after the Palomino—he laughed as he used the word: "no pal o' mine," he said—left. It wasn't worth it to her, she told him; no black man would take her out if she was seen with a white; they would have to talk about it, she said. As they cruised down Claiborne, then along Carrollton, her body still angled away from him in line with the left head-light, she overshot Hickory and continued on down to St. Charles. In Audubon Park she pulled in under a live oak festooned with Spanish moss, and turned to face him . . .

"I give a violin lesson downtown in twenty minutes, so let's make this brief. How was your AA meeting?"

"Like a bloody reunion of the bloody Dekes. Billy Bland was there, so was Hart Davis."

"You don't mean it."

"I was assigned to Hart—he's my 'sponsor.' Picture, if you can, Hart Davis and me drinking coffee all evening in a Methodist church and exchanging pleasantries. He's about fifty pounds overweight and works for Waguespack-Pratt realtors over on Maple."

"Did he marry that Fuller girl?"

"They've got four kids, live in a townhouse out in Metairie, swimming pool, guards, the whole bit."

"Jimmy . . ." Her voice was husky and her eyes glazed. As she spoke he could hear in the background the subdominant chord from *Lulu.* "I'm going home to visit my Daddy. I'm leaving tomorrow. There aren't any jobs here—I've looked,

God knows I've looked . . ." Her voice broke and the fateful
D Minor chord lengthened; it spread as her hands groped
toward him then fluttered down to her sides.
    "You figure you'll find work in Gulfport? At Gryder's
Shoes, maybe, or Salloums' department store? How about the
Vipond Gas Works?"
    "I'm going home, Jimmy. I . . ." She shook her head from
side to side, sadly.
    "You didn't call my goddamned mother, did you? To keep
me busy while you cruise around Gulfport? Of course, your
old man can always ring up the FBI. Isn't Keesler Air Force
Base out there somewhere?"
    She shook her head up and down, side to side, her eyes
shut tight. With eyes shut tight, and making little fishlike
gasps for breath, she hissed: "You've . . . shamed me . . . and
your family, Jimmy, with that . . . riding around with that
. . ." She gave a little convulsive gasp, and could scarcely
bring herself to say the word: "nigger!" she whispered, and
blindly waved her hand toward the street. "I'm going,
Jimmy, and I won't be back, this time I won't!"

. . . night after night after work stealing into his place,
leaving her car parked around the corner, on Short, or two
blocks away on Green, and when her mama asked where she
was disappearing nights, lying, crying, promising and swearing that she wasn't going out with that white man, the one
across the street, that she wouldn't disappoint her mama . . .
and lying, crying, promising and swearing to herself, too, but
never to him—with him she was always truthful, as he was
with her:
    "Honey, do ah look like a black hole in th' sheet?"
    "You look like an oil-slick on ice."
    "Is it true that all whites are perverts?"

"It's blacks who'll do anything."

"Are there really women who can't?"

"My wife never could, with me."

"If she could do it, honey, she could've done it with you."

"I never could, before . . ."

Lying with Valerie he was able to isolate what was wrong between him and Lee Anne; it had been wrong since the beginning, the very beginning in the back of Billy Bland's Ford and in the yacht on the north shore of Lake Pontchartrain and at the Viponds' cottage that first vibrant summer—sex: their love-making was never quicksilver, genital, and direct; it was always confused and off-center—a fierce skirmish in which each sought to sidestep the other and nip in for a crippling blow—he to nail her down, she to surround him— before settling down to the protracted ordeal which would exhaust them both and leave them gasping like spent swimmers on a beach, no good for anything else that day and leery of their next meeting. Whereas with Valerie sex was contained to the genital regions: once she got him in she wouldn't let him go, and she could modulate, within moments, her orgasms with his. She was simply a pro (the thought occurred to him), who was able to do what she wanted when she wanted as she wanted to; and sex for her seemed independent of love, merely a way of giving and getting pleasure. The center of Valerie's being was indisputably between her legs, which when he touched it liquefied; whereas Lee Anne's center, if she could be said to have one, was not hidden on her person anywhere, nor was it in her mind or heart or any other organ—it was him: love-making with Lee Anne was like grappling with himself, not a simple matter, and one in which his mind and heart and, possibly, his soul also was up for grabs.

For now though, lying with Valerie night after night he

could forget the soul's journey through limbo, the soul crying out from beneath the bridge and from beneath his uncle Antoine, the soul—his soul and that of his progenitors— crying out to him in anguished arias and midnight walks; could forget himself and concentrate on the body before him: a body swart and satiny and self-possessed and intent on possessing him, by squeezing and extracting from him all his vital juices six and seven times a night. But possession of his body he did not fear. He did not worry even when his nervous edge was shot, when at the mere smell of Valerie he broke out in a rash, a systemic reaction of desire mixed with revulsion. Until, coming into his place one night around midnight,

"Droopy seen me."

"What'd he say?"

"He jes' looked sad-eyed and shook his head."

"Com'ere."

He was sitting up in the bed in his shorts, no light on, only the shadowy arc light, broken in fragments and waving patches by the hickory tree, of the solitary streetlight outside. He had a drink in his hand which sloshed as she slid in beside him, but he neither moved nor quit peering intently out the window at a point across the street, toward her house.

"Wha's wrong? What chu lookin' at, honey?" she said, alarmed.

"I'm watching those people," he said, nodding his head in the direction of her mamma's house. "They've been there all evening."

"What peoples?" she said, crowding up close and searching intently. "Tha's Jackie an' her boyfren', they won't do you no harm."

"You sure? I mean, are you sure it's Jackie?"

She peered again. "Sure ah'm sure. Ah knows my own sister, even if she do blend in. Since when you scared o' black folk?"

He leaned back against the wall and sipped his drink. "I'm moving, Val."

"Movin'?"

"My mother called today. Somehow she got wind I was here. She's rented a place for me, and the movers are coming tomorrow. I have to go, Val. It's either that or DePaul's."

"DePaul's? Why you say that?"

"Mother's got this idea that I'm an alcoholic. She could do worse than send me to DePaul's, she could send me to Mandeville, or let my father-in-law call the FBI—I told you about that. The Palomino's in on it too, she's moving in with me, I'm told." He finished his drink, set down the glass, and put out his arm to draw Valerie closer, but she shrank back.

Her mouth was set and her eyes mere slits as if she'd been slapped, as though the tide of her blood had risen to gorge in her throat, mouth and brain. She looked explosive as she drew away. "You doan' have nothin' to fear from black folks, you got your own folks to fear. We doan' do things like that to each other." Shaking her head, she backed off. Backing away as if from a rapist, she blundered into the front door. "Ah'm nothing' but your free whore!" she cried suddenly, then turned and bolted, running across the front porch and down the street to her car. Through the open door he heard the car start and rubber peel as VAL burst into motion. The two people on her mother's front porch heard it too; in the shadowy arc light he watched the whites of their eyes, like tigers' eyes in the darkness. Then they went back to kissing, or eating shrimps, or whatever it was they were doing.

Wearily he got up and closed the front door, padded to the bathroom and peed while staring at the sign Lee Anne had tacked up:

> If you sprinkle
> When you tinkle
> Be a sweetie
> Wipe the seatie.

Then, feeling high and a little dizzy, he lunged in to the kitchen where he poured another drink, stopping on his way to position *Lulu*, Act 3, Scene 2, on the record player. Then he made his way back to the bedroom, releasing the needle to the record as he went, and crawled back to the place where he had been before Valerie, like a flung grenade, had burst in on him, bounced around awhile, then burst out, being careful as he crawled in bed not to spill his highball.

The music washes over him: Lulu and Jack the Ripper unknown to one another encountering each other, each seeking to get over on the other. Lulu is killed. As she expires in a series of death shrieks, which are drowned in the chromatic sea of the *Lulu* chord, it comes to James Antoine Girard, sitting on his bed nursing a drink, that he is no better than his father, and his father was no better than the Jack the Rippers, Don Giovannis, and E.T.A. Hoffmanns of opera—a weak man: fearful of, dependent on, and dominated by women. He pictures the Palomino: an Olympia, a Donna Elvira, a Lulu if ever there was one. He thinks of her as a virtuoso soloist, a saxophonist who has left the big band, and who in a series of one-night stands with pick-up bands has run out of riffs, and wants to return. He, of course, is the big band. Levering himself off the bed he replaces *Lulu* with a Brubeck album,

Brubeck after Desmond had come back. The music of "Blue
Rondo à la Turk" comments ironically on *Lulu*, Brubeck
trivializes Berg. Girard feels better, mellower, less doomed.
Maybe it will all work out this time, this one last time, he
thinks. He has one trump left to play, one weapons system
still in reserve, and he considers putting on Albert King, B.B.
King, Big Mama Thornton, Bessie Smith. But the situation
wasn't terminal; he wasn't ready yet to play the blues.

CHAPTER 4

The house on Pitt Street was behind his mother's house on Henry Clay. It was a self-contained bungalow set back from the street, approachable by a narrow walkway which ran beside his mother's bedroom, the windows of which were always open, so that whenever he ventured out or came in he felt himself under his mother's eye. At one time the building had been a slave quarters attached to the town house that had gone to his mother (in lieu of some shares to NORCO—the New Orleans Oil Refinery Company—which she inherited); it had been laid out facing Pitt Street to afford the slaves, as well as their masters, a modicum of privacy. There were two rooms and a kitchen and bath: a large main room entered by the front door, which he relinquished to Lee Anne; and a smaller side room, where he installed himself.

In this room—so small that his record player and records had to be set up in Lee Anne's room—he had a desk made from a door perched on stereo speakers, a mattress, and a chair. Within a few days he had compacted himself even further, sequestering his bed beneath the desk. Now he had a self-contained, coffinlike unit: bed beneath, desk above, music at head and at foot, and he slept and crept and listened below the level of the windows, which in addition to shades on rollers had heavy drapes on rods. Though his comings and goings to and from the small house were visible from the big house, and he had to cross Lee Anne's bedroom to get to his own, once inside his own little room he was inscrutable. He

116

could go to the bathroom directly from his room; he could enter the kitchen without trespassing on her room; but he could not change a record without encountering Lee Anne, especially at night.

After ten o'clock at night, when he began to drink in earnest while Lee Anne read herself to sleep, changing a record meant an encounter and, after midnight, a confrontation. In slippers and bathrobe he would pad softly toward the turntable, rehearsing in his mind the changing of the record— from Janácek to Ray Charles, or Bartók to Miles Davis— when suddenly Lee Anne would snap on all the lights and order him out of her room. Or, if she was reading by the small bedside lamp, she might put down her book, turn out the light, and wheedle: "If you have so much energy, James Antoine Girard, after lyin' around all th' livelong day while I'm workin', the least you can do is scratch my back!" And she would promptly turn over, presenting her backside. And gradually as he kneaded her broad back and cold buttocks, as her kneaded parts warmed and her legs parted, he would touch her vulva and finding it wet would lie down beside her, then with her. But even as he mounted and she yielded and they moved more or less in concert—she half asleep, he half drunk—he felt pity and contempt and revulsion for the woman beneath him who out of some ingrained sense of honor, duty, shame, would resort to such devices, and for what—to report to his mother and her father that she had slept with her husband? Love was such, the love of a good Southern girl like Lee Anne, that he would resort to tricks that Valerie would never stoop to: such was love among the upper class.

So this was where he had got to, where the love of good women had brought him: his mother's big house dominating all access to the little house in which he and Lee Anne lived, or appeared to live; Lee Anne's big room dominating all access to the little room in which he lived alone. Bath and kitchen were equally accessible to them both, but since there was no back door he was cornered in his little room of the little house and doubly imprisoned—or protected, depending on his outlook—from the outside world: Lee Anne in her larger room guarding him from his mother; his mother in her larger house guarding them both from everyone else. For him it was like solitary confinement in a minimum security prison, with the two dominant women in his life his guards: his mother his warden, whom he seldom saw; his wife, whom he glimpsed daily, his feeder and keeper. Both were devoted to their charge and to his welfare, within limits—Lee Anne, for example, brought him Early Times, a quart every second day; and his mother supplied her with money for groceries, $150 a week (they'd told him that much)—but he knew that if ever he kept the wrong company, or ventured out into the freedom of the city, or took a trip of which they disapproved (to Homewood, for example), or got drunk, or ran away, he could be sent in a trice by either of them, and probably both, to DePaul's for the twenty-seven-day cure including shock treatment or to the state asylum at Mandeville, or, worst, turned over to the FBI to stand trial for draft evasion. And well he could picture, in the first two scenarios, their solicitious visits to him while bamboozling the doctors; and in the trial scene their public posturing, ads in the *Times-Picayune*, and crocodile tears.

Weekdays while Lee Anne was out teaching he would take a walk upriver along the levee as far as Ochsner Clinic. Sometimes he would break into a bit of a jog, but the enforced inactivity and heavy drinking had begun to take their toll: his weight was up a hundred pounds from the "Big Sleep" period to two hundred and fifty, he felt bloated and heavy, slow-witted and dull, and broke into a sweat easily. From Ochsner Clinic he could see the bridge, its span and trestle veering off like flying buttresses above Bridge City, the railroad trestle arcing on at least a mile in a rollercoaster turn toward Westwego. He would stand on the levee and watch the bridge until a train had passed over, and the long unbroken locomotive line converged with the pulsating flow of cars where trestle and span intersected, while barges and tugs plied upriver and crossed under the bridge at precisely the spot where his father had vanished forever. Then he would cut across the Ochsner Clinic parking lot and up Coolidge or Harding ("Dis 'ere's Cooledge an' dat dere's Hardun, no confusin' dem two," the old Negro porter at Ochsner would say, and hailing him into his shack would offer him whiskey. "Silent Cal de one were call't, an' Warrun de udder. When Cal come home frum church his wife say, 'What'd th' preacher preach on, Cal?' An' he say, 'Sin.' 'An' what'd th' preacher say, Cal?' 'He's agin it.' Now Warrun, his Daddy say he glad Warrun ain't a girl, 'cause if Warrun be a girl he be in a fam'ly way mos' de time!") and on to Jefferson Highway (no jokes: "Jeff weren't a 'Publican, were he? But Wilbur Mills, now there's a Democrat! You wants to find th' 'Publicans, look where th' money is. You wants to find th' Democrats, look where th' pussy is. Why you wants to waste yore life along this levee? When you goan to get yore fill of that there Hoopalong bridge?") through Metairie Country Club Golf Course, where he would enter the clubhouse kitchen by the servants' entrance each morning at ten to have chicory coffee and hot croissants with Diane, the eldest of the Negro porter's nine daughters ("When first ah seen you joggin' crosst th' san'trap on them little sticks—mah Daddy called an' say, 'He comin', Di'—ah say, 'That boy needin' feedin'.' You fattenin' up now. You gitten big on black Diane's croissants!") and on to the Metairie Cemetery and Mausoleum, where passing the Confederate Cavalryman's statute—his mount with one hoof raised: the South was wounded in battle, but not killed—he comes to the corner crypt just down from the Army of North Virginia cenotaph, where generations of Girards are buried, including his father. And gazing at the sealed white crypts ("Sealed Forever," "Gone Forever," "Pure and Chaste as Morning Dew, One More," "One Less at Home, One More in Heaven") in the white marble mausoleums with the bodies buried above ground and the names inscribed as on foot-lockers (Agricole Armand 1843–1916, Jms. Gilbert Girard 1857–1922, Jos. Amilcar Girard *aetat.* 25, Jn. Morris Girard b. IX.25.02 Lost at Sea in Airplane Crash II.14.53), it comes to him that though they may be better off than he, he is better off for being here. Here no tormentors pursued, no jealous women guarded, no uncles taunted him. All around him lay in little urns the ashes and on steel shelves the remains of the most celebrated families in New Orleans—Morales and Delgados and Peyrefittes and Eberts and Girards—a silenced city of adulterers, idolaters, effeminate and many more who died in the midst of their pleasures. He himself was a pleasure-seeker, as was his father who was at rest here (James Allemands Girard 1917–1961), or was he in torment? Was his father in the torment he was in, or was his father's torment tolerable? Did God punish the disbeliever, pleasure-seeker, opera-lover? No. God loved absolutely, without question. Could *he* love absolutely, without question? Could he love? That was the question—fuck the how. If one could learn what love was by enduring its perversions—jealousy and vengefulness, tyranny and spite—he was learning . . . When he got home he had a minor set-to with Lee Anne about the record player. To punish him she played scales on her violin all night. . . .

Next day the sky was cloudless. He was jogging instead of

walking his circuit along the levee toward the bridge to Ochsner Clinic where he would cut over—feeling clumsy, coffee-logged and old beyond his twenty-eight years—when a girl darted out of the willows along the river's edge and started running beside him. Her hair was black and braided, her skin olive-colored and tanned, and in runners, shorts, and halter she looked lithe and fresh and young. Graceful, too, her movement, as a young gazelle's, and effortless. They ran together on the levee for a mile or more, Girard sweating and forcing himself not to gasp but to breathe through his nose like a horse, the girl panting slightly through parted lips and glistening with a fine sweat along her hairline and across the bridge of her nose where her freckles were clustered. Then as abruptly as she had joined him she turned off at Carrollton, while he pounded on up the levee. He noted the place of the sun in the sky, and watched her trim little ass out of sight.

Next day, another perfect running day, he was out pounding the same course at the same hour. This time the girl slipped out from a different clump of willows and they ran along together without speaking, as though they were partners and the levee was theirs, as though they had run there for years. When the girl turned off at Carrollton, Girard veered off with her, and at the railroad tracks at the base of the levee they slowed to a walk, the girl striding on ahead of him, hands on hips and breathing hard, to the shade of a magnolia tree where she knelt, and he squatted beside her, panting. In the shade of the tree, with the heat of the day and the flush of exertion upon her, the girl, he could see now, was strikingly pretty: long black hair braided and bound at the nape of her neck, large brown almond-shaped eyes, soft sloping breasts that quivered slightly as she caught her breath.

"Can you run that far again," he asked, "for a shower and drink?"

She looked at him appraisingly. "Sure," she said.

Taking his outstretched hand she hopped up and they jogged along the neutral ground on St. Charles, then through Audubon Park, to the house on Henry Clay where he led her down the laneway past his mother's window to the little house on Pitt, and through Lee Anne's front room to the little room where until now he had lived as a captive. As the enclosed space they entered grew smaller and darker, and the area of interdiction narrower—Girard leading her on by the hand—the freckles on her nose blended into one dark blotch and she seemed younger, fresher, more exotic than she had in sunlight. She stood in the shuttered dark of his room, appraising his cubbyhole bed.

"You really live here, in this little room?" she said, her eyes wide and almond-shaped in the dark room.

"I really do," he said.

"All by yourself?"

"All by myself."

"But don't you get lonely?"

"You might say I had a happy childhood."

"Who lives out there?"

"The Palomino."

"Who's that?"

"My keeper. She's also my ex-wife. But it's hard to talk to the cowgirl when you're standing under her horse."

"That's weird."

"You want to shower first? Or shall I?" Then, when she hesitated, "Want me to flip a coin?"

"Why don't we both go?" she said, and began unbinding her hair.

As he watched her freeing her hair and wriggling out of her T-shirt and pulling her shorts down, he asked, "How old are you, anyway?"

"I'm sixteen," she said petulantly. "I can do what I want."

He nodded.

"And my name's Magdalena."

"Okay, Magdalena. You go ahead. The shower's in there." He pointed toward the bathroom. "I'll fix us a drink."

"Oh, do you have orange juice? Just orange juice for me."

"Sure. You go ahead."

In the kitchen, fixing Magdalena her orange juice and himself a gin and tonic, he could hear the water running and pictured to himself her naked form; small sloping breasts, taut nipples with the water running off them, perhaps a birth mark on one hip or a webbed toe on one foot. Then he heard, or thought he heard, Lee Anne arriving home from school, though it wasn't time for her, unless it was Wednesday. He tried to remember what day of the week it was, but couldn't. He took the drinks into the bathroom.

"What day of the week is it?" he said, keeping his voice low.

"What?" Magdalena's drenched head appeared like an otter's from behind the shower curtain.

"Here's your orange juice. What day of the week is it?" he said again.

"Wednesday, I think. Thanks." She took the drink and disappeared again.

Aware that things might turn out badly, he sipped his gin and tonic and, peeling off his shorts and jockstrap, entered the shower. The girl, with water running over her, resembled some exotic, tantalizing fruit—a South Sea Island virgin bathing in a grotto? The BVM splashed by her fountain at the Sacred Heart Academy?—her olive-colored skin ripe to bursting except for two white stripes where sunlight seldom penetrated; and when as naturally as he might pick fresh fruit or pet a kitten he touched with his hands her breasts and dark-tufted crotch, she did not resist him. He could feel her dark cleft already wet, and her entire face—eyes, nose, mouth

—registered receptivity when he touched her nipples.
Without moving, she took his cock in one hand and began
soaping it with the other, then held it slippery with soap at
the lip of the opening where it would fit. They clasped each
other tightly and rocked to and fro, careful not to slip on the
wet tiles, until Girard placing a hand on her buttocks thrust
himself in. She gave a little scream, but he was ready to come
so he thrust on through—something tore—and as he came
inside her and she moaned he became aware of a cool breeze in
the bathroom, then as he shriveled and began to slip out, of a
disembodied hand inside the shower curtain, turning knobs.
The water on them went suddenly hot, then scalding. Girard,
whose back was to the showerhead, yelled and ripped open
the curtain. There Lee Anne stood, the Palomino rampant—
this cowgirl and her mount meant death to traitors!—nothing
in her hands or face but outrage. Girard leapt out with a
bellow, Magdalena close behind. Lee Anne stalked out of the
steaming bathroom, slamming the door after her.

Later that night, lying on his stomach, his back slathered
with Oil of Olay administered by Magdalena (whose scalded
front he had doctored before she went away), he realized he
was locked in a struggle whose outcome could only be bleak.
The lives of his mother and Lee Anne had narrowed down to
interdicting him, and his to circumventing them. They had
command, control, and communications on their side, as well
as massive retaliatory capability (even now he was awaiting
the crushing blow they were bound to deliver), while he had
only surprise, which he had squandered, and the simplicity of
small numbers—the smallest of numbers: one. As he lay with
the hot chills in his Pullman-like bed which had been shunted
by mischance into this siding—between DePaul's and the
Home for Incurables, downwind of the zoo and within sound
of the river—the stench of caged animals combined with the

stink of the New Orleans night, and the maddened roar of old Caesar the lion in response to boat horns on the river, made him nauseous and wakeful and aware of his chances, which were about those of old Caesar. Was it love that made the lion roar, the child's hand disappear? If he were to repay his Mumsy and old Pal for all their love to him, the cross and doublecross of Christ and Judas, or maybe the swastika of Parsifal, the ankh of Cleopatra might suffice. "Hail Mary, full of grace," he muttered, as a hot chill seized and shook him. The blast of the tug and an answering roar from old Caesar sounded contrapuntally, their deep diapason reminding him of some desperate cabaletta after all the arias are sung and doom is certain. Painfully he extricated himself from his coffinlike bed and padded into Lee Anne's room to put on a record.

All of his records were there, but not as he had left them, in an unholy jumble on the floor. Filled with foreboding he picked up an album and pulled a record from its jacket: it was scratched. A deep scratch scored with some sharp instrument cut across both sides of each of the records of *Parsifal*. Quickly he checked *Tannhäuser, Lohengrin, Tristan and Isolde*: all of his operas had scratches and X's and double X's scored in them, both sides, every record, all ruined. His *Norma* and *Lulu* and *Lucia* and *Electra* would never sound the same again, never. Frantic with loss and outrage he surveyed their maimed corpses beneath him—as at the end of a mega-opera, in which all the world's beauties are slaughtered—and searched for an opera unharmed. The blues which were off in a pile to themselves lay untouched—Big Mama Thornton, Bessie Smith, Billie Holiday: quickly he pulled and checked them— more intact on wax than in life. They were all there in their jackets ready to console him; and he was ready now to play the blues.

Shakily he put on Julia Lee with the Kansas City

Stompers. Julia Lee had "Trouble in Mind" back in 1944, but
the blues hadn't changed:

> *Sun gonna shine, ooh,*
> *Sun gonna shine in my back door someday,*
> *Wind gonna howl and blow my blues away.*
> *I'm gonna lay my head on some nearby railway line,*
> *An' let that midnight train satisfy my weary mind.*
> *Sun gonna shine, ooh . . .*

Her blues enter him and he is aware, as he would not be
with opera, of the thirty years' lapse between her singing and
his playing the blues, of how pain does not go away, does not
even diminish, but lurks and waits to be transmitted from
person to person and city to city until it is crushed on the
railroad track, or drowned in the river. Julia. Julia Lee. A
blues singer in Memphis, in Kansas City, in Harlem; a black
Baptist choir mistress in St. Francisville, Louisiana: just a
sittin' and a rockin' on her front porch while pickaninnies
play on the hard packed dirt beneath her chinaberry tree.

> *I'm blue, my poor heart is bleedin' sore,*
> *Never had such trouble in my mind before.*
> *Sun gonna shine, ooh,*
> *Sun gonna shine in my back door someday . . .*

And hearing Julia Lee and Jay McShann trade the age-old
talking blues, her telling him how "I'm goin' to Chicago,
goin' to Detroit town," and him telling her how "Detroit is
on fire and Chicago's burning down," it comes to him, the

blues he heard in hiding as a child outside Love's shack—
Jasper on the front porch with his battered old Stella, and
Love from inside the kitchen:

> J: I'se settin' here a thousand miles from nowhere
>   in this one-room country shack.
> I'se settin' here a thousand miles from nowhere
>   in this one-room country shack.
>   L: I'm here with you.
>   J: I wake up ever' night 'bout midnight, Love,
>   I jes' cain't sleep.
>   I wake up ever' night 'bout midnight, Love,
>   I jes' cain't sleep.
>   L: Yore Love's beside you.

And Jasper taking him aside and telling him, "Now Love,
she's sanctified. I done a trick when I married 'er. I pretended
I was sanctified to get 'er. Well now she stay with me
because it's jes' like if you was singin' the blues right now an'
you die, well they say you goin' to hell 'cause you was singin'
the blues." Then, striking a chord on his battered old Stella,
Jasper's eyes glitter fiercely: "How 'bout chu, boy, you goin'
to hell, now ain't chu?"

Methodically, he laid out his father's World War Two
Navy greatcoat with the New Orleans Opera Club medallion
pinned to it, the hand-tooled cowboy boots his mother had
given him for his twenty-seventh birthday, and the sweater
Lee Anne had bought for him when he was living with Les
and weighed a hundred pounds less, telling him he would
grow into it. Well, he had. These he laid out neatly on Lee
Anne's bed, then padded to the front door and opened it a

crack to see if the lights were on in the big house: something he never did when he was in his room, something he didn't need to do. They were on, though it was well past 2 A.M. The lights had gone out all over the South, but in his mother's town house they were on. With a vengeance. The big house was brilliantly lit as Homewood used to be on warm summer nights—every light, countless candles, and the three chandeliers—his mother out prancing the levee and his father locked in his room. His mother, it occurred to him now, left them blazing to make his father think she was there, his father who couldn't care less where she was: his father, and this was the worst he could say of him, his negligent father; his mother, and this was the best he would say of her, his hysterical mother. He was both, but it scarcely mattered now; only the light bill was left, and no one to pay it.

He was closing the door when a piece of school notepaper fell down between the screen door and its lattice. It had been cannily stuck between the two so as not to attract attention. He opened the screen door, stooped to retrieve the note, and hastily closed the front door. A child's scrawl, Magdalena's.

After I left your wife took me into the big house. She was sorry she hurt me. Gee, she's nice. Just thought I'd leave you this note to tell you she loves you a whole lot. She was just mad, that's all. I won't be running tomorrow. Looks like rain.

Love, Magdalena

P.S. She says you've decided to commit yourself for child molesting, and that you've done it before? Is that true?

P.P.S. What's molesting? Is it bad?

Love again, Magdalena

A hot chill shot through him as he read the postscript, a great thirst. So the lights burning bright in the big house were those of a council of war: his mother and uncle and wife. He was taking his own little counsel. He wondered what shock treatment felt like, and broke out in a sweat at the temples. He padded into the kitchen and fixed himself a highball, downed it in one lusty gulp, and poured himself a second. Another hour and a half would bright first light—*Sonnenaufgang!*—morning of the last day. If he stayed around, if he slept a wink, it was *The Cabinet of Dr. Caligari* for him. He retraced his steps into Lee Anne's room and put on another record, the last. This time it was Robert Johnson, dead of a stab wound in a roadhouse at age twenty-four.

I believe, I believe my time ain't long.
I believe, I believe my time ain't long.
I gotta call Mr. Harris, tell him send my sow back home.

The music pulses out from Robert Johnson, and into James Antoine Girard. "Dust my broom" Robert Johnson belts out, and there is no answering voice. A boat horn blasts but there is no answer from Caesar, who sleeps, no doubt, as only the innocent can sleep. Should he sleep he would wake up wired at DePaul's to lose 50,000 brain cells in one jolt, or get sent to the state nuthouse at Mandeville for child molesting. Then he could meet Magdalena on the levee doing the Thorasine shuffle. Slowly he got up to fix one last drink, a triple bourbon, went to the toilet to make room for it, and entered Lee Anne's room for the last time: his drink refreshed, his bladder relieved, his spirit fortified. Holy Mary, Mother of God, pray for us sinners now and at the hour of our death, amen. He put on the clothes he had laid out on the bed, tossed off his drink, and went out leaving the turntable running.

The New Orleans night was heavy with pollution. No light, except from the big house. He crept along the walkway beneath his mother's bedroom window like a shadow in his father's Navy greatcoat; a shadow, and a sizeable one, he skulked past the brightly lit front room from which he could hear, like a concluding cabaletta in some luckless *opera buffa*, the voices of mother, uncle, wife:

"But Mandeville, I'm not sure . . ."

"Hot damn, you're not! DePaul's, then."

"It's such a shame I'm thinking, Jimmy . . ."

—with his mother as contralto, his uncle the *basso buffo*, and Lee Anne as an overextended coloratura. For an instant he considered bursting in on them, singing at the top of his lungs a cavatina: "*Una furtiva lagrima*," for example. His father had done that with his mother once or twice; his mother had then thought it charming. Times had changed. "New occasions teach new duties/Time makes ancient good uncouth"— where was that from? He skulked past. Past the house lit up as the plantation used to be, past lugrustrum and Japanese plum heavy with scented white and pink blooms, and his mother's enormous live oaks which arched out over Pitt Street, carpeting both pavement and parked cars with buck-moth caterpillars. The yellow devils squished underfoot as he crossed Pitt, glancing anxiously over his shoulder; then he began to walk down Henry Clay—beyond his mother's grasp for one block only—until the solid ten-foot-high brick wall around DePaul's loomed on his right. He walked beside it, stooped and in its shadow for three blocks: past DePaul's, where his mother and his uncle and Lee Anne were intent on sending him, if not to the state nuthouse at Mandeville, then crossing Magazine he skulked along beside the ten-foot-high brick walls of St. Clare's Monastery. Crossing Constance—a brief, deserted street between more blind brick walls: New

Orleans here had architecture after Auschwitz, or was Auschwitz modeled on the Garden District—past the Home for Incurables (lights out, no councils of war in there) and, finally, turning at Tchoupitoulas at the entrance to the Crip- pled Children's Hospital and, flanking it, behind its own brick wall, the Blind Hospital ... or was it? It was a question he'd often wondered, and had gone so far as to ask. No one, not even the people who lived across from its blind brick wall and sat out evenings swinging on their verandas, watching the 120-foot-high brick incinerator stack belching black smoke, knew what went on inside. All they could tell him was that from time to time truckloads of the blind were trundled in and, presumably, trundled out again, but no one would even hazard a guess as to what the foundry stack resembling a crematorium was for. Something Catholic, no doubt, like monks making cheese. He would never know now. Behind him forever the Blind Hospital, whatever its function, and behind it the levee, the river. Turning toward Audubon Park Zoo where Caesar slept the sleep of the brave, he came to the end of Tchoupitoulas and entered the park where he had run and wept the day his father died.

He began to feel light-headed, euphoric, like a man with a mission, a man of fact. The man of fact waits in grim silence —where did that come from?—to make the throw and score the point. Only, his wouldn't be a throw, but a fall; and there wouldn't be any point to score because there wasn't any opponent.

Past the park, on the levee again, he passed a clump of willows—dark and indistinguishable from other clumps along the river's edge—similar to the one behind which Magdalena had lurked, and from which she had darted like a ... like a what? a faun? an undercover agent? a co-respondent in a divorce suit?—into his life, his miserable life, and out again. He broke into a bit of a run to clear the place of ambush, then he was walking again along the levee with the lapping of the river like the sloshing of a drink around his ankles to his left and off to his right the steady hum of houses and neighborhood bars, dog-runs and cages, in which human beings drunk or sober and dogs and lions slept and struggled toward the light, or rested from it, snoring. A few lights blinked on now, in addition to the street lights, in squalid and yardless dark houses—city bus drivers, dock workers, security guards—and he could imagine the groggy inhabi-tants, men slain by alarm clocks which ticked like time bombs all night, groping their way toward toilets for the first pee of the last day, fumblingly lighting first cigarettes. A baleful pink light was visible above the black water, mists rising like sulphuric acid from the river which flowed swift and slick into the pinkness behind him, Gulfward. There were islands in the Gulfstream, had to be. The levee shored the river, the river flooded the delta, the delta debouched into the Gulf: the Gulf was that of Mexico, another country. Amazing what the mind can do, when pressed. It can make a hell of heaven, it can make a heaven of hell, but it cannot create something out of nothing, only God can. Who said that? Holy Michael the Archangel defend us in battles—Fr. Durieu, S.J., Catechism—and cast into hell all who wander through the world seeking the ruin of soul amen. Bundled in his Navy greatcoat to take a long journey, the longest of journeys in; his father's greatcoat heavy and warm and warmly oppressive the air as he strode the levee toward the long curve. He glanced at his watch—nearly 5:30.

Ahead he could glimpse as he approached Ochsner Clinic, and as he passed Broadway, Cherokee, Dante—names replete with missed appointments, mistaken identities, failed encoun-ters through his growing-up years: each street he had taken had dead-ended here at the levee—the shadowy arc spanning the river, which was visible now, of the bridge. All hope dead-ended there, at the bridge: the bridge his father had jumped from, the bridge built by Huey P. Long. It was narrower than the bridges built now, than the Sunshine Bridge Jimmy Davis built above Homewood too late for his father. His father, had he jumped from the Sunshine, would have been the first to do so; from the Hoopalong he was neither the first, nor would he be the last. A train toiled up the mile long trestle leading from Bridge City: boxcars, flatcars, tankers, dusky silhouettes chugging infinitely slowly —twenty plus the engine, no caboose—out over the river to the apex of the arc above the flat black current slithering beneath. Names indistinct, but he knew them: Missouri Pacific, Illinois Central Gulf, Burlington Northern, St Mary's Railroad, Louisiana & Arkansas—places he had been or longed to go, places he had never been and had no yen to go, places he would never go. Had he been passive? The alternative was war, from which he flinched. What honor in fighting with women? Women were a moral force you couldn't fight, as General Butler found out when he occupied New Orleans. The South was proud of its women, lacking men. Was he proud of the South? Was the South proud of him?

At Ochsner Clinic he left the levee and broke into a little downhill scrimmage as he cut across the parking lot and past the Negro porter's shack: *"Why you want to waste yore life along this levee? When you goan to get yore fill of that there Hoopalong Bridge?"* He was sweating now, all 250-poundweight of him jostling and sloshing in the confines of the Navy greatcoat, working up a great thirst. Ruefully he realized he hadn't any money: if Agostino's was still open . . . which he doubted. If it were, maybe he could wangle one on credit, long term—

credo: would Agostino believe?—very long term, or . . . his watch! Briskly and with renewed purpose he covered the two blocks on Coolidge, then swung left onto Jefferson Highway at the corner where the package liquor, barred and shuttered against vandals, bristled with alarm warnings and police-protection stickers. Jefferson Highway was almost deserted at this hour—5:42 by the watch that might survive him—overcast by pink-streaked clouds as the sun rising behind him bled down shopfront windows: Hire's Root Beer, Tasty Do-Nut, Church's Chicken. He could almost make out Agostino's beyond the Causeway overpass, about a mile down the desolate stretch of junky, neon-lit motels and fast-food joints: squat little dirty-white stucco growths, hardly buildings, thrown up maybe twenty years ago to be marooned on this highway when the expressway was put through. He quickened his pace, feeling good, even euphoric, now that he had a purpose, even a temporary one: a creature comfort, even an uncertain one, to bend his steps toward. A drinker needs a drink, a Christian Christ . . . heartily sorry for having offended you and I detest all my sins . . . St. Agnes Virgin Martyr Church and School—nobody he knew ever went there: an old and poor church, you could tell by the façade and the crude *Christus Victor* out front; an integrated school, Spanish Catholics, overrun since Castro by the Cubans, since Eisenhower by the Negroes. Discipline in St. Agnes, even for the nuns, impossible; he'd heard stories, notches on their rosaries . . . Still, if you disbelieved in something long enough, it ceased to exist. Agostino's ahead. But above and beyond Agostino's and dwarfing it, swathed in a bandage of cloud, Mercurochrome-colored, the bridge caught the rays of the sun rising over the delta. Like a man shot from behind, he hurried forward . . . firmly resolved with the help of your grace to sin no more and to avoid the near occasions . . . past

Agostino's, a dirty oasis blinkered and shuttered, brief little diversion to propel him up Jefferson to the last lap and homestretch of junk yards. His watch said fourteen minutes till six but there would be no last call. With the last near occasion behind him, he made the dogleg south where the highway becomes a fronting road, crisscrossed with shunting tracks, for lumberyards, iron works, and dry docks. At the New Orleans Scrap Iron and Scaffolding Yard, stony-faced and sober he turned onto the bridge.

He was thinking, as he started up the pedestrian walkway on the outside of the car lane, the lane divided by train tracks, how narrow it all was. The entire bridge, to accommodate eight lanes of traffic—two rail, four vehicular, two pedestrian—was less than an end zone across. He had a good quarter mile to go, most of it over scaffolding yards and piles of rusty scrap iron, and cars were speeding toward and swishing past him on their way to New Orleans at intervals of every minute or so, at a distance of less than a yard. This was not the broad way that led to perdition, this was the towpath that led to Westwego, and like a man on his way to Westwego he had no desire to arrive. Westwego would not miss him, nor he it. The only place he had ever missed was Homewood, the only person his father. He could see as he passed over them a warren of warehouses, then willow bottoms, shacks on stilts and fishing boats tied up at the banks, then the river—he was now at least one hundred feet above the water—mud-colored, whitecapped, and swift. A black buoy bobbed in mid-channel, whipping up whitecaps. The river was up, so was the sun—over the delta, over the islands, over the Gulf—not so high that the Bonnet Carré spillway was open. Downriver he could see the Sugar Bowl and Ochsner Clinic at the bend, the smoke and froth of barges plying upstream pulled by tugs, and far across the city at the base of Canal Street the Greater New Orleans Bridge, where others had jumped. Behind, on River Road—he didn't need to look, didn't want to—blighted elms shrouded the shame of Elmwood, that ruined plantation, and shipyards and dry docks cluttered the banks all the way to Harahan. No reason upstream not to jump; none down, either. Not that honor demanded it, and sex wasn't worth dying for . . . his father, drink in hand, gazing down from the balcony on Chartres Street at the procession of gays: "You know, the problem with having a good time is that it always leads to pain. I haven't yet learned to eschew the one so as to avoid the other. I've never learned to enjoy Mardi Gras." And raising his glass to the gays in the street, who made obscene gestures back: "No pleasure but opera," he said. And then he was gone. That was the same Mardi Gras when, eating purple and green and gold King Cake with his father, he had bitten the baby inside. "Now you must give the next party," his father had said quietly. "But I will give the one this year, to show you how it is done." And then he was gone. His father, his negligent father . . . He wished there were some way of soaring out over the causeway, of making it right for those he had wronged . . . made a list of all persons we had harmed and became willing to make amends to them all—Step 8; Step 9—made direct amends to such people wherever possi-ble except when to do so would injure them or others . . . The river slid past at 25 to 30 mph 100 feet below him; 100 miles downstream—past oxbows and hairpins, dead-man's channels and bayous—the Gulf awaited. The sun was . . . the sun, no *Christus Victor*; he was himself, a drunk. The sun was up and still rising—over the delta, over New Orleans, over Metairie Cemetery and the Negro porter's shack and the bridge on which he stood, mocking time. The sun when it set would rise again; he would plunge and would stay down,

drowned—no *Christus Victor* he. If he had swallowed the
sentiment for thirty years it was because he believed in the
dogma; he still believed in the dogma but the dogma would
not save his soul; divers and dredgers would salvage his body,
his body that did not believe . . . A mile distant he spied and
then heard a train coming, the plume of its smoke puffing up
over Westwego as it commenced the long, slow, rollercoaster
ascent over Bridge City. The trestle vibrated beneath him.
The train would pass on its way to New Orleans at a snail's
pace, nearly a standstill, when it reached him. When the
shadow of the bridge struck the oncoming engine he would be
in the shadow struck by the train . . . geometric pattern that
would not be repeated: the train was and would be, *ibid.* the
bridge, *ibid.* the sun; he was and would not be—not that it
mattered. No more than a piece of flotsam, trembling as it
shot from beneath the bridge, turning once or twice on the lip
of whitecaps, riding up a wave, sliding down a trough,
abruptly disappearing: sucked into the vortex of a whirlpool.
How they suddenly leave the surface, dead sticks. "You're a
lost soul, Girard," Les had said. True, but it rankled. Who
but God had a right to say that? . . . The train puffed nearer.
Hello fodder. Goo'bye mudder. Goo'bye Lee Anne, Maggie,
Val . . . and goddamned soul. The train chugged nearer, its
labor deafening, the narrow walk he stood on with its outside
metal railing just above waist high vibrating like the pipes of
a pipe organ. He waited, watching out the corner of his eye
the train puff toward him, while out over the river a scrap of
newspaper cavorted like a kite caught in an updraft. The train
toiled up the steep grade toward the apex of the trestle:
downhill from there, nearly there. Both hands on the railing,
shoulder width apart, in readiness; the railing singing, swaying, vibrating, but not hot: he gripped the railing as the train
came on. When the shadow of the bridge struck the snub-nose

of the engine he placed one foot on the railing and with a
thrust of his shoulders vaulted over as he used to vault the rail
gate down the dirt lane leading to Love's house, only this
time there was nothing on the other side—no lane, no house,
no Love—only windless space he plummeted down in a wake
of terrifying blasts the train gave forth like a man shot from a
cannon but in such a way that he sped faster and faster the
further he hurtled from the cannon's mouth—see Jim jump,
see Jim fall—an astonished object falling and accelerating
amazingly as he fell toward, then struck, the swiftly moving
water, the impact thrusting him down, down, down, in
motion still, but in a different medium . . . he relaxed as he
had not done in the air . . . He was aware, not acutely
conscious, but pleasantly aware of *moving*: he wondered
vaguely whether he was moving up, or down . . . *moving up*: he
looked up through water dark and muddy above him and
further up less muddy, and wondered vaguely whether he
would break the surface sooner, or later . . . *breaking surface*:
encircled by a maelstrom of white water, undertow clutching
at his legs and lower body, the wake of the whirlpool
buoying him up, just barely, and feebly turning him inside a
disintegrating circle against the current of enormous suckage
downstream. And he felt *pain*: such as he had never felt before,
through his abdomen and chest and head as he attempted,
lungs half-filled, to choke in air, air, air . . . he sucked a
strangled half-breath, then another, then a breath as the wake
of the whirlpool by which he was buoyed up played out and
he began to be swept down and under—against which he
made feeble swimstrokes: who would have thought he would
fight so hard to live?—but the undertow suck was terrific,
like tug-o'-war against a train, and the pull of the current
irresistible as his mother's arguments . . . he began to be
pulled down and under . . .

Muted colors, muted sounds, browns and grays and moans
and whispers. Had he been here before? He thought not. He
was not here now. His body was, lying on a bed, surrounded
by Lee Anne. She was talking, not to him, never to him,
always to some image of herself which she confused with him,
but in this case not even to that since his eyes were closed,
closed and would not open, his mouth too; to someone else,
then: ". . . his Daddy's World War Two greatcoat. He jus'
flapped down in th' breeze. It kep' him up, too, all that air.
Tugboat captain says they jes' reached down an'gaffed him by
that greatcoat, neat's you please, no struggle, good job they
were there. I always worried 'bout him jumpin' off that
bridge. I knew he was gonna jump off that bridge, 'cause of
his Daddy, you know. An' thank you, doctor. Ah 'preshiate
it, Jimmy an' I do." Silence. Not the absence of sound, but
the presence of someone not speaking. Surrounded by silence,
Lee Anne's. Her hands do something with the covers, he
flinches. A burning pain in his abdomen, here, there, everywhere, like the pizzicatto passages in Penderecki's *Threnody*,
stippling his stomach, abdomen, and groin. "Adhesions," she
says. He lies very still, not even breathing, until the pain in his
groin causes tears to start from his puffed-shut, bruise-black-
ened eyes; he feels the tears trickle down his swollen face,
along his neck, and then he feels them no more. He hears a
hum. Lee Anne talking: "I know you're there, Jimmy Girard.
You can't fool me, you never could fool me. Jes' you look at
yourself! Your body all bloated, your face all pocked. You're
not the tiger I married, those piercing eyes, that stealthy
walk. A panther walk, but you had tiger eyes. You gonna be
all right though, th' doctor says you're one in a million. Little
does he know! But you gonna be all right. Your momma says
after you come back from Mandeville she gonna wash her
hands, you gonna be all mine an' I'm never gonna let you out

of my sight, I'm gonna love you an' watch over you an' you're gonna be jes' fine. Maybe you'll get back that panther walk, but if not it don't matter. You gonna be my tiger again, an' I'm gonna love you forever."

He heard her words as though from a great distance, underwater. He was traveling on a flatcar through a watery tunnel, his hands and feet and arms and legs outstretched, his hair swept back, as fragments of her meaning and even entire meaning-units, like underwater mines exploding, shrapnelled into him with deadly force: "Momma," "Mandeville," "tiger . . . love . . . forever." He could not see an end to the tunnel, all he knew was he was *moving*; then he remembered he was *moving up*. He moved up at an intolerable speed through shredded fragments of depth charges and blown buoys to *break surface*, but the surface where he broke through was a boat hull, *Pride of Dixie. Pain,* good for the soul. He went to sleep again . . .

III. HOMEWOOD

There is no such thing
as desire of the body.

Plato, *Philebus*

Melancholia is an infection that
hath mastry of the soule . . . and as the
causes be diverse, the tokens and signes
be divers. For some cry and leape, and
hurt and wound themselves and other men,
and darken and hide themselves in privy
and secret places. . . .

Bartholomaeus Anglicus,
De Proprietatibus Rerum

CHAPTER 1

Girard! Girard!

The dreadful day of exquisite suffering has arrived. I am a pediatric intern at Charity. Yesterday was my first day. Of course I was on call for the nursery. That meant staying up all night and taking care of sickly babies in intensive care. Surprisingly, none died. One got better.

You'll want to hear of Joe, our suicidal friend without the face. My last day in Emerge (before the switch to pediatrics) I stopped in to feed him and found old Joe—get this—with his head down in the toilet, his artificial blowhole too, drowning. Afraid I saved him. Had to—I'm just an intern after all. Joe will have to be more resourceful. Told him so. He can't talk back, but he can hear. If he'd come to me for advice, earlier, with all his senses and his face intact . . .

Since you too are given to great suffering, Girard, not to mention bouts of self destruction, this happy thought appended to the fridge (more below) may see you through your next dark day. The facial nerve, seventh cranial, provides motor/muscle innervation to the muscles of the face and the superficial muscle in the neck. It emerges on the face just anterior to the ear after traversing the inner and middle ears. A well-placed gun shot could wipe out

this nerve, leaving a generally sagging face—the condition,
I conjecture, of certain politicians. If this happens, one is
unable to close one's eyes, or eye. The cornea dries out and
ulcerates, becomes infected, until the eye is a runny hole in
the head. I doubt that doctors today would let it go
beyond the ulceration stage. But—and here is the beauty of
my plan—the same blast, without in itself being fatal,
could destroy the nerve plexus supplying innervation to the
tear glands. Hence, no tears.

No tears, Girard!

Which brings me to Sears. Remember the fridge? It
broke, was fixed, and broke again. Both times while I was
away. What an unholy mess! Stink! I believe freezer un-
derwent spontaneous generation—crawling with scuzzy
little bugs. Back to Sears. Seems the second breakdown
was due to inadequate repair the first time. Wrote Sears
claiming $72 damages. Sears responded they were check-
ing service record. In sum: fridge does not work, so don't
use it. Don't even open the door. Otherwise, make self at
home. My schedule's screwed, we may never see each
other, keeping tabs on Joe. Keep you posted.

Ciao, Larry

The letter, Scotch-taped to the terrible fridge, meant that
Larry had been in sometime since he'd been across the street,
propositioning Valerie. What time was it now? The next day
certainly, hopefully morning. Without opening the door of
the infernal machine, he took down Larry's note and scribbled
a message on its back:

Ah, Larry! Ah; Charity!

Whenever the weeping urge wells up, I will recall your instructions. Whenever the yen to self-destruct compels, I will open your fridge. Convey my condolences to Joe. Tell him we're monitoring his attempts. I go meanwhile where Joe has never gone, where now he'll never go. Be away a day or two. Hoping for a moment of lucidity between here and where I haven't been for twenty years—Homewood.

Chimo, Jimmy

Reusing the Scotch tape proved futile: in the humid atmosphere it would not stick a second time. Finally he was forced to open the fridge door, just a crack, to insert the end of the paper. The odor wafted out, muzzy and sulfurous, like a fat man's fart. He quickly closed the door. New Orleans had smells unidentified and unknown elsewhere in America: oily and putrescent smells among magnolia blossoms. He would likely smell today the whole range—Creole cooking, cane fields, river silt, the mustiness of his mother's horsehair love seat—things he hadn't smelled for twenty years. He peeled one hundred dollars off the wad he'd got from Floyd, stashed the rest beneath the Christmas cactus blooming in the next room, and ambled down the back stairs through the tangle of mirliton vines, jaunty, almost cheerful at the prospect of the trip.

> "*Alouette, gentille alouette,*
> *Allouette, je t'y plumerai . . .*"

He hummed to himself as he walked up Hickory, past the Mt. Moriah Baptist Church and rows of shotgun houses, not squalid but not quite respectable either, each of them laid out like Valerie's mother's, with a little fence, a little porch, a swing on the porch in which sat in the shade an old black, and in front of each little house a big yellow or red or two-toned Chrysler or Lincoln or Cadillac parked in the street. He had determined not to take the trolley downtown, but the Freret Street bus instead; that way he hoped to reach Canal by ten o'clock when the tour buses left, and he would be spared the ride down St. Charles through the Garden District where his mother lived. In New Orleans only one night, and already finding his way! Maybe he would be able to live here this time, by hiding and watching, picking and choosing, tiptoeing his way as through a mine field—

> "Je t'y plumerai la têt'—
> —Je t'y plumerai la têt' . . ."

At the "Whites-only" bar, white stucco blockhouse with bars like a guardhouse, he crossed over and cut through the cemetery where Valerie's father would lie. A ghoulish live oak dominated the pavement where two promenades intersected the marble and granite, domed and decorated mausoleums; and next to the live oak an angel. This angel of stone stood guard on the blockhouse of "Capt. Joseph Bisso." As Girard passed the cemented-shut mausoleum—"Sealed Forever"—a grounds attendant emerged from behind it, almost as though he had come from a back door, rake in hand and lustily singing the tune Girard was humming:

". . . Je t'y plumerai les yeux—
—Je t'y plumerai les yeux.
Et les yeux—
—Et les yeux.
Alouett'—
O! . . ."

With elaborate mock surprise at meeting Girard, the attendant—Cajun, in his sixties, and wearing a brimmed cap
that announced "N.O. Saints"—planted his rake and leaned
on its handle.

Girard, whose jaunt through the cemetery was a shortcut,
paused impatiently. *"Quelle heure est-il, s'il vous plaît?"*

"Il est neuf heures, cousin. Le temps est à la pluie. When it rains,
y' know, the dead float—those ones do." The old fellow
pointed beyond the live oak to the city's side, where rows of
small mounds, marked by crosses, hummocked half the cemetery. "Bisso here," he said, placing one hand familiarly on the
mausoleum, "'e was a real 'eller, 'e stays put."

Girard regarded the old Cajun, then the mausoleum where
Capt. Joe stayed put, then the Cajun again.

"A real what?"

"'eller, 'e was a real 'eller."

"Heller?"

The old fellow winked. "Tha's th' secret," he confided,
and recommenced raking and singing:

"Je t'y plumerai le bec—
—Je t'y plumerai le bec.
Et le bec—
—Et le bec.
Alouett' . . ."

Girard hurried now, intent on boarding the Freret "jet" in time to catch the tour bus on Canal. He did not bother on Broadway even to glance at Newcomb College, where the ghost of another hellion, his beloved ex, might still be stalking rampant or stirruping her Palomino from desk to desk and classroom to classroom, giving herself, reserving herself, nice shaky buttocks, while he drowned his sorrows; nor did he when a black woman boarded the bus and flounced past him to the rear—dark breasts jiggling like clusters of ripe grapes—remember Valerie in the dawn, holding and milking his scrotum, massaging him toward a second (or was it a third? fourth? or fifth?) climax. He simply sat and registered as though he passed them daily, the Tulane NROTC unit, the Loyola fieldhouse, Tip-Top Ice Cream, Alcee Fortier High, Our Lady of Lourdes Elementary, its ballfield razor-wired to keep the Catholics in, the junkies out, the Brown Derby where once he'd gone with Valerie and got thrown out. The Freret jet sped past Valence, Cadiz, Jena. On Napoleon an old school bus with letters four feet high, REPENT or PERISH!, large wooden cross mounted on its rear above the license, with a lake of burning fire lapping at the windows which were blacked-in to depict those (heads up) who had and (heads down) those who hadn't heeded the scripture verses scrawled in flames; driving it a wild black man in bathrobe and black turban. Right on Simon Bolivar—2nd King Solomon Baptist Church, Shelley's Social & Pleasure Club, Majestic Mortuary—blacks boarding at each stop— "We Serve With Reverence." Gathering speed to hurtle down Dryades, packed in with blacks like shock troops, he entered without warning a landscape under siege—the Dryades Merchant District—with wire-meshed windows on store fronts, steel-bar-latticed doors, palms studding narrow grassless neutral ground like stubby thumbs lopped off at the first joint; the H.L. Green department store where once he'd bought a shirt . . . Thalia, Erato, Clio, Calliope. Bode's Venus Gardens, Deli and Rink; the gilded, domed and placarded Masonic Hall. Downtown. A blind man with a basket, zigzagging in front of cars on Canal Street, boarded the bus. Tapping his way into the seat behind the driver, he started biting his hand.

"Felicity Street, please." Biting his hand.

The driver stopped the bus abruptly in the middle of the block.

"This bus doan' go to no Felicity, feller."

The blind man sat, viciously biting his hand.

The bus driver shrugged, as if to say "I warned him, you heard me," and resumed driving.

Girard got off at Burgundy, colliding with a rummy dum —"Hey, buddy, you wanna buy a radio?"—a rummy dum with a filched radio—"Hey, buddy!"—and shouldered his way through the throng of freeloaders, panhandlers, and early shoppers outside D.T. Holmes waiting their turn at the 9:45 free coffee being served by an attendant from the two-tiered silver service to the twenty or so bag ladies and others who sit on folding chairs just inside the big glass double doors. No sign, but people in New Orleans know—9:45 A.M. to 5:40 P.M. daily except Sundays, a warm place and free coffee—for over fifty years. He pushed on past the coffee hopefuls and arrived with time to spare on the corner of Canal and Rampart, where halfway down the block a bus marked "River Road Plantation Tours" was parked. Tourists were already in the bus and on the sidewalk by the door three drivers, fat men in Salvation Army uniforms, black with red trim but without the SA on the collar, tour-guide caps upon their heads. A pencil vendor, holding up his wares and throwing out his arms, delivered a set spiel to the three

captains. But no sound of the pencil vendor's routine reached
Girard. The tour guides seemed amused; one bought a pencil
from the vendor while another, the fattest of the three, sold
Girard a ticket, and he saw now that the pencil vendor was a
deaf-mute. Not the tour guide.

"Right in there, right in there. Get this show on the road
right away. Where you frum, son? Don't tell me. See'f ah
cain't figure it out. Step right in, right in, we're 'bout
ready."

Girard entered the parked bus, his wrinkled windbreaker
and travel-stained pants, his dirty, tobacco-stained teeth and
ex-boozer's pockmarked face the momentary focus of twelve
to fifteen blandly curious, slack-mouthed, well-fed white
faces, mean age about sixty-five. He lurched to the rear of the
bus, not because it was moving, but because he was accustomed to boarding buses with a wine bottle tucked under his
jacket while half-drunk. One woman, as he lurched past,
looked at him with eyes unlike the others. The others, with
their little red pigs' eyes encased in flesh, their avid gazes
darting from glossy brochures clutched in pink hands to
Girard's pitted face, were what he expected to find on a tour
bus, tourists, and they were in couples. The only single on the
bus besides himself was the woman: about the same age as the
rest and white haired, but tall and thin, with freckles all over
her face and ice-blue Irish eyes. If the bus filled up, he would
sit beside her. He slumped down on the back seat by himself
and studied the woman, who now by a sudden struggle of sun
over D.T. Holmes was clothed in light. Then the driver got
on, the bus started up, and the tour began.

The tour guide, who announced himself as "Charlie Spagioni, atcher service!" had an irritating manner of repeating
his nouns, and of breathing into the microphone, which he
didn't need. "Now in justa minute we're gonna take th'

expressway, th' expressway was built in th' sixties, one 'a th' first, folks, first of its kind. An' in justa minute we'll pass under th' overpass, th' overpass was built in sixty-nine, sixty-nine, no dirty minds here! No-sirree-bob, not a dirty mind in Nu Awlins!'' To the mock-shocked tittering of sexagenary tourists, there followed an extended comparison of the Superdome with the Astrodome, to the Astrodome's disadvantage. Numbers impressed Charlie Spagioni mightily, and stuck to his mind like burrs. That the Superdome cost $167,000,000 rather than the $63,000,000 it was designed to cost, was adduced several times as proof of New Orleans's greater corruption and general grandeur. Girard, having tried and failed to stop his ears, settled into a Protestant slump sort of passive resistance, gazing idly out the window at the ho-hum Superdome while envisioning the Sugar Bowl it had replaced. And suddenly it came to him: the Sugar Bowl was gone! It had been demolished when the Superdome was built. In its place there would be housing, office buildings, or just wreckage—another spot he must declare off-limits to himself. . .

"Now, folks, off to yer left you see th' Huey P. Long Bridge, a semi-cantilever bridge built in 1935. It handles vehicular, rail, and pedestrian traffic, an' occashunally th' odd suicide, but what bridge don't? In just a minute we'll be leavin' Orleans parish, ah said parish, an' ent'rin' Jefferson parish. We have parishes here in Loosianer, just like you have counties in—where ya frum, lady? Arkansas? Well, in Loosi-aner . . .''

He hated this. Once before he had taken this bus, the only bus that wended its anachronistic way along the almost abandoned River Road, from which traffic had been diverted decades ago to the Airline and Veterans highways, and more recently to the I-10. Only once, and once on this bus was enough; even Jesus walked his valley only once.

"Here in Nu Awlins we got forty-two cemeteries. Plots start at $80 and go up to $83,000. Now in just a minute we gonna pass under that Huey P. Long Bridge off t' yer left, an' you gonna see sumpin' sad, moughty sad, yes-sirree!"

On Jefferson Highway now, the tourists checking their brochures and feeling, doubtless, disappointed as they pass St. Agnes Virgin Martyr Church and School, Cuban and slummy, then the dirty stucco of Agostino's Bar, sleazy and shuttered against ante meridian light, and finally past the New Orleans Scrap Iron and Scaffolding Yard, before passing under the Huey P. Long access, whose rail and road (but not pedestrian) traffic had been visible off to the left the whole time.

> To and fro across the Hoopalong
> cars go:
> Few to, but many fro
> Westego!

It was his sister's, sing-songed by the two of them together (*aetat.* fifteen and eight) in the backseat of his father's 1947 twelve-cylinder Chrysler on frequent trips to town (usually to deliver or retrieve his mother); for a brief embattled year or so it had replaced "Shilliky pooky, pull out your horns! Shilliky pooky, put out your eyes!", before it was itself replaced by silence. On River Road alongside a dirty old man river, Charlie Spagioni citing statistics, of tonnage, draughtage, and freight, for shippage, dockage, and rail, in among the elm trees and wisteria Girard sighted the bill-board: "Vote Girard U.S. Congress!"

"Folks, ah gotta call yer 'tenshun now t' sumpin sad. It's Elmwood Plantashun, an' you can catch a glimpse of it off to th' right there. This is th' oldest home in th' Mississippi Valley, built in th' early 1700s on a land grant by Bienville to th' father of Nicholas la Frenière, first attorney gen'ral of Loosianer. An' look at it now, folks, a eyesore, hippies camp in it, broken beer bottles an' used whatchamacallems an', well, you name it. It's a shame.''

"Can't the Heritage Society restore it?" a white-haired suffragette at the front of the bus asked.

"What say, lady?"

Can Linda be her own woman and your representative?
Vote Girard U.S. Congress!

The larger-than-life-sized picture of his sister smiled in faded beauty from the ruins of Elmwood upwards at the Huey P. Long Bridge. Why had he never noticed it before? It was tucked in between the derelict plantation and the levee, left unmolested because she had a pretty face and no one coveted the space for advertising. But it must have been there when he had taken the narrow pedestrian walkway, placed both hands on the railing as the train shook the trestle, and jumped; why hadn't he seen it? He vaguely remembered now an article seven or eight years ago in *Life*, no, *Look*, saying Linda finds it not impossible to be a woman and a person, or somesuch . . . with pictures of her as a young girl, as a debutante at McGhee's, as a hostess in front of Homewood, as Miss Louisiana, as runner-up to Miss America, as a young attorney on a civil-rights march . . . so it must have been after the beauty contests and law school, the year she articled for Billy Bland's law firm—'69? '70? . . . "Look out on th' left there, folks. That's th' levee there. Now, look at th' water, then look at th' road we're on, folks. What ah'm tryin' to show is we're always two to eighteen feet below sea level. We'd be in a boat 'stead of in this bus. That's why we don't have no skyscrapers here in Nu Awlins. Lately though we been gettin' some pretty tall buildin's—th' Shell buildin', it's fifty-one stories, an' th' Sain' Charles Place, it's fifty-three stories, but it's actu'ly shorter."

The tour guide rattled on, machine-gunning the busload of tourists with inanities which Girard half-heard or heard fragments of, little dum-dums of misinformation, bigotry, and Southern self-justification detonating in the close air of the bus and dinning at his ears. Of the Negro: "Now, I have to tell you th' black man is very emotional, 'spesh'ly when he gits into voodoo. They bring out them bones an' 'fore you know it we have a grand s-e-x urgy. Jes' a bunch of ni . . . no, I ain't gonna say that word. Very primitive, they very primitive." Of Fat City: "Up that canal there you see that tile roof, that's a pumping station, pumping station. Now th' homes out there are goin' for $150,000, up to half a million. That's what they're goin' for out there—doctors, lawyers, politicians—they don't pay no taxes. Any a' you folks a doctor or lawyer? Anybody here a politician?" Of the race track: "That's Jefferson Downs, folks, now this is jockey racing, we don't have no dogs. Now th' Nu Awlins racetrack broke a record this year, averagin' one million six hundred thousand an' seventy dollars a day. That's a day, folks! Pretty good, huh?"

While the tour guide kept up his non-stop patois of homespun witticism interlarded with bad grammar, the bus departed from the River Road to take the elevated highway over Good Hope Swamp and Cross Bayou, cypress trees in the distance, swamp waters studded with duck blinds. "Huey Pierce Long, th' Kingfish, tha's th' man." Swamp waters, brackish and shallow, merged imperceptibly with

Lake Pontchartrain in the distance. "This here's th' Bonnet Carré Spillway, folks. Pretty good, yeah, pretty good, folks." Strong smell of sulfur all along the bayou, marsh gas and duckweed covering the whole submerged area between Bayou Lebranche and Bayou Trepagnier, where Irene Trepagnier (before she became Irene Girard) used to fantasize as a girl that gold lay buried. "That's natch'rul gas you see burnin' in them flues. That's Norco, folks—Nu Awlins erl refin'ry cump'ny. Now ain't that sumpin?"

What did he hope to accomplish by this trip? or had he, like the aspirants in front of D.T. Holmes, been cured of the disease of hope, unless for something like a cup of coffee, a swig of wine, or a spot to sleep? Even those commodities he could do without; there was little that he couldn't do without, almost nothing, and nothing that couldn't do without him. So it went when you departed this life. "We gonna turn off now just 'fore Boutte, where you gonna see th' Waterford nucle'r plant." If he had departed this life, why was he here? Was he in hell, or was this a daytrip through purgatory, was the abyss yet to come? "Yep, we got ev'rythin' here in Loosianer." The tour guide, having spared his group a closer look at the refiner's fires of Norco and the floodgates of the spillway, left the Airline Highway at La Place and at a bleak roadhouse named Paradis swung the bus back onto River Road.

They had now entered St. John the Baptist parish. Barrels of blackstrap molasses beside the hard-packed country roads, with here and there an old iron-wheeled wooden wagon still standing and shattered sugar-cane stalks lying in the furrows of fields recently stripped by machete. To the left less than a quarter of a mile away ran the levee, its brown grass slopes conjuring for Girard images of bonfires, Christmas Eves, and his mother prancing; of insidious crawfish for the red-eyed tourists. Crawfish a threat, Spagioni conspiratorially confides: dig in mud, undermine the levee. Annually since 1926 the big game isn't Tulane vs. LSU, it's crawfish vs. Army Corps of Engineers. Score 2–0. The father of waters, meanwhile, silently swishing down its 2552-mile course, the levee marking its homestretch, and before he knew it they were passing San Francisco with its gabled gallery overlooking the river and, directly above, its widow's walk and weeping porch. "Not Open to the Public" a sign read. Directly across the river was Oak Alley.

The last time he had taken this bus, nearly twenty years ago, it had stopped for a tour of San Francisco, then crossed on the ferry (the Sunshine Bridge was still under construction) to tour Madewood, Oak Alley, and the Edward Douglas White Home in Assumption parish. He was a schoolboy then, in the hated uniform, and his father not yet dead. He had got off the bus at the bridge site (to the consternation of the tour guide, he remembered now) and walked the four miles to Homewood, taking the shortcut through the cane brake by Love's house. Homewood, though in decline since his parents' divorce and his father's bankruptcy, was still his father's home; his father's room still resounded with opera (no longer the lush nineteenth century sounds of Verdi, Rossini, and Wagner; his father's new music was twentieth century, starker: *Salome, Dialogues of the Carmelites, Lulu*); and returning to Homewood was still for him then an escape from his mother's town house.

Now he did not know what to expect. Would the bus turn at the bridge to tour Madewood, Oak Alley, the White Home? Maybe it would go on past Homewood to Hermitage House, Mrs. Bringier's old mansion, or maybe to Ashland Plantation, where his sister used to stay when his parents were quarreling. No telling which of these old plantations had been "restored" by absentee heirs or holding companies, and which had been allowed to run down like Elmwood. If the bus crossed the river, he was crouched to get off, Spagioni or no Spagioni. Off to his left now he spied, in desolate splendor, built as a payoff to corrupt politicians, the toll bridge: linking nothing to nothing, no traffic on it or traveling to it from either direction. The high arched span over batteur and levee, dignified neither by rail, nor vehicular, nor pedestrian traffic, was not even ready in time for his father to jump from.

"Folks, you know that song, 'You Are My Sunshine'? You know who wrote it? Jimmy Davis, Gov'ner Jimmy Davis, an' this here's th' Sunshine Bridge. It don't go nowhere, frum Union to Donaldsonville, but they's just names, don't nobody live there 'cept some . . . I almos' said that word agin . . . some tenant farmers didn't have no place to go when we freed 'um, back in 1865. Now, let me tell you 'bout emancipation, folks . . ."

The Irish woman with ice-blue eyes seemed uncomfortable and turned in her seat to stare at him, but Girard had already stood up and walked to the well of the rear exit. He saw Charlie Spagioni—full-faced and swarthy, with a crease across his brow from the tour-cap brim, and eyes like chalcedonies—staring at him in the rearview mirror. "We us'd to go to Madewood, 'cross th' bridge," Spagioni said into the microphone held to his mouth, "but that's another tour, folks, for another day. We goin' to Homewood," he announced, his little glo-eyes riveting Girard's in the rearview.

At that very moment Burnside, Louisiana, zoomed up on both sides of the bus to unman him. "*I accuse!*" trumpeted St Michael the Archangel from his cypress-boarded church, the plaques commemorating miracles "Closed to the Public." "*We accuse you!*" the derelict shacks and store and cypress mill

erected by his dead grandfather's slaves and wretched freed-
men cried out at him through glass. The half-dozen tenant
shacks and general store stood tenantless and untended, mute
evidence of monumental decadence and gross neglect. "Now,
folks, we passin' through Burnside, don't blink. It's got
85,000 acres an' 2,000 slaves. Did have, in 1857, when ol'
man Burnside owned it. Fam'ly lost it all in th' Depression.
Now if you look out yer left . . ."

He wanted to interrupt and correct the odious tour guide:
his fulsome generalities, his tiresome spiel . . . But the futility
of setting straight the record restrained him; the record was
of failure, the land registry entries did chronicle decline: from
the megalomaniacal acquisitions of the old man through two
generations of epigones, who by mismanagement and market
force ("but that's another tour, folks, for another day") were
brought at last to bankruptcy, divorce, and suicide.

"You mind sittin' down there, mister? Standin' in th' rear
there makes me nervoos."

Girard lurched to his seat, legs shaky and the palms of his
hands sweaty, as the bus, having jounced across the Sunshine
Bridge access and passed in silence the dilapidated mansion
Tezcuco, Narcisse Landry's old homestead, entered without
fanfare Ascension parish. Out the window to his right old
sugar-cane stalks lay in the furrows of Miss Louisa Conway's
field, flanked by fallow bottomland and bordered, at the
canebrake concealing Love's tarpaper shack, by the curtain of
cane more familiar to him than any other dark spot on earth.
To the left the levee hid the father of waters as it carved a
channel two hundred feet deep to deposit new batteur: the
levee along which from bonfire to bonfire his mother paced
when she was prancing; the river flowing as it always had
flowed to the Gulf it had always flowed into.

CHAPTER 2

"They be a small boy sit right here in the corner. And on a very hot day they would sit a block of ice on the table. The ice come from unner the groun' there, where you already seen. And the boy, he move his fan made of feathers, mebbe chicken, mebbe guinea, over the ice there, like this . . . an' there be air-conditionin'. You welcome. As we move now to de secun flo', y'all please to note the pettipoint tapestry on the wall there, fi' by six, 'Turn from th' Chase.' It's done by th' nuns, yes'm, over here at Convent. Sixty years it taken. Tha's right, y'all go right ahead on up that staircase."

Who was this Aunt Jemima who had modeled herself on Hattie McDaniel in *Gone With The Wind*? Got up in a white lace apron and a little doily cap, she had herded them like a gaggle of geese from the *porte-cochère* where the bus had unloaded and in through the kitchen and dining rooms and the Empire sitting room, and now was shooing them up the stairs to his own room, or what used to be his own room. The strangeness he felt in entering room after room and finding familiar objects—in the sitting room the baby Steinway his mother used to play, in the front hallway books laid out and some left open as though time had stopped, in the main dining room the huge oak table where the family ate dinner—roped or curtained off, or, in the case of the Thomas Jefferson desk his father did his accounts on, covered in plastic, was akin to the sensation he had when walking through a mausoleum, where "Gone Forever," "Sealed Forever," "One Less at

Home, One More in Heaven" separated him from the cemented-shut foot-lockers, urns, and caskets; except that the cordoned-off objects surrounding him here—in the sitting room
his mother's horsehair love seat, in the dining room the rose
jars filled with scent, and the huge gilt-framed federalist
mirror in the hallway reflecting the tapestry of slaughtered
deer with hunters—were more real, more familiar to him than
he was to himself as he traipsed dutifuly up the massive
staircase, a glossy "Tour Homewood" brochure in hand,
disguised to himself as a tourist.

"This young lady y'all see over th' landin'," the Negro
guide was calling up the stairs from behind them, "is Miz
Jurard's auntie. She made ninety-three years old on October
'leventh, an' she still stay at New Orleunz. At th' head of th'
staircase you be see Miz Linda Jurard's armoire an' further on
down on th' right her bedroom. Th' chirrun, when they reach
aged twelve, was considered men and women. She's Miz
America not long back, and representin' us now in th'
Congress."

The portly mammy, having given the tourists something to
gawk at, came huffing her way up the stairs past Girard, who
had not yet reached the landing. As she bustled up the second
flight, saying "'Cuse me, 'cuse me, m'am," the Irish lady in a
quiet voice asked as she drew alongside, "What order of nuns
is at Convent? And isn't that tapestry needlepoint, instead of
petit point?"

"M'am, I'd have to axe. I don't rightly know. 'Cuse me,
now."

They shuffled along the upper hallway, following their
leader past the paired convex and concave mirrors ("Dis
here's the chap'rone, an' dis the petticoat. Doan axe me why.
You welcome") and entered what was called "the chirrun's
room," Girard at the rear of the group barely squeezing into

the room dominated by the mahogany four-poster bed with its tigerwood canopy posts, and the tin washtub at the foot of the bed with its own small canopy, and beside the bed the holy-water fountain with guadalupe flowers floating in it. "This here, fo' it 'come Miz Linda's room, was both the chirrun's, an' this here's called a 'married bed.' Now, doan you go gettin' no idees. Tha's 'cause this bed's made of two woods, 'hogany an' tiger maple, see?"

A titter of prurient humor rippled through the gaggle of tourists who stood gaping at the bed where he had lain, some nights with his sister (until she moved into the room next door), and others with his mother (who never had a certain resting place), but most often alone, gazing at the medallion in the white waste and middle of the sixteen-foot ceiling which revolved, as he lay on his bed in the dark staring at it, round the mysterious medallion faster and faster as the top of the room spread wider and wider in spiraling arcs spinning further and further away, until he became a whirligig, the plaything of terrible forces, clinging spread-eagle and sweaty to his tigerwood bed, all the while sensing behind him and hearing the river's ceaseless flow seven hundred yards distant.

". . . th' 'riginal medallion, made of horsehair and plaster," the Negro maid was saying, "an' now we gwine enter wha's called on your pamphlet the 'master bedroom'"—a shuffling of papers as tourists consult their brochures— "though Mister Jurard hisself al'us slep' out in the C'lonial wing 'yond th' carriageway. We be seein' it after th' widow's walk. You welcome. Right this way. . . ."

Instead of following the tourists into his sister's room, Girard stepped back into the hallway, where the chaperone mirror thinned and the petticoat mirror fattened him as he moved stealthily down the hallway. Spying through the open door to Linda's room the black maid facing him, he reversed

his course and walked—fat, then thin again—to the front end
of the hall and out onto the gallery. The gallery ran along
three sides of the house and was in fact a loggia, interrupted
at the rear by the *porte-cochère* which joined the main house to
his father's quarters (the so-called "Colonial wing") and,
beyond that, to an atrium, where his mother kept her garden.
Before him now lay the alleyway of eight massive live oaks
holding their ground and marking the centuries against the
river's incursions. Above the arch formed by their gnarled and
intertwining branches he could see, less than half a mile
distant, the levee, and beyond its gray clay flattened top the
river: black jetty rocks, brown shallows, backwashed flotsam
caught in willows mud-colored and yellow. Here was the
site, and this the scene that characterized all that had been
amassed, possessed, resided in—fertile bottomland, field
slaves (black) and servants (brown) and concubines (hi-yaller), and self-subsistent mansion—then squandered, mort-
gaged, lost by the southern planter class from which he came.
A way of life both elegant and excessive, repressive and
refined: to have once been party to its privileges and abuses
was always to remain in that position, or wish to. As Girard
stood leaning against the banister of the upstairs gallery,
gazing out at the river and the alley of live oaks (eight now,
but in his father's time there had been twelve, twenty-four in
his grandfather's day), and hearing at his back the chirruping
of tourists consulting their brochures and being led by a
pancake-makeup Aunt Jemima whom he heard behind him
counting, ". . . thirteen, fo'teen, now where that feller go to?
Y'all see where?", at the same moment as the tourists shuffled
out into the hallway—mumbling, tapping, and clucking—
Girard's eye caught the hexagonal *garçonnière* and just beyond
it, in the shade of the three-hundred-year-old live oak where
once upon a time he had watched the future runner-up to Miss

America sunbathe, the water turret in which he had hid as a child: brick-lined, cubic and cool.

"We gwine to view the widow's walk now, up the floatin' staircase. On your way you gonna see th' plantation bell. It's rung for prayers, for dinner, for a steamboat dockin' down't the levee. This-a-way, Suh . . . Suh!''

But Girard had disappeared from view, or, rather, he had scuttled round the gallery and descended (as he used to do as a child, when escaping the big house) by means of the bougainvillea trellis, which weaker than it used to be, as he was heavier, broke under him with a loud crack and ripping of old vines. He fell the twenty feet into a hibiscus bed, shattering the dried-out papier-mâché-like red and yellow flowers into fragments, sat among them for a moment, stunned, then picked himself up—but it was long enough for one of the tour group to come running out on the gallery and find him there.

It was the tall and slender freckle-faced Irish lady. "Are you all right?'' she called down, anxiously.

Girard scowled. Then, as he picked himself up and began checking for broken bones, she laughed. It was a gentle, confidential laugh and, since none of the other tourists had witnessed his fall, he took no offense at it.

"It just struck me,'' she said, leaning over the banister directly above him, "that this is Ascension parish, and . . .''

"I do this every day,'' he said, brushing himself, "just to keep in practice. And, in answer to your question, the tapestry is needlepoint, but the faces are petit point, and the Convent nuns are St. Joseph's Sisters. Most nuns in Louisiana are.'' Then, seeing that none of the other tourists had followed her out, and hearing the tour-mammy approaching around the front and summoning him—"Suh . . . Suh!''—he gave a conspiratorial shh, finger to lips, and pointed her to the rear of the gallery. "The spiral staircase," he soundlessly pronounced. The freckle-faced woman looked questioningly at him, then where he had pointed. "Staircase," he whispered more loudly. She nodded. Without waiting to see what she did, Girard limped from the hibiscus bed to the cane sugar boiling kettle used as a planter for amaryllis. He leaned on it and scanned the grounds—the coast was clear— and, skirting the *garçonnière* where Linda's suitors and Uncle Antoine used to stay, entered surreptitiously the water turret.

Inside the water turret all was dark and cool and cubic. The tank itself, suspended by a scaffolding of struts ten feet above ground, did not hold water anymore. Its metal bottom formed the ceiling of the brick-lined cubicle he'd limped to and entered by a little door. But once inside he felt safely hidden, out-of-bounds as he did when playing hide-'n'-seek with his sister (never once had she caught him here), almost as though he had entered the world of the *ancien régime* to which the books in the big house, laid out and left open, pointed—a timeless zone in which *ancienne noblesse* reigned forever.

There was a diamond pattern in the brickwork, where bricks had crumbled and had been removed, and he could hear outside in concert with the lazy hum of late bees in the shattered hibiscus the quack of the tour-mammy and little chirrups from the tourists and could see, by standing on tiptoe or by stooping and peering through the highest or the lowest of the diamond-patterned slots in the brickwork, as through slits in a gun bunker, the procession itself winding up the spiral staircase, or standing at funereal attention on the widow's walk, or waddling across the *porte-cochère* en route to his father's hideout which was now merely another station in the tourists' pilgrimage. With Floyd's Sten gun he could easily have machine-gunned the whole group.

But for what? It was he who was dead, not the tourists. They were fascinated with this ruin, and avidly awaiting lunch. So was Charlie Spagioni, over by what used to be his mother's garden house behind the atrium, but which now bore the legend "Tourist Shop." Through a knee-high diamond-patterned slit, like a loophole in a Confederate revetment, he could see the greaser lounging beside his bus, checking his watch. A well-placed sniper shot would finish him.

Girard settled into position, half crouch, half sitting down, beside the lowest loophole looking out. He could see no way out this time: no gap in the barbed wire, no no-man's-land, no enemy trench, no enemy. It wasn't just the past, it was the future. There was none. He didn't even feel himself in a dilemma . . . he didn't feel himself . . . he didn't feel. . . . All his human instincts had been stretched like strings on Lee Anne's violin, then popped! pinged! severed . . . There was only now a sound-box and a bridge. . . . Somehow it didn't make sense to perform from the Sunshine the same ludicrous maneuvers he'd rehearsed from the Hoopalong. The Hoopalong at least had class. The Sunshine was for Donaldsonville blacks; or Charlie Spagioni, who never felt remorse . . .

". . . remove in my heart . . . Ah! I cannot smother remorse . . ." The great quartet from *Lucia di Lammermoor*, Act two, Scene two—Henry's plaint—and was he hearing it now? He was. Locked in his place of concealment in the water-tower, the music wafted out to him from his father's room, poignant wave on wave, as it used to do when he was a child in hiding from the big house and his mother:

Edgar
She lies twixt life and death.
I love you, ungrateful one, love you still!

Henry
She is of my blood! I've betrayed her!
And she lies twixt life and death . . .
Ah! I cannot smother
The remorse in my heart!

Lucy
Betrayed by heaven and earth,
I would weep, but cannot . . .
For tears themselves forsake me!

Raymond
She lies twixt life and death;
He who does not pity her
Has a tiger's heart in his breast!

The music (faint, but he hears each word distinctly) enters
every diamond-patterned loophole of his turret like plunging
or reverse fire riddling him, but, oddly, he does not think of
Valerie ("*I have betrayed her!*") or of his sister Linda ("*She is of
my blood!*"); he thinks of Lee Anne and the shattered hibiscus,
of his mother prancing all night while the plantation bell
rings and bonfires flame on the levee, of his father in his room
drugged with opera:

Lucy
Not till you join me
Shall heaven be heaven for me!

Henry
Endless days of suffering,
Remorse, are in store for me.

The music stopped as abruptly as it had begun. And now
he saw the tour-mammy poke her doily-pated head out the

carriageway entrance and the whites of her eyes scan the grounds. Almost at the same moment a swatch of sunlight drenched his turret: the little door was opened and peering in and blinking, radiant with sunlight, stood . . . "Lee Anne!"

No one else could touch him. Not his father—"Gone Forever"—nor his mother, who had shrewdly cut her losses long before (perhaps as long ago as she smelled black gold in the bayous) by taking up with his Uncle Antoine, leaving him and all he mourned in a vast limbo of remorse and lamentation; and not his sister, certainly, whom nothing touched—no blemishes on Linda, no flies either. . . . Only the face of Lee Anne, his ruination and redemption, which he had shattered like hibiscus when he leaped from the Hoopalong, could come back to haunt him now. She only who had goaded him to suicide could guide him through the limbo he was in.

"Praise be to Jesus!" she exclaimed, stooping down and poking in her head. "So this is where you've got to. That woman is chasing me just like a goose!"

His immediate sensation was of a beetle attacking his brain, boring in through his ear. Then he heard at his back through the brickwork the tour-mammy's summons: "Y'all out there? M'am? Yore bus leavin'. You, Suh! Y'all come on, you hear?"

"Close the door," he said, and when the tall and slender Irish woman with the freckled face stood there smiling, hesitating, he said again, "Come in and close the door!" She did. Girard felt a sudden loss of interest in her, as little as in the meaningless scene confronting him as he peered out the brickwork at the mammy, in conference now with Charlie Spagioni, while tourists traipsed from "Tourist Shop" and atrium to board the bus: Charlie Spagioni, who stood beneath the bell in the *porte-cochère* anxiously conferring with the black-face, checking his watch; the woman squatting by

Girard at a loophole in the tower turning his wrist and checking his. Nearly noon. Lunch for the hungry pilgrims; home, or maybe Jefferson Downs, for the weary driver. The bus would not delay long now. Briefly Girard glanced at the woman next to him, who was studying the tourists' departure in the *porte-cochère* and steadying herself as she squatted to peer out by continuing to hold lightly to his arm.

She was not so old after all, ageless rather, and not so tall as thin, almost weightless. Her hair was not white after all, but wispy and fine and a very faint cream or wood color, and summer sprouts speckled not only her face but her neck and her arm and her hand resting lightly on his.

He cast a forbidding look, and moved his wrist.

She withdrew her hand.

"You're disappointed that I'm not the person you mistook me for—Lee Anne?—the woman you were expecting . . ."

"I wasn't expecting anyone."

"I'll leave as soon as the bus leaves. You don't mind?"

He was ready for her to leave. No one had ever entered his water turret before, except the once when he found Linda there rocking and holding herself in a fetal position and crying "Mamma . . . Mamma!" That had only happened once, in all the times he'd hid here as a child, and even now his hideaway was off limits to tourists. But she was here, and the bus would be gone soon. One thing puzzled him.

"You said something when you came in."

"She was chasing me, I said, just like an old goose."

"No, before that. Something about Jesus."

"Oh! 'Praise be to Jesus!' that's what I said, and you're supposed to say, 'Praised-and-blessed-be-the-holy-and-imma-culateconceptionoftheBlessed VirginMarymotherofGod!'"

"I am?" he said archly.

"You are. And if you don't say it snappy, like that, it might happen to you."

Girard turned away in disgust.

"Well, I guess it wouldn't. You're a man. We were always afraid it might happen to us. That's how we got up every morning."

"What are you talking about?"

"About how we got up every morning for twenty-three years. Every morning the nun would come and say, 'Praise be to Jesus!' and you had to sit up in bed and say, 'Praisedand blessedbetheholyandimmaculateconceptionoftheBlessed VirginMarymotherofGod!' We always ran it out like that, afraid if we said it slowly, thoughtfully, it might happen to us. Though one girl went mad, and got married."

"You're a nun." Then, when she didn't say anything, but continued squatting there by his side, steadying herself with her hand which, forbidden to touch him, fluttered in the air until it finally returned to his arm, "You're a nun, aren't you?"

"I have been," she said quietly. The brightness of madness in her ice-blue eyes, which he saw now were depthless, made him wonder if maybe she'd been shot in the seventh cranial. No tears. She continued to balance herself, but without exerting any pressure. "Until now," she concluded in a tone of certainty, surrender, and repose.

The plantation bell rang twelve o'clock, and the bus horn honked a full minute, then ceased. They watched the tour bus, Charlie Spagioni at the wheel, disappear into the carriage-way and emerge from the far side, the little O's of tourists' mouths gaping at the windows, lunch bound. Beneath the big plantation bell stood the big tour-mammy, standing as Hattie McDaniel stood when Rhett Butler spirited away Scarlett O'Hara: arms akimbo, hands on hips, hmmph on her lips and hurrah in her heart (for Homewood was a museum that closed down at noon, and today a man and woman had got lost, or run away, or hid themselves— mebbe in th' garsonere, mebbe the water turl, unner th' live oak there, now ain't that sumpin'?), shaking her head and laughing to herself as she went back into the big house.

CHAPTER 3

"God, says St Sylvester, is an onion. He is good and He makes you cry."

"He doesn't make me cry. God absconded long ago—from the South."

"He might return at any time."

"The past prevents Him."

"Change it."

"The present keeps piling up more past, which prevents Him."

"Change that, too."

Girard shuffled uncomfortably.

The woman, kneeling on the hard-packed earth inside the water-tower, hands folded in her lap, stared schoolmarmishly at him. She was, he was convinced, daft. Not like the St Joseph's nuns who ran Lee Anne's school. They were all docile, dowdy, and deferential (at least in the presence of St Michael's priests), though Lee Anne said they were fishwives at school. "What order of nun are you?" he asked.

"I was a Faithful Companion of Jesus. I still am. I consider myself still faithful, though . . ." She searched for a word.

"Divorced? Separated?"

"You're speaking of yourself. I'm here because I saw on the bus, from the moment you got on, that you were desperate. I'm sure I should be here, I'm sure God sent me to you—whatever His relation to the South—and I'm sure that the pain you are feeling is connected with the lives of others, who feel pain for you."

Girard, hearing her words, suddenly remembered the great VD scare—an interconnection of mammoth proportions, which according to Larry swamped the facilities of Charity Hospital. He, Girard, had been at the center of the vast cobweb Valerie had started spinning when her longshoreman developed an itch. Names given, tests run, involving hundreds, thousands, black and white, male and female, until the tests showed simple vaginitis: Lee Anne's.

"The South has its own tolerance for desperation," Girard commented wryly. "You shouldn't preach the Gospel south of God."

Her unflinching stare wavered. She gazed out through one of the diamond-patterned slits. "The greens here are different from the greens in Ireland," she said quizzically.

"Are the greens there more green, or less?"

"The greens in the grass are more brilliant, but the greens of the trees more pastel."

Girard hesitated. He wanted to leave, but where would he go? Back to the beginning, or forward to the end? There was a drowned man in the river, a man with a gun in the streets. Here at least was a breathing space, and the woman was here to help him. "You were in Ireland," he said.

"I was in a convent, it hardly matters where. At one time the novitiate of my order had its headquarters in Brussels, and they had these great stories about Brussels. They never saw a thing of it, they were enclosed the whole time, but they had great stories about the gardens in Brussels. They had a garden in the convent, inside the walls, and they went out every morning to collect earwigs."

"My mother kept a garden," Girard said, "right over there." He pointed to the atrium. "It was the only thing she

did herself, around the house, I mean; Love did everything
else. But we didn't have earwigs, we had aphids.''

"Who's Love? Is Love a person?''

"Love was my mammy.''

"Was she good to you?''

"Very good.''

"Did you love her?''

"Sure.''

"You were lucky.''

"Very lucky—up to a point.''

"When was that? What happened?''

Girard, who had been feeling expansive, demurred: "You
wouldn't be interested.''

"I would. I never had a mammy, I never had a mother,
even, that I can remember. I was the eldest of seven. We were
poor. Tell me.''

"Well, it was when I was about seven. I was in here,
exactly as I am now, and I was watching the big house. It
was a game I played.'' He learned forward on his hands to
peer out one of the slits. "Love had just crossed the carriageway to take my father his supper, back in his room there, and
my Uncle Antoine arrived in the carriageway, crunching the
gravel underfoot, he had parked his car at the front, and my
mother, my beautiful mother—I always said that: whenever I
said 'my mother,' I always said 'my beautiful mother'—my
mother came out of the big house into the carriageway, and
they kissed . . .''

"Your mother and your uncle.''

"Yes. And I knew.''

"You knew what?''

"I just knew.''

"What did you do about it?''

"Nothing.''

"And your father, did he know?"

"Yes. He did nothing, either."

"So you chose to do nothing, you and your father. What happened then?"

"My mother left for New Orleans, and took me with her, and my father committed suicide."

Both were silent. The hum of late bees around the hibiscus was barely audible inside the water tower. The afternoon sun, declining past the atrium, drenched the plantation grounds with brilliance, heating the water-tower bricks. In the speckled gloom rhomboids of sunlight illuminated here a patch of hair, there a portion of a sleeve, two lips, a mouth. The mouth, isolated in the spectral gloom, was curiously like his mother's.

"Let's suppose it was your father who had the affair, moved to New Orleans and took you with him, and your mother who committed suicide."

"That's inconceivable."

"Why?"

"Because . . . because my mother is a bitch!" Even as he framed the words, and before he spoke them (but voice is consciousness, words are acts; he entertained no other thought between the act and the announcement so it must have been a premonition) Girard had the ridiculous sensation that he was speaking to his mother! The calves of his legs cramped as they used to do when he sensed she was out prancing on the levee. He would wake up then and find her gone, and only later would he actually hear her come in, then the cramp would go away. His calves cramped now, so violently he had to scramble up and stamp them out.

"And your father is a saint."

Girard continued to do what resembled a little rain-dance in the confines of the empty water tower, while the woman, who more and more resembled his mother, looked on.

"You misremember, James Antoine Girard, that it was I who bore you, suckled you, and raised you from a baby. Until you were full three years old, I let you sleep with me. Your father was off in the city runnin' around with Narcisse Landry, and later with that slut whose name I vowed never to sully my lips with . . ."

Was he hearing this, this diatribe, this catalogue of old wounds, old names, old alibis? It was his mother's voice— how could he mistake it?—but those did not seem to be her very words. Instead the words seemed to be these:

". . . the crucial decision, all other decisions flowed from. I had to accommodate myself to the whims of [your] father. To virtual chastity, obedience in every particular, and watching the [plantation] decline; and, of course, silence . . . but not choices, I never made choices, after that one. And making choices keeps you human. . . ."

In the claustral gloom the woman raised a finger—for emphasis, to drive her lesson home. It waggled disembodied in a shaft of light: a long, Napoleonic, index finger. . . Was he going crazy? Was he losing the power to distinguish one from another, the same from the similar, his mother from a nun?

"Sit down," she said.

He sat, more or less collapsing in the place he had stamped out.

"I used to look at Sister Corita and Sister Angelina, and think: she couldn't be a mother, she couldn't be a mother. And if she couldn't be a mother, she shouldn't be a nun. That's what celibacy came to mean for me: you couldn't have a baby, yet you must. You had to be a mother before you could be a nun. But that would never do. God wouldn't let you . . ."

As she spoke he had the vivid sensation of shrinking, not only in his outer parts but inwardly collapsing; or was it simply *vertige labyrinthique*, the infection of the middle ear which disturbs one's sense of balance, that distorted and conveyed her voice as if from a great distance, so that not just his understanding but the words themselves were altered?

"... *it was me all along, Jimmy, not Mommy. I was the one you slept with till you were seven, crawling out of your bed and into mine in the middle of the night, and it was on account of me you started hiding in here, to spy on me through the little peepholes. I knew you were here, I could sense it, that's why I sunbathed right over there, by the big tree. I could have found you time and again when we were playing shilliky-pooky, but I wanted you to think you were hidden because I liked being looked at. I always gave you something to look at. I knew you liked looking at me. ..."*

"One girl, a gorgeous looking girl, after six years covered with boils. The only question was whether the decision to enter was right. We were trained not to feel, not to consult our feelings. Is it reasonable? we asked; not, How do you feel about it? But since we never had to make any decisions anyway, just accommodate ourselves to the decisions made for us, it really didn't matter how we felt. When Charles Stewart came, she went completely crazy. They got married on Shrove Tuesday. You could never get married in Lent."

"... *that was why I went to Ashland—not to get away from Mommy and Uncle Antoine, I didn't care about them, and Poppa never noticed—it was to get away from your watching me, spying on me all the time. I couldn't have a boyfriend, I couldn't read a book, I couldn't dress, I couldn't undress, I couldn't go out on a date without you waiting up for me, it got to where I couldn't hardly breathe or go to the washroom in private. You were a little tyrant, Jimmy, a terrible pest, a spoiled brat, a silly little brother in short pants. That time Claude Labiche came and stayed in the garçonnière, while you hid in the water tower, I was mortified! And whenever my friend Clarissa Landry would stay overnight, she'd say, 'We'd better watch out for your little brother, his eyes are everywhere ...'"*

The index finger points to the diamond-patterned slits in the watch tower. Can what he sees be happening? Are there

really such creatures at Homewood? The tourists are marshal-
ing on the plantation grounds, in lunch formation, by twos:
two wings hide their paunches, and two arch over their
heads, and with two their backs are humped. A man in a
Salvation Army uniform, black with red trim but without the
SA on the collar, approaches the head of the column and
shouts, "Who are these? Have they paid?" And a Negro
woman in white lace apron with a little doily cap steps from
the column and shouts, "These be th' ise o' the Lord. They
done paid." And the tourists, numbering more than the sand
in the sandbags of the levee or the drops of water in the father
of waters, open their little O's of mouths to shout in one big
O . . . "Lunch!" he expects them to yell, but no sound splits
the sun-drenched air except the buzzing of a bee and the
droning of the nun.

   ". . . we could never go by twos, we went by threes on the
crocodile with a nun in front and a nun behind. We had to be
three. Otherwise you might have a particular friendship, and
that came from the Jesuits. With the Jesuits you could never
have a particular friendship. They never told you why, but
the reason of modesty and the vow of chastity said you must
not touch. That was why you had to flatten yourself against
the wall when the nuns passed at night and repeat with your
eyes closed as fast as you could the litany of aspirations . . ."

   Girard sits stunned on the hard-packed earth, like a man
who has suffered a seizure and survived: glassy-eyed, gasping
for short little breaths, and sweating profusely. His familiars
have been struck dumb, like the redeemed, and he is sure they
are ghosts. Only the woman drones on, with a rapt ecstatic
gaze on her face as she recites and exhorts and confesses, but
he scarcely hears her, or hears her words only, the sound of
her words without meaning, for the shadow of another aveng-
ing archangel—like a little rain cloud the size of a hand—has
loomed on his southeastern quadrant (away from the river and

toward the riding paling where his sister used to sunbathe
and twirl her baton, beyond his mother's atrium) and is
galloping powerfully toward him. He braces himself for the
onslaught.

". . .also called the litany of ejaculations—little spiritual
darts aimed at Jesus and Mary—so short there was no chance
of distraction, ten of them. The exact words were

> First-sweet-heart-of-Jesus be thou my Love,
> Sacred-sweet-heart-of-Mary be thou my Salvation,
> Third . . . until you had a decade, then . . . a happy death.

But because we were saying them as we moved and in a sort
of singsong, emptying water into pails or brushing our hair or
flattened up against the wall at night when the nuns passed,
they became

> Swe'art of Jees be'ou my love,
> Swe'art of Mary my salvation. . . .

Whenever I recited the ejaculations I imagined I was dandling
my baby and rejoicing in her and uttering a fervent thanks to
God for blessing me with her."

"But there wasn't any baby. You never had a baby, you
never knew a man, it was all prayers and fantasy."

"No! I begged God, please don't let me die until I've
known the love of a man. And God, who is all powerful, and
who never denies the prayers of His faithful . . ."

The punishing virago is almost on him now. He can hear
her crashing through the canebrake, the booming of a giant's
strides with a terrible rustling of skirts. Her palomino clatters

across the riding paling, splinters like a cyclone the three-hundred-year-old oak, invests the tower. Her arrival is a sudden storm of wind and fire and water. The sun is immediately blotted and the trees lash wildly. There is nothing he can do to hide himself or Homewood. Bricks are not enough and prayers are futile. The reenactment of electroshock zaps Girard like lightning, leaving him giddy. He remembers everything: all—betrothal, betrayal, conspiracy, committal—surges to remembrance in a single incandescent burst, accompanied by such crackling, buzzing, and humming as of Lulu and Electra and Julia Lee all at once exploding in his ear:

"You gonna be all mine an' I'm never gonna let you out of my sight." "I believe, believe my time ain't long . . ." "Mamma, mamma! . . ." "I've called your mother. She's coming tomorrow." "Oh, do you have orange juice? Just orange juice for me." "Sun gonna shine, ooh . . ." "Nobody is a friend of yours, let's face it—you're a lost soul, Girard." "You gonna be my tiger again, an' I'm gonna love you forever." "Does she like sucking cock? Boo Mason told me . . ." "There ain't no light! There ain't no light!" "Ah'm Baptist. We're all Baptist." "My name is Roy and I'm an alcoholic." "Come in sometime an' ah'll make you lunch, a dollar ninety five." "No pleasure but opera." "Love lift-ed me-ee." "Now you must give the next party. But I will give the one this year. . . ."

The whole silenced city of adulterers, idolaters, effeminate and many more who fitfully slumber or suffer torment in the mausoleum of his mind suddenly leap to life, scream in his ear, dart to and fro like sparks among the stubble when the cane is burnt, while outside the sudden storm (is it merely that? it seems a hurricane!) rages, threatening to uproot the three-hundred-year-old oak and topple the tower. The rain, slashing

at a nearly ninety-degree angle from the southeast, the direction of the Gulf, splatters on the edges of the many little
windows, spraying in the tower and muddying its floor. The
tower is a sieve; it is like being in a grotto underneath some
powerful Niagara. The nun with the Napoleonic finger (nothing else about her interests him) presses up against him and
presumes to be familiar, talking more and more obsessively—
oblivious to the storm outside—about her room, her secre-
cies, her vows: "Each of the cells had a curtain in front and
metal partitions on three sides; the crime was the windows
were so high you had to be over six feet to see out. My room
was the sacristy, the priest's room was my bathroom, and in
the wall of my bedroom, which was larger than the cells,
there was a dumb-waiter with a slide-door. When you slid
back the door, that was the confessional. You spoke into the
wall, through latticed louvres. In that room Sister Winnifred
was dying a whole year. She used to come to me at night, in
the infirmary, like this . . ." Rising slowly as she talks, like a
cat in languid motion, the long bare legs move forward
toward Girard, who sits soaked on the muddy floor in his
filthy pants and scuzzy underwear, until her crotch meets his
face, her hands hold his head, she presses him against her.
"And even as it happened, God, God, I was praying, please
don't let me die until I've known the love of a man . . ."
    She was walking out of the humorless procession where
nuns huddled, their pallid features veiled, their limp hair
covered, their pale flesh mortified, even the habits they wore
black and bulky and inscribed "I have known the use of . . .,"
out of the long and lightless dormitory where there was no
ownership, no possession, no identity, and no possibility of
anything other than a happy death—happy because, after such
a life, death was no misfortune. On ungainly girlish legs she

was stepping across the chasm she had never ventured over, not only because Satan and unspeakable filth lurked beneath, but because Jesus had called early and detained her on this side. But she was ready now to break ranks, cross over, and make a full, perfect, and sufficient sacrifice: the sacrifice of her virginity, her vows of silence and obedience, to this man for whom her whole life had been conscious and painstaking preparation.

She was gliding without effort from one state of grace into another, her feet and hands and hair trussed up, her mind (but not her face) made up, bound by solemn vows and aspirations to the spokes of a prayer-wheel, while little darts of jealousy and lechery and wrath, thrown by Sister Corita and Sister Winnifred and Sister Angelina, struck and wounded her and gave her pain, but on she walked, confessing the whole time the ease with which she crossed to her confessor Father Benoit, who seemed troubled and who, suddenly, was not there anymore. Neither Sister Corita nor Sister Angelina, not even Sister Winnifred was there anymore to taunt and torment her. She was far from any human face or form now, all alone, with eyes all around her and blood in the eyes that saw through and undressed her everywhere. The walls had eyes, and she was in a wheel whose rim seemed enormous and had eyes all around the rim, and she was in the wheel. When she moved, the eyes around her moved, for the spirit of some animal was in the wheel. When she stopped, but she could not, for the spirit of the animal was in her, too, urging her forward toward the eyes that formed the axletree and had the most blood in them . . .

"You doan' have to come. I'm already in a fam'ly way with yore baby, honey."

The whiny voice strikes the tangled snarl of strident,

snapping, biting voices, bounces back, strikes again, then snuggles in between Valerie's and that of the anonymous woman in the Fontainbleu.

Holy Michael the Archangel, it was the woman from the bus.

"*Tha's why I followed you all the way here, honey. Ain't you proud?*"

Girard flung her away and lunged forward, slipping in mud. He was struggling to get out, out of the plantation dominated by women, out of the slave quarters behind his mother's house, off the bus with the tramp whining at him. All his life he had been trying to hide—to hide from women —and always he had been followed, found out, cornered . . . now once again he was fighting for a way out, and there was no way, he'd led them right into his lair, but by that curious inversion by which men always lose—gentlemen always lose —it was *her* lair he'd led *himself* into, and he was trapped, grappling with his captor in the mud and stifling her strident, ingratiating, quavering nun's voice with both hands, throttling it with all his strength.

The voices of nuns buzz like bees all around him, sting his face and arms and hands like buckmoth caterpillars—nuns faceless, featureless, disembodied, invisible but for their voices ascending from behind the ten-foot-high brick wall of St. Clare's Monastery on Henry Clay. He, too, is behind a brick wall, a wall as thick, as high, but he is at the bottom of his plunge and still descending, while they are floating upward toward the light, scattering fragments of attenuated laughter, shouts and laughter from the cloistered sisters drifting up like smoke from the foundry furnace in the Blind Hospital over the Crippled Children's Hospital, over the Home for Incurables, over DePaul's. He is in DePaul's, just two thicknesses of brick wall away from the nuns' laughter, and, in the opposite direction, just one block from his mother's house. He is in DePaul's, put there by his mother, his uncle, and his wife, not for the twenty-seven-day cure, but to undergo electroshock treatment, Thorasine injections, harassment by the guard Ernest White—"Miz Jurard asked me to take care of her boy-o, seein' as how all the other guards is niggers, an' I know what she means"—forever. He is in the clutches of their combine, asphyxiating underwater and descending still, struggling to turn the vortex of the whirlpool pulling him down, to reverse the entire direction of his life and surface for a breath, a mouthful of free air with which he can shout "How good it is to be alive!" when the cries and whines and whispers from the nun-tramp-goodwife break on him like clouds of smoke spied on a torrid day ascending from the furnace of the blind . . .

"Swe'art," the voice croaked, but not struggle. "Swe'art of Jees," it rasped when he released it. At his feet she slumped down in the mud. Fistfuls of rain drummed on the water tower.

CHAPTER 4

"I gave up on Girard. I'm studying a new genre—silence."
The failed playwright moves from the little table on which
his ancient typewriter sits, in the slope-roofed garret with
the rampant lions out front, forepaws clawing at the neutral
ground. Through the open stained-glass dormer window he
can see through a light drizzle of rain the Southern Baptist
Hospital across Napoleon Avenue, and on the neutral ground a
parked tractor with "Department of Highways, State of
Louisiana" in bold letters. He pours himself a bourbon, neat,
and offers one to the doctor, who waves both hands almost
frantically in refusal. Les shrugs, sits down on the bench
beside the little alcove which looks out on the hospital. His
back is to the tractor, but he is aware of it in the street
below.
"Then why all this interest in him?" Larry asks. "It's
unnatural, it's like a post-mortem."
"'The Golden Boy?'" Les says, closing his eyes as he sips
his bourbon. "Let's just say there's not another like him. I
mean, how many people do you know who've died twice?"
"Clinically?" asks Larry. The doctor pictures old Joe, as he
does whenever the subject of death arises. Though he has seen
his fill of corpses and watched his quota of patients die,
always when he thinks of death he pictures faceless Joe and
Joe's protracted passing, which merges in his mind with
Girard's furious exit. "Anyway, you should talk to Billy
Bland. He's the executor of the estate."

184

"Estate? There's an estate?" Les opens his eyes. "Girard didn't drink it all up?"

"Not by a long shot. In fact, once he became an AA he tried to make up for all the harm he'd caused others. What's the phrase? 'Made direct amends to all persons we had harmed, except when to do so would injure them or others.'"

"You know it by heart," Les remarks, taking another sip of bourbon.

"I'm a doctor."

"I know it by heart, too; it, and the steps leading to it: 'Admitted we were powerless over alcohol, that our lives had become unmanageable'; 'Came to believe that a Power greater than ourselves could restore us to sanity'; 'Made a decision to turn our will and our lives over to the care of God as we understood Him'; 'Made a searching and fearless moral inventory of ourselves'; 'Admitted to God, to ourselves, and to another human being . . .'" Les reeled off the resolutions like a litany, emitting little burps along the way. "There you have it," he said, with a loud, oleaginous belch, "the church in its purest form in the twentieth century."

Larry looked at the long-haired, nearsighted, alcoholic playwright. A fraud. An aging hippie, now that hippies were passé; before that a beatnik; a bohemian before that. Fashions had changed, but Les had always been locked in his little garret with the lions out front, writing the great American drama. Living on grants and writer-in-residencies with his perpetual work-in-progress. His few one-acts, produced at Tulane and at Le Petit Théâtre du Vieux Carré, were—it was generally understood—mere technical exercises: fragmentary, preparatory to the big work he had been laboring on for ten years. Its title had changed: first, The Big Sleep, then The Bridge, at last report Golden Boy. Girard and his furious entou-rage—his keepers, his black and white girlfriends, the Naval

officers and FBI agents chasing him—were the only real
people who had ever broken in on Les in his garret with the
stained-glass windows. Still, there was something about
those icy blue Scandinavian eyes behind the thick glasses and
shrouded in hair like a woman's, some indefinable something
that made Les, though a failure, formidable. "You're an AA,"
Larry said softly.

Les nodded imperceptibly. "I have been known to be.
Now, you see . . ." He held up his nearly emptied glass as
though to toast. "Let us say I find the example of Girard . . .
instructive. And you . . . ?"

" 'My name is Larry and I'm an alcoholic,' " the Charity
doctor confided. "One has to be in this town. It's either that
or drown in your own vomit."

Les turned abruptly to look out the stained-glass window.
The late afternoon rain had covered the neutral ground with a
flat matte finish. He had sensed, as he sometimes did, the
tractor shift behind him; but it hadn't. "Like Girard," he
said.

"No, not like Girard. At the end I think he was sober."

"At the end he was dead. Does it matter whether you're
drunk or sober, if you're dead?"

"It matters to an AA," Larry said.

"AA, my ass! Girard was no more an AA than I am," said
Les, pouring himself another finger of bourbon and tossing it
down in the same motion. "On that, you can ask Billy Bland.
He attended those bleak little meetings at the Methodist
Church. Bland knows, it's his business to know. He's not
only Lee Anne's lawyer, he's her lover."

"Bland?" The doctor said it warily, without surprise. He
had already attended one autopsy on Girard: DOA of gunshot
wound, the coroner had ruled.

"Bland was there when Girard came rushing into the

Paradis roadhouse that night. According to Bland, he was sloshed and guzzling down everything in sight."

"The night of the flood?"

"The same night he strangled the nun. The same night he went to the black church. The same night he broke into Floyd's . . ."

"Why?" The word had escaped the doctor, and he was standing up now, agitated, his empty arms raised up in an I-am-not-responsible shrug. Arms a little higher, palms a little more forward, and he would be protesting at gunpoint. Billy Bland had done that at the autopsy. At the autopsy the doctor had seen and heard things he never thought possible, from people he'd known all his life, people like Bland, who weren't accustomed to perjuring themselves. What had come over them—Bland, Lee Anne, Irene Trepagnier, this fraudulent playwright, and even himself? Was Girard's death their one and only opportunity to define their lives, to make or break themselves? Were they so impoverished? And if so . . .

"Why?" Les repeated, sensing the tractor behind him, not shifting, but getting ready to shift. On that tractor Governor Earl Long, brother of the late, lamented and detested Huey, tried to make his getaway from Southern Baptist hospitality. Naked as a jaybird and crazy as a loon, he failed. Even though he was assisted by his girlfriend, the stripper Queenie Caesar. "Might as well ask why he went to the black church, why he broke into Floyd's—a suicidal act if ever there was one: that place is an arsenal—why he was born. . . ."

"But the nun?" Larry said, letting his arms drop suddenly.

Les finished off the whiskey. "He was crazy, wasn't he? Schizophrenic, or something like that? You're a doctor, you should know. Was he crazy, or wasn't he?"

Girard on that night throwing open the back door, bursting into his place on Short Street . . . Larry remembers the

curtain of rain behind him and the sharp reports, like pistol
shots, of mirlitons falling and striking and rolling down the
metal stairs at the back. Girard was shaking all over, standing
drenched in the doorway alongside the fridge, and Larry
remembers as though it were last night transposing (was it
the two rectangular shapes, or did he have a premonition?)
the hunched and shivering creature framed in the doorway
before him into an upright corpse in an upright coffin, the
dysfunctional bridge beside him, and saying, "Joe died."

The blank face in the black hole of the doorway does not
say "Joe?", says nothing, just stands there abstracted, de-
mented, in shock, like a man in a catatonic trance, except his
eyes are not glazed, they are glowing.

Is he on coke? Larry thinks, and hurriedly glosses, "Our
friend without a face. Our blob without a friend. He
managed to asphyxiate himself. Cream of wheat—or maybe
grits—down his blowhole."

And Girard standing there in the doorway, having just
strangled the nun, and broken into Floyd's (was that before
or after?), plus the zany prank he pulled off at the holy-roller
church—"The Original Morning Star Black Baptist Church
of New Orleans," he always called it, with a sort of reverence—and on his way to what for him must have been the
acid test—his confrontation with Lee Anne—Girard looked
him straight in the eye and said, "Poor Joe." Like that. "Poor
Joe." And then he was gone. One instant he was standing
there like a duck or a roadrunner in an animated cartoon, and
the next instant . . . vanished, so quick and so startlingly that
the man trained in science after a moment's stunned silence
opened the refrigerator door. . . .

"Well? What do you say, Doc? Was he, or wasn't he? And
what does it take in these days of 'discontinuous personality'

and 'temporary insanity' to qualify as truly insane? I mean old-fashioned mad like Hieronymo, not like Hamlet."

"Again, you'd have to ask Billy Bland. I'm no expert on the law, not even the medical side of it. At Tulane Med School there's a professor of forensics, a Dr. Myron Fishbein, who claims that the legal definition of insanity, purportedly established on clinical evidence, is actually a political variable which varies from jurisdiction to jurisdiction, by regions, by administrations . . ."

Was he crazy? At the autopsy—Lee Anne and her lawyer, Billy Bland, present—he had testified he had known the deceased twenty years, that Lee Anne and Girard had not to his knowledge cohabited for the last five (to legitimize under an antiquated *Code Napoléon* their divorce, which was still *nisi*), and that Girard was not *non compos mentis*. Was he sane, then? And, if sane, a murderer? And if a murderer, insane? Perhaps to murder someone you had to be insane, temporarily at least. But what if that someone was a nun, and you were Catholic? Wouldn't it be like murdering . . .

"I'm not political," he heard himself saying.

"You had a mother, didn't you?" Les says in the same flat tone he achieved in his one-act, *Refrigerated Deathlessness.*

"What does that have to do with it?"

"Didn't you?"

"Of course I did."

"Girard had three."

"Three mothers?" exclaimed the doctor.

"At least three. There was Irene Girard, *née* Trepagnier, whom you've met, surely. A lovely lady, a New Orleans saint. One of those who live only for others; you can tell the others by their hunted look. Then there's Love, Girard's mammy. Have you met Love?"

The doctor, a pained expression on his face, shook his head no.

"Well, you must. She's a dear, Love is. I met her one hot August afternoon fifteen years ago, back behind the cane-brake. Girard was making one of his sentimental journeys to Homewood . . ."

So the nun must have been the third, Larry thinks. She must have reminded Girard of his mother when he was there at Homewood: confused him, provoked him, maybe even maddened him, especially if he was drunk, to a state of homicidal, rather than suicidal, insanity. So it was a simple matter of displaced violence . . . he'd already tried suicide . . .

"You've seen this, I trust?" Les tosses to him the Times-Picayune with the banner headline, "Ex-nun slain at River Road Plantation," with photos of the water tower, a body bag with men standing around, and the nun.

"I've seen it," the doctor said, without looking.

"But the picture, have you examined the picture of 'Sister Dierdre O'Hara, 41, until recently a member of Faithful Companions of Jesus'? Cover the veil with your finger and look at the picture," Les ordered the doctor. "Don't you see the resemblance?"

"No," he said. The photo—probably the only picture ever taken of the nun, printed "By permission of the Archdiocese of New Orleans"—showed a neophyte, no more than twenty years old, gazing serenely and eagerly out on a world of which she was ignorant. How could that wimpled beatific face, with weak chin and trusting eyes, possibly be mistaken for Irene Trepagnier Girard, the shrewdest, most calculating woman in New Orleans high society? Especially by her son, who sometimes called her "My mother, my beautiful mother," and other times "Ferocia"?

". . . it's a toss-up, actually, between Linda Girard and Lee Anne," Les was saying, "but I favor Lee Anne. We have to remember that when Girard met her the nun was twenty years older than this photo depicts her . . ."

"And she wasn't wearing her wimple."

"And she wasn't a nun."

"She was an ex-nun."

"I think you've got the picture," said Les. "Lee Anne, don't you see?"

"No," said Larry.

"Never mind," Les shrugged, "it will all come clear . . . in purgatory." Les wheeled suddenly and with surprising speed lurched to the stained-glass window. The doctor watched as he gripped the sills and peered down at the street; then, his vigilance relenting as he relaxed his grip, Les turned and shuffled back into the low-ceilinged garret, stumbling over his own chair. Dusk had fallen like a shroud on the playwright and the doctor and the rain-soaked city. There was no light in the garret, no streetlights lighting the neutral ground. The rain outside which had ceased falling hung in the uncertain air, threatening to resume at any moment. In the room made darker by stained glass the doctor sat sweating, watching the distraught and drunken playwright lurch and stumble from one station of the darkened garret to another.

"I have this . . . obsession, I suppose you could call it," Les intoned, slumping into his chair beside the ancient typewriter. "It's that they might move the tractor."

"The tractor?" said Larry. He did not recall any tractor.

"The tractor down there," in the near-dark room Les pointed to the alcove, "on which Governor Earl Long, the last of his kind, tried to make his getaway." The playwright's voice disintegrated into silence. "He failed, of course. As they all do, as Girard failed—twice. And Girard is probably the last to even venture the effort, to put himself in such a no-win situation that we can say, 'he failed.'" The playwright's flat, inflectionless monotone insinuates itself into the darkness, the words issuing forth without color or timbre and requiring no sustenance, only a source, like the skitter of cockroaches. "That's why Girard continues to haunt me, and why Governor Long's tractor has become my talisman. Not that there's any achievement involved—no bridges built, no pictures painted, not even the neutral ground groomed—but there is a certain attitude maintained . . ."

In the humid gloom of the garret the fraudulent playwright's mutterings seem to the doctor somehow obscene, if not deranged—at the very least the off-scourings of a disturbed and misanthropic consciousness. The entire afternoon's excursus on the etiology of Girard's disordered acts and possible derangement upset the doctor immensely. He could not say why; perhaps because he avoids probing, or provoking, failure and defeat. He is, and knows himself to be, a doctor for the wrong reasons, but he does not consider changing it. The massacre of a surgical convoy by the Viet-Minh on Bastille Day, 1962, determined his vocation—the courses he took, and didn't take, in high school, college, med school; the dates he didn't go on with the girls he never had; the loans he had to take and was still paying off—all, his life down to the minutest detail, was programmed by an event that happened half a world away to his father who was in charge of the surgical convoy and who ever since had been symbolized by the Officers' Cross of the Legion of Honor conferred *in articulo mortis* and sent to the widow and son by the French government. So he knows what it is to live vicariously, to maintain for nearly twenty years an attitude defined by someone else. Is that why he finds this probing, this unofficial autopsy conducted by a fraudulent playwright, so disturbing? *His* vocation, where he touches it, feels soft, unwholesome. His whole existence at Charity seems to him a dark and spreading bruise, a malignant carcinoma, a diseased smear magnified. But because a part of him continues to be curious, objective, unconvinced, despite himself he hears his voice, thin and fretful, though he spits the words out like boracic acid: "Your play, the one about Girard, did you ever finish it?"

The playwright stares at him with resignation, as though he has been through this before. "I didn't," he says finally, "and I never will. I told you: I'm studying a new genre."

"Silence—right? Then why did you ask me here?" the doctor says. Again, his words taste like boracic acid, cock-roach killer.

"Because," says Les, "after fifteen, or is it twenty years?, I want to know the truth about Jimmy. I was with him through the 'Big Sleep' and never could get inside him. When he was in DePaul's I visited him—once, and once was enough. He might as well have been asleep, never said a word, just kept staring at this white guard, who stared back at him."

"Maybe he was homosexual."

"I think not. I think toward the end he came out of some closet, but not that one—the closet of his own mind, his own . . . *melancholy.* I think that toward the end he showed himself, maybe for the first time, maybe even to himself."

"And you think that I . . ."

"It was from your place on Short Street that he went to Homewood, and it was to your place he came back. You saw him both before and after he killed the nun and all the other bizarre things he did that night. You were one of the last to see him alive. You also testified at the autopsy."

"And I also was with him," thinks the doctor, "at the

very end. All the pranks and high jinks of a lifetime compressed into one final frantic night. I was with him then, too,
at the unexpected curtain, at the sudden unfulfilment, at the
impoverished anticlimax of his death." But he does not say
this; he says instead, "Why don't you talk to Lee Anne?"

"Lee Anne wouldn't see me," says Les. "Can't say as I
blame her. We used to fight over Girard's nearly comatose
body during his 'Big Sleep'—her trying to rouse him, me
trying to rout her. But I picture them in their last moments,
Girard's last moments anyway, haggling over whose parents
were upper-class and whose middle-class. Here! here's an
argument they actually had while I was sitting right here, and
. . . Wait." Les lurches across the room, rummages through
papers, stumbles back and switches on a lamp. He thumbs
through pages of a manuscript, attentive as he has not been all
afternoon. "I took notes," he says with a self-mocking grin,
"but I never used it. It never went anywhere." He begins to
read.

—Jimmy, your Momma's on th' phone.
—Tell her I'm out.
—She knows you're here. She wants to talk.
—Tell her I'm busy.
—I know what she wants. She wants you to dress up an'
go to Longvue Gardens with her.
—That shit place! I wouldn't go there if my life depended
on it.
—She wants to show you off, Jimmy, show ever'body
you're alive an' still your Momma's little boy.
—Tell her "Mother's only half a word," tell her I'm not
going.
(*Lee Anne leaves the room, talks on the phone, comes back.*)

—I told her you didn't feel up to it.

—What'd she say?

—Said she'd pick you up at four. She's got her heart set on this, Jimmy, showin' you off.

—Well, it's better than your father, "the Colonel." At least she phones to warn me!

—Daddy doesn't like to bother you.

—Yeah. He sends the FBI.

—He never!

—He threatened to.

—He never did. Daddy wouldn't do a thing like that.

—Why would he? I'm in prison here. Besides, it'd be bad publicity for the Vipond Gas Works.

—Daddy's above that.

—Is he? He's *nouveau riche.*

—What?

—He considers the metric system vulgar.

—You must be out of your mind!

—He told me himself. That time we had the "little talk," when he warned me not to marry you.

—His only concern was that you wouldn't support me in the manner I was accustomed to.

—That's not what he told me. He said I'd wind up being your chauffeur, your chaperone, and your cook, which is pretty much the case.

—That's a boldfaced lie! How dare you attribute such things to my father!

—Your father, the Colonel, said, and I quote . . .

—Don't say it! I don't want to hear it! You can degrade me all you want, you can curse your mother if you want— that's the way your family talks—but I won't stand here while you insult my father! . . .

The doctor, during the reading, had stood up from his chair and was pacing back and forth in the narrow space between the dormer-window alcove and the ancient typewriter, from behind which Les had read. The doctor was visibly distressed and gestured agitatedly as he spoke.

"No! It wasn't that way, it wasn't at all like that at the end. You weren't with him when he died. And you weren't with him because you weren't his friend. Your only interest is in writing his obituary."

"His obituary?" Les repeats. "That's easy." And he rattles off a set piece, the doctor is sure it's a set piece, though it sounds so like a child's rhyme that he wonders if he's heard it before:

"Goodbye marriage, so long strife,
Here lies Girard, a victim of life.
They hitched, she bitched,
And he left bereft;
Now he sleeps with the worms
Instead of his wife."

The playwright shakes his shaggy head. "How's that?" A question, but his flat monotone turns it into a statement.

The doctor, who has stopped pacing, just stands there— saying nothing, doing nothing, to relieve his own tension—as unwilling to give a dismissive shrug as he is unable to exit.

"Jimmy never had any friends," Les observes in that flat monotone, not without a trace of menace, "just witnesses, spectators, keepers—those who tossed the dice a certain way and watched him jump, and bet on whether he would jump this way, or that. Me, I was the odds-keeper, his bookie, for a while. I gave up trying to write about Jimmy."

"You wouldn't have got away with it. Not in this town. you'd have been sued. If not by Billy Bland acting for Lee Anne, then on his own; or by Girard's mother, his uncle, his sister . . . she has friends in high places and her reputation to consider—"

"Friends in low places, too, and deals to cover up," Les interjects.

"—or by Knox over at the University, or Lee Anne's father, Colonel Vipond, at Gulfport, or by the corporation that manages Homewood—"

"Which Linda Girard controls."

"—or by . . . any of a dozen others," Larry finished weakly.

"You, by chance?"

"Me what?"

"Are you one of those 'dozen others' who would have sued me?"

The great VD scare leaps to the doctor's mind: blacks by the dozens coming to Charity to get checked; and the Tulane contingent, whose names had been given and their phone numbers traced, refusing to come, declining to answer, flocking instead to their own family doctors, the University health clinic, to out-of-town gynecologists and the Naval base doctors at Algiers. "The Harvard of the South" they called Tulane and Newcomb—but Girard had already crossed over.

"I might be," the doctor concedes, and slumps back in his chair.

"Tell me what you know," Les cajoled. "I told you, I gave up on Jimmy. But I lived with him for so long I'd like to know how he died—whether whining or cursing, with his head above water, or drowning. Or did he die, perchance, a happy death?"

"I can tell you how he died. I was with him."

"Good God, then, tell me," Les pleaded.

The doctor studies the playwright in the pool of light surrounded by darkness. In the damp room, both are sweating. The doctor himself sits in darkness, and by acceding to the playwright's demand—to tell how Girard died, really died—he fancies he will extend the damp darkness until it covers again the whole room, perhaps the entire city. "But that's silly," he admits. "Girard was just a man—a son, a husband, a would-be suicide, a murderer—and now he's dead: like faceless Joe, or Valerie's father, or . . . so many others, so many. . . . God grant me, at the last, a different death," the doctor thought, "as different from Girard's as day from night. . ."

IV. DEATH IN DESIRE

"I have to live, even though I died twice
and the town went half mad on water."

Osip Mandelstam

Many waters cannot quench love,
neither can the floods drown it.

Song of Solomon, 8:7

CHAPTER 1

Night was falling when he crawled out of the tower, wet with sweat and spray and hot with exertion. The storm had settled into a steady pelting rain, and within minutes his mud-splattered pants and sweat-stained shirt and windbreaker were thoroughly soaked. He could still hear voices, music—all the voices and music he had ever heard, it seemed, vying for the same wavelength (or was it he who was open to all frequencies and unable to distinguish between past and present or to tune out the least snatch of song or trace of voice he had ever heard, however insignificant?). The voices and arias and songs were flattened by the rain, as were the amaryllis and hibiscus and bougainvillea about the grounds. The cacophony of opera and blues and his own overheard, unfinished libretto was concentrated in a steady inner hum as he began to walk swiftly and then to run along the alleyway of oak trees, beneath a canopy of branches beaten by the rain, toward the river which dominated all other sounds he could hear—crashing lightning, rolling thunder, strings, woodwinds and brassy oak leaves, canebrake and his own convulsed hum—the river's deep diapason orchestrating both rhythm and momentum to the compressed energy humming in him.

He crossed the road at a run and reached the levee. Here as a child he had lain in the grass gazing at clouds before clambering up to the sand-bagged top; here, too, his mother, his beautiful mother, had ascended by night to pace up and down on the thin narrow strip that held back the river from Homewood. Her guilt and his innocence were as irrelevant now as the shattered hibiscus or the strangled nun; a jury of flattened witnesses in the wake of destruction behind him, urging him on, up and over. He ran full tilt—legs pumping, arms churning, his runners slipping on the drenched and tangled grass—to the top of the levee, and stopped. There before him flowed the father of waters, its force immense and terrifying, its destination sure. Screaming banshees of rain slashed at its surface, but did not deter it—nothing did—on the contrary, each new attack augmented its force and momentum. The river, swollen with recent rainfall and higher than he had ever seen it, swished past within a foot of where he stood and surged and boiled up higher, uprooting willows and eroding sandbags while bludgeoning the bank with an enormous piling it had carried from upstream. The shock to the bank threw him to his knees and almost into the water. He staggered to his feet, alert now as never before to the narrow verge between the bottomlands and plantations and low lying canebrakes behind him and the voracious river just inches away and rising.

—How many inches of rain will it take to bring the river up over the levee?

—There is a spillway. You've forgotten the Bonnet Carré, built for just such emergencies.

—When will they open the spillway?

—It may already be open.

—If it is already open, then what?

—The river will burst its banks.

—And then? What then?

—The Flood, you fool. It wouldn't be the first time . . .

Girard, on his feet, had begun to run along the top of the

levee—where his mother had paced, where the bonfires were
held, where the water was already lapping. Running alongside the river, downstream, pacing himself by the piling—its
dark hulk shearing straight and true through the waves
thrown up in its path, the piling stiff and straight like a
corpse, like the stiff he had found early one dawn at the end of
his Big Sleep down from the *Café du Monde* and had planted
his ID on, the face all eaten away and the fingers and belly
and genitals missing, the fishes, the little fishes, how they
disfigure a body! Whose? His. From that day forward . . .
"Lee Anne," he thought; and on every fourth step he croaked,
"Lee Anne!" to encourage himself as he ran.

He had long since lost sight of the piling and passed the old
Tureaud place, Miss Louisa Conway's field, and Narcisse
Landry's homestead Tezcuco, when the Sunshine Bridge
loomed up ahead. Arc-lit and bustling at both ends with
sandbagging pygmies, the span with more traffic on it than
Jimmy Davis had forecast resembled half of a ferris wheel in
motion, except that the truck lights were going both ways—
the evacuation of Burnside? or of Donaldsonville? or of each to
the other? The wheel was turning, the flood was coming,
whirl was king. It was Burnside that had been written
off. . . .

"*Poor Burnside. After Antietam he was never the same.*" U.S.
Grant in the guest room at Homewood.

And his grandfather, his rich and ruthless grandfather: "*He
should have resigned his commission!*"

"*Or been cashiered. If I .had been president then, I would have
cashiered him.*"

"*Court-martial the son-of-a-bitch and save God the trouble!*"

His grandfather's words, as related by his mother, to the
President of the United States.

"*And the President did what he was told,*" his mother would finish her tale, "*as presidents should.*" And then she would smile her pride of Dixie smile: his mother, his terrible mother. . . .

He was on the right side, but it was not the side that won; the winning side was . . . "U.S. Army" . . . He passed the first truck, khaki-colored, "U.S. Army Corps of Engineers" stenciled across its canvas canopy, "La. Regiment" on the mud-stained door. The convoy of trucks was parked all along River Road, extending beyond the arc-lit, cordoned-off bridge, beyond Burnside, a hundred or more trucks.

"My God," he thinks as he runs past truck after truck, "the entire Louisiana outfit is here—at Burnside."

And the unprecedented magnitude of the emergency, the absolute uniqueness of this concentration on Burnside thrusts him into the present, where he has not been for so long that he scarcely knows how to cope. He thinks as he runs past camouflaged trucks toward the knot of men laboring ahead, directly beneath and on either side of the bridge, of the strangled nun, the river rising, Lee Anne . . . running straight into the first bunch of men—Donaldsonville blacks stripped to the waist, some filling, some toting sandbags, a helmeted and holstered Army engineer in charge—Girard grabs a shovel out of the hands of a black man, who looks up surprised, rolls the whites of his eyes toward the white man in charge, then falls back and sits on a sandbag. He starts shoveling furiously, filling towsack after towsack with the sand which, as bag after bag is toted away by the black men, disappears at his feet like time running out, until at last his shovel strikes earth.

A whistle blast.

"Awright men," yells the engineer, a swarthy, heavy-set Cajun, fiftyish and fat, "we'll cross over the river. There's more sand where that come from—at Donaldsonville." The engineer starts to walk off.

"Wait!"

The engineer stops; the engineer turns. The black men are gathering up their shirts and belongings and shuffling off toward the trucks. This engineer is a sergeant; he wears sergeant's bars on his pocket flap and chevrons on his shirt sleeves. Though disguised in a sergeant's uniform and sha-dowed in the arc-light, Girard knows now it is Charlie Spagioni: by day a tour guide, by night an army engineer. And facing this greaser with chevrons he searches for the right question, the question whose answer will provide key and cornerstone to the entire sagging, sandbagging situation.

Nothing comes.

"Awright," says the sergeant, and starts walking away.

"What about Homewood?"

The sergeant halts again, turns halfway about. His face silhouetted by arc-light looks less like the tour guide's and more like Ulysses S. Grant's.

"What about what?"

"Homewood."

"Doan' know no Homewood, son. You're tired, like th' rest of us. Le's go."

"The Bonnet Carré—when will they open the Bonnet Carré?"

The sergeant looks incredibly tired, though he has not been working. Shadows line his face and exhaustion shows in every line and angle of his body.

"It's done been opened, son, about 20:00 or so, earlier this ev'nin'. Like ah said 'fore you come, this' ar last dang hope. Cain't keep them trucks waiting ."

This time he turns and shuffles off toward the truck in which black men are already sitting slumped and softly moaning, waiting to be transported, to shovel and tote. Flinging down the shovel Girard begins to run away from Donaldsonville and the Sunshine Bridge, past other trucks,

some filled with blacks, some empty, on the River Road
beside the swollen, surging river which strains at its retaining
walls and here and there pops through like a strangulated
hernia. And as he runs he strips away the soaked and stinking
windbreaker and shirt that cling to him, and as he flings them
off he laughs and gasps like a death's-head: "Ar last dang
hope! Ar last dang hope! ..."

". . . to encourage himself, I suppose. Anyway, in such a state
he entered Paradis naked from the waist up, in his running
shoes, his muddy pants, and scuzzy underwear."
   Larry has poured himself a drink from the bottle which Les
has pushed toward him./ Now he picks up the tumbler,
scrutinizes it in the light of a candelabra which Les has lit.
The tumblerful of bourbon sweats in his hand. He sniffs it.
There is the odor of incense, too, in the garret: a butterscotch
smell, sickly sweet and cloying—a prop from *Golden Boy*. The
doctor scarcely notices these stage props, or the claustric
closeness inside the garret, or the rain pelting noisily on the
roof and against the dormer windows, he is so immersed in
the story he has been telling, and in the whiskey he has just
poured for himself and now, having eyeballed and sniffed it,
tosses down in one swallow.
   "You mean he was laughing, or do you mean to say he was
mad?" Les, who has been listening for over an hour, asks
insistently. "Why, it must be thirty-five miles from Burnside
to La Place. You mean to say he ran all that way in the rain?"
   "I mean he was . . . That's good, that's really good. You
know, that's the first bourbon I've taken—the first alcohol,
except for a sip of champagne to toast Lee Anne and Bland at
their wedding—in over a year." He wipes his mouth.
   "Have some more." Les nudges the bottle toward him.
   But the doctor sits staring, abstracted. A full minute later

he notices Les and says, "Laughing, he was laughing at some joke, that's all. Girard was like that. And Bland, though he knew Girard was like that, didn't know what to make of it. Bland was some scared, I'll tell you . . ."

"I remember Paradis," Les says, "you don't need to describe it. . . ."

Paradis. The bleak roadhouse at the by-passed juncture of La. 44 and U.S. 51. From this point south La. 44, the River Road, ceases to exist. If it did exist it would have to span the Bonnet Carré spillway, nearly four miles wide, which drains the flooding Mississippi into Lake Pontchartrain. In summer at low water table the Bonnet Carré is a stagnant swamp concealing a huge drainage ditch; at floodtide it is a raging torrent—a shallow spillway four times as wide as the Mississippi draining seven miles across the isthmus on which New Orleans sits to an enormous, man-made sump, Lake Pontchartrain. On the north shore, at the western edge of this huge open sore, the sign announcing "Paradis" surmounts a squat, unprepossessing roadhouse. More recent neon signs— "Jax Beer," and "Drink Dixie"—adorn its paint-flaked clapboards, but the old sign of block wooden letters (from which the "e" was lost so long ago it is not missed) atop the roof identifies the place, once a post-house for rich planters' carriages, now a bleak and by-passed roadhouse at the elbow of the River Road and the highway to the causeway that leads to New Orleans.

Why is he stopping at Paradis? It isn't water he wants, or warmth, or food and drink, or anything the noisome, noxious roadhouse has to offer. And he is into the rhythm of running, so it is much harder to stop than to go on. Is it Billy Bland's car? It is not; Bland no longer has the '55 Ford that Girard might have recognized—a car such as Ida Lupino might have

come rushing out of the roadhouse and driven away in, with
Cornel Wilde in hot pursuit; but those days are decades past
—and, besides, Girard is in no state to notice cars. Nor is it
to ask permission for the boat, the skiff across the road which
he will steal, oars and all, and drag to the Bonnet Carré's
locks and launch on its turbulent current: the rowboat which
will ferry him down past La Place and across the enormous
sump pit of the lake, past Kenner and beneath the Lake
Pontchartrain Causeway, to the very edge of the breakwater
where, just as it looks as if he and the boat will be smashed—
the water roaring and waves up to fifty feet high surging and
breaking beneath and behind him, and riding the crests between troughs he looks to the land and sees nothing but
darkness and sorrow, the light darkened and the land flooded
—he remembers the slot to the Southern Yacht Club and
with a ruddering sweep nips in to City Yacht Harbor where
he ditches the boat among hundreds of bunched and banging
boat hulls, their shrouds snapped loose and whiplashing and
their spars against the black water stabbing the sky like
drunken picadors or drowning pikemen. So it is no ratiocina-
tion that brings him to a halt before the "Drink Dixie" sign
above the weathered door of Paradis. Nor does he ask himself,
"Why am I stopping here?" or hesitate before entering,
despite the sign which reads "No shoes, no shirt, no service.
This means you!" He enters Paradis at a dead run, and
immediately upon entering he spies Lee Anne, and without
slowing for an instant even to orient himself continues in that
same dead run across the dingy dance floor toward Lee Anne,
who was sitting with Billy Bland. . . .

"It was something he was altogether unprepared for," Larry
says, "and he didn't notice it at first."
    "Really?" says Les, incredulous. "You mean to tell me
. . ."

"I don't mean to tell you anything," the doctor bristles. "Girard had a way of seeing what he wished to see. If he'd wanted to see Ida Lupino waiting tables in that roadhouse, she'd have been there. He wanted to see Lee Anne—Lee Anne as he remembered her—and that's who he got, more or less."

"So the two of them just resumed their bad soap opera where they'd left it five years earlier: one long middle, without beginning or end? How romantic!"

"That's what Bland said. He was sitting in the booth when they spied this creature from the black lagoon bearing down on them: wild-eyed, wet and naked from the waist up, running in a dead heat toward their booth with such unerring purpose that it looked like murderous intent. Bland says he would have shot him if he'd had a gun, and pled justifiable homicide. He didn't recognize Girard, but Lee Anne did . . ."

The instant she saw him she was up and running toward him, as she always did when stopped by the police: veering to the shoulder, jumping from her car and running to theirs before they had a chance to open her door or ask the first question. But because she wasn't traveling alone she was distracted, apprehensive, confused. It was him, all right, the tiger she'd married, with pockmarked face and piercing eyes and not an ounce of fat; but the stealthy panther walk had given place—not to a Thorasine shuffle: that, thank God, was gone, as was the bloated flesh and puffy face and nerveless, hanging hands of his mother's son—to a steely-eyed concentration of purpose she had never seen in him before. It scared her, even as she said his name, "Jimmy," and asked the first question, "Why did you come back?" Her voice, even as she framed those few words, trembled: like a sparrow greeting a hawk. She was scattered, she was divided, she was watching herself from four corners—as though all this were happening after an accident and she lay scattered in several pieces, unable to function or, if she appeared to be functioning smoothly, it was a sham for the crowd's benefit and she was in shock the whole time. But what scared her more was that the wild, half-naked figure bearing down on her with panther walk and tiger eyes and murderous intent was not in control of himself. She was not in control and neither was he. Nobody was. There had been an accident; it was all a bloody accident. She had somebody else's baby inside her, and the somebody else was hiding behind her, and the tiger she had married was bearing down on her, plus there was this shadowy figure she couldn't quite see and didn't have time to focus on off to the side. She was in the dance square and center of this quincunx, surrounded yet appealed to from each corner, compromised. It was a limited warfare she waged in the no-win arena of the dingy Paradis dance floor, with the shadowy figure off to one side, her cowardly consort behind her, and her tiger-man who looked as though he had harrowed hell and crossed high water to get at her bearing down on her and her baby like an assassin.

"He'd just run thirty-five miles," Les murmured, shaking his head. "He must have looked like he did during the Big Sleep."

"But somewhat more energetic, I should think. Probably he was in shock, too: massive and prolonged adrenaline surges with hypothermic reaction, enhanced nitrogen balance, increase in respiratory rate with a decrease in arterial oxygen saturation—well down below ninety percent—probably by now he'd lost his night vision. I learned at the autopsy that Girard had a trip-hammer—what they call an athlete's— heart. He was past the wall that runners speak of, between peak performance and burn out. "Like a straight-edged razor," Bland described him, "coming right for me."

"A heat-guided missile more likely," Les glossed, "intent on his mummy's tummy."

"Or Lee Anne's," said Larry.

"Or Lee Anne's," Les nodded.

"She was seven months pregnant, remember, and wearing one of those frilly maternity dresses. It didn't take even Girard all that long to notice that something was different."

Immediately he saw her extract herself from the arm around her, the arm attached to the terrified face and trunk and asshole in the corner, and come running to meet him he knew he'd made a mistake. She wouldn't come with him, she couldn't, and if she did she was a fool. They were both fools, but she was not free, never had been. He had been fooled, and she would be fooled again, but not by him, not again; and all that would come of stopping to talk would be that she would turn things around so that it wouldn't be her not coming with him, but him not staying with her. He should leave, must turn, would go without exchanging names or excuses or, worse, pledging love or casting blame. But he was ahead of himself and had been zeroing in a straight line on this corner for hours, days, months, for five years. How could he turn? Where would he go? Who in the world was there left? He had run like a chained dog to all the four corners and pissed on them all and now like a cur he was back at the piss-post to which he was tied, had been tied all along, and would stay tied: the post at which he would surely die and beneath which he would be buried, so why raise his leg, why argue, why cry, he was beaten. Lee Anne in all her winsomeness, with that impish look on her face like a little girl who has peed her pants, was out from beneath Bland's arm and up from the booth, unfolding like a flower or a switchblade to receive him, to caress or slice him to ribbons with her tongue,

to bemuse or bang him to dumbness with denials, explana-
tions, accusations . . . It was then that he noticed the shapeless feedsack covering her body and concealing, or announcing, her condition . . . Holy Mary, Mother . . .

—Why did you come back?

—You said . . . I thought . . . it would always be the same.

—It'll never be the same again, between us. Something's
died inside me, something's dead. You're not the man I lived
with, cooked for, worked to support, the only man I ever
loved or thought of having children by.

—The only?

—That just slipped out. That's what I've always thought,
what I believe.

—But it's not true.

—It may not be true.

—You may be pregnant by Bland.

—I may not be. Legally, it's yours, you're my husband.

—But Bland is your lover.

—He was. He's not anymore. He's a friend.

—A good friend.

—My best friend, my only friend.

—You can hardly live without him.

—I can't live without him.

—What am I supposed to do?

—Share me. Share my love. I have love enough for you
both, and you both love me. Let me love him, come back to
me, and I'll love you so much better, I promise I will. Because
then I'll be able to, I won't be divided.

—Sure. Love him.

—Are you just saying that?

—?

—Can you imagine what it's like to do without someone
you love?

—!

—I used to deceive you. I was dishonest with you. I gave in. I did what I wanted, and didn't bother to ask your permission, knowing you'd never give it.

—And then told me what you'd done three years after you'd done it.

—Was it three years? Always three years?

—You said exactly the same thing six years ago—about Phil: remember Phil?—same sentiment, same words, same syllables, same vowel sounds, only a different consonant. It's Bill now . . .

—I've been trying to get away from you for six years; I'm still trying to.

—What's kept you?

—I don't know, I honestly don't know. You never loved me. You turned away from me a hundred times.

—Not a hundred.

—What about your little librarian? What about Summer Crawford, the blonde bombshell of San Miguel? And your black concubine with the fire-engine car—what's her name: Val, or Sal, or Chevrolet—what about her? I could go on, I can count to a hundred.

—So can I.

—We're killing each other with quarreling. It's got to stop. I don't want to do with you anymore.

—Fine with me.

—I want a divorce.

—Why not?

—Let's talk out the terms. Here's my lawyer.

—Your lawyer!

—I don't love him any more than I loved you. But he returned my love, he loved me from the start. While you were saying "I love you only, you only I love," and screwing your little sixteen-year-old!

—That's past.

—We fight because we can't make love. We never could make love.

—We haven't always fought.

—We've been fighting for twelve years.

—Not twelve. Seven.

—I submitted for the first five. I admit I thrust myself on you.

—And on Phil, and on Bill, and the garbage man in Frisco, and the furnace man, and God knows who else.

—You've had plenty throw themselves at you. What about the child who popped out of the bushes, the one who liked orange juice? Didn't you love her?

—If it weren't so important to you, I could accept this arrangement with Bland.

—I know.

—But how can I? It's intolerable, it's decadent, it's . . .

—I know.

—I've got no one else. Lee Anne . . .

—Stay with me. Jimmy, stay. But I can't just run out on him. I loved him, and he loved me back. I can't live with myself if I don't honor that love.

—Honor! You speak of honor?

"And then Bland, who all this time had been listening intently and edging his way out from the booth, stood up beside Lee Anne . . ."

"Not behind her?" Les, who has stood up and is moving toward the window, jibes sarcastically.

"According to him he stood up beside her and, to the astonishment of both Lee Anne and Girard, put in his two cents' worth: 'Maybe honor is too strong a word; it suggests "obey"—you know, love, honor, and obey? I'd rather think in terms of "celebrating the relationship."'" That's the gist of what he said. And Girard stood there glaring at him, dumbstruck; they both did. And Bland went on (he told me this himself): 'If you're worried about who'll be the father of the baby, let's decide it right now once and for all. Let's flip a coin for it.' And fishing a quarter from his pocket, he placed it on his thumb. Girard, he says, just stood there rooted to the spot, with such a look of horror on his face that Bland was afraid Girard might kick him in the groin, or Lee Anne in the stomach, or fall down on the floor frothing at the mouth and bite his own tongue. Then, Bland says, like a dog that's been cowed and has no fight left in him, Girard turned around as though he was in pain and limped across the Paradis dance floor, while everyone in the whole place laughed (the atmosphere had been tense and the outcome uncertain, and they were applauding Bland's ploy, his bloodless coup), except Lee Anne, who was making little gurgling sounds that might be mistaken for laughter, and probably were by Girard . . ."

"Poor bastard . . ."

"And with the laughter still ringing in Girard's ears, the sounds of Lee Anne and Bland having a good time together, making him suffer and relishing it, and being applauded for it, Bland yelled out after him: 'The reason you can't stand the thought of our being together is that you were always miserable with her. I've done you a favor, Girard. Someday you'll thank me! Girard!' And the next time anyone saw him he was running in that same dead run through City Park."

"Poor, dumb bastard," said Les, who was standing in the dormer staring down at the tractor on the middle ground. "He got what he had coming, didn't he?"

"Don't we all?"

"Yes, but some get more than others."

"Girard's suffering marathon had only just begun," said Larry.

"Poor, dumb, lovesick bastard," said Les, staring down at the tractor that had not moved.

CHAPTER 2

"How could someone have seen him running through City Park? That end of the city was flooded. I kept a file on that flood—for *Golden Boy*—and I seem to remember . . ." Les moves from the little balcony outside the dormer, where he has been standing in drizzle gripping the wet railing, to his desk in the corner, switching on lights as he goes. He pulls open one drawer, then another, rummaging quickly through file-folder contents, until he finds the folder he wants, pulls it, and brings it over to where Larry is sitting, switching off lights as he comes. In the pool of light made by the flickering candelabrum he drops the *Times-Picayune* clipping. Drops of water glisten in his shaggy mane and drip on the newsprint photo, blurring its aerial view of a partially submerged residential district, with rescue boats drawn up at the house fronts, and a dog on a car top surrounded by water. "This was taken in Lakeview, right next to City Park. Can you see Girard running through there? Even Jesus couldn't run through that shit."

The newspaper photo, with its banner headline "New Orleans Braced for New Flood," lay reproachfully like a piece of evidence controverting the tale just told. Larry read its brief text in silence.

NEW ORLEANS, La.—Residents of New Orleans braced for another onslaught of storms that weather officials predicted could be as bad as those that left up to ten feet of water standing in some parts of the city.

Phone service and electrical service was partly restored by yesterday to many of the city's residents who had been virtually isolated from each other and the rest of the world since early Thursday morning.

American Telephone and Telegraph officials said this was the first time in memory that a major U.S. city lost all telecommunications services. "It is extremely, extremely rare," said AT&T spokesman, Gail Purpura.

More than 10,000 homes were without electricity after six feeder lines blew out.

City and civil defense officials said no accurate counts were possible on the number of city dwellers forced from their homes by flood waters because many sought refuge with friends and relatives rather going to official shelters.

However, Governor David Treen said at least 25,000 people north of Lake Pontchartrain, about 35 miles from New Orleans, were moved out as rain-swollen streams overflowed their banks, rushing through residential neighborhoods in Baton Rouge, Amite, Folsam and Covington.

New Orleans lies about 6 feet below sea level and massive pumps are used to keep floodwaters outside the 40 miles of levee ringing the city.

The pumping stations, capable of removing 25 billion gallons a day from the city, were overburdened.

The Bonnet Carré spillway, opened Thursday night, relieved the immediate threat of rising waters in the Mississippi, but portions of the city were flooded from the lakefront.

"If the rains continue," a U.S. Army Engineer Major was quoted as saying, "the levees will go and New Orleans will get it from all sides. It's a hell of a place to have a city."

The doctor looked listlessly up at the playwright, who was sitting behind his typewriter. "So?" Larry shrugged. "The rains did continue. The levees did break. New Orleans was flooded. But that was two or three days later—May 5th, remember?—the May 5th flood. I was in emergency at Charity the whole time, or almost the whole time. The situation in Desire was so bad—looting, riots, tenement fires, the whole bit—we had to move our emergency unit to it."

"You mean the Desire project?" the playwright says, his eyes half closed.

Larry nods. "It was then I saw New Orleans underwater . . ." The doctor shakes his head sadly. "Cars submerged and people stranded everywhere, people driving cars along the streetcar tracks—that's how our ambulance got there—dodging trolleys and buses, even houses that had floated to high ground. I watched one guy electrocuted when he touched a broken power line—he was standing in knee-deep water. We picked him up on our way back, his corpse was floating around the neutral ground. We laid him out alongside Girard."

"Girard?" says Les, coming out of his chair. "You mean to tell me Girard made it all the way to the Desire Project? I thought he went to Floyd's, in the Garden District, then . . ."

"He felt the need for a little walkabout, I guess," Larry said wryly.

"Walkabout, hell, we're talking marathon, we're talking madness . . ."

"Anyway, after Floyd's he went to the black church in Desire."

"But they're miles apart, they're in opposite directions from City Park, and the whole city was flooded," Les objected.

"Not the whole city, not yet. There was flooding—in

Lakeview, Mid City, Gentilly—but it wasn't until May 5th that the levee gave way."

"Even so, how . . ."

"He made a big circle of the city, beginning in City Park —at Beauregard Circle to be precise—and ending in Desire. That's where I found him. That's where he died. He was DOA at the hospital, along with the other stiff who electrocuted himself."

"But why?" shrugged Les, visibly perplexed, "why circle the whole drowning town and run interference with thousands . . ."

"Tens of thousands," the doctor corrected.

". . . who are trying to save themselves, trying to get out of the rat trap, when all he was after was a sleazy place to die? Why go to so much trouble?"

The doctor shrugged. "There's one period of time unaccounted for," he said slowly. "I don't know whether it was before or after he broke into Stone's, but he saw someone, I'm not sure who, I'm not even sure where—it was probably in the Garden District. God knows who it was or what he was up to . . ."

The Angelus bell of Mater Dolorosa—Our Lady of the Drowned—spreads through the air like a depth charge as he sloshes past the amputee-parts shop on Carrollton, water up to the display window: in the window a plastic leg with leather harness, a truss, a plastic arm, a disembodied hand:

> Come in and See Our Selection
> Finest Craftsmanship
> Guaranteed to Fit

Might a soul go in and be refitted, a lost and violent soul, a ruined life? The Angelus bell sounds again and Girard sloshes on, avoiding the deeper pools and block-long lagoons which have formed along the gutters of the street since the city's sewers backed up. The rain, unrelenting, pelts the flooded streets with such velocity that bubbles form in the puddles, burst, form again. The water covers everything, or almost everything, at ground level, and the lay of the land is a surprise to him: the Church's Fried Chicken where Valerie once worked has tilted, is nearly afloat, whereas Manuel's tamale shop which he would have expected to be submerged is high and dry, surrounded by a moat of standing water. Crossing Claiborne at a dead march, the same dead march he has maintained since City Park, the guttering water knee deep, then ankle deep, then knee deep. No one out on Claiborne, not a soul on Carrollton, cars abandoned on the neutral ground, a trolley off its tracks, it must be nearly midnight. The bells again. At Hickory he turns and wades the block to Short, but he can see from the corner without wading across: the front door to Valerie's house stands open, they've fled, as has every other family on the block except the one old Negro woman in her frowsy yellow housecoat, sweeping leaves—sodden, pulped-up piles of leaves and silt the water has washed up—from her front porch into the water lapping at her porch. And now he hears, even as the church bells echo across water and the rain falls all around like flattened hands, he hears the gospel singing from the church. They are singing "Love Lifted Me," loudly and with gusto, with belief. The Negro voices, palpitant and tonic in the sodden air, uplift him for a moment even as they exclude him from the ark they strive to launch. And standing knee deep in flood waters, hearing gospel hymns, it comes to him as something he already knows that Valerie and her mother and all the other Negroes would be in church singing and praising God for His great works (though many of the men would be out working on the levee: not Pooky though, not Droopy—they'd be in church, Pooky at the organ and Droopy with the women and the Reverend Reed).

"Frobena!" he calls across the flooded street, "Fro-be-na!" The frowsy neighbor-woman with the faded skin and yellow housecoat starts, then spies him. "Where," he yells, and mimes each word, "are . . . they?" She gives a little Stepin Fetchit shuffle, and calls back, illustrating with her broom that it is not next door she means, but across town: "They be at church!"

When the Angelus bells sound again he has already crossed Plum Street, wading waist deep across the low corner rather than detour, and before the echo of bells in the air has detonated more depth charges in his mind, he has slithered up the steps and opened the oak door and entered the church of Mater Dolorosa. . . .

The sudden hush of plush and padded furniture and muted silence. Few worshippers in the enormous semi-darkness, their hunched and kneeling silhouettes cast like figures in *film noir* on the cavernous sixty-foot walls of stucco hung with stations of the cross, candelabra aflame beneath each station illuminating here and there a patch of wall, a hunched and silent worshipper. The silence and repression are infectious. Girard stands just inside the huge oak doors, at the stem of the nave which far ahead transects the chancel in the form of a cross with ceiling domes. There are frescoes on the domes depicting hermaphroditic angels: angels bearing banners that say Sanctus, angels crossing swords with winged cupids, angels holding symbols of the forge and crucible, the scythe and furnace. The massive support columns along both sides of the nave are decorated with plaques and with lavish trefoils of gold leaf where they join the domed ceiling. On both sides of the chancel life-sized statues of the Virgin Mary, Jesus, the apostles stand on wooden diases banked by candelabra and cut flowers. Girard, shirtless and standing in the puddle that has formed around him, moves zombie-like toward the life-sized statue of the BVM, down the far left aisle along the nave, passing stations of the cross with, overhead and partially obscured from view by columns, frescoes of scrolled banners proclaiming, "Woman, Behold thy Son! . . ." "It is fini . . ." "My God, My God, why . . ." when, at the jointure of nave and chancel and confronting at the corner a confession booth, he comes smack on "the little king"—in satin bridal dress, with golden crown, two fingers of its raised right hand linked by a wedding ring, its left palm holding a blue ball. The doll surmounts a donation box inscribed,

> "The more you honor me
> The more I will bless you."

With darkened sight Girard regarded the divine infant of Prague, brazenly soliciting for marriage. Then, returning the little beggar's glassy stare, on a sudden impulse he sidestepped around him and pushing past the velvet drape and through the knee-high gate he entered, as he might his mother's garden, or a pay-toilet, the middle booth of the confessional.

All was dark inside, except the latticed speaker's grate, which emitted thin bars of pale light. Groping, he found a built-in stool and sat down, facing out, his forearms resting on the sills of the speaker-grates. There was a shutter above each armrest which could be slid across the grate. He slid both shutters closed. Heavy red velvet curtained him off; the short gate clicked behind him.

When the gate clicked shut, a red light came on outside. Why was he here? To confess? To what? To whom? He had never practiced confession, only when forced to at St. Stephen's: the boys called out by classes and queued up to confess to skipping chapel or—once he had tested the old priest, Fr. Lilloquet, the one with bad breath—masturbation:

—*Father, I have committed, you know, self-abuse.*
—*That is a very venal sin, my son. Next time you feel the urge, try three Hail Marys.*

What would he say now?

—*Father, I have committed . . . fornication. But it was in hell, and besides, I killed the slut.*
—*Three mortal sins, my son. Say three Our Fathers.*
—*She was a nun.*
—*And three Hail Marys.*

It was restful in the priest's box after all he had been through: sitting in the total dark and sensing—what did he sense?—God's absence; and hearing through the grate which he had shut—what did he hear?—God's silence. Restful; reminiscent of the water tower, which was out of bounds to him now; safe. At this rate all the world would soon be out of bounds to him, not even a crawl space left in which to sleep, he was so tired, unless it sank before he drowned,

unless it drowned before he sank, he was sinking, making
confession to old Lillouquet whose breath smelled sweet and
who, when he slid back the grate had the face of his father,
his father biting the king cake—purple, green, and gold—
with a baby like the little king in it, then floating down in
the Navy greatcoat that he always wore but did not wear
that day, through a stridency of gulls, a swarm of bees from
his mother's atrium, a wonderment of fishes, down and down
. . . the voice at his right ear, low, insistent, neither his
father's nor old Lillouquet's, but a woman's, kept repeating
the same phrase over and over through the grating at his ear:
". . . for I have sinned. Father? Bless me, Father, for I have
sinned. Father? Bless me, Father. . . ."

He slid back the grate to say he wasn't a priest, but before
he could say anything she began barraging him with broken
words, low murmurs, interspersed with little moans and
cries. He started to slide shut the grate, to leave, but her
anxious voice rose hysterically, cajoling, pleading, begging
him to hear her out. He listened as the woman in the booth
confided to him that she was in love and wanted to get
married, but was not a virgin, having committed fornication
"long ago" with an older, married man. Her fiancé, from "a
good Catholic family, Father," was outraged when she told
him, because she had never let him closer than . . . another
priest had told her . . . they had made a pact, she and her
boyfriend: whenever they got carried away kissing, in his car,
watching TV on her parents' sofa, one time in her bed, she
would make the sign of the cross on his arm and he would
quit kissing . . .

"This is lunacy," Girard thought, and remembered his
sister Linda, long since lapsed, being told by the nun at age
seven that if she took communion before confession the host
would explode in her mouth.

"But Father, Father, when I told him I was technically a virgin, that the older man and I had always done, you know, that other thing, he went really crazy. He screamed at me: 'Magdalena, you slut!' he said that. Now he cries all the time and threatens to kill himself. Father, what should I do?"

At the grate Magdalena's voice—richer and fuller than he remembered it, but still hers: she must be twenty-one now, twenty-two—fell silent while she waited, expectant and submissive, for some magic word from him to make it right: negate the past, insure the future, at the going price of three Hail Marys, maybe less.

"Magdalena," he said through the grate, "do with your boyfriend what you did with me."

Silence. In the silence the girl's breathing.

"What . . . what do you mean, Father?"

"Do you love him?" he asked.

"Ye-s," she pronounced, hesitantly.

"Then don't be afraid to show it. Love him. Don't be afraid to love."

She was waiting again.

"Is . . . that all, Father?"

"That's all. That's all there is. Everything else is . . ." He closed the grate before he could think of what everything else was. What was it? Hell. Love was hell, and the absence of love was hell, too. Hell was where he was. He himself was hell.

"Father . . ." He heard her muffled voice through the closed grate, and opened it a crack. "Thank you, Father." He clicked the grate shut and sat hunkered up and sweating in the small, hot, dark, closed booth. Through the wall Magdalena getting up from kneeling, preparing to go out and love with sanction, with abandon. He had a mad impulse to rush out and—what? Hug her? Horrify her?—good Catholic girl . . .

with a name like that. It gave him some slight pleasure to think that somewhere tonight, in the wilderness of waters New Orleans had become, a man would be loved as he had not been loved before.

Magdalena's footsteps through the empty church. A soul refitted, a dove released on the flood. Hawkish he sat in his little cage, the selfsame coffin he had contrived for himself again and again, time out of mind—in the water-tower, in Les's garret, in the apartment in Frisco, under the desk in his little room on Pitt, even at Larry's apartment on Short. He had been in hell a long time, but it was a hell of his own making, his own hell, having nothing to do with . . . Unlatch-ing the little gate, he stood up, cramped and stiff: prepared to come out on the run, to keep running until he dropped . . . Lee Anne: their obsessive passion had had its own momentum: two trains hurtling head-on at full speed. But now that love was dead, by comparison with it, everything else was dying footsteps in an empty church. . . .

"Wherever it was, and whoever he talked to, it turned him around," said the doctor. "Toward the end he seemed to be rushing around trying to right all the wrongs he'd committed, and then some."

"The tenth step," Les murmurs.

"Tenth step?"

"You know, in AA: 'Made direct amends to all persons we had harmed, except when to do so would injure them or others.' You were the one who quoted it earlier. Maybe you've had too much . . . My God!" says Les, reaching for the nearly empty bottle, "you've been cadging drinks all along." He closes his eyes and takes a swig.

Larry absentmindedly receives the bottle back from Les and empties it. "Of course!" he says. "That explains the sudden burst at the end, his break-in at Floyd's and his performance at the black church. He was in a hypothermic state by that time, must have been, running on sheer nerves and adrenaline surges. Floyd described it in his usual bluff manner . . ."

"That bastard Floyd," said Les. "The world would be a better place without his fat ass."

"Wait!" said Larry, excitedly. "Even Floyd was turned around by Girard's last act. He says Girard was 'incandescent' when he broke in—and, remember, this is Floyd, Floyd 'Dragon' Boudreau, talking—'like a flaming bloody angel, or I would have shot the little snot.'"

"Floyd said that?"

The doctor nodded.

"Well, he must have got religion or been high on coke," Les said. "I'll leave it to you to guess which."

"I think he felt sorry for Girard," Larry said. "Beneath the fat and gunsmoke, Floyd's always had a sentimental streak."

"Right. How many blacks did he finish off that day?"

Larry sat staring at the empty bottle like a man resisting drink. But he had not resisted drink, and there was none left to resist. "Just one," he said.

CHAPTER 3

In the hour he'd been in the church, the water had risen. He descended the steps of Mater Dolorosa to enter a thick soup of water the color of mud with debris floating in it. At the corners of houses and at the intersections of streets were little swirls of debris with black sticks, a red oilcan and empty glass bottles, and swirling and bobbing and bouncing off fences and house steps a scattering of checkered volley balls which must have got released from their net in the schoolyard. In its sweep through the city the river had carved its own channels, ignoring the man-made streets and venues laid out for it and cutting through backyards, flattening fences and submerging cars, while rushing through houses and buildings and alleys in a pathway of its own choosing, braided and deep. It was easy to see where the low spots were, and where the high water was: houses which seemed on a level with the structures they flanked were submerged up over their porches to the second floor, while next door, or down the street, a small house on slightly higher ground sat like a raft on an island; a few houses floated, with a dog, or a cat perched on their gables. The slave-quarter house on Pitt Street, behind his mother's house on Henry Clay—he was sure it would be under water, and with it his records and books and bed, maybe even his mother! The thought gave him a sense of grim jubilation as he waded waist deep through the orange soup of water—trying to keep to the street, where he figured the street should be—down Carrollton and, avoiding the suckage of undertow caused by the gutters, up Hickory Street.

He passed Valerie's place—no Frobena in sight: had she jumped?—and the Sibyl's: the junked car seat in the vacant lot where she normally sat was surrounded now by water sludge—colored and slick. But the Sibyl was not in the sludge and the old motor oil. Had she ascended? Was this the event she'd foretold time out of mind? Girard wagged his head as he slogged through knee-deep water past the clap-board side of Mt. Moriah Baptist, brilliantly lit and awash with an old preacher's voice, the doors shut tight, the faithful inside their ark casting off with a sermon on Noah.

The lights had gone off in the Whites-only bar, the water was up to the grillwork. All along Hickory the lights had gone off, except at the church two blocks back. As he sloshed past the open-front laundromat, machines upended and float-ing, and approached the curb—where the curb should be—past the squat, white stucco, Whites-only club, a desolation of water extended from the high picket fence before him, with brooding angels and Confederate horsemen surveying the damage beneath them. Inside the mausoleum beside the live oak a bus, marooned, had been overturned. The large wooden cross mounted on its rear, that anchored it fast in the mud, marked it as the bus that read "REPENT or PERISH!" —the lettering now upside down—with the lake of burning fire sketched on its side in high-gloss lacquer; but the mur-derers, idolaters, effeminate, and many more who were caught in the wavy sea of burning fire, were no longer upside down, but right side up, while the blessed hung head down-ward plunged in mud. It was then, as he slogged along the picket fence and turned in at the gate which led to the live oak in the center of the cemetery, that he saw the keeper—the old Cajun, with the N.O. Saints cap—trussed up and depending from a live oak branch like fruit; while perched up in the crotch of a slightly higher branch sat the wild black preacher who went with the bus and now sat watching it.

The keeper, Girard saw now, was dead. The preacher, dressed in a dirty old robe with a gunny sack vestment and a black turban, though sitting hunched and silent like a vulture, was very much alive and vigilantly watching both his up-turned bus and prey and the godless, shirtless man approaching him. Suddenly he turned and shouted, pointing a bony finger: "Woe to Shem an' Ham an' all them Shitites! He wouldn't let the Gospel-bus come in among th' saints! He wouldn't 'low salvation thru' them gates! 'Hold 'im now, an' hear: as he be, yo is! Jest yo look at yoreself!"

Girard looked at the black man perched in the tree, then at the sightless, strung-up keeper, then at the upside-down saints and right-side-up sinners portrayed on the bus. At himself he didn't look.

Girard sloshed on, beneath the drowned live oak with the dead man hung from it and the madman perched in it, down the lane the bus had trespassed to the gates the bus had burst through and on out past Hilary. At Broadway he stopped. Across Broadway was Newcomb. To his right were the frat houses, many lights and much activity; to his left, Broadway was like a bayou that had overflowed its banks, long and lightless with two rows of flooded houses fronting it. Like Venice. Like Newcomb's Junior Year Abroad on which Lee Anne had gone.

> Blinds are a menace,
> Return them to Venice.
>
> Blondes are a menace,
> Return them to Venus.

In every direction, water.

There was no longer one place to go, there were many, but many amounted to none. There was one place to stay away from—Paradis—but he was cut off from there anyway. A waste of water islanded him in the city; it was futile to try to go back. She was there, in Paradis, he was here. Nothing that he might do here was of any importance to him. Between her and him was a great gulf fixed—he'd been lucky to get across it—and now he was here, on the inside, and she was out there.

Turning neither to the left nor to the right, he slogged on across the canal that had been Broadway and waded up the little slope to Newcomb campus. Like a Marine taking a beachhead twenty years after the war, he braced himself for machine-gun fire and checked dorm windows for snipers. The campus seemed deserted. He slogged on.

—Do you remember me mentioning a fourth at Paradis?

—There was Girard, Lee Anne, Bland . . .

—And this fourth guy sitting in the shadows in the corner. Lee Anne knew him, she knew he was there.

—So she wasn't playing to the crowd?

—Nor to Girard.

—But to this guy. Who was he?

—This prick used to be a guard at DePaul's, then at Mandeville. Before that he'd been a policeman in South Africa. Besides that, he'd seen Girard with Valerie.

—Wait a minute. Whoa! You say Girard . . . But what does it matter? By the time he got to Paradis there was a spillway and a lake to get across. The whole evacuation movement was away from, not into, New Orleans.

—Not for Girard. He went the other way, into the city.

—Girard always went the wrong way. But who besides Girard would want to go to a flooded city?

—Ernest White. And White was just as driven as Girard, as events would prove. It was Girard he was really after.

—But why? Why would . . .?

—Girard's mother. That's why White was there, in Paradis. He was tailing Lee Anne.

—Lee Anne? I thought you said the mother . . . ?

—He was tailing Lee Anne for the mother, he was in Irene Trepagnier Girard's employ.

Les gave a low whistle. He cast a quick glance out the dormer at the tractor on which the Governor of Louisiana once sat and yelled, "Ah'm still Gov'ner! Ah'm still Gov'ner of the State of Loosianer!" The tractor had not moved.

"So, even paranoiacs have enemies," the playwright said.

"Girard did," said the doctor. "He was paranoid. And he had an enemy in Ernest White . . ."

Watching from his corner in the Paradis bar, seeing the girl who was pregnant by the first man bawling out the second, Ernest White remembered the time Girard brought Valerie to his little slave-quarter house, just off the Garden District. The little house was just behind his own big house, which he was renting with an option to buy from Mrs. Girard, the boy's mother. Girard and the black girl marched right through as if they owned the place, while he watched from inside the big house. Two hours later they marched out again, but this time their line of march was interrupted. It was then, as he stood blocking the narrow alleyway, that he recognized Girard. The girl resembled a thousand other coloreds in New Orleans: brazenly decked out, an affront as she stood in God's sun giving off her powerful Negroid stench while hiding behind her protector, black hoof in his white hand.

"I'm Jimmy Girard," the nigger-lover said as they drew abreast, thrusting out his hand.

White hesitated, then shook hands.

"Sure's a hot day, Mr. Girard."

"Sure is."

"Your mother know you're here?"

"Maybe not," Girard said.

"Well, I suppose the place is clean enough. You folks comin' from church, you an' the maid?"

It was 2 P.M. on a Sunday, and they had arrived around noon. The black girl had on a cheap yellow crepe, all fluted and frilled at the armholes—a ten-year-old's dress on a grown woman, the elastic sizings stretched out of shape by her powerful arms.

"You know, the Bible's got somethin' to say about coloreds and whites gettin' mixed up with each other."

Now the black girl was glancing wide-eyed over her shoulder and trying to pull Girard away. The elastic sizings seemed ready to burst, but Girard didn't budge.

"Tell you what, the Bible's not somethin' I'm keen on hearin' just now. Had my fill in church this morning. You keep it in mind, Ernie, an' maybe I'll come for the lecture."

"Tuesday nights, seven o'clock."

"Yeah, I know. At the Whites-only club."

"You'd be welcome."

"Yeah, I know. Well, we won't be detaining you any longer here in this hot sun. Ready, Val?"

White continued to stand stockstill in the middle of the alleyway. He was a big man, and there was no way around him. "Not on my authority, but on the authority of truth I tell you, you have committed fornication, adultery and, worse, miscegenation, which is an abomination in the sight of God and man."

"Yeah, I heard it all before—haven't we, honey? Well, Ernie, nice meetin' ya. And get some slats for that bed, will you? Me an' th' maid here nearly fell through, know what I mean? Nice talkin' to ya. Give my regards to your mother, I mean my mother, I mean . . . you know, Miz Jurard.''

Three months later Girard had jumped from the bridge and his mother and his wife had committed him to DePaul's, where White was a guard. . . .

Now as he watched from his corner in the Paradis bar— the blonde girl, who was actually married to this nigger-lover who had reappeared after three years, though she was pregnant by the rotter in the other corner—Ernest White was not surprised, he was not dismayed by Girard's reappearance, he was just disgusted. For the past three months, ever since her pregnancy had become public, he had been hired by Irene Girard to ''keep a watch'' on Lee Anne. So long as there was no direct contact between her and her estranged husband, whom he'd been paid to ''take care of'' in DePaul's, there could be no question of inheritance. But the nigger-lover had escaped, gone missing for three years, and now . . .

As a policeman in Johannesburg, Ernest White had been more successful than anyone else at getting coloreds to confess. No marks, just threats, reinforced with pressure applied in the right places: the groin, the kidneys, the soles of the feet, and on family members who could be rounded up on suspicion or anonymously beaten up. Psychological pressure —terror, not torture—and it worked every time. But at DePaul's there had been constraints, and the colored attendants had complained against him that he brutalized the patients, especially black patients, in ways that didn't show. He would, for instance, go into a rage every time he saw a colored patient and punch him in the kidney with the swagger-stick he always carried; no bruise showed on their velvet hide but terror glazed their eyes when they saw Ernest White approaching. That was all he wanted: acknowledgement, that could not be faked, of the superiority of whites and the inferiority of coloreds, whom God created to be slaves and servants of the whites, and the swift and certain punishment of nigger-lovers, who like traitors crossed the color-bar and contaminated the race, spawning half-castes and hi-yallers and mulattos, bred from pleasure to give pleasure and to perpetuate corruption from one generation to the next, down to the seventh generation, as the prophet Ezekiel warned. And many other scriptures, too, confirmed his gut response and justified his treatment of coloreds, though he hadn't understood why until he became a British Israelite and read the Bible—*Genesis* and *Exodus* and *Leviticus* and *Deuteronomy* and the little book which summarized the law and refuted the black Baptists: *Philemon.* But nigger-lovers! There was not a place ordained for them, they were like the rebel angels, fallen, damned, and unredeemable, breeders of half-castes and vermin, traitors to their race and to society a plague, like parasites. He remembered vividly a lecture he'd attended in Johannesburg, delivered by the grand vizier of British Israelites, in which whites who crossed the color-bar, or who encouraged blacks to cross it, were likened to ichneumon flies that lay their eggs in a host body—usually a fat, white caterpillar, which the ichneumon paralyzes. The helpless white host lies, sentient but immobile, while ichneumon larvae hatch in its innards and begin their grisly feast: fat stores and digestive organs first, the essential heart and central nervous system saved for last—just like the ancient British penalty for treason, drawing and quartering, with the intention of inflicting as much torment as possible by keeping the victim conscious to the end.

All this Ernest White had learned as a policeman in South Africa, where he'd had ample opportunity to practice what he preached, and had carried with him, first to Trinidad, then to New Orleans, as a missionary carries tracts or a planter seeds, the certainty that someday he would be called on to act as an avenger for the Lord. He was head of the New Orleans chapter of British Israelites, which met weekly in a little room behind the Whites-only bar on Hickory—six to eight men, all middle aged or older, most of them former policemen somewhere in the Commonwealth—and he was willing to take any job, preferably police work, which did not conflict with his belief in white supremacy and his mission of disseminating the British Israelite Gospel. These were to Ernest White, a British subject with a British passport, more important than family or fortune, recognition or even respect from the degenerate and corrupt society which required that he report annually as an alien because his visa was renewable only on the grounds that he qualified under Special Category 2.b. of the Immigration and Nationality Act:

> Certain practicing ministers of
> religious denominations whose services
> are needed by a religious denomination in
> the United States. (Spouses and children
> included.)

But he was a bachelor, aged forty-eight, whose only certain achievement thus far was that he had not burdened the world with any godless progeny. The world was overrun already with vermin and indeterminate creatures, neither this nor that, not certain who spawned them, or for what purpose, or to what end.

Now as he watched from his corner in the Paradis roadhouse the pregnant woman having words with the man without a shirt, the other man in a suit coming out from his corner and standing beside the woman, and the two of them driving off the interloper—Girard, who had forfeited his birthright and betrayed his heritage, who had been contaminated and now carried like a virus the contaminating darkness—Ernest White was neither pleased nor displeased at the ridicule heaped on Girard, nor at the defeat on his face as he turned and limped away—off the dance floor, out the door, into the night. It wasn't enough, it was never enough; heretics had a way of nursing their wounds and turning up, after five years, on trial dates, out of the blue, up from the dark . . . With a quick pat to his businesslike Smith and Wesson .38 Special revolver, to make sure it was still there, snug in its belt holster on his right hip, White lunged from his seat in the corner and made for the doorway. In uncertain light from the blinking Jax sign he could barely make out a shadowy figure moving toward the Bonnet Carré spillway; then, as he ran toward the rush of water that cut off the whole of northern Louisiana from the city to the south—moated by the flooding Mississippi, the Bonnet Carré spillway, and Lake Pontchartrain—he saw a silhouette across the water like a negative of Jonah, or the fugitive slave Onesimus in *Philemon*. Immediately, with the uncanny certainty that directed all his movements when his job coincided with his personal mission, White ran to his car outside the Paradis, jumped in and headed north on 51 toward Ponchatoula which, though he hadn't thought that far yet, hadn't needed to, trusting in the instinct that drove him as automatically as he drove his car, would bring him to the Lake Pontchartrain Causeway, heading south. . . .

"Shit," Les muttered. "I might have known that creep would show up. That's the guy I spotted at DePaul's, the guard who was always hanging around Girard, remember? South African —I knew it! And now he jumps out of the woodwork of a sleazy roadhouse—named 'Paradis,' for Chrissake!—with a gun in his hand." Les shook his long shaggy head disbelievingly. "Cee-riest! Do you know how crude that is, how incredible? It's *deus ex machina*, it's 1590s revenge tragedy, it's completely insupportable and unacceptable and . . . We're as likely to see Governor Earl Long on his tractor brandishing a sword and wanking off while the water rises."

"Why not?" said Larry. "It happened, didn't it? You wanted the story of how Girard went out, didn't you? I warned you it was untidy, I told you it was messier than Blowhole-Joe's, or did I?"

"Who's 'Blowhole-Joe?' Some dago hit man helicoptered in from Chicago, for Chrissake?"

"Nevermind, nevermind, Blowhole-Joe doesn't figure in," said Larry soothingly. "You've got me going now, I want to finish. What time is it, anyway?"

"Fuck the time," said Les, reaching over to a bookshelf and removing books by the handful, exposing to the candlelight a stash he had concealed. "Here, here's some Grand Marnier. The last, the absolute last round." He poured a finger for Larry, then one for himself, in shot glasses which he produced from the same cache. Les raised his shot glass to the light and peered through it. Already the glass was sweating. "Here's to 'Golden Boy' *in extremis*," he proposed.

"*In excruciatis extremis*," answered Larry.

The glasses sweat in their hands. They clink glasses.

The doctor and the playwright raise their glasses to their lips and drink, gazing fixedly at one another, draining the whole drink, but slowly, ceremonially. Then, like mirror-twins, they place the empty glasses on the table, blink and swallow, and sit back. The rain outside has ceased to fall, or falls noiselessly. A clammy silence settles on the garret.

"Now tell me where Floyd figures in. Or does he? With

all these Johnny-come-latelys emerging from the woodwork
. . ."

"Floyd figures. Girard went to Floyd's first, because he
and Floyd arrived together at the black church. What he did
at Floyd's I can't imagine. Whatever it was, it didn't prevent
. . ."

"Wait!" Les interrupted. He had leapt up and was gripping his chair back, shifting from one foot to the other like a
bear on a chain. "Maybe Girard was on a sentimental swing
through his old haunts. That'd be like him. Floyd lives just up
the street here, a block off Napoleon and St. Charles."

"Fat Harry's is at Napoleon and St. Charles," the doctor
offered.

"He lives behind Fat Harry's, and Fat Harry's . . ."

". . . is across the street from St. Stephen's, and St.
Stephen's is just up the street from . . ."

"Sacred Heart! That's it, Lee Anne! He'd already back-
tracked to Homewood and killed his mother—"

"What do you mean 'killed his mother?'"

"I mean the nun, the mother superior, the mother-figure—
fuck! We already discussed it, don't throw me off!" Les was
stalking bearishly in the narrow cage between the typewriter
table and the bookshelf by the window, arms flung out
expansively, shaggy mane hanging in his face. "He may even
have swung by here, who knows? But I don't see how. The
water was over the lions out front, the neutral ground was
submerged, and the Governor's tractor . . ."

The statue of the BVM looms white and phosphorescent in
the deserted courtyard. Rising from the middle of the fountain, which is flooded and submerged, only the head and torso
show above the murky water which extends in every direction and covers with a flat opacity the flagstones on which, a

dozen years ago, Lee Anne had stood surrounded by a flush of gabbling girls. Not just the flagstones but the stations of the cross in their little glass-paned shrines about the grounds and every other landmark has been erased, except for trees, the tops of fences, and the Sacred Heart Academy itself. Even the stairs where graduating classes posed are sunken past the bottom row, the tall girls, and the robed and wimpled sisters flanking them as guards flank prisoners are chopped off by dark water at the waist. The BVM stands solitary in the flooded courtyard, sole surviving emblem of the choirs of virgin girls who, not favored and not blessed, have declined into the flood and been swept off. Serene she stands, her enigmatic face and folded hands above the flood, neither blessing nor condemning, neither curious nor distressed, as though about to enter the deluge whose source she is, beside whose bank she stands aloof, impassive, while men drown.

Girard was on a makeshift raft. At the corner of St. Charles and State Street he'd found it—the announcement board for St. Charles Avenue Presbyterian Church, which as a schoolboy he'd passed time out of mind on his way between his mother's and St. Steve's—still standing, though canted, with the water (waist high as he worked to pry it free) nearly past its two legs. In large white letters on a black background, it read: "Hosea—The Pain of Love." It carried him, not entirely satisfactorily, for it sunk six inches under-water with his full weight, so he had to scuttle forward with it as a shield, his feet touching the spongy ground in shallow spots. Through deep pools he poled with one of the legs, which he had managed to pry free. It had not been too difficult down the neutral ground along St. Charles, where there were few obstacles, but it was awkward on corners, and tended to get sucked into back eddies wherever solid walls channeled the current. He was moving toward the slot between two solid structures now: catty-corner from the BVM, across the intersection of Napoleon and St. Charles, which he had managed to negotiate by running interference with a hydroplane which roared along St. Charles at fifty mph, and two old weatherbeaten *bateaux*, each with a family of Negroes, being poled along Napoleon.

He swung the raft toward the narrow alleyway between St. Stephen's gym and school. On the street side by the gym was a tennis court, submerged up to the net, and in the high wire fence which bounded it a yellow tennis ball, driven on a drier day into the mesh above arm's reach. He passed the ball and plucked it from the fence, then let the current float him on into the alleyway.

From the muddy watermark along the old brick building, he could see the water was receding. He stopped along a row of windows looking in on the school lunchroom, Fr. Durieu's classroom, and library. Shielding with his hand his own reflection, he peered inside. Lunchroom tables and chairs floated lopsidedly in a sea of bread and plastic wrappers and milk bottles. Two large refrigerators and a freezer had upturned, spilling their contents into the watery desolation that had been St. Stephen's lunchroom, and the chromium food counters, from which the water had receded, were covered in silt. He pushed his awkward raft along, trying to keep close to the building under the eavestroughing, out of the rain, to the end of the lunchroom and a view of Fr. Durieu's lab. Here where students sat on stools the desks were higher, covered in silt as the lunch counter had been. But the watery mass surrounding the floating, upturned islands of desks, stools, and glass-covered cases, was cluttered with a thousand sample bottles leaking acids, anatomical displays, and formaldehyde into the murky waters. The stench, released from so many bottles and contained in one small room, was terrific.

He moved on, approaching with a sinking feeling the library. This was the only desolation he regretted; of the school's destruction he was glad. But books . . . He peered through the windows of the library: silt-covered counters, muddy water-damaged books (the new-releases shelves, from which the water had receded), the books, many books, awash, afloat, their spines broken and their pages mushed. Of one or two of them, the dust jacket sheathed in plastic, he could read the titles: *The Birth of Purgatory, The Hour of Our Death,* and *Who Is My Mother?* He blocked out his reflection with both hands in an effort to peer further: beyond the desolation of waters the shelves stood, the top three above water, the fourth halfway under, the lowest shelves submerged. Chilled, and feeling colder than he could ever remember having felt, he let go and let the current carry him, still partially submerged, on through the narrow alleyway and out onto the wide watery murk, where rain still fell, which fronted on Napoleon. He felt a coldness in his soul comparable with what he'd felt the day his father's death was in the papers. He'd sensed himself, that day, alone—no place to go, no one to run to—and had blamed it on his uniform. Naked now, or nearly so, he was still alone.

No one was following him, but he felt that someone was. No one cared enough to go to the trouble; there was nothing on him of interest to anyone, and he posed a threat to no one. As for promises, he was past making them and those he had made were broken—like the bridges behind him, the spines of the books through the window, the desolation all around him through which he scuttled like a large reptile, as ill at ease in water as on land.

He had seen New Orleans as a city underwater when he arrived by bus—only three days ago?—it seemed aeons. And now it *was* a city underwater. A wave of destruction had followed in his wake, and he was neither outraged nor surprised; he wasn't even interested. He had difficulty think-ing where to go next, what to do last. He didn't want to be picked up, identified, committed . . . he didn't want to sleep. He could be mistaken for a bum, some other bum, and the last thing he needed was "the cure," "the treatment" . . . Having drowned once and suffered the cure at DePaul's and the treatment at Mandeville, he had appeared a second time . . .

"*You're a glutton for punishment, Girard,*" a familiar voice told him, grinning as it said it.

"*You sure do get around,*" a second voice purred. "*A man with a purpose, anyone can see that.*"

"*Listen, Jimmy, you've got friends in this town, you still have,*" voice #1 said earnestly.

"*Nobody is a friend of yours, let's face it,*" said voice #2.

The second voice shrugged while the earnest voice grinned. The grinning voice was no friend of his, the shrugging voice either. But were they enemies? Not having friends was one thing; having enemies was something else . . . Still, he couldn't shake the feeling that someone was after him—Mor-mon elders, maybe, or the FBI, like the time in San Francisco —and that he ought to have a gun. . . .

At Fat Harry's he poled past wrought-iron chairs and tables, where disguised as a Crusader he'd sat and read in the newspaper the action brought against his father by his mother; then around the corner and past a swirling eddy of newspapers, pop bottles, and beer cans, he poled his platform down the alleyway and came out in a nidus of interconnecting garages with cars flooded, garden tools and gas cans floating, back stairs leading into a commonwealth of water, criss-crossed by different kinds and colors of fence tops, demarcat-ing backyards. One of them was Floyd's, who had a gun.

He spotted the Mercedes. It was canted at an angle, trunk

down, front end up, as if someone had jacked it up to keep the motor above water, then despaired of it and quit. The back stairs were unguarded and Girard washed up against them, pulled himself out on them, crawled up, tried the back door, smashed his fist through the glass pane nearest the lock, which gave way. The door opened and he fell inside.

CHAPTER 4

"I'm at one end of the process, the bottom of the scale. From the confessional, where the poor, conscience-stricken, fear-tormented girl (or so the priest portrays her to the faithful, but her actual words in confidence and confession were, 'But, Father, it gives him so much pleasure, and me so little pain') shares with only one other man, the priest, but he represents the communion of saints—not the New Orleans Saints, Girard . . ."

It was Floyd's voice, Floyd's sarcastic rhetoric, Floyd's enormous bulk—and was he lecturing on Valerie? It seemed he was—seated high and dry in decadent comfort in a chromium-plated, neon-lit and many-windowed living room, up above the drowning city. The voice droned on.

". . . to my pornographic pictures, in which potentially millions of viewers may share in the lucky girl's fortunate fall. It's all part of the process—the transformation of sex into discourse—in which the minimum number of sex acts yields the maximum number of words . . ."

"And images," a feeble voice croaked. Girard, on the verge of exhaustion, lifted heavy lids and glanced to right and left to see who'd spoken. It was he. He, too, who was seated on a chrome and white sofa, dressed in clean and dry, but baggy, pants and shirt. The pants were held up by a belt, the shirt was starched.

"And images," Floyd boomed back, pleased.

"So you're her pimp," Girard said wearily.

"Pimp's so coarse. I prefer 'agent.' As her agent, I market

what she has to sell to the maximum numbers of buyers with a minimum of effort from her. Rather than letting out her favors little by little, to one client after another, she is consumed all at once, in a single act''—Floyd enacted with fat hands a small explosion—"Poof! A perfect paroxysm of sex and violence, pleasure and pain: viewed over and over, time out of mind, by millions . . . Lee and Mavis bathed and dressed you, by the way. If the duds are a trifle roomy, complain to the 'Big 'n Tall Shoppe.' ''

"Much obliged.''

"They're good, warm-hearted, country girls—Lee's from Jesuit Bend, Mavis from Naomi—La., of course. Where's Val from?''

Floyd peered from behind his horn-rimmed glasses like an owl.

"Donaldsonville,'' said Girard.

"Another good, warm-hearted, country girl,'' Floyd leered. "But poor, unfortunately poor. She contracts to sell a little of herself, a portion of her favors. I compute at the market value her lifetime output, I put up forward money, I buy her all. She needn't know this; the fact that's she's marketable, and has put herself on the market, is enough.''

"But you haven't put forward any money.''

"Let's not forget the five hundred—your finder's fee, Girard. Anyway, forward buying works like this: one man promises to provide at some distant date effects he does not possess, and the other commits himself to paying for them with money he does not have.''

"But she hasn't agreed to sell.''

"She's sold, or contracted to sell, one lump of sugar; we've paid for it. Now we buy up in advance the whole crop and all future crops. Let me explain it to you in terms of sugar. That's a commodity you understand.''

Floyd heaved his vast bulk upward from the chrome and

white chair in which he had been sunk and moved noiselessly
across the carpeted floor to the bar. "Drink, James?" he said,
putting out and half-filling two glasses.

"I want a gun, Floyd."

"The last time you asked me for a gun, and didn't, I regret
to say, get one, you jumped from the Huey P. Long Bridge.
This time the river's come to you. If Mohammed cannot go to
the mountain . . . Faith, Girard. Your little faith has already
flooded the city. Have more: Valerie will be declared a Saint,
Lee Anne will float by on a yak . . . whatever your little heart
desires . . ." He held out the drink to Girard.

"Somebody's following me."

"*Ibid.* the last time, if memory serves. But a gun, no, it's not
your style, Jimmy. It short-circuits the process of faith. Faith
is a process, you know, like the transformation of sex into
discourse; but with faith it's the opposite—the manipulation
of objects by thought. Let the mountain come to you, Jimmy
. . ."

"A knife, then."

"We have food and Jack Daniel's to last the duration. No
need for weapons, Jimmy. Put on the breastplate of faith. Let
every man sit under his own vine and tend his own fig tree."

Girard took the drink, frosted and sweating from Floyd's
clammy grip, and sipped it.

"Cheers," said Floyd. "Now, sugar. And I know whereof
I speak, James, for, like you, I had an ancestor in the sugar
trade, but he was not a planter like your father and grandfather; Simon Boudreau was what they call a 'merchant usurer'
—a perfectly lawful occupation by means of which he
managed to make piles of money at small risk and with little
exertion. Here's how it worked. This old fox would buy at
Rio de Janeiro bills of exchange from the Brazilian sugar
planters who were sending their product to Europe and who
were in a hurry for their money. Simon Boudreau would

advance it to them against a bill of exchange drawn on the purchaser of the sugar and payable in three months' time. If possible, he would buy the bill at less than face value and send it to his friend Leander Beaugez in Paris. Beaugez would collect the money, use it to buy another bill of exchange this time drawable on a bank in Rio, which Simon Boudreau would cash three months later. This final operation, at the end of six months, represented the closing by Simon Boudreau of the circuit. It was because the sugar planters could not tolerate the usual delays of transport and payment that Simon Boudreau handled it for them, making a clear profit of eighteen percent in return for credit over six months.

"But deals could always go wrong. In any given money market, paper and specie operated in a certain relationship. If specie was abundant, paper appreciated, and vice versa. The direct return with a regular profit on the second bill was sometimes difficult, if bills were quoted in Paris at too high a rate. Leander Beaugez would then be obliged to draw on his own account—or, rather, on the account opened in his name by Simon Boudreau—that is, to 'launder' the money via Antwerp or Venice. Thus the money would make a triangular trip, taking another three months. This was still acceptable, but Simon Boudreau would be furious if at the end of nine months he had not made the interest he counted on every half-year. He wanted to play the market, but only on a safe bet. As he wrote in 1584—his letters are all there, my most prized possessions," Floyd pointed to an old, round-top trunk at the end of the room and out of keeping with the other furnishings —"he preferred, he said, to '*retenir son argent dans un coffre, au lieu de risquer le perdre dans l'échange,*' 'keep his money in a chest rather than risk losing it on the exchange.' So said my ancestor, Simon Boudreau, in the year of our Lord 1584, and what Simon says . . ."

"Really, Floyd," Girard protested. He was exhausted,

stiff from the air-conditioned cold of the room and, generally, disgusted.

"Patience, Girard, patience—the point . . . yes, the point. It's that one had to have confidence in one's agents then, and instructions had to be obeyed. Simon Boudreau had learned this the hard way, for in 1562 he'd had an agent in Bordeaux named Lauré Berthelot, a young man not unlike you, Girard. One day Simon Boudreau lost his temper with his agent and accused him, rightly or wrongly, of some fraudulent dealings. Lauré promptly disappeared, since the Bordeaux police were after him. But before long he turned up in Rio de Janeiro, where he flung himself at his master's feet to beg his pardon. When I was reading some of my ancestor's letters dating from 1570, I came across the name of Lauré Berthelot again. Six years after the disgraceful incident he had become a merchant specializing in wine, back in Bordeaux. Was he successful? Who knows? One thing is certain: he could not have got back into trade without the blessing of that old fox, Boudreau. This, Girard, throws light on the issue before us: the reliability that a merchant—be he a merchant in sugar, money, or flesh—expects, and has a right to expect from his agent, his partner or his employee."

"Simon Boudreau wasn't a merchant of death, Floyd. You are. Thanks for the drink." Girard was still rising from the sofa when he was tipped back in by the big man, who moved across the floor with the speed of a cat and the force of a rhinoceros.

"You misunderstand, Girard. Boudreau forgave the young man not because he repented, but because it was in Boudreau's best interests to use him again. Get the picture?"

Girard closed his eyes and settled back in the sofa.

"I'm talking about the shift from a command structure to a market commodity one. Once that shift is made, the transfer, even the promise of money is binding, the profit motive is determinative. There's no mercy. It's the only way to break out of the Southern planter matrix, into which you were born, Girard. Girard?"

"I'm listening, goddammit."

"First, the old patriarch amasses power and prestige, abuses his privilege; under his son accounts decline, production shrinks. There's only one sale a year, but expenses are daily. The plantation needs maintaining, the workers' conditions are improving—not much, but they're not slaves anymore—if he doesn't give them what they want, they'll move to town and work in the mills. The planter can't afford to wait to sell, he has to borrow for supplies. Finally he's at the mercy of his creditors. The women, who stave the creditors off, take over, while the planter hides out at his club or, in your father's case, in his room. Now comes your generation —here you come, Girard, a little dandy in short pants—into a thoroughly woman-dominated world. The matriarchate is in place. The women have taken over. Your mother, your sister, your wife, they've read the writing on the wall and the figures in the account books. They've wrested from the grip of mortmain and the grasp of the profligate son the title to plantation, goods and chattels, servants and tenant farmers— all: all for your sake, in your name. These they get, either by inheritance (the way your mother came by shares in Norco) or by lawsuit (the way she acquired Homewood). Having converted land to liquid assets, the women move to town— where they always wanted to be from the beginning, but they had to do their time, too, in the boonies. They get out of sugar, though they use it on their tables; they break out of 'weaker sex' roles—wives, mothers—though they use them, too, in law courts and in bed. They bid adieu to the feudal planter structure, with its guilt-loyalty, its master-slave mentality. They play the stocks, they control the banks, they enter the market."

Girard did not open his eyes. "Selling what? What have they got left to sell?"

"Themselves. Your mother's retired now: she sold herself to your father and your father's brother, a limited market, admittedly, but she sold high. Your sister markets herself from billboards and *Look* magazine. She sits with congressmen and sleeps with senators. Just as Valerie becomes a prostitute to millions, so your sister becomes . . . what?"

"A celebrity fuck?"

"Your sister's more in control of her market, I'll admit, than Valerie is, but . . . Here, allow me to instruct you with a little parable."

"A parable? You?"

"Why not? Didn't Our Savior, on occasion, use parables?"

"Our what?"

"Our Saviour. Yours and mine. Well, maybe not yours and maybe not mine, maybe that's the point of the parable. The Saviour, then."

"Really, Floyd, this is too much . . ."

"A certain man had two sons . . ."

"I find that offensive."

"You break into my goddamned house, you steal five hundred bucks from me, you try to welch on our goddamned deal, and you find what I say offensive! I don't care a Christly fuck what you find!" Floyd heaved his bulk up from the sunken chair and strode quickly across the bar. "Never bloody mind, he didn't have two sons, he had a son and a daughter. What's the matter? Why are you snickering?"

"Floyd, whenever you quote scripture, it offends me."

"You think I give a Saviour's fart? You think I care a fig?"

"You're really too obscene for words."

"Then hold your bloody tongue while I tell my tale!" Floyd thundered. He freshened his drink and held the bottle up toward Girard, who shook his head.

Girard's eyes were fully open now, as he watched Floyd go to the shuttered window, peer out, then pace back and forth across the chrome and white room with the drink in his hand. To Girard, sitting impassive and exhausted on the sofa, it seemed an elaborate display of nonchalance, masking impatience, anxiety, what?

". . . a son and a daughter, both of whom he loved very much. But he had a wife, too. And a very shrew of a wife she was—like my first wife, the bitch . . ."

"The one who gave you the Mercedes."

"The same. Don't interrupt. Home he would come at night to his dark house and dread wife, and as soon as he entered the door she would light into him: the kitchen tap's leaking, my mother's coming for a visit, the children are quarreling, I need money for shopping—a hundred things daily she found to complain of, and besides, she had lovers. She denied it. She lied like a senator and whined like a fishwife, but she had lovers, plain enough—the children let him know—and sometimes these lovers ate at table with them, and sometimes they slept over (on this or that pretext: the house was in the country and they couldn't get to town, or they wanted to stay and help around the house while he went to work—the various excuses Jodies always give, always have given) and no one much cared what he thought or said or did because it was plain the wife would leave him if he objected, and take the children with her. How'm I doing?" Floyd stopped to ask.

Girard who in spite of himself had been listening, nodded.

Floyd resumed pacing, talking while he paced. "So now, in the face of all this high-handed treatment and hen-peckery, taking into consideration that he loves his children, and that they're still young and need their mother, what would you say is the most spiritual response our man could make?"

Girard screwed up his face in concentration.

"He can't get rid of the wife, right?"

"Right."

"And he can't just leave with the children . . ."

"They're too young. Besides, under our archaic Napoleonic Code, he'd never get custody."

"Disappear, I guess," Girard said finally.

"Exactly! You know the spiritual thing to do, Girard, because you're the type. It's the oldest trick in the world—to disappear, leave no trace, call it quits and vanish, vamoose, scram"—Floyd snapped his thumb and fat middle finger together—"and that's just what the spiritual types have been doing ever since the world began . . ."

"Giving up."

"Sacrificing themselves."

"I see."

"Or being sacrificed," Floyd added quickly. "After all, it's not easy. Sometimes you need help."

"You're helping Valerie."

"I'm helping her fulfill her . . . destiny: what she and no one else, when she was created, was created for. She's religious, isn't she. Isn't Valerie religious?"

Girard looked disgusted.

"Protestant or Catholic, Girard—which is she? I know she's religious, I can tell."

"You know she's Baptist. She's black, she's Baptist."

"Well, I'm facilitating her religious vocation, which according to Luther is 'to annihilate oneself.' What's more important? 'What profiteth a man' (or a woman, Girard, even a woman, even a black woman) 'if he gain the whole world and lose his own soul? Or, what can a man give in return for his soul?' What, Girard? Isn't the answer . . ."

Floyd held both fat hands palm up, handing over the answer of thin air.

". . . nothing, Girard, nothing. . . ."

Having handed over the answer, his hands collapsed in mid-air. His eyes, however, remained on Girard, whose mood had shifted from disgust to serious, even alarming, introspection.

"But surely," Girard said slowly, hesitantly, "to fulfill one's destiny, free will is required. Any act you're forced to do is meaningless, it's hollow. It's only what you do for love . . ."

"Or money, Girard. Most things are done for money."

"That's why most acts are meaningless. Only the few done out of love are worth anything, and love can't be bought, it can't be coerced, it can't even be earned."

"Now you're getting there!" Floyd said, clapping his fat hands together. "You ain't just whistling Dixie, boy! Now you're hummin', you're pledgin' allegiance, you're singin' Th' Star-Spangled Banner!"

Girard sat impassive, disdainful of this last outburst.

"What you've described is how things used to be, how we thought things were when loyalty and obedience and guilt still had some claim on us, when the church was something other than a sixth-rate power. But the world shifted, Girard. We've moved to a market economy, baby, and you and all those values are out with the bathwater. Speaking of which, it was the battleships and super-battleships and dreadnoughts built around the turn of the century, by the Brits and Krauts and Japs—or more precisely their financing—that tipped the scales to a market economy worldwide."

"There are pockets of resistance," Girard objected weakly.

"There are. There always will be. Jesuit Bend and Naomi, where Lee and Mavis hail from, are two such, and I doubt not that Donaldsonville is another, but . . ."

"*Suffisant!*" Such a weariness had come over Girard that he had broken into a sweat. His ears sang, vertigo and giddiness seized him by turns, his shoulders and shoulder blades ached and he had that grief in the mouth of the stomach—accompanied by short breath, hard wind, strong pulse—which made him think it was his heart that ached. "Enough of this . . . *talk*, Floyd—what have you *done*?"

Floyd regarded him quizzically, as a doctor might regard a patient whose reason is darkened but who has lucid intervals, as if pondering which this was and how to address it. "What do you mean, what have I done?" he pronounced finally, flatly.

Girard, still gasping for breath as if suffocating, rasped: "*with . . . Val . . .*"

"Ah, yes, the ebony lady!" Floyd said breezily. "Man does, woman is, Girard."

"And . . . has things done . . . to her!" Girard got off.

Ignoring him and glancing at his watch, Floyd said: "I met with the ebony lady. We struck a deal, of sorts. She agreed to pose once, and never pose again; I agreed to pay the price—to certain beneficiaries she named: one *Jackie*, a certain *Sheelita*, someone named *Yulanda*, and . . . *Pooky*," Floyd pronounced the names distastefully. "It's notarized."

"She understands," Girard began, getting back his breath, "what's being asked of her?"

"Really, Girard. Who am I to say what someone else understands? Especially one of the fair sex? Especially a black? What do I know of their reasoning process? A hundred years ago they were throwing spears at each other."

"And what were we doing forty years ago? What are we doing today—in Guatemala, Salvador, Nicaragua?"

"Ah!" The fat man moved swiftly to the bar to freshen his drink, glancing at his watch as he did so. "What I wouldn't give to catch it on film? A village massacred, an archbishop assassinated, American nuns raped and murdered—it boggles the mind, Girard! But closer to home, if I could just felicitously find myself at one race riot—and, God knows, our lovely city is ripe for one—then I wouldn't have to rent a room, I wouldn't have to buy a woman, I wouldn't have to pay out money to welfare cases with such names as *Pooky, Sheelita, Yulanda.*" Floyd spit the names out with the lemon seeds from his gin and tonic.

"You're disgusting, Floyd."

"I am, am I? Well, listen now to what your Miss Black New Orleans went and did. She backed out on me. She signed the contract, she took the forward money—and, no doubt, spent it—then she backed out. Not only did she not show up . . . here I am, struggling up the stairs to a hot little room—an upper room, Girard, to simulate that other upper room—but this hot little room is in Desire, and rented, not by the day, but by the hour—you can guess what for— Negroes are a nefarious race, Girard, nefarious and avaricious, yes they are . . . here am I struggling up the stairs with all my equipment, lights, camera, actor, I had to hire an actor, and the alligator, I had to *lease* the alligator in its tank, along with the paraplegic that goes with it . . ."

"The paraplegic?"

"His feeder. Now *I'm* the feeder's keeper. Anyway, here I am struggling up a hot little staircase in Desire with alligator and accoutrement—no easy job carting an alligator around, Girard, try it sometime, try pushing a paraplegic in his wheelchair up two flights of stairs while balancing your alligator in its tank . . . and what does your lovely lady do? Your Miss Black New Orleans? You know, beauty is an affliction, Girard. What does it get you? If you're beautiful, as the ebony lady is, what have you got? Men ogle and lust after you, women envy and scorn you; you're prey to the wiles and deceits of every Dick who wants into your pants, and the distrust of all other women—it's an affliction, Girard! Worst, have you ever known a beautiful woman who wasn't vain? of course not, because being pretty is a full-time job! I'm doing your lady a favor relieving her of a burdensome existence, I'm committing euthanasia—pulchrathanasia, if there's such a thing; there ought to be—while *paying* her, or her idiot family . . ."

"Here I am, trying to do her a favor—pushing the paraplegic and carrying his alligator up the stairs, the actor has already carted the klieg lights and camera up to the next landing and has come back to help me—and what does *she* do? Sends this cretin in a kango cap and rehabilitated suit, this bullet-headed, no-necked preacher with a note that says '*Ill return yure money.*' Hot damn, Girard! And then this idiot nigger preacher starts ranting and raving, he sees the alligator, I guess, and gets excited and goes into what can only be a seizure of some sort. It starts with facial tics, then his arms and legs start leaping uncontrollably, his eyes start rolling, neck muscles bulging, nose bleeding, ooze coming out of his ears . . . I'm watching this, the actor's run upstairs and the paraplegic's huddled in the stairwell, and I'm thinking 'What's this madman gonna do?' and 'I'd better get a shot of it,' when all of a sudden out of his mouth comes, just like an explosion, this . . . utterance, this . . . howl, whatever you call it, this '*Uba-dooba-dooba*' sound, like scat-singing at 50,000 megahertz, and the guy's face is coming apart, like in a slime movie, I swear, I never . . ." Floyd paused to pluck from the pocket of his silk suit a silk handkerchief, to wipe the sweat from his brow. Taking a long pull of gin and tonic, he shook his head incredulously. ". . . and then, Girard, this nut case, this mad-dog nigger preacher with spittle flying, mouth frothing, nose bleeding, arms flailing, and leaping up and down in little jerks, just like those circus freaks and religious fanatics you read about plunges his arm into the alligator tank. Only this is not a tame alligator with all its teeth pulled; this is a genuine Louisiana swamp 'gator that's been thrashing about for raw meat. Christ! I expected something to happen. Wouldn't you? And this alligator that's been starved for two days—for the film, you know—never opens its yap. It just lies there, sleepy-like, as if it and this old preacher had some kind of deal. Anyway, that's what your Miss Black New Orleans pulled on me—me, her Diaghilev, her Hugh Hefner, her Bob Geldof, her . . ."

"Judas."

"No, Girard, you're that. After all, I scarcely know the girl. She's your find, Girard, you got the finder's fee, I couldn't have done it without you, she believes in you, believed enough to sign on the dotted line, then had second thoughts, as women will. She's ambivalent, Girard"—Floyd once again looked at his watch—"but when she sees you she'll feel better, more secure, knowing that you of all her past lovers have her best interests at heart . . ."

"What's the point, Floyd? And why so nervous? When a man as fat as you are gets as nervous as you are, it makes me jittery."

"Eleven twenty-five," Floyd pronounced precisely, peering at his watch. "In exactly thirty-five minutes your Miss Black New Orleans sings with the angels, cavorts with the 'gators, Girard. It's arranged, there's nothing we can do to stop it. We can watch, though."

Floyd peered owlishly, dispassionately, at Girard, who with half-closed eyes regarded from the couch the fat man peering at him.

"Fine with me," he answered with a shrug. "And where does this dismemberment take place?"

"You know the place," said the fat man affably, "and the way you know. Desire Project, not far from a certain black Baptist church you've been known to frequent."

"How do we get there?" Girard was standing now.

"The N.O.P.D. has a hydroplane," said Floyd, glancing at his watch, "due any minute." Even as he said it, the faint high whine of a distant motor became audible in the room.

"You coming, Girard?"

Like a condemned man Girard marched ahead of Floyd toward the door through which an hour earlier he had broken in. *Hosea—The Pain of Love* blocked the steps down to the driveway where the hydroplane idled with a driver and another policeman in it. The water was now visibly receding everywhere.

Floyd came up behind Girard, whose way was blocked by the sign. "Life's a morality play, Jimmy: yours is. Even the church signs pursue you." He kicked at the board, which was wedged into the banister and would not yield.

"Hurry up," he said gruffly, planting his foot on the board and making a way for Girard to pass through, "and give me a hand here, goddammit. We don't want to be late for the last show."

CHAPTER 5

HOLY GREETINGS TO
MISSIONARY INEZ GILMORE and
THE YOUNG WOMEN'S CHRISTIAN COUNCIL

May God lead and guide you to higher heights and deeper
depths.
May you do the things that aren't worth doing better with
Christ's help.
May you be godly women.

From THE MOTHERS' BOARD
MACEDONIA CHURCH-OF-GOD-IN-CHRIST

The banner and other congratulatory greetings to Sister Inez
and the Young Women's Christian Council drape the walls
inside the building on Louisa Street where the saints are
gathered singing, sweating, halleluing as Valerie pushes her
way inside and a program book is thrust into her hand.

"Glad you could come, Sister Val. Moughty wet, ain't
it?" Elder Griffin smiling: black lips, red tongue, gold tooth
with star inlaid.

"Glad to be here, Brother George. You seen Momma?"

Elder Griffin braceleting her wrist, powerful grip, pointing up the middle aisle of halleluing saints where she spies

Pooky's legs, pumping the old organ between jumping up and dancing, alongside Rev'run Reed and the massed choir with Sheelita, Yulanda, and Jackie, all three of her sisters and the nine Lacy sisters—Jowlanda, Demetria, Darnise, Patrice, Creola, Orvella, Jamesetta, Alvaida, and Alma—in purple robes. Momma can't be far.

"Much obliged." She twists free, Elder Griffin holding longer, tighter, than his station or the flood calls for. "Lem'me go," she says, turning in a tight arc so the hot breath of this Behemoth blows down her neck. Instinctively her hand goes for the Smith and Wesson Terrier .32 in her purse—lunging ladylike for an item businesslike. She hesitates. In her red Chevrolet with the old guy who wouldn't let her go or let her out, she pulled her S&W .32 and shot his kneecap off. But this is church—The Original Morningstar Black Baptist Church of New Orleans—her momma's church. Valerie summons up a *Matthew* 5:44 smile and Elder Griffin, leering, lets her go, his huge paw sliding fannyward and propelling her on up the aisle and into Isaac Jones and Lula Sanford and Elder Lindell Brown like a shot pinball. To the sheltering side, like the shade of a mighty oak, of Sister Ethel Washington, who while she sings and stamps her foot points with her hand: in bold red letters underneath "Processional," "Prayer," "Mistress of Ceremony," and "Choir," "AGENDA SUBJECT TO THE HOLY GHOST" leaps out and Val starts singing lustily and holding up her hand to the Holy Ghost before recognizing the song she sings or noting the expression change on Jackie's face, then Sheelita's, then Yulanda's: from rapture to bewilderment to alarm.

"God Never Fails" with Pooky rising above his pump-organ to wail the tenor solo wondrously, with his sisters' backup and the double bass (the electricity is out, so are the lights and the electric guitar) and tambourines and trumpet,

while Mother Delores starts into her cataleptic seizure by the
Holy Ghost, prancing marvelously for a woman of her age and
treading down the Evil One as strong men in Moab and the
Bible lands tread grapes, while the Rev'run Reed bows down
his bullet head and holds both strong arms rigid, summoning
the Enemy—*petit* or *grand mal*, snake or Satan?—to slither
toward the threshing floor of The Original Morningstar Black
Baptist Church of New Orleans:

> "Let God arise, and let His enemies be scattered!
> Depart from me, ye wicked! I will keep
> the commandments of Our God!"

The Rev'run Reed bellows, and commences shaking, shimmying on the podium. "God Never Fails" throbs on, Pooky at
the organ, Fred Turk on double bass. Mother Delores pro-
phesying, Jowlanda and Yulanda and the massed choir singing
now but Jackie's birthmark registers alarm and Sheelita's
broad-faced, big-lipped O of a mouth is open, silent; their
gaze is on the far end of the church where trouble-lights hang
from the wall in little plastic cages with clips attached to
twelve-volt batteries.

From the side of Sister Ethel Washington Valerie looks
back. Elder Brown and Elder Griffin are looking at a scuffle
at the church's rear beneath the butcher-paper banner:

GREETING TO OUR GREAT YWCC LEADER
YOU ARE DOING A GOOD WORK, DON'T COME
DOWN
"FOR A CHILD SAVED IS A SOUL SAVED PLUS A
LIFE!"

And now she sees them, white men, two of them—one of them fat, fatter than Droopy, the other a policeman—against the wall beneath the trouble-light. They're scanning with their eyes the sea of blackface look-alikes, like perverts at the edge of a schoolground staring at the children at recess, is it one in particular they want, or just the plumpest little boy, the prettiest pickaninny . . .? Valerie shelters closer in to Sister Ethel Washington, whose Elvin is in Algiers with Valerie's brother Tyrone. Tyrone: that's why their Mother Delores comes to church, the sisters come because their Momma does . . .

—*Sister Delores, lots of th' saints prayin' for yore Tyrone, how's he makin'?*

—*I'se sayin' he's a good boy, but he got in with the wrong crowd. Ever since age ten he's had that short foot, since he got that knife stab. Now 'is leg's cut off above th' knee.*

—*That's in Algiers, is it, Sister?*

—*Tha's right. He got ten years heavy labor, with his foot.*

Now Momma's stompin' with both feet while Pooky pumps the organ to tread the devil down, but none of it will bring back Tyrone's leg or Tyrone's wife or pay for his appeal, not even Miz Black Nu Orleens could do the first two an' the third, well, ther've been offers but since I got myself mixed up with Jimmy all the offers have been really low, like suck off these old cocks at the Whites-only Club on Hick'ry, an' definitely against my religion which is Baptist. That's why when Jimmy come to me with his proposition—a few pictures for a few dollars—I said maybe, maybe I'll think about it, it wasn't for myself, it was for Tyrone. And, of course, Momma. Then when this guy Floyd called and said $10,000, I said sure, why not, they're only pictures and you're only Miz Black Nu Orleens once, once only, a full perfect and sufficient sacrifice, like it says of Jesus. Then I got to thinking, that's not what God means, He wants me to serve Him in purity and fear, not like Tyrone whose leg's lopped off above the knee and his spirit twisted into bitterness. I got to thinkin', an' I took it to th' Rev'run Reed . . . down Florida Avenue to Desire, past the bucks in brim hats and high heels who flagged her car as she passed, to the Project beyond the bleeder canal choked with weeds, and up the stairway cluttered with broken toys to where the Rev'run Reed stayed.

The thick black man whose bullet head with the bloodshot eyes sat flat on his neckless shoulders, if she were to meet him at night on the street and not know him to be the Rev'run Reed, would terrify her—but such terror she knew, had grown up with, and carried a gun in her purse; the terror she felt now was different, was vaguer, was dreadful. She only prayed the Rev'run Reed, whose epilepsy had been sanctified, could tell her what to do. He listened, the reds of his eyes rolling and his facial muscles twitching, as they always did, while she stood before him and tried to explain; his long arms twitched too, and his hands. Finally, when she'd told all there was to tell, and asked him what to do, he grinned horribly:

—Yo *remembers th' Revrun Reed. Lak th' nigger gal that yo is, yo forgits when yo takin' yore pleasure, then yo remembers th' Revrun.*

She hung her head and averted her eyes and went through the ritual:

—*I remembers when Ise in trouble,* she moaned.

—*An' yo is in trouble, nigger gal, yo sholey is. Is yo in trouble?*

—*I is,* she moaned.

—*But yo is also sanctified, Sister. Is yo sanctified?*

—*I been sanctified, by th' water an' th' blood.*

—*Yo c'n smoke, drink, whatever yo wants, but one thing yo cain't do is fool aroun' with no white mans. Ain't no white mans been born who never done no nigger gal no good. Jesus waren't no white mans. Yo*

been sanctified, Sister; but yo's a nigger gal, too. Yo's gonna have a
monstrance, a monstrance gonna come crawlin' right outa yore womb,
'cause a monstrance been in yore womb, an' where a monstrance gone in
a monstrance gonna come out. . . .
It was the same advice the Rev'run Reed had given her
when she was pregnant, before the abortion, except he hadn't
sent her this time to the voodoo deaconess. Maybe he misun-
derstood that she was talking about pictures and thought she
was talking about sex. Or maybe, just maybe (it occurred to
her as she ran down the stairs and tripped on a doll with its
head torn off) it could be the Rev'run Reed in his idiocy
knew more than she did about this fetish, this perversion (it
was sure to be one or the other, probably both, for $10,000),
and had given up on her. Hadn't he looked hard at her with
that look of his straight out of *Hebrews* 10? *"For if we sin*
willfully after that we have received the knowledge of the truth, (th'
knowledge of th' truth! daughter, if yo sins willfully!—not slide
sidewise into sin, but sashay straightway fer it—willfully!) there
remaineth no more sacrifice for sins (no more sacrifice! yo hear? yo hear
that, nigger gal, yo listen good!), but a certain fearful looking for of
judgment (of judgment, gal) and fiery indignation (fiery!), which shall
devour (shall whut? Devour! Lak when yo gobble up them shrimps, so
th' judgment gonna gobble you up when you sin, 'cause you been
sanctified, you unnerstan'?)."
Hoping that he hadn't understood and that she'd imagined
it and that the Rev'run Reed was an epileptic pure and
simple and that all the hours she had spent in church were
wasted—hollering and holy-rolling, sanctifying nothing—
but fearing in her heart of hearts that he might have fore-
known and forewarned her, might even because he was
afflicted and a saint have forecast her fate, Valerie watched
the two white men at the rear of the church, the grotesquely

fat man and the normal-sized policeman beside him in uniform, only he was no longer beside him, they had spread out
to different sides of the church, scanning the congregation,
peering over and around heads black and kinky and hunched
down in their search for someone, one in particular, just one,
she knew who it was and she knew who they were . . . now
the fat one was talking to Brother Andrew Magee and Brother
Andrew was shaking his head, not looking up at the white
man . . . to Sister Berita beside Brother Andrew, same response but he wouldn't give up . . . now the cop in uniform
had Elder Griffin by the paw and was taking him around the
outside to the fat man who was squeezing past people and
between chairs to meet them, and Elder Griffin was pointing
toward her, like that Greek word for righteousness, *dike*,
which Jesus drew in the sand as a hand with a finger pointing
. . .it wouldn't be long now . . .

Now! . . . Sister Ethel Washington turned round to look
and it was like a rushing mighty wind shaking the tree and
making a vacuum, like when you tailgate a huge semi on the
expressway and the semi turns and you break free, so Sister
Ethel Washington turned round and left her open, in the dead
zone and center of the saints, with saints before, saints
behind, and on both sides saints, but she was bull's-eyed by
Elder Griffin's pointing right hand as by a gun. Then Sister
Ethel Washington (for when she turned, the saints turned,
the focus of the Holy Spirit turned, the attention of the
congregation pivoted with Sister Washington as on a ful-
crum), Sister Washington stopped singing and the massed
choir stopped their singing and Delores and the Rev'run Reed
collapsed like two rag dolls in little jerks and twists, and
Pooky quit playing and Sister Washington confronted Elder
Griffin, her baby brother, flanked by N.O.P.D. (for the fat

man now had flashed his badge); and Sister Ethel Washington looked her baby brother in the eye and said, "Who're
these turkeys?", and Elder Griffin dropped his pointing hand
and the fat man with thick glasses answered, "N.O.P.D.,
Ma'am. We're looking for that woman right beside you, the
one in red." And Sister Washington: "Jes' you look at yore
ownself! Though her sins be as scarlet, she be white as snow.
Though they be red like crimson . . ." And Pooky who'd
already started pumping the old organ when she prophesied
the first line, started playing as she cited him the rest, the
massed choir and the entire congregation of the saints coming
in on "They shall be as wool, oh, they shall be as wool,
Though they be red like crimson, They shall be as wool. . ."
And Sister Ethel Washington stood firm as a mighty oak, as
big around as the fat man she faced-off—him with a little
badge of tin stamped N.O.P.D. and a gun, her with the
breastplate of righteousness and the word of truth—and she
was heartier than him, as a mighty oak beside rivers of waters
is stronger than second-growth sweetgum. . . .

Beside the water she sits, the Sibyl of Salcedo Street, under
the shadow of the expressway, on Perdido. She has had to
move from the junked car seat in the vacant lot where she
usually sits to this backwater behind the Criminal Court and
Jail, on higher ground. She was moved by her son onto a dry
couch, then picked up
   (—Mah boy, he work for th' City.
   —What he do?
   —He do pick-ups, yas, an' he do dee-liv'ries),
then deposited from the rear end of the garbage truck her son
drives onto this new vacant lot behind the city jail, where the
temporary morgue has been set up. From where she sits, she
can see the headlights of the traffic up above on the express-

way, jammed all the way from the Superdome to the Country
Club, as far as she can see in either direction, headlights, and
further, too, from Algiers across the bridge to Lake Pontchartrain, across the causeway, almost all the way to Ponchatoula
. . . seeing, having seen in the last forty-eight hours, houses
floating and washed down half a block, an' a white man
floatin' who they thought was black, find out later all the
corpses look like that, greasy an' black an' th' look on their
faces is th' look they had when it hit 'em, open eyes an' little
guppy mouths gaspin' for air . . . and over there, just the
slightest turn of her head and her eyes, unblinking, rheumy
and yellow with age and weary with so much seeing and all
of it gloomy (like this li'l doll, only it weren't a doll but a
li'l boy, no more'n five or six—you know them dolls with th'
big legs all bent out?—his legs was like that), see the bodies
being brought in, cars and boats pulling up and people
getting out and going in, women crying, men supporting
them, then both men and women leaving, driving off, making
the water in her vacant lot to ripple like a lake in a soft
breeze. Where she sits, marooned on a couch with a tarp
thrown over her, she sees
    (—*How you makin'*, *Granny, you all right with just that tarp?*
    —*Ise fine. Mah son, he work for th' city*),
all the ones from Hick'ry Street she used to see, scattered
abroad like bread on the water but returning to her one by
one and still in her mind's eye like pieces of a puzzle, only one
or two missing: the white man with th' wagging head, the
pretty black girl who stays next to Frobena, lost somewhere,
she's not sure, like pieces of a puzzle moving an' ever'body
wanderin' round an' askin', You seen so-an'-so? An' people
jes' stoppin' to go to th' turlet right there on th' sidewalk,
church folk too, an' dogs that had been washed down and
weren't dead springin' up an' shakin' theirselves, an' they

were wet. Then th' Preacher come drivin' his ol' hellfire an'
salvation buggy right up Hick'ry Street, an' swung in through
th' cemetery gates an' it turned over, an' there wasn't anything to do but jes' sit there. Looking out over that dark
water, past th' Whites-only Club an' th' laundromat an' past
th' cemetery with th' Cajun hanging' from th' tree an' that
old Preacher squattin', God-forsaken. An' th' water up to th'
Mount Moriah Church steps, th' top step, an' surroundin' mah
old car seat an' seeping through th' floorboards, mud and
water. The mud was away up in mah backseat an' mah
clothes, they wasn't no good. Ever'thing was wet an' black.
That's when mah son come an' pick me up an' ferry me 'cross
town. . .

It came to her in the drive across town as she lay staring up
at the dirty yellow sky lit here and there with little yellow
spurts like a yellow-bellied dog lifting his hind leg, while she
lay on her back on her couch on the garbage, smelling the
pollution above and the corruption below, the dark warm
wet slimy substance beneath and the yellow-bellied dog up
above, it come to her as she lay puzzling it out, trying to fit in
the odd pieces—here a patch of fur, there a dog's ear—where
all them people went to: the purty gal who stay next to
Frobena, the white mans with th' acned face who always
wag his head, an' Pooky, Droopy, Jackie 'n the rest—she seen
them all an' others too as she was ferried like a Zulu queen on
a parade float through the flat black streets of sump and glory
to the morgue: Jackie in her wine choir robe and Sheelita and
Yulanda singing "Who Shall Overcome," Fred Turk playing
double bass and Pooky pumping the old organ, while Chevrolet—tha's the girl—Chevrolet's seized by the Holy Spirit
with the white man, white men, looking on, but they can't
do a thing . . . some hostile presence smudges the picture but
not like usual—the center indistinct and the edges crisp—

here the center holds but the edges are fuzzy: it's another man, men, white men, got their own row to hoe an' their own hoes to work it, white folks switchin' partners more often than niggers change churches, but this is no work-bee, no church dance neither. . . . As her son swings the stained-white garbage truck like an armored ATV reeking of putrefaction and corruption off Euphrosine onto Salcedo, and she feels the load of garbage give while her couch slides to one side, and she sees the expressway overpass loom up like an overhead gate, entrance to the place she's prophesied for others and lied about to herself, she spies for the first time those two men, pursuer and pursued, and the Whites-only club comes up to the edge of her mind's eye, and the upstairs of the house on the corner of Hickory and Short, and she sees clearly now, as the armored ATV bears her past dog-headed sentries beneath the gate to the morgue, she sees as through a window underwater or a periscope the acne-faced young man with his wagging head surrounded, his accusers' fingers pointing like handguns, the head—no longer his: it is the City's now, her son's—wags off in multiple directions like a pumpkin splattered on a pavement, the Sybil of Salcedo sees that too, and is filled with a great sorrow for the waggle-headed man who never stopped to talk but always spoke to her, and for every lost and violent soul borne by the flood away like trash or garbage, whose pride and pain and foolishness will not return, no, they will not return. . .

Between the Pompey red altar and Pooky's pump organ, beside the boarded-up window with gold-plated fuchsias and directly beneath the old banner "Jesus Christ wants New Orleans to go to heaven!" (partially hidden by the new banner congratulating Sister Inez), Fred Turk stands at his double bass, having switched from Jesus Christ the Light of the World, where in a year he had moved from the back to the third row, to The Original Morningstar Black Baptist Church of New Orleans, where he was straightaway placed in this corner—directly behind the Rev'run Reed and with a view from the rear of the nine Lacy sisters and Jackie, Yulanda and Sheelita, especially Sheelita.

Now, with the Rev'run Reed humming in his head, and the sisters in their burgundy robes belting out a blood-rock beat: "... she be white as snow ... though they be red like crimson, she be white as snow," getting *down*, as if the Holy Ghost, defenseless, were dependent on them, Fred Turk was trying to take his eyes off Sheelita and to train them on Pooky. Pooky—that boy was always changing keys, said the Holy Spirit made him do it—had paused for a two-beat and switched in mid-chorus, and Fred had had to change his fingering. Not that he minded, just that the Spirit didn't come to him when fingering, the full revelation didn't come till he got home and studied it, then th' fullness comes an' ah'm there in a wonder like Pooky's in all th' time, 'cause that boy's *gifted*, no denyin' it, an' his lungs is *pink*, an' if you doin' good seems like all the dogs be at chu, as at this moment they were at Pooky's sister Valerie, roaring up outside on that thing the police be ridin' on and barging straight on in during th' singing of "God Never Fails," until Sister Ethel Washington, with the little spikelike mole just below her eye, faced down the fat man and the massed choir started singing "They shall be as wool, oh, they shall be as wool ..."

Now they were singing "I'm Going Back," which what the Holy Ghost told Pooky to switch to, when Terracina started jumping like a rag doll in between the rows an' banging herself on the pew seats, till Francine could squeeze herself inside to help her out. And the fat man prowling up

and down the aisles, making Sheelita nervous, Fred could tell
—her back, that powerful back he loved to slather with
Sunscreen, went rigid and her buttocks, those magnificent
buttocks and wraparound thighs he longed to be inside of,
flexed and stopped swinging, because the fat man had drawn
back his white linen coat an', yes Jesus, there was a holster
strapped under it, then he whipped out his gun and started
pointin', and that was when th' Spirit struck th' Rev'run
Reed an' he started prancin' and' preachin' on a incident
what happened in Bethel, prancing an' roaring into the microphone and flicking the microphone cord, and yelling, "It
happened in Bethel! Where did it happen?" And everyone
yelling, "Bethel!" And "'member when there didn't used to
be nothin' here. Now they's drug stores, liquor stores, drug
pushers, junkies—got ever'thing here in Bethel!" The Rev'run
Reed getting down now, too, frothing and slavering and
yelling into the microphone—the mike was dead, the amp
was dead, the only thing electric was the trouble-lights
hooked up to Elder Brown's car battery—shaking his head
and roaring "*Uba-dooba-dooba*" like the roaring of the sea, like a
raging lion, till all Fred Turk wanted to do was bury his face
in Sheelita's backside and burrow on down to her bottom and
listen to God . . .

Then it looked like everything was going to work out, as it
always did for the saints, not the New Orleans Saints, the
answer to every other football team's prayers, but the saints
of Morningstar, except that the Devil was on the outside,
prowling around and trying to get in, flicking his tail and
pointing his gun and roaring to deceive. Then Sister Helvetia
ran forward to the Rev'run Reed and grabbed the dead mike
from his hand—he was in a wonder the whole time—and
flinging it aside like it was a snake said in quick little
commands, "I want Larry and Corey and Linell and Shinell

to come forward now, ax him to pray for you." And while they traipsed forward—Larry and Corey and the twins—the fat man all this time holding his gun and pointing it at Pooky's sister, and that other policeman standing back beside the trouble-lights against the boarded-up windows . . . while the children traipsed forward the Devil, who'd fought Fred ever since he switched from Jesus Christ the Light of the World, made his move. . . .

Fred was watching Pooky when Sheelita's back went stiff, like it did when her ex walked in, and he looked past the heads of Yulanda and Creola and Jackie, Jackie's crimson birthmark glowing like the oil light in a car that's about to throw a rod, past the Rev'run Reed down on his knees in a prayer huddle with Larry and Corey and the twins, and see somebody run in at the door, and it was like when he approached Sheelita the first time, feeling black inside from playing the blues and sweaty and all thumbs:

—*Where 'bouts you live in Nu Orleens?*

—*I stays in the Ninth Ward, 'bout a block from where th' Mississippi takes a bend an' 'comes th' Industrial Canal.*

—*The Ninth Ward's moughty depressed.*

—*I stays in th' lower ninth, too.*

Only this *passe en blanc* be from the seventh district, like Sheelita's ex, else he be white, and he be runnin' straight for Valerie beside Sister Ethel Washington, and the minute he seen 'im Pooky started pumping an' I knowed *something* was coming, but I didn't know what 'cause I couldn't see his face, but Sheelita and Yulanda they could see and started singing, hitting the first high note with a sound that pierced my heart and set me tingling, "Jee-sus!" And Jowlanda and Demetria and Darnise and Patrice and Creola and Orvella and Jamesetta and Alvaida and Alma and Jackie commenced singing and swinging in their burgundy gowns:

Jesus, not Noah!
O, Lord, wudn't that a flood? a turble flood?
Wudn't that a day, wudn't that a turble day?
Who's gonna save them creatures, two by two?
Who's gonna save th' whole wide world frum drownin' on
that day?
Jesus, not Noah! Jesus, not Noah!
Jee-sus!

Ever'body standing up to give Jesus a standing ovation,
Floxina jumping up and down and giggling, when suddenly
it comes to me an' I'm there in a wonder like when I was
studying at home an' see where the real danger lies: th' real
danger lies in what comes at you from inside, not what comes
from th' other side. Like th' Rev'run Reed say—an' he saying
it now: his little crappie mouth gaffed open by th' Holy
Ghost an' spewin' foam an' spittle ever'where: "Be not
deceived to disobey th' Lord!" An' I knew before it happened, a quarter-note before anybody else knowed what was
gonna happen an' I just wanted to lie on the floor on my face
and listen to God . . . Larry and Corey an' the twins up there
with th' Rev'run Reed gettin' slain in th' Spirit; the fat man
wavin' his gun, a big police model, at Valerie, an' her wavin'
her little lady's gun back at him, right at his belly; and
running toward Valerie (to save himself, or her?) Jimmy
Jurard, who I hadn't seed since DePaul's—when he was a
patient an' I was a orderly there—an' suddenly the man I
knew would show, 'cause wherever Jimmy Jurard went, there
went Ernest White, mebbe ten foot behind 'im, mebbe a
mile, but sooner or later here come Ernest, an' if it's later he's
feelin' mad, an' if it's sooner he's jes' natur'ly that way . . .
and sure 'nuff, *here come Ernest*, right into th' house o' God,
running, only he's not eager for salvation, he's not hankerin'

for the horns of the altar to hold to, he's right behind Jimmy
Jurard an' gunnin' for 'im, an' it was just like that shoot-out
they had at th' Brown Derby—I was on the bass then, too,
an' Preston on tenor, an' Bunk he was on drums, with Taft
Jordan sittin' in on piano—cleared 'em out so fast you
wouldn't know th' diff'rence tween th' devil an' th' deep
blue sea, or whether we was playin' blues or gospel, or if it
be th' holy Ghost or Beelzebub—ever'body rushin' for th'
gate an' tramplin' ever'body else an' people fallin' here an'
there, guns poppin' ever'where an' saints bein' slain an'
drunkards reelin'. An' if I hadn't seed it once before, I
wouldn't have believed. An' now I seen it twice, I cain't . . .

So blinded by fury was Ernest White when he entered the
black Baptist church, so automatic his response as he opened
fire on the huddle of faces and figures surrounding Girard,
that he did not notice they were black. He might have burst
into the New Orleans Country Club, or the Whites-only
club—so tunnel-visioned his sight and single-minded his aim
for Girard, Girard only, only Girard. Anyone sheltering
Girard—preacher or policeman, black or white—and anything shielding him—fire or flood, church or tenement—was
peripheral to Ernest White's self-imposed mission, an obsta-
cle to be got round or gone through. So he did not even
register the terrified faces surrounding Girard, much less their
color. Nor did he see the two policemen over to one side—
the fat one pointing a gun—and though he noticed her, he did
not pay much attention to the girl directly in his line of fire,
who was holding and pivoting to fire at him a little purse-
model S&W Terrier .32. None of these things registered on
Ernest White or, if they did, they did not deflect him from
his purpose. If he had not waited all his life for this moment,

he had waited five years. And the forty-three years before that had been filled with frustration enough to last him a lifetime. Ever since Mrs. Girard had commissioned him to "take care of my boy," he had been a man with a mission, never doubting what his mission was. And here at last was the fulfillment of that personal mission and his apotheosis, long delayed, as a British Israelite. But unerring as his aim was as he came barreling into the black Baptist church blasting away at Girard, fourteen hours earlier when he'd lost Girard and been forced to outflank him—first by way of Pontchatoula, then all the way back to Westwego—the outcome of the chase had been in doubt.

He had come running out of Paradis prepared to finish Girard, only to see him enter the boathouse and launch a stolen boat on the swollen Bonnet Carré. With darkening sight he had watched the solitary figure bob and spin on the flood-crested spillway, then disappear from view. Not feeling out-smarted, only out-maneuvered by Girard's lucky escape —a fluke, which rather than discouraging him would make sweeter his turn, when it came—he had jumped in his car and without hesitation taken La. 51, avoiding the larger U.S. 55 which would be jammed, to Ponchatoula. At Ponchatoula he took La. 22 through Madisonville en route to Mandeville, where he had worked as a guard after Girard was moved there from DePaul's. But even as White drove the last few miles through swamp and willow brakes on the deserted state highway, driving slowly on the road which was submer-ged beside the lake which frothed and raged like a maddened animal just to the right of him, he sensed that he had taken the wrong road and was trying (as the British had attempted to turn Boers holed up in river beds that ran forever) to turn the wrong flank. The feeling became stronger in him the closer to Mandeville he got, until, when he passed the swollen

Tchefunta River and saw across the dark north shore of Lake Pontchartrain the narrow-span causeway glistening like a spider's thread and lit by myriads of cars, all heading in the same direction, north, he knew not only that the causeway would be blocked, but that for him to keep on going east—to the I-10, or the Gulf Coast Highway 90—would be to try to turn a flank that would turn with him.

At the Lake Pontchartrain Causeway state troopers were diverting traffic northward; they waved for him to join in the thirty-four-mile-long traffic jam, but he refused. Even as he turned the car, not wasting breath to curse, he knew that an identical exodus would be taking place on all the major arteries out of the city, on all the major highways that led north, northeast or northwest. His only chance lay in the opposite direction, the way from which he'd come—back nearly to Paradis and across the Mississippi at the Sunshine Bridge and along the River Road to Westwego—the way no one would go, for no one wanted *into* New Orleans and south of the city would be only submerged subdivisions, intra-coastal waters, delta—the soft underbelly of the stricken city, its south flank. . . .

By midnight Ernest White was splashing along the West Bank Expressway, his 1975 Dodge Royal Monaco the sole vehicle moving cityward while thousands of cars crept out. He could see them ahead exiting over the Greater New Orleans Bridge, a thin double line of little glo-eyes evacuating the flooded city like rats leaving a ship. He was passing through Marrero now, a bedroom suburb of New Orleans, where he had had his first run-in with immigration and customs officials years ago. He passed half-million-dollar houses flooded to their picture windows, pathetic little malls completely submerged, and just across the neutral ground hundreds of cars headed in the opposite direction, away from

New Orleans. He drove on, the only car on the divided
highway, the only man with a purpose, through Harvey and
Algiers then over the Greater New Orleans Bridge, past cars
stalled and abandoned, threading his way through the almost
stopped traffic heading out, on he drove into the Irish Channel district of New Orleans.

He knew Girard wouldn't deviate from his old haunts, and
Girard's old haunts he knew: in DePaul's and then at
Mandeville he had taunted and probed the yellow-bellied
nigger-lover until he had divulged all the places he would go
back to, once freed. It was simply (simply! nothing was
simple in this Venice of cisterns, this Atlantis of flooded
lagoons) a matter of determining, as he had rightly targeted
Paradis by tailing Lee Anne, which place Girard would home
to, and when; his mother's house on Henry Clay, the doctor's
house on Hickory, or . . . the black girl's place on Hickory
was directly across from the doctor's! Ernest White headed
there first, turning off Canal onto Carrollton and passing
Manuel's Tamales, then a Church's Chicken dislodged from
its footings and beginning to float. He passed Jim's Fried
Chicken, noted for the clutter of condom dispensers in its
men's room, then on past the amputee-parts shop on Carrollton. Six years ago White had purchased a truss there for the
egg-shaped hernia which had strangely appeared in his groin;
then, just as strangely, the hernia had disappeared, but they
wouldn't take back the truss. Now as he bumped across
Earhart Boulevard—the truss, rusty at the hinges, in his car
trunk—he cursed the amputee-parts shop and the AmVet
with a wooden leg who ran it, as he passed. Leaving his car
on the Carrollton neutral ground, he waded up the sidewalk
along Hickory, where he had walked a thousand times to the
Whites-only club.

Sloshing across Short, Ernest White marched right up to

the shotgun-style house where the new-model yellow Olds used to sit. It was not there now, nor the red Chevrolet which usually sat at the curb, which was not visible either. In its place a pond of dirty water eddied sluggishly around a leaf-clogged drain. Suddenly the name of the strong-armed girl in the cheap yellow crepe came to him: Val. Details— names, addresses—surfaced unbidden when he needed them. And he needed the young negress's name now, for perched in the swing of the row house next door, watching him, was the hi-yaller woman in her colorless wrapper. Ernest White, who had overheard the old woman's named called out once, remembered her color, chrome-yellow, and said without the slightest hesitation, "Frobena," as though he'd been greeting the toothless old woman every day for a decade. "Any idea where Val and her folks went to?"

The old Negro woman in the colorless wrapper stares at the large white man as a frog might regard an alligator. "You the third white mans been askin' today," she says, and shakes her head.

"You seen that white man used to mix with her? Used to live over there," White says, nodding toward the house across the flooded street where a baby carriage hangs strangled in mirliton vines.

"Ah tol' 'im lak ah gonna tell you. She be where they all be gone, to cherch."

"Any idea what church Val and them go to?" White says solicitously.

"No'm." The old woman has mistaken White's question for banter. "Somebody got to stay. Ise th' only one aroun'. Eben th' old lady cross't th' road done lef', her son come cart 'er off."

"You tell me what church they're at!" White shouts, suddenly pulling his S&W .38 Special from its holster and cradling it in his hand. "You tell me, or I'll put a bullet through your toothless head. Tell me right now!" he yells, aiming.

"Mornin'star! They's at Mornin'star, over't Louisa, in . . ."

Before she could finish White was sloshing down the sidewalk, pacing himself as he broke into a little run toward Carrollton where his '75 Dodge with the truss in its trunk waited for him. . .

"It's still not clear to me," Les says, "how Girard went out. He was with Floyd and the other cop, and they went after Valerie and didn't get her, while White went after Girard and got him—is that right? But where? How? I've given up on why."

Les looks at the doctor and waits. This is a new technique: witnessed speech. But Larry has not spoken. Is the doctor, too, studying the new genre, silence?

The doctor sits in the lightless garret holding in his hand the smooth shot glass and staring straight ahead into the dark and at a stairwell. There are stairs below which he seems to have ascended, and stairs above which go up and out of sight, but something lurks on the landing just above him and the interrogator in the shadows who mixed his drink mixed it too strong. Sleep hovers all around the stairwell, and he cannot remember . . . anything, except the black hole in the center of the stairwell. He does not respond.

"Valerie's church is on Louisa. You found Girard's body where? In the project somewhere? How did Girard get from St. Charles and Napoleon to Florida and Desire? Don't tell me, I know: the ATV or motorboat or hydroplane or whatever. But what about White? Where was old Ernie all this time?—waving his .38 at the rats and dogs? There must've been thousands of rats from those bleeder canals swimming around in the project."

There were . . . thousands, twenty thousand, or so his father said, in the human-wave attack that smothered the surgical convoy and plummeted him, the son, into Tulane med school; as though something that happened in a Laotian swamp could transmit an impulse to a Louisiana schoolboy which causes his whole world to shift . . . only the message got garbled in transmission and refined, from the gesture of futility and mercenary dandyism that it was to one of gallantry and bravery and anachronistic valor awarded the Officer's Cross of the Legion of Honor . . . not like Girard's gesture . . . no Legionnaire's Cross for Girard, not even *in articulo mortis*. . . .

"Where exactly did you find Girard?"

Screaming down the neutral ground of Franklin, then of Almonaster, the loop-the-loop ambulance siren driving him crazy. . . Like riding with the *Groupement Blinde* his father always talked about, plowing through rice paddies in the Tonkinese delta and along the dikes, shaking off human-wave attacks and bazooka salvos at ten yards, hell-bent to pick up casualties then return to base to fuel up, unload the dead and wounded, patch up the tanks and roll off again. . . By the time he found the church (he was navigating: a city map in one hand, the radiophone in the other) and the driver got to it, the carnage had already happened. Ernest White had opened fire on the black congregation, leg-wounding Girard who had barreled in and tackled Valerie, sheltering her from White's spray-fire and from the shots fired by Floyd, who either had returned White's fire or else fired into the blacks charging pell-mell for the exit (there was only one exit, the windows were all boarded up), and the resulting casualties—one dead and seven wounded—were the reason the emergency unit was called in the first place, by police radio, because the ambulance he was with was at St. Claude and Franklin, less than a mile from Florida and Desire. So by the time he arrived the worst, if it had not already happened, was happening . . . like his father's arrival at the massacre of the surgical convoy on Road No. 19 by the Vietminh on Bastille Day, 1962, with time enough only to survey the slaughter and take the highest ranking walking-wounded with him into the swamps which were swarming with armed Vietminh . . . the swamp in this case being the bleeder canal which bounded the low-rent, ill-built tenements of Desire project, swarming with angry and rioting blacks, where Ernest White, too, had taken refuge and was holed up waiting with his .38.

Because he'd had to leave the ambulance on the other side of Abundance, the driver with it and the stretcher-cases they'd picked up (they'd managed to stuff five wounded in the ambulance bed built for three) with instructions to go on, not wait for him, then wade with Girard across the flooded bleeder canal, at any moment expecting to stumble on submerged rake-heads, broken bottles, rusty nails in old machinery like Vietminh caltrops, which would pierce a foot through jungle boots, or to be stitched across the chest by machine-gun bursts, or doubled over by poisoned darts fired from blow-tubes . . . you had to be a savage to survive in this jungle, but the six-storey tenements of Desire were the only high ground around.

So they'd had to come here . . . Clambering and crawling past the bleeder canal and through the vacant doorway where no door had ever been (if there had been a door, it wasn't there now) and up the tenement stairway cluttered with broken toys and mushed food and water-damaged, unidentifiable junk while Girard who was leg-wounded crawled and clambered beside him . . . like his father leading Colonel

Barrou, wounded in both legs, from the flaming hell of Kilometer 15 on Road 19 into the swamps and up into the mountains, not to safety, no, nor comfort, due to the arrival of the Air Force's B-26s and their aerial strafing which froze everyone flat, friend and enemy alike and only feet apart, then the Vietminh's renewed assault with machine-gun bursts that cut the standing grass in which his father and the colonel were hiding, remembering only and so selectively as to be lulled into unguardedness the single image which had catapulted him into med school: the gallant medic rescue of the colonel by his father, for a few moments only, twenty minutes maybe, from Kilometer 15 to a point in the swamps not far from Kilometer 16 . . . when Ernest White from the landing just above them opened fire in the narrow stairwell, emptying his weapon into Girard, and Girard slumped down ragdoll-like beside him while White yelled "Nigger-lover! Yellow-bellied nigger-lover!" and was himself struck from above, by an unseen hand on the landing just above dropping an old-fashioned flatiron, black and heavy and cast iron, which required no electricity and not much aim. It struck White on the head and felled him suddenly among the junk and clutter of the narrow stairwell. . . .

"I found Girard on the stairwell of a dirty tenement in Desire Project. He'd been shot four times in the chest, and twice in the legs. He wasn't dead."

"Wasn't dead! Why not? My God, man, why wasn't he dead?"

The doctor shrugged.

"Who shot him?"

"White."

The playwright blinked behind his glasses and sat silent at his desk in the almost lightless garret. The garret smells of

whiskey, stale smoke, and burnt almonds. The dirty light of
New Orleans dawn has begun to filter through the stained-
glass windows on the eastern side, and sounds from the
Southern Baptist Hospital across Napoleon Avenue can be
heard indistinctly through the dormer. "Five o'clock," Les
muttered, "shift change."

"White shot him, then got struck by some falling object—
a flatiron, I believe."

But Les was gazing abstractedly out the dormer toward
the hospital.

"Got to go," said Larry. "I'm on duty."

"One last thing," Les says slowly, getting up lazily,
drawn obsessively toward the dormer, gazing down. "Did
Girard say anything—famous last words, you know, like 'the
horror, the horror' or 'more light! more light!'—anything like
that?"

He was looking down at the tractor now, its gray paint
speckled with blisters of water from the night before, while
the doctor stared down a dark stairwell. The tractor had not
moved, not since that day . . . and the tenement stairs stank of
carbide, the headless dolls and waterlogged cushions with the
stuffing protruding and two bodies in the stairwell—one
dead, the other not quite dead—were sticky with blood and
smelled acrid and sweet, with the carbide, while he looked
down: nothing had moved, no one was stirring.

"Well, did he?"

"No, he said nothing."

"Nothing?"

"Nothing."

Les stands at the dormer gazing down at the neutral
ground, the doctor staring down the dark stairwell: they will
stand that way forever, witnessing a black hole at the center
of their vision which they cannot penetrate, much less plunge

into. Whenever the doctor is confronted with a gunshot wound or a failed suicide or a mangled leg or a maimed arm requiring amputation, or the playwright with a tale of waste and beauty, it will fall into that black hole and be swallowed up by it, for, in comparison with the wastage and lost promise and futility they glimpse now—Les gazing down at his neutral ground, the doctor staring down his dark stairwell —each into his own black hole, the same black hole at bottom, linked as by an underground sewer, nothing and no one can ever be taken seriously again. Les, gazing out the dormer at the tractor and stone lions, neither of which has moved or been moved since the flood, listens as the doctor leaves the garret, hears him stumble on his way to the first landing then descend the stairs, open the double doors downstairs, close the doors, then silence. The hunched figure of the doctor as he passes between the lions and along the sidewalk seems smaller, less purposeful than it has ever seemed before. Perhaps this enquiry into Girard's last days was not a good idea, after all. Perhaps Girard was not, after all, worth looking into. The only words worth writing are engraved on stone, Les thinks; he wonders what would be Girard's true epitaph?

James Antoine Girard, 1945–1978
beloved son, devoted husband

read the burgundy ribbon on the evergreen wreath, below a cameo portrait of J. Girard, #44, QB, cropped from an old Greenwave roster.

"It's like Jimmy his ownself's with us, it's that lifelike."

"It's Jimmy to a T, Momma. Here, you take my arm. This ground's uneven."

"I needn't soil your nice lace, Lindy Lou. I'm just fine, really."

"Now, Momma . . ."

"Here, take my arm, Miz Jurard," Senator T. 'Timmy' Theriot said, "I'm black-banded."

"Like a titmouse," Linda said.

"Well, I prefer to think like the American eagle . . ."

"There she is—over by the Army of North Virginia—y'all see her?" Irene Trepagnier Girard, processing in mourning from the Fountain Gate of Metairie Cemetery, supported on the left by Antoine Girard and on the right by United States Senator Theriot, called across the rows of silent dead, "Lee Anne! Annie! Over here, Honey!" Extracting her arm from the crook of her brother-in-law's elbow, she waved. "Here! She sees us now," she said, and to her daughter: "Run over there, Honey, an' meet her. We'll proceed together."

They pass the Confederate Cavalryman's statue in their march to the Army of North Virginia cenotaph. Low-lying nimbostratus clouds blanket New Orleans and a chill wind blows in the cemetery, drying the ground. Piles of dead leaves from the pin oaks and detritus from the flood dot the raked and tended landscape. Irene Girard gives a little shiver; Antoine Girard attentively pats her hand which holds his arm, contracts his brow into a little query—does she want his coat?—she shakes her head, the party proceeds on to where Lee Anne Girard, swathed in a shapeless wool tunic and escorted by Billy Bland, half walks, half runs from the Army of North Virginia cenotaph to join them.

"Lee Anne, you stop that running this instant! You hear?"

The two women meet, embrace, the three women; the three men stand back behind them, shaking hands with one another on the outside of the group the women form. The women finish greeting, they stand tentative, escortless, opening out gradually to make room for the men who fall in between them and edge forward, at first in a loose and ragged scrum, then, as they turn the corner to the Girard family crypt, passing the white marble mausoleums and sealed crypts with urns of ashes and steel shelves and nameplates marking Morales and Delgados and Peyrefittes and Eberts, in decorous procession: the mother of the deceased escorted by her brother-in-law, followed by the wife of the deceased escorted by her friend, with the deceased's sister, still carrying the evergreen wreath, escorted by a friend of the family.

Father Henri du Charbonnet, O.M.I., meets them on the curbed and graveled path marked "Metairie Avenue" between two rows of square and dark stone mausoleum vaults, like shrunken tenements with nameplates; the mausoleum on the left is marked "Girard."

Father Henri shakes hands all around, comforting the widow of the deceased, the mother of the deceased, and those who mourn. He is seventy, dressed in an old-fashioned black cassock with a new-fangled stole denoting the church season —white—and refers as he ushers them into formation to a small urn set in an open slit, the only slit open, in the otherwise cemented-shut mausoleum. As he speaks he refers now and then to the urn, and to the white linen cloth set before it, on which are a paten with seven wafers, one of which he takes, breaks, blesses, and eats, then offers to the mourning party, one by one, the other six. All but one partake. The deceased's sister, clutching a wreath, shakes her head. Father Henri, left holding the paten with the seventh wafer on it, returns it to the linen cloth. All pray, even the sister prays the Our Father, the Hail Mary, the Gloria, and Father Henri delivers the Prayer to Saint Michael Archangel, calling on the prince of the heavenly host by the power of God to cast into hell Satan and all evil spirits who wander through the world seeking the ruin of soul, especially the soul of James Antoine Girard, Amen. Then he shakes hands with the mourners all around again, ending with the mother, reassuring her. She is crying a little, so is the young widow who is pregnant. Their menfolk lead them off while the sister steps forward to place the wreath, arranging it just so around the urn, then goes with them. The Senator stays back to pass the envelope to him, with sincere thanks and a firm hand-shake, then turns to join the departing family group. Father Henri approaches the urn bearing the ashes of the deceased; he folds the white linen cloth around the solitary wafer, pockets it. Then he tears open the envelope to see what it contains: seventy-five dollars. No written requests for prayers for the deceased, no instructions regarding masses. He pockets it, too. The affair is at an end, finished. He looks about him to make sure he has not forgotten anything; then he turns down the graveled path that leads out to Metairie Road.

It is then he notices behind the Girard family mausoleum the solitary Negro woman dressed in white, her uniform the color of the linen cloth he carries in his pocket and of the Easter season. It may be she is on her way to work, cutting catty-corner through the cemetery, and has stopped so as not to interrupt the mass for the dead. Or she may be waiting for someone. She loiters, it seems to Father Henri, disconsolately —though that could be due to a domestic squabble, or financial troubles, or the weather . . . He wonders if he should notify the cemetery office, then decides against it: there is nothing she can take, no damage she can do, no reason to object to her being there. . . .

A sudden impulse seizes him. He strides across the sodden, squishy ground, wetting his oxfords. The woman shrinks a little before him.

"Are you Catholic, child?" he demands.

The negress, who is young and pretty, shrinks yet further from him, terrified. The whites of her eyes are enormous. She looks on the point of running, but stands her ground and answers: "N-no, fa-father, suh. I'm black an' I'm Baptist."

"I can see you're black, child. Did you overhear the mass I said just now?"

The woman rolls her eyes toward the mausoleum. "Jes' now?"

Father Henri nods.

"I heard some. I doan' understan', though. My auntie's Catholic, she's a Lesbeen. Like I said, I'm Baptist."

Father Henri thrusts his hand through the slit in his cassock, encounters first the envelope with money, brings it out, then rummages in his pocket for the folded linen cloth. He extracts it gingerly, and thrusts the money back. Opening carefully the folded linen cloth and holding it with the wafer on one hand, he asks the woman: "I offer you this bread, which is the body of Christ, in memory of Our Savior and the boy we just buried. Will you take it?"

Valerie gazes wide-eyed at the host, baffled, fascinated, terrified . . . like when Jimmy first got in the car with her, and she drove with the angle of her body in line with the left headlight, expecting him to lunge across the seat and rob or rape her, with one eye on the road and one on him, and one hand on the wheel and the other on her purse, ready to pull her S&W Terrier .32 and start shooting . . .

Father Henri holds the host, having taken, broken, and blessed it, proffering it to this black Baptist girl who has never before seen a host and doesn't know the meaning of it, or the risk he runs in doing this, or the importance of this gesture, so how can she know what to do, much less why she should do it, being completely uninstructed as she is?

"You eat it, child," he says.

Valerie, her mind in turmoil, reaches for the pitifully thin, small, white wafer, which the old priest calls the Body of Christ. She is under no illusions. It is nothing but Jew-bread, which when she helped to serve receptions at the Metairie Country Club, the white folks with the spindly legs and enormous bellies ate. It is nothing. Besides, all the others ate one too. Then why this one? What is special about this one? Why is it alone remaining? She touches it with one finger, takes it between her thumb and index finger, lifts it off the cloth; the old priest watches her, a glazed expression in his eyes. . .

"You too," she says, holding it between them, up above the cloth. "You have some too."

The old priest looks surprised.

"I cain't eat all this by myself," she says, "no-suhree." She grins.

The old priest with his other hand breaks off a piece, his forefinger and thumb touch hers. They eat.

"Do you know the 'Our Father,' child?"

"Th' what?"

"The Lord's Prayer."

"I guess so."

Without waiting he begins mumbling rapid-fire, "Our Father, who art in heaven . . . ," and she joins in and goes a little longer than he does, and when she ends he says, "Bless you, child," and turns and trudges back across the grass and along the graveled path and out the gate to Metairie Road without a word more or a look back or a wave. A funny old priest, but she didn't mind doing it for him after all God and

the saints at Morningstar had done for her, and she remembered now what her Momma said about Catholics, and
especially priests, that unless they had a witness when they
did it, it didn't count.